D1237530

THE
LANGUAGE
OF
FOOD

THE LANGUAGE OF FOOD

ANNABEL ABBS

SIMON &
SCHUSTER

London · New York · Sydney · Toronto · New Delhi

First published in Great Britain by Simon & Schuster UK Ltd, 2022

3 5 7 9 10 8 6 4 2

Simon & Schuster UK Ltd
1st Floor
222 Gray's Inn Road
London WC1X 8HB

Simon & Schuster Australia, Sydney
Simon & Schuster India, New Delhi

www.simonandschuster.co.uk
www.simonandschuster.com.au
www.simonandschuster.co.in

A CIP catalogue record for this book
is available from the British Library

Hardback ISBN: 978-1-3985-0222-2
Trade Paperback ISBN: 978-1-3985-0223-9
eBook ISBN: 978-1-3985-0224-6

Typeset in Palatino by M Rules
Printed and bound by CPI Group (UK) Ltd, Croydon, CR0 4YY

MIX
Paper from
responsible sources
FSC
www.fsc.org FSC® C171272

PREFACE

This is a work of fiction based on a handful of known facts about the life of the poet and pioneering cookery writer, Eliza Acton, and her assistant, Ann Kirby. Between 1835 and 1845 Eliza and Ann lived in Tonbridge, Kent, and worked on a cookery book that has become known as *the greatest British cookbook of all time* (Bee Wilson, *Telegraph*), *the greatest cookery book in our language* (Dr Joan Thirsk CBE) and *my beloved companion ... illuminating and decisive* (Elizabeth David). It was a bestseller in its time, internationally as well as in the UK, selling over 125,000 copies in thirty years. Eliza Acton had a profound influence on later cookery writers including Delia Smith, who calls Eliza Acton *the best cookery writer in the English language ... a great inspiration ... and a great influence on me.*

To my daughter, Bryony,
fellow writer and kitchen companion

Life has dark secrets; and the hearts are few
That treasure not some sorrow from the
world . . .

L.E.L.,
'Secrets', 1839

But oh! the bitterest griefs of all,
Are nurs'd in tearless anguish still.

ELIZA ACTON,
'Yes Leave Me', 1826

I would venture to guess that Anon, who wrote
so many poems without signing them, was
often a woman.

VIRGINIA WOOLF,
A Room of One's Own, 1929

PROLOGUE

1861
GREENWICH, LONDON

Ann

Before Mr Whitmarsh leaves for work, he does something quite out of character. He gives me a gift. Wrapped snug in brown paper. No ribbon, just string. But a gift all the same.

'This is for you, my Ann,' he says, even as his rheumy eyes are on his pocket watch. He likes to call me 'his Ann', although I think 'Mrs Kirby' would be more appropriate for a servant of my age and experience. I do more than serve, of course. Like keeping his bed warm at night and braiding the sleek hair of his motherless daughters.

As soon as the lift and press of his leather soles on the marble floor is gone, I prod curiously at the package. I know it's a book. I can tell by the shape and heft of it. I untie the string and pull at the paper, my mind racing and dancing. As if someone has climbed inside my head with an egg whisk and turned my brain to a fine froth.

Will it be a volume of poetry? Or a novel? Or a book of

maps? And why has he bought me a gift anyway? The paper falls in clumsy shreds to the floor. Not like me to be so ... I pause and search for the word. *Exuberant.* I smile, knowing exactly who taught me the word *exuberant*.

Mr Whitmarsh knows I like reading for he has caught me at it. Red-handed. First, he caught me in his library examining his map collection. Then he caught me at the stove, deep in a poetry book. And after that he found me with my nose in a novel when I should have been waxing the floorboards to a shine. But isn't that why he took me so readily to his bed? And why he calls me, with such affection, *his Ann*?

A little twitch flirts at the corners of my mouth. But then the twitch sets fast. And the whisking in my head stops. For all the wrapping paper is off now, lying round my feet in scraps and rags. The book is a colossal tome that's neither poetry nor novel. Nor is it a book of maps. I turn it over, sniff its calfskin bindings, feel its leather spine as smooth as skin. Then I run the tips of my fingers over its cover, over the raised gilding of its title. *Mrs Beeton's Book of Household Management*.

Why would I want such a book as this? Disappointment rushes through me, making my fingers slip so that pages turn, crackle, crumple. And words flicker and spin before my eyes ... knuckle of veal with rice ... tartar mustard ... turnips in white sauce ... gooseberry pudding ... A snorting gasping sound, most inelegant, escapes from my mouth. Mr Whitmarsh has bought me a book of recipes! The man is more of a buffoon than I thought.

My fingers move less hastily, my gaze slows and lingers. Until I am stock-still and reading – word for word – a recipe for crimped salmon with caper sauce. A most peculiar sensation passes over me. My mind, which a few minutes ago was whisked to a foaming peak, goes very small and tight and still. Like a hazelnut.

Every word, every ingredient, is uncannily familiar. I turn the page. And read. And turn another page. And then another. Slowly it dawns on me. These recipes are mine. And *hers* too, of course. I recognise them because I cooked them. Because I wrote down my observations of them on a slate. With a stub of chalk. Day after day. Year after year.

Our recipes have been plundered, rearranged upon blank new pages, emptied of *her* elegant tilt and turn of phrase, *her* sly humour. The bones remain – cold graceless lists of instructions and ingredients – assigned now to a Mrs Beeton, whoever she may be. Yet they belong to me and to Miss Eliza, who is barely cold in her grave.

I read on, tasting each dish upon my tongue: sweet slippery leeks, new-born peas swirled in butter, meringue as fresh and light as snow. And gradually, recipe by recipe, I'm returned to the kitchen of Bordyke House. The air smoke-thick with roasting pigeons, frying onions, softly stewing plums. The sing of it all: the water pump cranking in the scullery, the logs spitting in the range, the jingle of pewters and the rattle of cutlery, the thump of a rolling pin, the endless bubble and simmer of the stockpot.

I push away Mr Whitmarsh's book of stolen recipes, and slowly stoop, kneel, to pick the wrapping paper from the floor. That's when I hear her. I recognise her tread – so neat and determined – upon the stone flags. She's moving towards me, her skirts swishing round her ankles. Her voice, at once purposeful and gentle, calls out: *Ann? Ann?*

I know her next words off by heart: *Today we shall be very busy, Ann.* I wait. But there's only silence. From outside I hear the faint notes of a dove, scraped thin by the wind. Then next door's cockerel starts crowing with great gusto.

And I know what I must do.

CHAPTER ONE

Eliza

1835
FISH BONES

Midday in the City of London, the carts and carriages rattling over the cobbles, the screech of costermongers, the jostle of barrows and handcarts, the thin-ribbed boys who are shirtless and swooping like starved birds to shovel every steaming clod of dung. It is the hottest day of the year – or so it feels to me, burning and corseted inside my best silk dress. On Paternoster Row the heat radiates from every brick, every brass bell pull, every iron railing. Even the wooden scaffolding that props up every half-built windowless property is stubbornly lodged with heat and creaking with thirst.

It is the most important day of my life, so to calm my

nerves that are all a-welter, I observe the scene and shape it into words. The crowds dripping along the side of the road where the taller buildings fling their shadows. The straining horses that are slick with sweat. The fans stitched from peacock feathers and fluttering from carriage windows. The wilting lash of the coachmen's whips. And the sun, like a vast golden orb in a dome of unbroken blue.

I pause, for the rhythm is not quite right. Perhaps *far-off bowers of blue* is more pleasant on the ear than *a dome of unbroken blue*. I mouth the words, letting them slip over my tongue and echo in my ear ... *Far-off bowers of blue* ...

'Look where you're going, you stupid old trout!'

I swerve and stumble, narrowly missing a cart of rotting cabbages. Suddenly I long for home, its familiarity and friendliness. I feel as though I have no place in the vast stinking skirmish that is London.

I leave the shaded side of the street with its fractious, melting throng. In the hot sunlight, the people are fewer but the stench is thicker: unwashed bodies, decaying teeth, human slops. All manner of debris lurks beneath my feet, wedged and rotting between the cobbles: bleached herring bones and cockle shells, rusting nails, spat pellets of chewed tobacco, a dead mouse bristling with maggots, the desiccated rind of oranges and gnawed apple cores fizzing with fruit flies. Everything is either dried hard or rotting softly, foully. I peg my nose with my fingers for I have no desire to turn this noxious reek into poetry.

Far-off bowers of blue, I say beneath my breath. A reviewer of my first poetry collection described my work as *neat and*

THE LANGUAGE OF FOOD

elegant, and I can't help thinking that *far-off bowers of blue* is similarly neat and elegant. But what will Mr Thomas Longman, publisher of celebrated poets, think? The thought of Mr Longman returns me – dizzily – to the present, to my mission. I look down and see the damp silk of my dress, veined a darker shade of green, with great black puddles spreading beneath the pits of my arms. Why did I not take a carriage? I shall arrive at the most important meeting of my life drenched and sopping, like a child with fever.

A brass plaque announces the offices of Messrs Longman & Co, Publisher and Book Seller. I pause, take a breath. And in that second my life, my past, the vastness of the skies above, the tangled mass of London – all of it telescopes into a single quivering point. This is it. The moment I have awaited for ten long years. *My starry dawning* ...

I peel the loose tendrils of hair from my neck and tuck them into my bonnet. A quick anxious rub at the damp creases in my dress and I am – tremblingly – ready. I pull on the intimidatingly long doorbell and am gestured through rooms toppling with books to a narrow flight of stairs. At the top is a single room so crammed with books there is barely space for my skirts. Mr Longman – for I assume it to be him – sits behind a desk examining an unrolled map, so that I am presented only with the luxuriant crown of his head.

He ignores me and I take the opportunity to observe him with my poet's gaze. He is weighted down with gold. A gold signet ring upon each hand and a gold watch chain that stretches into the black folds of his frock coat. His hair is steely grey and sits in a thick drift over the plates of his

skull. When he raises his head I see his face is florid, its rosy
hue exaggerated by a cravat of lavender twill silk on which
the folds of his chin rest. His eyes are set very far back in his
head, beneath a scrambling pair of brows.

'Ah, Mrs Acton ...' He looks up at me through half-
closed eyes.

My cheeks flame. 'Miss Acton,' I say, my voice lifting defi-
antly on the word *'Miss'*.

He nods, then pushes away the maps and books and ink-
pots to make a channel through which he thrusts a hand. I
look at his pale cushioned palm, bewildered. Am I to shake
his hand, as gentlemen do? He makes no motion to take my
hand to his lips, or to rise and bow. And when I shake his
hand I feel a curious excitement, a dim thrill of something I
cannot explain.

'You have something for me, I believe.' He rummages in a
lacklustre way at the papers sprawled across his desk.

'I explained it in my letter, sir. A volume of poems I have
worked on diligently for ten years. My last volume was
published by Richard Deck of Ipswich, and indeed you sold
it from this very shop.' As the words slip from my tongue –
more steadily than I expected – an image swims into my
head: Miss L. E. Landon reading aloud from *my* book of
verse, which is beautifully bound in sealskin with my name
embossed in gilt. The picture is so sharp, so bright, I see the
hint of a tear in her eye, the appreciative curve of her lip, her
tender fingering of the pages as if they were as delicate and
precious as goose down.

But then Mr Longman does something most baffling,

most distressing. And Miss L. E. Landon, along with my published book, is swept immediately from my mind. He shakes his head, as if I have muddled my facts in some inexcusable way.

'I assure you, sir, it was stocked by Longman & Co – and many other reputable bookshops. It was reprinted within a month and—'

Mr Longman interrupts me with a loud impatient sigh. He withdraws his hand from the desk and uses it to mop at his forehead with a handkerchief.

'I raised the subscriptions myself and received orders from as far afield as Brussels and Paris and the island of St Helena. My readers are quite convinced I need a publisher with the universal might of yourself, sir.' I hear my voice and am startled by its note of desperation. And conceit. Mother's words rush into my head ... *too hungry for recognition ... too ambitious ... no sense of propriety ...*

But Mr Longman is shaking his head more emphatically than ever. He shakes his head so strenuously the folds of his chin bob and small drops of sweat spin from his forehead scattering carelessly over his map.

'Poetry is not the business of a lady,' he growls.

I am so taken aback every inch and ounce of me stiffens. Does he know nothing of Mrs Hemans? Or Miss L. E. Landon? Or Anne Candler? My mouth opens, as if to remonstrate. But he swats at the air as if he knows what I am about to say and has no wish to hear it.

'Now, novel-writing ... that is a different matter. Novelettes, Miss Acton, are splendidly popular with young ladies.' He elongates the word *young*, making his voice rise and fall. I feel my face scald a second time. And all my feelings of excitement and defiance vanish.

'Novelettes of romance. Have you none of those for me?'

I blink and try to compose my thoughts. Has he even read my letter? Or the fifty poems in my best copperplate that I delivered, by hand, six weeks ago? If not, why did he write and invite me to meet him? To my chagrin, I feel my throat close up, my bottom lip waver.

'Yes,' continues Mr Longman, speaking as if to himself. 'I could consider a gothic romance.'

I brace myself, biting down on my wavering lip. A spark of something – fury? Irritation? – leaps inside me. 'Some of my poems have been published more recently, in the *Sudbury Pocket Book* and the *Ipswich Journal*. I am told they are good poems.' My burst of audacity surprises me. But then Mr Longman shrugs and his eyes slide to the ceiling, which is low and sagging.

'It is no good bringing me poetry! Nobody wants poetry now. If you cannot write me a little gothic romance ...' His palms are open and splayed upon his desk in a gesture of helplessness.

I stare at his empty palms and feel my insides – my spirit, my audacity – being scooped out and cast away. Ten years of labour – in vain. The emotion, the effort, everything that has been sacrificed in the writing of my poems, all for nothing. Perspiration runs in rivulets down the sides of my ribcage and I feel a shortness of breath as if my throat is constricting. *The painful beatings of a breaking heart are hush'd to stillness ...*

Mr Longman scratches noisily at his head and continues staring at the ceiling. The soles of his shoes tap at the floorboards beneath his desk, as if he has forgotten my presence. Or perhaps he is deciding whether I can be trusted to write a gothic romance. I give a discreet cough which sounds more like a harried gulp. 'Sir, could I possibly have my poems back?'

He claps his hands and jumps to his feet so abruptly the gold chains of his fob watch jangle and the silver buckles on his shoes rattle. 'On second thoughts, I have sufficient novelists at present. So do not bring me a novelette.'

'My manuscript? Did you not receive it, sir?' The words limp from my throat, barely audible. Is it possible he's lost my poems? Carelessly mislaid them among his maps and papers? And now he is about to dismiss me ... empty-handed. Not even the promise of a commissioned novelette. *I told you so*, whispers my voice of doubt. *Imposter ... imposter ... Surely your puny efforts at poetry have been put upon the fire ...* I scan the room, instinctively seeking out a grate, a wisp of my verse among the ashes.

All of a sudden Mr Longman claps his hands a second time. I look at him, wondering if this is his manner of dismissal. But he is staring at me, his eyes alight, his hands clasped. 'A cookery book!'

I frown in confusion. The man is both rude *and* obscure, I think. Who on earth does he think I am? I may be thirty-six and unmarried, my dress may be streaked with sweat, but I am no aproned household servant.

'Go home and write me a cookery book and we might come

to terms. Good day Miss Acton.' His hands splash over the detritus of his desk and for a moment I think he is hunting for my poems. But then he gestures at the door.

'I do not – cannot – cook,' I say lamely, moving like a somnambulist towards the door. The inside of my head is dulled with disappointment. Every bit of bravura slipped clean away.

'If you can write poems, you can write recipes.' He taps on the glass face of his pocket watch and puts it to his ear with a grunt of irritation. 'This infernal heat has lost me valuable time. Good day!'

I have a sudden urge to be gone, away from the monstrous stench of London, away from the humiliation of having my poems spurned for something as frivolous and functional as a cookery book. I hurry down the stairs, tears crowding in my eyes.

Suddenly Mr Longman's voice rings out: 'Neat and elegant, Miss Acton. Bring me a cookery book as neat and elegant as your poems.'

CHAPTER TWO

Ann

TURNIP POTTAGE

Today is my most shameful day ever. I fall asleep by mistake and for no more than a quarter hour, only to waken with the vicar looming over me. Like a black shadow.

'Oh, Reverend Thorpe,' I stutter, stumbling to my feet. I know instantly why he's here. In truth I've been waiting for this day to come.

His eyes swivel round and round, like windmills. Well-fed windmills. He's inspecting our cottage: the cobwebs in the chimney, the piles of rank rags that I'm too busy to wash, the black balls of dog hair that have collected in the corners. At least the hearth is swept clean and all the ashes taken out.

Behind him Mam is clawing at a sheet which has been

knotted around her. I recognise the knots – they're the handi-
work of Mrs Thorpe. So I know Mam was found unclothed.
Likely by the River Medway, where she tries to wash herself
and forgets to put her frock back on. The thought makes me
flinch, all the narrowboats passing by, all the men watching
from the gunpowder mills ...

'Enough is enough,' says the Reverend Thorpe, one hand
circling his belly that has grown soft and round on patties
and pies and boiled puddings.

'Did she go wandering? She was tied to me but I fell asleep.'
I don't tell him that all night she had me up and down, want-
ing this and wanting that, pulling on the ropes, pinching me,
kicking me, shredding her nightdress with her nails.

'How long since she ... ?' He jerks his head towards the
ground, towards Hell, as if to say this is the Devil's work.

But I know God loves all his flock, so I answer in a most
determined way, jerking my head towards Heaven. 'It's five
years since she became ... absent-minded.' I don't tell him
that she is worse now than ever, that after the last full moon
she does not know her own daughter.

'She must go to a lunatic asylum, Ann,' he says. 'There is a
new one, over at Barming Heath.'

'I will tie her to me more tightly,' I say, avoiding his eye. My
face is hot with shame. Did he find her or was it someone else?
Someone who took her to the rectory rather than bringing her
home. Or did she take herself to the church? All my insides
cringe into a little ball at the thought of it, at the picture of
her naked, or in her ragged under-things, sitting in church,
mad as a March hare.

'What have you eaten today, Ann?' He stares at Septimus, who's stretched upon the hearth with one oozing eye open and one closed. The vicar's look is wary, as if he thinks our poor skinny dog is next for the pot.

'Better than Mam would eat in the workhouse or in any lunatic asylum.' I ease her down to the floor, loosening the knots on the sheet and hoping she will stay quiet. I want the vicar to go, but he presses me to answer, repeating his question three times.

'Bread and an onion, each of us, with a scraping of lard too,' I say at length. I don't tell him the bread was as stale as a baker's broom. Or that the onions had sprouted stalks as long as my arm. 'And a little turnip pottage,' I lie, as an afterthought.

'Your mother can go to an asylum – there will be no cost and she will be well cared for. I can give your father some work tending the graveyard.'

I pause, confused by the Reverend's words. I can see that he might want Mam gone, but to find work for Pa too ... Surely the man is a saint, for it's barely three years since he found a place for my brother, Jack, in London, turning spits in the kitchen of a gentlemen's club. I remind him that Pa has only one leg, that he lost the other fighting for King and Country.

'Yes, yes,' he replies, flapping his white hands like I'm a mongrel with the mange. 'God does not want your mother running naked through the fields. It is not good for ... for ...' He pauses and narrows his eyes. 'For the morals of this parish.'

Has God spoken to him? Has God complained about

Mam's lunacy? Perhaps God has told him of the other night when I found Pa with his scraggy knuckles gripping Mam's neck, twisting his two hands like she was no more than a Christmas goose. He'd been in a rare temper, with the ale upon him so strong I could smell it on every reeking breath. Fortunately, the drink – and the lack of a leg – had weakened him so that he'd fallen to the floor wailing, 'She remembers nothing, Ann. Not even me ... she's lost control of every bit of herself. She ain't human no more.' All the while Mam lay on the mattress, a long gummy smile on her face, no notion she'd been half throttled by her own husband.

The Reverend Thorpe begins to back out of the cottage, keeping his eyes high so he won't see Mam, who is crawling across the floor. Her scalp is like yellow parchment now, her hair thin and matted. I put her on the mattress, arranging her scrawny limbs so she's curled like a cat. The sheet is bunched and tangled round her with big knots at her shoulders, knees and hips, so she looks more like a twist of dirty laundry than a human being. All at once I know it's only me who can look after her, only me who can calm her. 'I promise to keep her clothed,' I plead. 'And I will learn to tie a firmer knot, a reef knot.'

At this the vicar pauses and looks round the cottage in a very pointed way. I watch his gaze travel over the shelf that once held Mam's books: her book of prayers, her book of Cookery Made Plain and Easy, the German Fairy Tales bound in ruby linen. The shelf is empty now. Bare and empty. I wait for him to ask why we have no prayer book, no bible. Instead he says something that stuns me, so that I cannot speak.

'Ann,' he says. 'You're a clever girl. A resourceful girl. You could be a housemaid. Or a nursery maid. Wouldn't you like that?'

I blink, like a fool.

'Your mother taught you to read and write, is that not so?'

He speaks the truth so I nod, and he says, 'If you are scrupulously honest and prepared to work your fingers to the bone, you could be a lady's maid. I can see that you are not averse to hard labour.'

Before I can stop myself, my most secret desire blurts from my lips. The words that run through my head every night, like fluttering ribbons. 'I dream of being a cook,' I say. I regret my words, of course I do. But it's too late to put them back, so I busy myself picking out a twig tangled in Mam's hair.

The Reverend Thorpe coughs, not a hoarse cough rattling with liquid like Pa's, but more like he has a breadcrumb stuck there. 'That would be ambitious indeed,' he says after a while. 'But perhaps in a small private family. Perhaps if you were to start as a scullery maid. How old are you, Ann?'

'Seventeen this coming Michaelmas.' I try to keep my voice sure and definite, but already my mind is straying. Before me float tightly crusted pies, buttery sticky puddings, birds turning on spits, shelves of ripe orchard fruit, fat barrels of sweet raisins, sticks of cinnamon as long as my hand – and all the other things Jack has told me of.

'You are old to go into service but I shall look out a position for you, regardless,' the vicar says. 'Everyone must pull their weight in God's world.' I should be cross, hearing him say I'm not pulling my weight. But my mind is only half here. The other half has flown clean away, to a kitchen where I'm chopping, slicing, stirring, fixing pigs to spits and trimming the fat from kidneys. Like Jack does in London. He says there's more food than I could ever imagine. Stockpots bigger than milk churns, Dutch ovens bigger than our cottage, larders the size of houses, mortars bigger than my own head. And then my stomach rumbles so loud I have to grip my sides for fear the vicar will think me too uncouth to work in a private kitchen.

He stoops beneath the door frame, which is barely high enough for a donkey. 'Your mother will be well fed and cared for, and you and your father shall earn some wages. So it's agreed.'

A tightness pulls and tugs at the back of my eyes. I can only be a cook if Mam is locked away in a madhouse? Is that what I've agreed to?

CHAPTER THREE

Eliza

OXFORD PUNCH

As the coach sways and rocks I try to distract myself by looking at the scarlet poppies and great mounds of hay, radiant and dishevelled. Crows rise, rags of black, from the dusty fields. But all this beauty only adds to my misery. Where once I would have exulted in finding the most accurate, the most fulsome words to describe such a scene, now every impression seems to taunt me. Besides which, I cannot stop thinking of everyone at home, waiting to hear of my meeting with the famous Mr Longman. His words of rejection have not left me once on this long rattling journey ... *Poetry is not the business of a lady ... nobody wants poetry now* ... And his final, demeaning request: *Go home and write me a cookery book and we might come to terms.* Terms indeed! I have no intention of repeating that particular line. Not to anyone.

As the coach approaches Ipswich, my shame and failure settle inside me like a brick. The sky blackens, peppered now with thousands of tiny silver stars. And when our house rears up from the dark – its windows flickering with candlelight, pale moths fluttering at the glass – I want nothing more than to disappear.

The front door bursts open, spilling breathless light and voices and the tumbling sounds of a pianoforte.

'Eliza's here! She's back!'

The pianoforte stops. Candles appear, wavering in the night air. And behind them, the eager faces of Catherine, Edgar and Anna. Even Hatty, the housemaid, is come to welcome me home.

Mother follows, squinting into the gloom. 'Eliza, is that you? We have all been waiting an absolute age. Hurry! Hurry! Or all the moths of Suffolk shall be making their nests in my new curtains.'

I am barely out of the coach before their pleas begin.

'What did Mr Longman say, Eliza? Oh, please tell!' begs Catherine. 'Tell us everything, from the beginning.'

'No, not from the beginning,' barks Edgar. 'We shall be here all night. Get directly to the point – how was Mr Longman?'

A sharp ache catches beneath my ribs. The disappointment of my family feels so much worse than my own.

Mother's will be tinged with I-told-you-so and a quiet pleasure at my failure, but not Edgar. Not my sisters. Not Father. Their disappointment will be palpable.

'Oh, Edgar, why must you be so impatient? Anna, ask Cook to bring a bowl of her best Oxford punch and tell her to be quick about it. John is still not home and it is making me fretful.' Mother wrings her hands anxiously. 'He was determined to be here for your arrival.'

I feel a sense of relief. Telling Father of my failure is what I dread most. He has always believed in me, always supported my endeavours. It was he who provided the money when I wanted to set up a school for young ladies. And it was he who funded my first volume of verse, insisting the paper and bindings be of the highest quality. 'No doubt he is delayed by paperwork or has misplaced his key,' I say, keeping my voice pert to hide the relief I feel.

'How was Mr Longman?' presses Edgar, spreading out his coat-tails and lowering himself into a chair. 'I am prepared to wager that Mr Longman thought your poems infinitely superior to those of that rascal, Lord Byron.' He rubs his hands up and down his thighs in mirth. 'We shall toast you as soon as the punch bowl arrives.'

'Please,' I say, in a thread of a whisper. 'No punch. There is nothing to celebrate.' I look down at my feet, at the streaks of London dirt on my boots, at the pearl buttons that are now black with coal dust. I have no appropriate words. Nothing to blunt the edge of their disappointment.

'Publishers no longer want poetry,' I say, eventually.

'Nonsense!' Edgar shuffles himself more deeply into his

chair. 'Is it because of your obstinate determination to use your own name?'

'Did you tell him of your last volume, of how it had to be reprinted in less than a month?' asks Catherine gently.

'Mr Longman did not propose I publish my poems under a nom de plume. He simply does not want them.' My fingers twine themselves in the seed pearls at my neck. My throat is hot and dry. 'I'm sorry.'

'Well,' says Mother, pausing to puff out her cheeks. 'I always considered your poems too frank – slightly indelicate, if you ask me. I expect that is why Mr Longman did not want them.'

My jaw tightens. I look down and see white salted rings beneath my arms and catch the stink of London on my dress and skin. 'He said no one wants poetry anymore. They want,' I stop and swallow, 'novels, romances, preferably of the Gothic kind.'

'Can you not write such a thing, dearest Eliza?' Catherine asks.

'This is all nonsense. You have no need of money. The poems were merely ... merely ...' Edgar's voice peters out, as if he isn't quite sure what the purpose of my poetry is.

'You exposed too much of yourself in that last volume,' adds Mother. 'There was an indiscretion that made some of our neighbours look upon me most curiously. You should never have published them under your – our – name, my dear. They were overwrought, too revealing.'

'So it is well enough for Mr Keats or Mr Wordsworth to reveal their passions, but not me. Is that what you mean?'

'I think Mother is merely asking if you cannot be content to scribble away in private,' says Edgar. 'True poetry has no need of an audience, surely?'

I grope, furiously, for the words that will explain why I want an audience, why I want my own name upon my own *scribblings*: that it is this – precisely this – that makes me feel part of a wider, deeper world, a richer world in which I am connected to others, a world in which I matter. How can I achieve this if I *scribble* only for myself? If I am blank, nameless?

Mother tilts her head to one side and nods. 'There is something a little ostentatious about seeking publication. For a lady, that is ... ungodly even.'

I stiffen, a burning behind my eyes. Mr Longman's words float before me ... *poetry is not the business of a lady* ... But for Mother to introduce God, to suggest that God's hand is at play is too much. I stare angrily at her but she has her eyes piously to Heaven.

Anna – sweet kind Anna – reaches for my hand, squeezes it. 'There are many other publishers, dearest Eliza. You must not despair.'

I nod gratefully, but cannot speak. My heart is too choked with the words of Mother and Edgar, mingling unpleasantly with those of Mr Longman. And beneath all my anger, beneath my justifications for an audience, hovers the perpetual doubt. *Imposter. Imposter.* But also something more, something hazy and obscure. A feeling of loss. Ebbing and flowing through the anger, the disappointment, the doubt. For what am I now? A spinster from Suffolk with a single small book of verse to my name ...

I stare at the silver punchbowl and my reflection glares back: a swag of dark hair, streaked with grey. A lattice of lines creeping round my eyes. Arcs appearing at the corners of my mouth. I am thirty-six. And I am nothing.

I excuse myself, mumble that the coach journey has exhausted me and bolt towards the stairs and up to my room, desperate to be alone. I want to plunge my head into my pillow and forget everything. I light a candle and lie on my bed, wondering if I should have taken a fortifying glass of Oxford punch. The smell of warmed spices and port wine seeps below my door, wrapping its fug around me like a shawl of softest lambs' wool. A glass of punch would have helped me sleep, I think. Helped me blot out the words of my family. But perhaps not the words of Mr Longman, which are altogether more tenacious, more shameful. Had I been a gentleman, I would never have been sent packing with a frivolous request for a cookery book. He spoke to me as if I were little more than a servant. Not even worthy of a novel. Or a book of botany or lepidoptera.

I sniff at the spiced air, as if for consolation, when all of a sudden my thoughts are sent scattering. From below comes a long, high wail. Like the piercing shriek of a barn owl. I sit up, startled. The house is alive with rising voices, slamming doors, a rushing heave of wind through the hall and up the stairs. As if a fire has slipped under its skin.

All thoughts of Mr Longman, of poetry, of myself, are gone. I grab the candlestick, run to the landing and look over the bannisters. Everyone is gathered in the hall, caught in a broad beam of lamplight. And such a ruckus! Father is back

and turning in flustered circles. Anna and Catherine are sob-
bing, Edgar is shouting, Mother has her head in her hands,
Hatty is watching with an open mouth.

Booted feet race up the stairs towards me. It's Father,
his white hair standing in wild peaks, his cravat hanging
loosely at his neck, his eyes flaring behind his wire-framed
spectacles.

'What is it?' I ask, confused and frightened in
equal measure.

'We are finished, Eliza! Finished!' He turns and runs down
the stairs to the drawing room, with me – bewildered – at his
heels. He catches sight of the punch bowl, its contents now
carrying a thin pale scurf, and staggers towards it. He draws
out the silver ladle, and drinks directly from its lip, so that
punch streams into his collar.

'We have lost everything.' He takes another mouthful, his
hand shaking. Crimson liquid runs down his neck, staining
his shirt, his cravat, the lapels of his frock coat.

'How?' I stare at him, assuming he's mistaken, or drunk,
or with fever of the brain. Every week the *Ipswich Journal*
lists a dozen or more bankruptcies, but none of the ilk of my
father, a gentleman, a Bachelor of Law from St Johns' College,
Cambridge.

'It's not my fault, Eliza. I was overcharged for the leases of
the Golden Lion and the King's Head. Grossly overcharged.
And the eight bushels of coal that were stolen left me severely
out of pocket. I had no choice but to borrow.' He plunges
the ladle back into the punch bowl and lifts it to his drip-
ping mouth.

'Borrow from whom? Can we not repay them?' I stare at Father and it's as if I'm staring at a stranger, a man I've never known.

'My debts are too huge … they'll declare me bankrupt, imprison me with common criminals. We are finished, Eliza!'

Just as I reach to take the ladle from him, Catherine bursts into the drawing room. 'Eliza, come quickly! Mother is in a swoon. Oh, what are we to do?'

CHAPTER FOUR

Ann

SEASONED GRUEL

I think of the vicar's words as I work our little patch of land that is no bigger than a tinderbox. Mam is bound to me with a rope that is three yards long. Together we hoe and dig and try to plant a few leeks. I say *together*, but mostly I am coaxing and cajoling. *Mam, will you not kneel now? Mam, please do not pull so on the rope. Mam, stop your griping!* All day long I am *Mam this* and *Mam that*.

Presently she begins to gnaw at the rope with her four teeth, which have become so loose I fear she shan't have them much longer. When I try to prise her mouth from the rope, I see her tongue has a mossy coating. I sniff at her breath. Her mouth and gums carry the thick low reek of sickness but there's no money for a doctor. All the money Jack sent has gone for Pa's new crutch that must be made with the sturdiest wood. The vicar says Pa can only work the graveyard if his crutches are of the very best quality.

'Mam, will you not sit still?' The rope cuts deep into my arm every time she strains at it. She raises her bony hand as if to strike me. I flinch and am about to call for help from Pa – who is asleep upon the mattress – when I hear a familiar voice singing in the lane. My heart leaps. I know that voice anywhere. Always so chipper, so full of good cheer. A minute later and he's swaggering through the gate like the cat that got the cream.

'Who is it, Ann?' Mam's eyes are full of the terror, darting this way and that. But I'm so happy to see Jack, I rush towards him, forgetting the rope. Mam is pulled roughly behind me and starts clawing at my back.

'For God's sake,' says Jack, all the song and swagger gone from him as he sees Mam and me lurching and tumbling. 'What's with the rope?'

I untie the rope and bind it instead round her wrists so that her hands stop their fevered scrabbling. Then I tell Jack how she has taken a turn for the worse, running away, taking all her garments off right down to her under-things, no longer recognising kith or kin. By the time I've finished, tears are pouring down my face and I can only gulp and choke.

'Mam? Mam?' Jack watches her squatting in the mud. 'I'm back from London with a few coins for you and Pa. I've walked two days with a drover and his goats, just to ... Mam?'

But she is staring at him, her eyes frozen with fear. 'I don't know you,' she says, and starts struggling with the ropes around her wrists. And when she cannot loosen them, she tries to jump across the earth, heading for the lane. I pull her back and hold her tight to me, weeping and stroking her scalp until she lies still against me. Her bones are as thin as a bird's and she smells like no mother should. It strikes me then that we have swapped parts, utterly and completely.

'Oh, Ann,' says Jack, shaking his head. 'Why must she be tied up like a donkey?'

I wipe at my eyes with a muddy fist. Finally, I whisper, 'The vicar wants her put in an asylum. He doesn't like her wandering around not properly dressed. He says it's not good for the morals of his parish. So I must tie her up.'

'Morals!' snorts Jack. 'Since when has a churchman had *morals*?'

'Hush,' I say. 'He's a godly man and well intentioned. Pa says so.'

'There's only one place you'll find God and it's not in a church or a vicar.'

'So where is it?' I pull myself and Mam up, and Jack helps manoeuvre the both of us inside.

'In a crust of bread,' says Jack, without the shred of a smile. 'Better still, in a good meal. I've always found him most present in a good hearty supper.'

His answer – and his voice so full of scorn – unsettles me. For didn't Mam raise us to trust in the Lord? I'm on the verge of telling him he's wrong, that sitting alone in church with the carved angels and the smell of burning candles makes me feel better, when I decide not to think about such things any longer. Mam is as quiet as a mouse now, all the terror gone.

'Tell me stories of London, of your work,' I beg. I have Jack to myself until Pa wakes up, or Mam starts her griping, or Septimus sets off with his barking, and I don't want to waste time talking about God or church, or anything else for that matter.

'I'm in the roasting kitchen now, skinning and trussing,' Jack says. 'There are two ranges as big as this mattress, and spits that can roast a whole sheep.'

'A whole sheep ...' I have a notion of tender roasted mutton, flavoured with woodsmoke and forest herbs. Saliva floods into my mouth. I put an iron pot of oats and water on a trivet over the fire, which is low and half-hearted. 'Tell me about the fine food you prepare.'

'Well, last week a gentleman returned a soufflé and Master Soyer let us taste it.'

'What's a soufflé?' I sigh, for that is how the word sounds. Soft and sweet as a summer breeze. I repeat the word in my head: Soufflé. Soufflé.

'You beat eggs as light as air. And you make a batter of cream and butter, very fresh and the butter as bright as possible and cut very small. Then you flavour it. Master Soyer likes to use an Italian cheese, or sometimes the finest bitter chocolate. And into the oven, where it rises so tall you cannot believe it. And when you bite in, it's like having cloud upon your tongue.' Jack smacks his lips together.

I stir absently at the gruel and wish we had a few currants to sweeten it. And as I think of currants, all manner of other dried fruits swim before my eyes. I've seen them at the market in Tonbridge. Great mounds of wizened shining prunes and raisins, orange peel crusted white with sugary syrup, rings of apple like the softest palest leather.

'There's a larder just for game. Snipe, woodcock, pheasants, grouse, guinea fowl . . . And a meat safe where great haunches of beef and venison are stored. And suckling pigs and whole sheep. And a stove where nine stew pans can be bubbling all at once.' Jack pauses and his eyes roll up to the ceiling, which is cracked and stained and has bindweed creeping at the corners. 'You should see Master Soyer. In his red beret, with a diamond ring as big as an acorn. It doesn't matter how hot the soup is, he plunges his finger in, diamond and all, and passes it across his tongue. And then he's shaking in this and that – more salt, more pepper, more cayenne. Until it is just so.'

'How grand,' I murmur, thinking of the drama of it all, and how a kitchen is like a puppet show, a fairy tale, and how good it must feel to have none of the violent hunger that comes on me and Pa and Mam when food and money are scarce. And how good it must feel to be in a room that is always warm.

'There are plenty of girls in the kitchen. But only pretty ones. The master says he wants no *plain* cooks in his kitchen.' Jack prods the dying embers with a poker and yawns.

I concentrate on the gruel, pushing the spoon hard against the iron pot. For a second I feel as if a huge door has been slammed in my face. For I am plain indeed. And for how long have I nursed my little dream of working alongside Jack?

Oh, months and months. Every night I go to sleep thinking
of Master Soyer in his kitchen whites with me at his side,
whisking, slicing, beating, tasting. That'll teach me, I think.
Dreams should be dreams and nothing more. I stir at the thin
grey gruel with extra vigour. Mam is sleeping now, curled up
on the mattress beside Pa. As peaceful as a pair of cats.

'Tell me more.' My voice comes out like the squeak of a
mouse. Jack narrows his eyes and looks at me very close,
but then he nods his head and starts describing all the
grand dishes that have swept beneath his nose on their
journey from the kitchen to the gentlemen diners. Pigeons
wrapped in the leaves of vines. Oysters in crisp pastry
cases. Whole Gloucester salmon in aspic. Yarmouth lob-
sters cooked in wine and herbs. Glazed tarts of pippin
apples. Paper-thin layers of buttery pastry spread with
greengages, apricots, peaches, cherries, served with great
gouts of golden cream.

'Well,' I say. 'It's gruel for us tonight, with a smidgen of salt
and pepper.' Whereupon he reaches into his pocket, pulls out
a twist of greased paper and opens it. Immediately I smell the
tang of heather honey.

'For you, Ann.' In his grimed palm sits an oozing chunk
of honeycomb as big as a plover's egg.

I clap my hands in delight, my tongue waggling with
greed. As we eat our gruel I make the clots of chewy wax
last as long as possible, pushing them round and round my
mouth, pressing them against my molars, sucking on them 'til
they slip sweetly down my throat. When my bowl is wiped
clean and the honeycomb quite gone from my teeth, I tell Jack

about the vicar wanting me to get a *position*, and thinking me *resourceful* and *clever*.

'And if Mam won't go to his asylum?' asks Jack. But I don't answer him. And I say nothing of Pa trying to strangle Mam when I have left them for barely an hour. Jack puts his bowl on the floor so that Septimus may lick it clean. 'And what do you want, Ann?'

'I want to be …' I pause, and then the word rushes from me. 'A cook.'

'A cook?' And he is doubled up, laughing so hard the tears stream from his eyes.

'Yes,' I reply, hurt. 'A *plain* cook.'

He points at his empty gruel bowl and starts laughing again. Then he wipes his eyes and says he's sorry and that even he – after three years of kitchen service – has only just moved up from turning spits. I want to remind him that I can read and write, and he cannot. That I can dream. And hope. But I hold my tongue. For what is the use?

My eye turns, of its own accord, to the shelf where Mam's books once sat. And that is when I know I'm all alone. A strange forsaken feeling comes over me. As if I'm standing on the very edge of the earth. Utterly alone.

CHAPTER FIVE

Eliza

BROWN BREAD PUDDING

I remove my books from their shelves, one by one, pausing to caress a particularly handsome spine or a binding of embossed Italian leather. Wordsworth, Keats, Shelley, Coleridge – I wrap each volume in a sheet of old newspaper and consign it carefully to a tea chest. I linger on the next shelf: the collected works of Ann Candler, seven volumes of Mrs Hemans' poems and three of L. E. Landon's. Every now and then I flick through the pages, reading a verse silently in my head, feeling wings sprouting on my shoulder blades.

When my small library is packed away, I grope beneath my mattress for a final volume ... neat, elegant and tightly bound in silk of sapphire blue. I sit on the edge of my bed and stare at it: *The Poems of Eliza Acton*. How slender and flimsy it seems. I run my finger down its spine, then lift it to my nose, inhaling its dry odour of dust and parchment. I open the book and feel the same sense of satisfaction as when I held it in my hands for the very first time, struck by how the neat orderliness of printing had transformed the inky sentiment of my verse. Moulded it into something with greater clarity. Bestowed upon it a weightiness and significance. And detached it from me, the final severing of an umbilical cord. The feeling had pleased me then, and it pleases me now. But as I look more closely, my insides curl and cringe ... *My first affections, and my last, were thine – thine only – fare thee well!*

How youthful those words seem now. Perhaps Mother was right. They are overwrought, brimming with exaggerated emotion. Or so it seems, a decade on. My new poems are better, defter, more mature. And yet Mr Longman ... An image of him comes to me, his plump ringed fingers patting at his pockets, the ticking of his gold pocket watch echoing in the swelter of his office, his vast polished desk that had sat between us like the Great Wall of China. He has yet to return my poems. Lost, no doubt. Drowned in the deluge of manuscripts – biographies, books of science, poetry, gothic novels – that come daily from the sweating fists of hopeful writers everywhere.

I slip the volume into the tea chest and look around my bedchamber: the empty grate, the damask curtains that have been taken from their hooks and folded in neat squares, the old Turkey rug rolled up and propped against the mahogany washstand. We are taking only the bare essentials: beds and linen, two tallboys, the elm kitchen table and the mahogany dining table with matching chairs. Everything else is to be sold at auction: the prints and paintings, the crystal, the silver plate, the feather mattresses, the wall clocks, the rugs and books. All except my collection of books which I fought to keep, offering up every piece of jewellery in its place. Much to the surprise of my sisters who declared themselves *flabbergasted* that I should prefer books to my triple string of pearls, or my diamond ear drops on gold wires, or my brooch of amethysts and rose quartz.

'Eliza! Eliza!' Mother's voice rises from the floor below.

I place the lid on the tea chest ready to be nailed down, and pick my way downstairs. The entire house is awry, with the heaving of furniture, the rolling of rugs, the lifting of portraits and maps from the picture rails, the dismantling of curtains, the wrapping and crating of china, books, mirrors and every piece of ornamentation from my past. All to grace the homes of others now. We are to leave for our new rented accommodation after dark, when no one will see us. Like thieves in the night.

Mother appears, her fingers chewing at the jet crucifix at her neck. 'Cook is in a terrible state. Do hurry down to the kitchen, Eliza.' She turns away and barks instructions at a boy standing idle in the hall.

'The kitchen?' I have not been below stairs for months and months. The kitchen, larders and scullery are the domain of Mrs Durham, the cook, who does not like visitors. Our previous cook was more open-hearted and as a girl I would cut pastry into oak leaves for decorating the crusts of pies, or punch my small fists into mounds of frothy dough. But Mrs Durham is decidedly unwelcoming. Only Mother and Hatty are permitted to take the back stairs now. Or Father, should he wish to check the contents of his wine cellar. But the wine has gone early to auction. And Father has fled to France.

Cook is sitting at the table surrounded by glass jars, tins of salt and loaves of sugar, baskets of eggs and onions. And at her feet, a circle of sacks – of flour, chestnuts, hops. 'Is none of this wanted, Miss Eliza?' Her eyes are pink, and her face washed through with the tracks of tears.

'It's all been so sudden, Miss Eliza. And to see the advertisement in *The Ipswich Journal*, even before we hears it from the mistress herself.' She pulls a fraying handkerchief from her pocket and blows noisily into it.

'But you're coming with us to Tonbridge. We shall need a good cook for our ... boarding house.' I frown at the words, new in my mouth. *Boarding house. Boarding house.* I don't like the feel of them in my throat or the sound of them in the air. I shake my head. But they hang there, like unripe fruit clinging to a windblown branch. 'Only you and Hatty are being retained,' I add, unsure if Mother has explained anything. 'Other servants we must find in Tonbridge.' *If we can afford them ... which is unlikely.*

Cook nods and blows her nose again. 'What am I to pack? I've received no instructions ... The jelly moulds? The cut-glass finger bowls? And what of all these spices? They're worth a pretty fortune.' She waves a juddering arm across the table, at the tins and glass jars and earthenware pots. All at once a shaft of thin northern light swoops over them, jolting them into luminous life: bubbled glass jars of briny green peppercorns, salted capers, gleaming vanilla pods, rusted cinnamon sticks, all leaping and glinting. The sudden startling beauty of it, the palette of hues – ochre, terracotta, shades of earth and sand and grass – the pale trembling light. All thoughts of running a *boarding house* vanish.

I reach for a jar, lift its cork lid. The scent of bark, earth, roots, sky. And for a second I am somewhere else. 'The mysterious scent of a secret kingdom,' I murmur. The jar contains little pellets, brown, spherical, unexotic. How marvellous that something so plain can have such an enthralling perfume, I think.

'Oh, Miss Eliza. Always the poetess! It's only allspice.' Cook gives a wan smile and gestures at the ceiling where long bunches of herbs hang from a rack. Rosemary, tansy, sage, nettles, woodruff. 'And what of these? All summer I was collecting these and they still ain't properly dry.'

'May I lower it?' Not waiting for an answer, I wind down the rack until the drying herbs are directly in front of me – a farmyard sweetness, a woody sappy scent, the smell of bruised apples and ripe earth and crushed ferns. Briefly, unexpectedly, I'm thrust back in time . . . pine needles scratch beneath my skin, light gushes through overhead branches, soft words fill my ears. Quickly I wind up the rack. 'Do you have family that could use these herbs, Mrs Durham?'

She brightens. 'Now there's an idea, Miss Eliza. And Mistress says all the books must be sold too, but not my own recipes surely?'

'We have cookery books?'

'Only a few.' She lumbers to the pantry, returning with

an armful of books. 'There's one here in French which I do believe you brought back from your travels, Miss Eliza.'

I pick up the volume, its corners worn, oily rings staining its leather bindings. *Le Cuisinier Royal* is stamped upon the tan spine. A second unwanted memory twitches inside me. I drop the book and begin leafing through another: *A New System of Domestic Cookery by a Lady*. I pause at a recipe for Pickled Oysters, scan it and frown. What messy strangled prose this *Lady* uses. Some of it is barely comprehensible. None of it conjures the exquisite sensation of a fresh oyster – briny and sharp, a rock pool at dawn – upon the unsuspecting tongue. 'Tell me, Mrs Durham, do these recipes make sense to you?'

'Truth be told, Miss Eliza, I can't make head nor tail of it. I'm not a good reader at the best of times.'

I re-read another recipe. The grammar is poor, the recipe unenticing, the entire thing flabby with half-formed opinions. 'If I read this aloud, will you tell me what this good *Lady* is attempting to say?'

'And why would you be asking?' She looks at me through half-closed eyes.

'It makes no sense to me, but perhaps that is because I have no expertise in the culinary arts. Unlike you, of course, who are so accomplished a cook we simply cannot imagine a future home without you.'

Mollified, she nods. 'Normally I use my own recipes, what I've collected over years and years of being a cook.'

I begin reading: '*Brown Bread Pudding. Half a pound of stale brown bread grated. Ditto of currants, ditto of shred suet, sugar and nutmeg: mix with four eggs, a spoonful of brandy, and two spoonfuls of cream. Boil in a cloth or basin that exactly holds it, three or four hours.'* I feel an inexplicable stab of annoyance. If anyone wrote a poem as imprecise and inarticulate as this recipe, they would be derided and mocked. 'Surely she doesn't mean half a pound of nutmeg? And what size is a spoonful? How are we to tell if she refers to a ladle or a salt spoon?'

Mrs Durham sucks in her cheeks and rolls her eyes. 'My own recipe is much better,' she says. 'Half a pound of nutmeg would take for ever to grate and it would cost a king's fortune too. And there's no mention of washing the grit from the currants, nor taking off their stalks.' She clicks her tongue, disapprovingly.

'And why does she say to boil for three *or* four hours?'

'Think of the waste, Miss Eliza. All that extra fuel needed when it might only take three hours and you've been boiling it for four hours.' She clucks again and shakes her head. 'Bad recipes to be sure, and yet every kitchen I ever worked in has a copy of that book.'

I scan the recipe a third time. Something gnaws at me. Something other than the implicit wastage and the irritating imprecision. My mind ticks through the ingredients: *bread, currants, suet, sugar, nutmeg, eggs, brandy, cream.*

'How do you imagine this Brown Bread Pudding would taste, Mrs Durham?' I close the book and, without thinking, tuck it beneath my arm.

'If it was me, I would be adding other ingredients. Salt to bring out the flavour ... just a pinch, mind you. And candied peel perhaps. And the zest of a nice fresh lemon stirred into the suet.'

'Indeed, Mrs Durham. Delicious,' I say softly. She is right, of course. This mysterious *Lady's* recipe is dull as well as poorly written, inexact, and scruffy in its presentation.

Cook swells beneath my praise and begins bustling round the kitchen, taking the herbs from the rack and binding them in twine.

'Take anything you wish,' I say, eager to escape with the cookery book. Mr Longman's words ring in my ears: *Go home and write me a cookery book and we might come to terms, Miss Acton.* Was I too hasty with my scorn?

'And these?' Cook holds up a clutch of books. 'I don't use any of 'em.'

'I'll take them,' I reply and hurry to my bedchamber, relieved the lid to my tea chest hasn't yet been hammered down. I slip the books inside, place a folded shawl on top and go down into the fray.

CHAPTER SIX

Ann

A BASIN OF BROTH THICKENED
WITH ARROWROOT

I'm at church a month later, when the vicar glances my way and nods his head at the vestry.

'Ann ...' His voice is a whisper, even though everyone has left.

'Yes, Father?' I try to look godly, hiding the pleasure from my face. Church has become the happiest part of my week, now that I may go alone and listen to the hymns and smell the white lilies on the altar and watch the coloured light coming through the stained glass in the arched window. All the while knowing that Pa won't yet have taken any ale and is securely bound to Mam. And then there is the walk home, through fields of corn and poppies. And although I must hurry, I always make time to nibble on hawthorn and dandelion leaves, or collect a few berries. As I used to when I was little and Mam – in her church best – would show me which leaves to eat and which blackberries carried the Devil's spit and must be avoided.

'I think there may be a position for you, as under-housemaid.' He rubs his thin white hands together and I see the bones moving beneath his skin. 'A new family is taking up residence here ... I couldn't recommend you to anyone familiar with your situation, of course.' He stops and gazes right over my head, looking for heavenly guidance I think to myself. I know only too well that no one wants a girl with madness in her blood. Nor do they want a girl whose father is a known drunk and whose mother roams the fields half-naked. But a new family is like a fresh clean canvas. They won't know of my shame.

'Where are they from, Father?' I ask, trying to stop my fingernails from jumping to my mouth in excitement. No one wants a girl who chews her nails.

'They have moved here from Ipswich. Might you be interested, Ann?'

'Yes, Father. If I can be assured my parents won't be alone.'

He is still sky-gazing when he replies. 'Leave that to me. Can you get to Tonbridge this week? Mrs Thorpe has an outgrown dress she is generously willing to lend you for your interview.'

My eyes go very wide, for Mrs Thorpe has never once smiled at me, let alone spoken to me. And then I wonder how her dress might look and my eyes stretch even wider – Mrs Thorpe has a bosom so ample you could trot a mouse on it.

I look down at my flat chest and see the vicar's eyes travelling in the same direction. As if he is reading my mind.

'You can sew, Ann?'

I nod.

'Good, good.' And he rubs his hands again as if he has a chill. 'A meek and pliable girl like yourself should suit them nicely.'

'May I ask the family's name, Father?'

'Their name is Acton.' He points at the vestry door, dismissing me in the way gentlemen do. I drop a curtsy and as I bob up he says, 'Do not disappoint me, or the Good Lord, Ann.'

'No, Father,' I say, but I'm not thinking of the Good Lord, for my head is full of other thoughts. Who is to look after Mam while I go to Tonbridge? The walk alone will take me thirty minutes there and thirty minutes back. In that time, Mam could have removed every shred of clothing and run naked all the way to Tunbridge Wells. Or Pa could have strangled her to death or beat her senseless with his crutch. I want to ask the vicar who will take Mam to the new lunatic asylum but I'm too late. The vestry door has closed with a clang and the iron key grates in the enormous iron lock.

A wind begins to blow up from the fields, shaking the leaves on the trees and making the hedgerows sway. Above me the heavens turn black. Needles of rain slice at my face. I gather up my skirts and break into a run.

At home there is no sign of Pa. The cottage is empty, even Septimus is gone. A feverish panic fills me. Where is Mam? My heart is galloping like a wild mule, and all thoughts of wearing a crisp white apron and stirring a silver cauldron with a long-handled spoon vanish. What was I thinking? Of course I can't go into service!

I stop and listen. And above the sounds of the wind, I hear someone moaning my name, very soft and sad. I rush to the back of the cottage and there is Mam, bound to a tree.

'Ann, Ann,' she wails, her hands pulling at her ears. I hurry to her side and scrabble at the knot, for he has bound her well and truly.

But then she turns on me, vicious, her eyes bulging like a frog's.

'You're not my Ann,' she shouts. 'Go away, you rogue!' A spew of vile language pours from her crusted tongue, words fit only for a drunken sailor. As her curses rain upon my head, I comfort myself by saying *the Acton family, a respectable family,* under my breath, over and over.

By the time I've untied the knots, rain is coming down in fat angry drops. 'Mam, we must go inside,' I say, all gentle and pleading, for she has such a fury on her now.

'No!' she shrieks. 'I must wait for my Ann.' And she lashes at my face with her uncut fingernails which are as sharp as blades, and ragged too.

'I am your Ann,' I plead.

'Liar!' She spits in my face, and as I step back she says something that strikes me cold. 'Ann is dead. Dead, dead, dead!'

That is when I know Mr Thorpe is right and I must get myself out of here, before I too go mad. I put my arms tight around her and manoeuvre her to the cottage. I can feel her sopping skirts against me as I pull her along and I thank the Lord she carries as little flesh as I do.

Later Pa returns from the tavern, his eyes a milky yellow but only a trace of ale on his breath. 'Ann,' he says and I notice his voice has the softest of slurs. 'I cannot go on like this. Mr Thorpe, God bless him, says if I stop the drink, he will give me a small stipend for keeping the graves clear of brambles and nettles.'

'So who will look after Mam while you're working?' I ask, keeping my voice light and steady.

'Ah, there's the rub.' His eyes fill with silver tears which he tries to wipe away with the backs of his hands. 'The lunacy is upon her stronger than ever.' He blinks very fast. 'She doesn't recognise us anymore. She has become little more than – an animal.'

I try to speak, to tell him he's wrong. But a lump the size of a quince has risen up my throat.

'The vicar says there's no cure for madness. And he says you have brains, Ann. Proper brains. He says he has found work for you. Not in an alehouse or on a farm, but in a private house with ladies of delicacy. Gentlewomen.'

I look away, fixing my eyes on the door, on the filthy muddy fingerprints that circle the latch and must be scrubbed away before they dry hard. I hadn't found the words to tell Pa what the vicar said. To repeat all that talk of *jobs* and *positions* would have doomed it, made it all vanish in a puff of smoke. 'Yes,' I whisper. 'I was going to tell you myself, but . . .'

I glance at Mam. She's sitting on the floor watching us blankly, as if she's someone else now, someone empty and gone. Not Mam at all. I put my arms around Pa and feel his wiry beard on my cheek. He smells of the tavern – drink and tobacco and woodsmoke – and clothes that need a good washing and airing.

'It'll be heavy work – carrying coal and water, scrubbing floors and beating carpets. But no more than here. And you'll be properly fed.' He indicates the pot on the fire which we both know contains nothing more than broth of peelings thickened with a pinch of arrowroot. From his mouth comes a long rasping sigh, so thick with defeat my heart goes out to him.

'I'll be paid, Pa. I'll send the money home.' I nuzzle my nose into his beard, thinking that I'll also get a good night's sleep at last, without ropes digging into my flesh or Mam's knees and elbows jousting with me every hour.

'Mr Thorpe is a good man, a godly man,' he says. I follow his gaze across the room to where Mam sits, all docile. And for a minute I wonder if we are both making a terrible mistake. Shouldn't I be here, looking after my mad mother and crippled father? What if this Acton family is no better? There's always a story or two in the village of some poor girl who has been beaten or locked up by her master. Or worse. Like the girls who return with bellies as round and full as a new moon.

'Pa, what do you know about this family that Mr Thorpe wants me to work for?'

'I believe you'll have two mistresses, a widow and a spinster. There is no man of the house.' And when he says that I know he's thinking just as I am.

Chapter Seven

Eliza

Crab-Apple Jelly

In spite of the fish vans that clatter through the town on their way to London and the hop pickers who arrive daily by waggon, Tonbridge does not have the hustle and bustle of Ipswich. This pleases Mother, who crows constantly about Tonbridge's *superior* inhabitants and its *superior* visitors. And it is these that she has her ruthless gimlet eye upon: the well-dressed ladies and gentlemen who come to take the waters of our neighbouring spa town, Tunbridge Wells, and are in need of *superior* rooms.

Our rented home is newly built and has its name – Bordyke House – carved into the lintel. As befits a *superior* boarding house, it is spacious, well furnished and situated far away from the town's open drains. And yet it feels all wrong, like a poorly cut coat. Perhaps this is because Edgar has set sail to make his fortune in Mauritius, and Catherine and Anna have taken up positions as governesses – all of us fleeing gossip and disgrace – so it is only Mother and me rattling around here. Or perhaps it is because no amount of *superiority* can disguise our future as the landladies of a boarding house.

We are in the morning room – yellow walls, armchairs upholstered in a shiny fabric featuring oversized yellow pineapples – when I finally muster the courage to suggest my plan to Mother. For three weeks I have worked on it. Night after night. Poring over cookery books by candlelight. Reading. Re-reading. During the days, as Mother busied herself arranging the furniture and placing advertisements for boarders, I loitered at the book dealer's, ordering books we could ill afford.

'Mother, do the lawyers have any claim on our remaining possessions?'

'I think not, my dear. I hope not. But we must make enough money to be independent.' She looks up from her ledger. 'We are woefully short at present. I have placed three advertisements for boarders and spoken to the vicar and the headmaster of Tonbridge School. We are in debt to the tune of ...' she pauses and scrutinises her ledger. 'Twenty guineas, perhaps more. The finances are muddled. Or I am muddled. I cannot tell which.'

'Can we afford to keep Mrs Durham?'

'We must have someone to cook for our boarders.'

'But we have no boarders. And this house is substantial – and costly.'

'Well, my dear, I cannot cook and nor can you.'

I take a deep breath. 'Mr Longman asked me to write a cookery book.'

Mother looks up, startled. 'You never mentioned that. What a rude man!'

'I've decided to accept his commission, if it still stands.'

'But you cannot cook, Eliza. You have never cooked. Besides, *ladies* do not cook.'

'I'm determined to make a contribution to the household costs.'

'You wish me to dismiss Mrs Durham and put you in her place? In the kitchen? Like a common servant?' Mother's mouth settles in a stubborn pout.

'Yes,' I reply shortly. 'We can pay her off – generously – and then I shall teach myself cookery and write the book Mr Longman has requested.'

'You wish to practise cookery on our paying guests?'

I lower my voice and look down at my hands. 'You forget, I have spent time in Italy and . . . in France.'

'But you were not cooking!' The word *cooking* bolts from her mouth as if she cannot get shot of it fast enough. 'Whatever else you were doing, you were not working in a windowless kitchen, below stairs.' She pauses, then screws up her eyes and stares at me. 'Or were you?'

'French food made a great impression on me.' For a second, a creamy vanilla pool collects sweetly in my throat. As if my body remembers where my mind will not. Then Mother squares her jaw and the taste slides away. 'I've been studying cookery writers and I can do better. Some of them are barely literate. The measurements are imprecise, the wording is inelegant. They lack clarity and even the recipes themselves are unappetising.' I glance at Mother – she is wringing her hands, her lips and jaws working soundlessly.

'I shan't be a cook. I shall be a cookery *writer*. It is perfectly seemly.' From beneath my gown I produce *A New System of Domestic Cookery by a Lady*, and offer it to her.

She flicks through the pages, her nostrils flaring. 'Your folio of verse was bad enough. But this . . .' She taps a fingernail on the cover. 'This is . . . unbecoming. If you wish to contribute financially I think you should find a position as a governess. With your experience, a place in a prominent family should be quite possible.'

Something cools and hardens inside me. I'm not the person who once ran a school, who inspired intelligent girls to excel, who accompanied wealthy young ladies on their grand tours. No – I am someone else entirely now and there can be no return. Sometimes I wonder if my past experiences have rendered me feeble. Frail even. For the merest thought of being in a schoolroom again fills me with exhausted dread. How much more pleasant a kitchen seems . . .

'At least let me write to Mr Longman and agree terms.'

'And you would publish anonymously of course, like this alleged *Lady*.'

A small sigh escapes my lips. I know Mother will be shamed by my – our – association with kitchen work, but I cannot forget my book of verse, *Poems by Eliza Acton*. I cannot forget the many times I ran a fingertip over my name, not from conceit or from pride but because it showed me who I was. Because, in some strange way, it placed me in the world. 'Only if Mr Longman insists,' I say after a lengthy pause.

She drops the cookery book in my lap and returns to her ledger. 'You are always so bellicose, Eliza. No wonder you have no husband.' She picks up her pen and prods at a column of figures. 'The saving on Mrs Durham will be ten guineas a year. I suppose we can try it ...'

'Thank you! Thank you!' I leap from my chair with such exuberance *Domestic Cookery by a Lady* flies into the air.

'Well, I can't have you mooning over poetry at your age. But you'll need help in the kitchen, a scullery maid. She can sleep in the eaves with Hatty.'

'I want someone quiet. And clever.' The thought of an ill-educated garrulous girl with dirty fingernails and not an ounce of common sense, in my ear all day, suddenly seems unendurable. I must have a modicum of seclusion and solitude, I think to myself.

'You can choose the girl yourself.' Mother swivels her arched eyebrows in my direction. 'What if it turns out that you have no skill for cookery?'

I don't answer her, for my thoughts are elsewhere ... the exotic spices arriving daily from the East Indies and the Americas, the crates of sweet oranges and bitter lemons from Sicily, the apricots from Mesopotamia, the olive oil from Naples, the almonds from the Jordan Valley ... I have seen and smelt these delicacies at market. But does any English person know how to cook with such foods?

I think back to my time in France and Italy, of all the delicacies that passed across my tongue. And then to the gardens I've seen in Tonbridge with their raised beds of sorrel, lettuce, cucumbers, marrows, pumpkins. Already the banks are starred bright with blackberries and rosehips, with damsons and sour sloes, the bloom still upon them. Trees are weighted down with green apples and yellow mottled pears and crab apples flushed pink-and-gold. Soon there will be fresh cobnuts in their husks and ripe walnuts and field mushrooms and giant puffballs.

I have a sudden craving for crab-apple jelly. A craving so sharp, my tongue aches. I turn back into the room. Mother's head is bent low over her ledger again.

'My first attempt at cookery will be crab-apple jelly,' I announce.

'Do you have the slightest idea how to make a jelly set fast?'

'With sage,' I add, as an afterthought. Yes, sage, I think. Such a muscular, earthy herb – perfect for the cruel tartness of those tight little crab apples.

'Eliza? Did you hear me?'

CHAPTER EIGHT

Ann

EXCELLENT PORTABLE LEMONADE (WITH LAVENDER)

Today is my interview. I'm all dressed up in Mrs Thorpe's cast-off frock, which is billowing around me, far too big and roomy for a scrawny creature like me. Mrs Thorpe has spoken to me for the first time, saying I will double in size once I'm working in Miss Acton's house. She also told me that I must call Miss Acton *ma'am* and reveal nothing of my *bad blood*.

I help Pa rope himself to Mam. She's quiet today, as if she knows I'm up to something. I walk the half-hour to Tonbridge, trembling like a leaf and my mouth as dry as sawdust. My nerves are made worse by the wearing of Mrs Thorpe's frock, for I'm afraid of damaging it and must lift the trailing skirts high. She made it plain she was only lending it because her husband is a godly man and the frock is worn-to-a-thread and fit only for the rag-and-bone man.

When I find Miss Acton's house my shakes get worse, for the house is very big and very grand. I slip through the carriage entrance, past a brewhouse, a wash house and a coach house. Fresh straw has been strewn over the cobbles, although there are no horses or carriages and all the doors are shut fast.

I'm standing in the yard, smoothing at my hair and at Mrs Thorpe's skirts, when a door bursts open. Out steps a lady, very tall, with dark hair that is swept up and twisted with pins. 'Can I help you?' she asks.

'I'm Ann Kirby, come to speak with Miss Acton.' My voice is all up-and-down squeaky.

'I am Miss Acton,' she says, which surprises me because Mrs Thorpe says gentlewomen sit in their parlours, out of the sun. She asks me to follow her inside, and as I walk behind her I get a good eyeful of her frock, which is pale blue and of the softest fabric, with real lace at the collar. She has no jewels – nothing at the ears or neck – and I wonder if this is to preserve me from temptation. Mrs Thorpe told me never to stare at a lady's jewels in case I'm thought a common thief.

'We will talk in the kitchen,' she says. I nod my head but cannot speak for my mouth is stiff with fear.

The kitchen is roomy and lofty, four times as big as our cottage. Copper pans hang from the ceiling and fluted copper moulds in every size run over the walls. In the middle is an enormous table all covered with fancy utensils, which I guess to be sugar nippers, dredgers, pastry prickers and cutters, butter

moulds and meat carvers. They are so beautiful, all embossed
and shaped and shining, I want to look at them for ever.

'This is where we shall be spending our days,' she says.
And I am so confused by her words I just stare at her, speech-
less. Who is *we*? I look round for the cook, but she must be in
the garden or gone to market.

'Tell me where you've worked, Ann.' Her voice is soft, very
gentle and kindly, so that I forget my nerves. But then she says
something that throws me even more. 'Forgive me, I have not
offered you refreshment. How rude of me! Would you care
for a glass of fresh lemonade?'

I shake my head, for it's not her place to be pouring drinks
for *me*. I will wait for the cook to return, I think.

But she presses me, saying 'I made it myself this morning.
I've been experimenting and this version includes a little
crushed lavender.'

I don't want her to think me rude, so I nod and whisper,
'Yes please, ma'am.' Just as Mrs Thorpe told me.

She pours a tall glass. And then I realise she's waiting for
me to drink it. Mrs Thorpe didn't mention anything about
drinks, so I'm unsure what to do.

'Drink!' Miss Acton commands.

I take a sip, and it's like nothing I've ever tasted. Sweet and
sour and sharp and blossomy all at once.

'What do you think?' she asks. I stare at her, forgetting that
Mrs Thorpe told me never to stare.

'Well, speak,' she says, but I don't think she's cross because
there's a little smile on her lips.

I don't say that her question makes me nervous, that Mrs

Thorpe told me I must never have an opinion. And nor do I tell her that the lemonade tastes of something I can't put into words, of Mam shredding lavender flowers and mixing them with the crushed leaves of verbena and lemon balm ... Tears prick at the back of my eyes, and I reach for the table to steady myself.

'Are you unwell?' Miss Acton comes to my side and helps me into a low chair where I sit, hot and ashamed and trembling.

'You need more lemonade,' she says, and pours another glass. Then she stoops beside me and holds the glass right by my face so I can see the pale cloudy liquid and smell the lemons and lavender all over again.

'Perhaps the heat has affected you, in that worsted dress.' She puts the glass on the floor and leaves the room. And I know full well she's gone to write a letter of complaint to Mrs Thorpe, that I have done everything wrong – and shown myself to be puny and rude and a disgrace. No doubt my *bad blood* has shown itself.

I drink the lemonade, and it's like coming from a grey dream and feeling the world lift and rise around me. Calming. So that when I hear her step in the hall, I jump up and stand very straight beside the sink. As if I'm ready for work.

'You're better,' she declares.

'The l-lemonade, ma'am,' I stutter. I want to make amends by telling her how delicious it is, but when I pause, Miss Acton leaps in.

'It made you unwell? Oh, that is terrible!' She frowns severely and peers into the earthenware jug. 'I think the lavender was a mistake. Perhaps cold milk and a dash of sherry would improve it . . .'

'No, ma'am,' I say, desperate now. 'It is the most delicious thing I have ever tasted and brought back such memories I was quite overcome. I'm sorry, ma'am. I'm normally strong as an ox, ma'am.'

She looks at me, very keen and solemn. This is it, I think. She'll ask me to leave now, on account of my impertinence. But she doesn't. She throws back her head and laughs, and I see her long pale throat with wisps of dark hair jigging round her ears.

'I think you and I shall get along exceptionally well,' she says once she's stopped laughing. 'Tell me, where else have you worked?'

I'm baffled and bewildered, but Mrs Thorpe prepared me for this question, so I answer quick as a flash. 'I've been looking after my parents who've been in delicate health until now. My father fought against Napoleon, ma'am. I can carry coal and water, and I can clean grates and black stoves, and polish and dust and run a hem. And I can scrub vegetables and peel potatoes and chop kindling and lay fires.'

'Can you read and write?' she asks, pushing a book towards me.

I nod, whereupon she asks me to open the book and read.

I turn the cover and see it's a book of recipes. All at once I feel a thrill run over me, as if there's a fire under my skin. But the fire blows up too quick, and turns to panic. 'Ma'am, I have not read for some years.'

'Go as slowly as you like,' she says, all the time smiling in a most encouraging way.

I open the book and begin reading, very slowly and concentrating very hard. 'To dress a hare,' I read. She nods and smiles and her eyes are warm and generous. 'Wash her in fair water, parboil her, then lay her in cold water. Then lard her and roast her. For sauce, take red wine, salt, vinegar, ginger, pepper, cloves and mace, and put these together. Then mince onions and apples and fry them in a pan. Then put your sauce to them with a little sugar. And let them boil together and so serve it.'

When I finish reading there's a short silence until my stomach growls with hunger. My face scalds again but Miss Acton just laughs and asks me where I learned to read so well.

'My mam taught me,' I say. 'She was most particular that I learn to read. My brother would not take to his letters, but I liked nothing more.'

'You must have an excellent mother,' she says, and her smile flows right across her lovely face.

I feel suddenly tired, as if the reading has taken all the life from me.

'I think you will do perfectly,' she says. 'We cannot pay much but would you accept five shillings a week?'

I am so blinded by this question that I freeze, like an idiot. It isn't that I don't believe her – although the house is so grand they are surely rich as Croesus – but more that I am flummoxed at her question. Mrs Thorpe said I would be informed of the wages and that I was to curtsy and say, 'Thank you, ma'am.' But I remember this too late and Miss Acton is speaking again, all flustered and concerned.

'The wages will rise, of course, as you become more

familiar with the workings of the house. Perhaps we can stretch to a little more. I can see that it's not a vast wage, but . . .'

'Five shillings is very kind, ma'am,' I say quickly, before she takes it away and writes to Mrs Thorpe that I am full of cheek.

'Excellent. Would you like to see the room where you shall sleep? You will be with our housemaid, Hatty, who has come with us from Ipswich.'

I look at her in alarm. Another question Mrs Thorpe said nothing of.

'I'm sure it's very nice, ma'am.'

'Good,' she says, and she puts her hand on my arm as if to steer me, gentle-like, to the door. And the feeling of her hand upon my arm makes me come over peculiar for no one has touched me with affection for so long. With Mam it's all tying and binding, or else she's shoving and prodding at me. And with Pa it's no different – either I'm bearing the weight of him or tugging at him, with the stir of his drunken breath in my face. But Miss Acton is so clean, so warm and pure and orderly.

'There is one final thing,' she says, as we enter the yard. My eyes go wide and stiff again, for surely now she has seen the truth of me – the *bad blood*.

'Yes, ma'am.'

She pauses and her hand flutters at her throat. 'We must find another way for you to address me.'

'Yes, ma'am,' I say, panicked. For I don't know what she means.

She laughs again, as if I've said something funny. 'You may

address Mrs Acton as ma'am, but would you be comfortable calling me Miss Eliza?' She reaches out and touches me on my arm again with her long pale fingers, very quick and light.

'Yes, ma'am,' I say, shaken. She laughs and I see what a dunce I am. 'Yes, Miss Eliza,' I say, speaking in the voice I use on Mam, my Napoleon voice. It bursts from me of its own accord and when I hear the force of it, I clap my hand over my mouth. But Miss Eliza only nods and smiles. And her blue eyes sparkle like dewy forget-me-nots with the sun flashing over them.

I dance all the way home, through the stubbled cornfields and the copse of oak trees, everything bathed in soft green light. It's only when I turn the final corner that I remember Mrs Thorpe told me to mention Jack – and how he works in the grandest kitchen in London. Oh, what a fool I am! My tongue was so tied by the beautiful Miss Eliza with her lemonade, and her kitchen all neat and gleaming like paradise, that Mrs Thorpe's command flew straight out of my head. I decide not to tell her. Nor shall I tell her how Miss Eliza touched me, like a friend. I put Mrs Thorpe out of my head – along with her trailing dress which is scratching and prickling at every seam – and hurry to the cottage, hoping Pa has kept his promise and stayed off the drink and not murdered Mam.

Chapter Nine

Eliza

Very Good Lemon Creams

The eggs are still warm and stuck with feathers as I count them from the basket. I pour grated sugar from the earthenware jar, then take a freshly whetted knife and pare the rind from two lemons. The world slips away. I feel my eye, my nose, my palate yielding, and I think how satisfying it is to scrape at a lemon, to lose myself in its sharp bright song.

I have started to see poetry in the strangest of things: from the roughest nub of nutmeg to the pale parsnip seamed with soil. And this has made me wonder if I can write a cookery book that includes the truth and beauty of poetry. Why should the culinary arts not include poetry? Why should a recipe book not be a thing of beauty?

My thoughts come quickly and smoothly in the solitude of the kitchen and as I beat the eggs I find myself comparing the process of following a recipe to that of writing a poem. Fruit, herbs, spices, eggs, cream: these are my words and I must combine them in such a way they produce something to delight the palate. Exactly as a poem should fall upon the ears of its readers, charming or moving them. I must coax the flavours from my ingredients, as a poet coaxes mood and meaning from his words. And then there is the writing itself. Like a poem, a recipe should be clear and precise and ordered. Nothing stray or flabby or inexact. And yet the recipes I follow now are like the very worst poems – sloppy, scrappy, disordered.

When Mr Longman wrote to me with his terms, he divulged a little more about the mysterious *Lady*, author of the successful but deeply frustrating *A New System of Domestic Cookery by a Lady*. The *Lady* (a Mrs Maria Rundell) has been dead some years. But before dying she sold half a million copies of her cookery book, a fact underlined twice by Mr Longman in his letter. As if to say that is what he expects from my modest efforts. Half a million readers!

I scan Mrs Rundell's recipe a third time, with a flutter of irritation. Why didn't the wretched woman arrange the ingredients in a simple list? It would be easier, I think, to list them myself rather than reading and re-reading the recipe over and over.

I shall write my recipes differently, I decide. I shall list the ingredients separately – and with precise measurements. Yes – with the most minute exactness! Surely women have

enough to juggle in their heads without having to memo-
rise lists of ingredients as they work? And it is women I
shall write for. Mr Longman has been most specific on this
point: *'Aspiring ladies from the growing merchant classes wish
to display their domestic qualities at dinners and the like. They
require assistance in the guidance of their cooks or so that they
themselves may be coaxed into the kitchen for the pleasure of their
husbands or to enable their husbands to entertain and impress
important persons.'*

I sigh deeply, for Mr Longman has yet to return my folio
of poems despite my asking twice, despite my accepting
his cookery book commission. I cut the lemons in two, then
squeeze each half into the mixing bowl, crushing them until
not a drop of juice remains – and until all thoughts of Mr
Longman have gone. My mind slides to Ann Kirby. Such an
odd little creature. Plain. Freckled. Bony. Her collarbones
jutting from a winter dress that positively ballooned around
her. And her shoulders stooped and rounded, as though
she'd spent her short life heaving sacks of coal. And yet able
to read ... and so responsive to my lavender lemonade. As if
she has a thread of poetry running through her. Her face, in
all its childish hesitancy, revealed traits I like: honesty, curi-
osity, intelligence. There was something else about her too.
A poignancy I can't explain. A feeling that we are united in
some odd and inarticulate way. Mother objected, of course,
demanding to know my reasons for hiring a girl who has
never been in service. She stopped her complaints when I told
her how inexpensive Ann was, how her letter of recommen-
dation came directly from a vicar.

'Wonderful news, Eliza dear!' Mother's trill interrupts my thoughts. 'Our first boarders arrive on Monday. A Colonel and Mrs Martin, from Spitalfields in London, come to take the waters for his gout. Will you be ready for them?'

A nervous excitement spikes inside me. 'I'm attempting jugged hare and lemon creams for luncheon, and spiced beef with dandelion leaf salad for dinner, followed by Apple Charlotte.' I suck at my finger where lemon juice has made its way into a knife cut, and silently curse my clumsy hands that have slipped upon the bread rasp, the paste jigger, the nutmeg grater, the herb cutter. 'If the dishes are good, I shall repeat them next week.'

'Goodness, Eliza – your hands! They are chopped raw! Who will marry you with hands like that?'

I roll my eyes. 'I'm not expecting any offers of marriage.'

'But what if Colonel Martin has an eligible brother?' Mother pats her hair with her fingertips.

'I would rather be a hated old maid than marry a gouty old man who needs nursing.'

'Oh, Eliza! An old maid has less value than a clod of dirt. Surely you want respect and dignity? Perhaps Colonel Martin will have a son who does not have gout.' She sniffs and looks me up and down. 'The blacksmith's wife is with child and apparently she is forty-three. Forty-three! Her hair is completely white, while yours is still a lovely shade of chestnut.'

'If you leave me in peace I can work on my cookery book which will give us an income quite independent of Colonel Martin and his possible sons and brothers.' I crack an egg on the bowl's rim and watch the yolk and its white slip free. Not a shard of shell escapes, and for a second I feel inordinately happy at this minor accomplishment.

'And do you plan to devise your own recipes? Or are you simply plundering the work of others?'

'I'm teaching myself to cook and then I shall write to all our friends and acquaintances and ask them to donate their favourite recipes.' My knuckles whiten beneath the whisk and the yolks spin a little faster round the bowl.

'So that all and sundry will know you have become a – a cook?' splutters Mother.

'And I shall create my own recipes,' I continue, keeping my voice steady and even. I don't tell her I'm already combining, pairing, mixing things in my mind – fruits with spices, fresh fish with herbs, meat with wild leaves and cream – for I doubt she would understand.

'Well, my dear, when you write to *our* friends and acquaintances, I propose you tell them that we need a varied menu for our boarders. There's no reason to say any more than that.' She folds her arms staunchly over her chest. 'At least that is respectable.'

'No, Mother. If I use their recipes I will credit them in my book. Unless they'd rather be anonymous.' I keep my gaze on the eggs, lifting the whisk high into the air then plunging it back into the bowl until my arm aches. 'You must have things to prepare for Colonel and Mrs Martin,' I say at length, wishing she would go away.

'Hatty is settling into Tonbridge very well,' she says. 'But

I think she will be happier when the scullery maid arrives and she has a friend.'

I think of Ann ... scrawny little Ann, rendered speechless by my lemonade. 'And so will I,' I say. 'So will I.'

CHAPTER TEN

Ann

ACTON GINGERBREAD

I arrive at Bordyke House on Sunday night but there's no sign of Miss Eliza. Instead an uppity housemaid takes me to the room in the eaves that we're to share.

'You may call me Hatty,' she says, looking at me like a starving cat come across a mouse. 'I've been in service before and this is my third job and I've come with the Acton family all the way from Ipswich, so I'm in charge here.'

'In charge of me?' I ask, looking round the little attic room. There are two beds, both of them narrow but properly raised from the floor, with sheets and blankets. The window is small and looks over the carriage entrance. There's a washstand with a basin and jug, a chest where I'm to store my belongings, and a chamber pot with a faded green bird on the side.

'Of course,' she says. 'Where's your box? Ain't you worked in service before?'

I feel so ashamed I open my mouth to lie, to say my box is coming later. But the lie won't come. I shake my head, mumble, feel my face scalding. Am I the only girl who has nothing of her own? Not even a change of clothes or shoes . . .

'No box? Every girl has a box.'

'It's all in my bag,' I point to the dirty canvas bag that contains my hairbrush, a set of rags for my monthlies, a cracked heel of soap and a whittled stick for my teeth. 'When can I meet the cook?'

'There ain't no cook here,' says Hatty, with a little superior smirk. 'There's only Miss Eliza and she won't be giving orders up here, will she?'

I frown, the shame of being without a box pushed aside by my confusion. Mrs Thorpe was most definite about me working for a cook. 'No cook? Who prepares the food?'

'Miss Eliza,' says Hatty and before I can close my mouth, which is hanging wide open, she tells me to get into bed because the first boarders arrive tomorrow and Ma'am wants us up at half past five.

As soon as I'm lying in bed, Hatty starts whispering, asking me questions about my family. Questions Mrs Thorpe says I must never answer. *Why are you so late into service, Ann? Are your mother and father still alive, Ann?* I mumble and mutter until she starts on questions I can answer without telling any lies.

'How many of your brothers and sisters have died, Ann?'

'All seven except me and my brother, Jack.' I don't say that four of them died of the sweats in a single weekend. I don't want to think about that now.

'Have you a fancy man, Ann?'

'No.'

'Why not?'

'I don't know. Have you?'

'Yes, a boy in Ipswich. He works for a draper and can get any fabric you want. Also cotton thread in any colour. We're to be married next year when I'm eighteen. D'you know everyone in Tonbridge, Ann?'

'No, not really. Just the vicar and his wife.'

'Don't you have any friends here?'

'My brother, Jack, but he's in London.'

Eventually Hatty falls asleep, right in the middle of an instruction about how I'm to do exactly as she says unless I'm in the kitchen with Miss Eliza. I listen to a scurrying creature in the rafters and try not to cry. Mr Thorpe took Mam away today. To the new asylum, where he says everyone is very godly. Tomorrow Pa will work in the graveyard, I will work at Bordyke House and Mam will – what will Mam do? Mr Thorpe says she'll have her own nurse who'll calm her when she has the terrors, and protect her modesty when she tears at her clothing. Eventually I stop thinking about Mam, Pa, home, and I start thinking about Miss Eliza, who is really a cook and not a lady at all. And I wonder why Mrs Thorpe didn't explain this to me. When my thoughts stop churning, I listen for the scurrying creature but it's gone. I wish Hatty would snore, or toss and turn, or shout out in her sleep. Like Mam and Pa do. But she just lies there very still.

The next morning I creep down to the kitchen. Everything is neat and tidy, clean and polished and in its place. The glasses stand in lines upon a shelf, ranged in size from those no bigger than my thumb to those I suppose are for jelly or wine, cut to dazzle and with trailing plants etched around the rim. Above them are earthenware flagons and pewter jugs, not like Mam's, but with great curving handles. The earthenware has no cracks or chips and the pewter has a gleam that ours does not. Freshly oiled oak spoons, with carved handles, stand upright in enamelled pots. On the table are three willow baskets: one contains two dozen brown hens' eggs, another has half a dozen white pullets' eggs and a third – lined with red cloth and fresh straw – contains speckled eggs no bigger than my thumbnail. The eggs of plovers or quail, I think to myself with a rush of hunger. I haven't eaten an egg since Mam got ill and we sold our hens.

But then I catch sight of a newfangled range and fear pours into me. I put my finger to it and it's warm as toast. I'm gawping at the range and wondering why I didn't notice it before when Hatty appears and asks me why I haven't raked the ashes.

'Oh, Hatty,' I whisper. 'I've never seen one of these 'til now.' I expect her to look all smug but she doesn't. Instead she kneels down and says Ma'am likes the cinders separated from the ashes and re-used.

'You must put the ashes on the blackcurrant bushes in the garden,' she adds. 'But first you move the fenders and the fire-irons, throw in the damp tea leaves to keep the dust down, then it's the raking and sifting. After that you clean away the grease, then black and polish the stove.' She opens a door at the bottom of the range and points inside. 'The lead and turpentine and brushes are in there. But always do it early while the range is still warm so that a good shine comes up. Then you whiten the hearth and lay the fire. Miss Eliza likes coal for the range. Have you used coal before?'

I shake my head. At home we use gorse and cow dung from the common, which makes our cottage stink half to death, although the Reverend Thorpe has said Pa can take the furze and pine cones from the graveyard now he's working. But I don't tell Hatty that, not only because I'm ashamed but because she might ask why the vicar is so particular about my family. And I'm not sure she'll believe Pa's answer – that he is a godly man. So I keep my lips tight shut.

'Are you still using a tinderbox at home?'

I nod.

'The Actons use matches. I'll show you how to strike one.'

I've never struck a match before and when I scrape the stick, it flares red and blue, and shoots sparks everywhere, and a foul smell like a rotten egg bursts into the room.

'I shall be glad not to clean this range anymore,' says Hatty, before telling me I must rise extra early on Fridays to clean the flues.

'And you do everything?' I ask, thinking of how big the house is, all the rooms and fireplaces and windows that must be kept clean.

'In Ipswich, there were seven of us and a butler. But

something terrible happened – I'm not allowed to speak of it –
and now there is just you and me. But Ma'am has promised
more servants once the boarders arrive. Which is today, Ann!'
And she claps her hands and beams at me, as if the boarders
are a great gift to us all. 'An army colonel and his wife with
their own housemaid – so I won't need to empty and scrub
their chamber pots. And perhaps they'll bring a boy.' She
winks at me when she says *boy* and I feel a flush travel up my
neck and across my cheeks.

By the time I've finished the stove – which seems to
take hours and hours and leaves my hands black as pitch –
the clock strikes eight and Hatty changes her apron and
says she must go to Ma'am. 'Don't forget that I'm in charge
and you're to do exactly as I tell you,' she adds, all bossy
again, as if she has slipped inside another skin. 'Oh, and
you can break your fast with bread and dripping from the
larder, but not too much, mind.'

I've been so busy I've barely thought of Mam. Or Pa on his
first day in the graveyard. And I've certainly not thought of
breakfast. But when Hatty leaves – having instructed me to
scour the shelves in the scullery – I think of Mam out walking
with her nurse in the asylum gardens that Mr Thorpe says are
flush with flowers. I told Mr Thorpe that Mam doesn't like
strangers or new places, but he said I was to put my trust in
the Lord. And so I do. Even now, as tears spill from my eyes.

'Why, Ann, you are weeping,' says Miss Eliza, who appears
as silent and sudden as a barn owl.

I wipe my eyes and shake my head. 'Oh no, Miss Eliza, I
have ash in my eye,' I say.

'No doubt it feels strange for you here. But if you feel an ounce of sadness, you will tell me, won't you?'

How to answer without telling yet another lie? I nod and say nothing, just look at my feet as Mrs Thorpe told me to. But I cannot keep my gaze upon my boots, with their watermarks and frayed laces and the soles that are coming away from the uppers. So I raise my head and see her observing me from her forget-me-not eyes, with their long dark lashes.

'We shall be busy today,' she says, putting her hand to her pale throat and stroking it in an absent-minded way. 'What are your thoughts on a stewed shoulder of veal with potato boulettes, followed by a baked plum pudding?'

Her question confuses me. What is a *boulette*? And how am I expected to have thoughts on a menu? 'It sounds very good,' I say, pressing my palm against my stomach to stop the growling.

'I think it's perfect for a Colonel with gout,' she says. 'And perfect for our first day together, as the recipe is not too complicated. Why don't you start on the plum pudding?' She sees the terror in my eyes and gives a reassuring smile. 'Find a loaf of stale bread, and then remove the crusts and grate it finely. Everything's in there.' She points to the larder. 'My mother only has China tea for her breakfast, which Hatty will make. You and I shall have a slice of cake a little later and I hope you will deign to give me your opinion on the flavouring.'

As I go to the larder, fear grips my insides. Why aren't I carrying coal and water – as Mrs Thorpe said I would? Mrs Thorpe made no mention of cooking. Worse, she made no mention of *giving opinions on flavouring*. And then it strikes me. She has mentioned Jack. And Miss Eliza has misunderstood. And I know immediately there's been a horrible misunderstanding. I'm about to rush from the larder and tell Miss Eliza everything – that my mother is as mad as a cuckoo, that my father is a cripple with a fondness for ale, that Jack does nothing more than turn spits and skin rabbits, that I have done little more than plant potatoes and scrub chamber pots and other dirty work – when I notice the air is dizzy with syrupy sweetness. The scent comes from a bowl of fleshy purple berries, dusty with bloom and crawling with drunken wasps. For a moment I can't think straight. I want only to breathe in the perfume of these peculiar berries.

'Have you found the bread? It is next to the Turkey figs,' calls out Miss Eliza. I stare at the fat dusty fruits, with their splitting crimson seams. Jack has told me of figs and how his gentlemen diners eat them stewed with port wine and cream. But I imagined them small and wrinkled, like currants.

I find the bread and the grater and a sharp knife. But when I scrape the bread against the grater, I'm clumsy and grate my fingertip so that blood drips into the bowl and soaks into the bread.

Miss Eliza asks me to weigh the crumbs and note the weight on a slate. 'I'm very particular when it comes to weighing and measuring,' she says. 'I must have order and precision in everything. That way we keep the chaos of life at bay, don't you agree, Ann?'

I wish she would stop asking what I think, for it flummoxes me when I have a throbbing finger and so many other things to think about. But this question is particularly flummoxing because her life *is* ordered and beautiful and I don't see a bit of chaos anywhere. Chaos, I want to tell her, is when your mother doesn't know who you are and cannot control her insides and takes the knife to her own hair for no reason. And when your father must be pulled from your mother before he murders her. And when you have a stomach that hasn't been filled for several days. And when your memories are nothing but dying brothers and sisters and a Father shaking and shouting in his sleep every night. But then I think of how her kitchen is like paradise, clean and neat. And perhaps this is what she means. And perhaps this is why I have always dreamt of being a cook, of taking edible things in all their messiness and turning them into tasty dishes. So I say, 'Yes, Miss Eliza.'

After that, we don't talk much until she brings out a ginger cake from the larder.

'An old family recipe,' she says. 'I've been experimenting with the quantities of cloves and Jamaica ginger. Tell me what you think.' And she pushes a slice towards me. I try not to gobble it, for I am starving.

'The most important thing with this cake is to beat in every ingredient, one by one, with the back of a wooden spoon,' she says. 'Simply throwing everything in together and then beating produces a most unsuccessful cake. I know because my first attempt was as heavy as a brick – quite indigestible!' She gives a rueful smile and asks if I think it needs more ginger.

I feel the crumb, dense and dark, melt on my tongue. My mouth floods with warmth and spice and sweetness. As I swallow, something sharp and clean seems to lift through my nose and throat until my head swims.

'I can see you like it.' Miss Eliza watches me and smiles.

And then I blurt something out. Something I know the Reverend Thorpe and his wife would not like. But it's too late, the words jump from my throat of their own accord. 'I can taste an African heaven, a rainforest full of dark earth and heat.'

The smile on Miss Eliza's face stretches a little wider and her eyes grow brighter. And this gives me the courage to ask a question that's nothing to do with my work. 'What is the flavour that cuts through it so keenly, so that it sings a high note on my tongue?'

She stares at me with her forget-me-not eyes. 'It's the lightly grated rinds of two fresh lemons!'

'It's very good.' I want to say it could take a touch more spice, but that would be rude and not my place. And Miss Eliza is so pleased I've spotted the lemon rind that she doesn't press me for my *opinion on flavouring*.

The rest of my day is spent helping Hatty prepare for the arrival of the boarders and then helping Miss Eliza as she prepares dinner. I can tell she's nervous because she moves in a quick anxious way and becomes a bit red around the face. 'My first real diners,' she says several times, and more to herself than to me. She has me chopping rosemary, sage and thyme for the veal. Then I measure and weigh ingredients for a sweet sauce she is making to accompany the plum pudding. The sauce is from a recipe that vexes her, for it has no weights so she must guess them. I pour a wine glass of Madeira, weigh out butter, sugar and flour, then juice a lemon and grate a spoonful of nutmeg. Miss Eliza dips a salt spoon in and out of the veal stew, tasting and adding a pinch more cayenne and mace and extra salt grains, and talking to herself in a low voice. In the warmth of the kitchen, with my hands busy and the smell of fresh nutmeg blowing up from the table, I forget about Mam and Pa. And for the first time in years I feel joy. And the feeling is even better than sitting in the quiet of church with the drone of Mr Thorpe and all the painted golden angels looking down on me.

Chapter Eleven

Eliza

Roast Calves' Liver with Lemon Pickle

There is something about Colonel Martin and his wife that I do not like. A coldness at the backs of their eyes. Mother is all over them like melted butter on a dish of parsnips. When I say they lack warmth, she snaps at me, accusing me of having airs and graces that I'm no longer entitled to.

'You can stay in the kitchen,' she says haughtily. 'But be discreet. I can't have our boarders thinking we're unable to afford a proper cook.'

I bridle at her words, for haven't my meals been as good as any *proper cook's*? 'It's a good thing I prefer it in the kitchen,' I reply tersely.

While the Martins take their carriage every day to

Tunbridge Wells, I cook and write. Mainly recipes, some of which I write over and over, for I am determined they be not only accurate and precise but neat and elegant. Sometimes I put my recipes aside and write a line or two of poetry. It is this – the constant switching between verse-writing and recipe-writing – that keeps my mind sharp and my ear attuned. So that I catch the rhythm, the cadence, of every line, be it verse or cookery book. But as the days go by, the words come so swiftly, so smoothly, I know something else is at play. The first time this thought strikes me, I look up and see Ann. And another peculiar thought comes: it is she, Ann, that is causing this surge of inspiration.

I had expected some disarray from her intrusion into my solitude. Instead her presence has set me alight. She is such a slither of a girl. Like a thinly flaked almond. Her shoulder blades jutting like stunted wings. Her large luminous eyes lighting up from pockets of darkness, like church candles. Her boots peeling away from their soles ... And yet she has a palate capable of distinguishing the subtlest of flavours. And it seems to me that her looks and gestures show meaning in the smallest and commonest of things. I cannot explain it but I feel it beneath my skin – and suppose it to be a wave of misplaced affection that must be kept hidden from Mother's prying eyes.

In spite of this, we quickly settle into a daily routine. We prepare meals for Colonel Martin and his wife, starting at first light so that we have time to make a dish two or three times if need be. Then Ann cleans up and I write. On our first day together I went to the drawing room to compose a recipe for a shortcrust paste which we had repeatedly undercooked, then charred to a cinder, wasting a pound of best beef kidney suet in the process. My nerves were on edge and the words refused to come, not helped by Mother snapping about the reek of burnt grease. So I returned to the kitchen and wrote at the pine table while Ann scrubbed and swept around me. The slop of water, the scrape of broom over stone, the scatter of sand and salt, soothed me, and now I write only in the kitchen. Afterwards I take a fractious luncheon with Mother in the dining room, and then Ann and I spend our afternoons preparing dinner. If the dishes are not too painstaking, my mind is able to swim between verse and recipe.

A few days after the arrival of the Martins I decide to submit a new poem to one of the more literary annuals, the *Keepsake*, which has the most embellished and loveliest of covers. I send my poem by express mail coach, with a feeling of . . . accomplishment . . . satisfaction. Afterwards, as I write a short recipe for roast calves' liver with lemon pickle, I see the poetry in my words and feel a tenuous thrill. A recipe can be as beautiful as a poem, I think. Useful and beautiful. It doesn't have to be a graceless list of barked instructions. *Take a fine white sound liver . . . steep it overnight with good vinegar and a sliced onion and branches of savoury herbs laid over it . . . roast it on a clear fire . . .*

For the first time since Father fled to Calais, I feel a sense of purpose, a sense of being myself. As if I have been given tacit permission to *exist*. Perhaps I'm not intended to live out some dim and broken life. Perhaps composing recipes can sustain and nourish me, just as writing verse does. Perhaps I can be more than an *old maid*.

I'm so wrapped up in my cooking and writing, in keeping tightly to the kitchen and my bedchamber, I barely notice the Martins and I forget entirely their peculiar lack of warmth. Only later do I wish I'd paid more attention, been a little less consumed by my own resurrection. But by then it is too late.

Chapter Twelve

Ann

A Jug of Water

For three days, Miss Eliza gives me instructions and I follow them to the letter. I scrape the sugar from its loaf, scrub the vegetables of mud and insects, scour the sink with sand and spread the tea leaves for drying. I fetch water, and firewood, and fish from the market. I slice and sift and grate and pluck. I stoke and sweep and black the range. I wash and dry and polish. And when I get a second to myself, I eat. I eat pie crusts burnt to a crisp and fit only for the pig. I drink cream that has curdled and is intended for the cat. I steal spoonfuls of over-salted sauces so that my tongue withers in my mouth. I eat the leftovers and lick the cooking spoons and even wipe my tongue around the batter basin. I cannot help myself for my insides are gnawed half to death from years of hunger and I've never seen so much food. Miss Eliza is very absorbed in her work and doesn't notice if a crumb goes missing or a wooden spoon is licked clean. Sometimes she stops and stares at me. But not because she's caught me chewing at a blackened pie paste from the pig bin or Colonel Martin's leftover crust of bread. More as if she's wondering why I'm in her kitchen. Or who I am.

Every now and then Ma'am appears with words of praise from the boarders. And me and Miss Eliza swell with pride. Only once does a kidney pie return, half eaten. Miss Eliza sees me ogling it, no doubt with drool upon my lips. She pushes it towards me and says I may eat it if I wish. The gravy is so meaty, so rich with rosemary and bone marrow and redcurrant jelly the whole world shrinks to nothing but my mouth. Afterwards my stomach is hard with the cramps. And bloated tight. I must remember not to guzzle, I think.

One evening, just as I'm collecting up the peelings for the stockpot, Ma'am rushes in. 'Hatty has been taken sick. Ann, you must go to the dining room and see the Martins have everything they need. Oh, Eliza, we are so woefully short of servants. This will not do!'

'Put on Hatty's slippers and change to a clean apron,' Miss Eliza tells me. 'Then go straight to the dining room and pour the Martins their water. And be careful not to spill any.'

She tucks a sprig of drying lavender into the neckline of my dress, saying it'll disguise the kitchen smell of me, and gestures me out with a flap of her hand.

I go to the dining room, feeling most unsure of myself.

Colonel and Mrs Martin are sitting at a round table covered with a linen cloth on which has been laid heavy silver cutlery, glasses of various sizes, striped napkins, a little dish of toothpicks and some silver cruets. Mrs Martin eyes me very strangely, as if she thinks I'm come to steal her jewels. Then she examines her hands in great detail. Colonel Martin looks at me and his eyes travel up and down me, as if he is measuring me by eye for a new frock.

No one has told me how to speak to boarders. So I pick up the water jug and say, 'Water?' It comes out more abrupt than I planned, for the line of glasses has flummoxed me. Which one is for water and which is for wine? Mrs Martin ignores me and continues to look at her fingernails with great concentration. But Colonel Martin points to a plain straight-sided glass and nods, in a kindly way, as if he knows this is my first time waiting at table. I start pouring the water, very carefully and very slowly. And then I freeze. Something is moving up the back of my leg. Chewing, squeezing at my thigh. I stay as still as a pillar, my heart pounding, my hand gripping the jug, which is poised and trembling above the cruets. A voice in my head tells me to move away, to walk round the table and fill Mrs Martin's glass. But I don't. Because another voice springs into another bit of my head, telling me not to cause offence, not to hurt the feelings of our boarders. I'm saved from indecision by the Colonel.

'To the brim, girl. To the brim!' He motions at the glass with his fat veined hand. His other hand – for so it is – stays on the back of my thigh. His fingers have stopped searching into my flesh, so I wonder if it's all a mistake. An accident.

Perhaps he doesn't realise his hand is on my leg. Perhaps if I was to shake off his hand – like a man brushes off an insect or a dog shakes off a flea – he would realise and be embarrassed, and return his hand to his own leg.

I know my arm is shaking – indeed all of me is trembling, like water after a stiff breeze has rolled over it – so I pour very slow, concentrating on the lip of the jug, keeping it centred over his glass even as it wobbles in my grip.

All of a sudden I feel his fingers again. Crawling up the back of my thigh, and moving in rough circles over my behind. Then he squeezes so hard the jug lurches in my hand and water leaps from the spout in a great rush, all over the table. It happens so quick, and the combination of my limbs set rigid and the hammering of my heart and all the little voices in my head, mean I lose my nerve and stand, deaf and dumb, like a pillar of salt, even as the water seeps into Ma'am's best linen.

'Oh, clumsy girl!' Mrs Martin looks up, a darting glittering look.

'Now, now, Jane,' chides Colonel Martin, whose straying hand is conspicuously stroking his whiskers. 'I suspect she is new to the establishment.' He takes his napkin from his collar and dabs at the spilt water. Then he waves it at me and asks me to bring a fresh one from the kitchen.

Still, I cannot move. The voice in my head tells me I must apologise but my mouth refuses to open.

'Get along, girl! A fresh napkin!' Mrs Martin's glowering words bring me swiftly to my senses, so I snatch the napkin from the Colonel and scamper to the linen chest in the hall.

When I return, Ma'am is talking to Mrs Martin about the weather. I pray she hasn't noticed the wet tablecloth, but she bustles off, saying she is going to the cellar for their wine. I bob a clumsy curtsy and offer Colonel Martin the new napkin. He points at his collar, as if he wants me to tuck it in for him. Then he leans his chest away from the table and I shake out the napkin, all fingers and thumbs. Keeping my arms outstretched I try to fold the corner of the napkin into his collar, fumbling like a blind man and waiting to feel his hand on my leg. But his hands are in his lap, so I edge a little closer and push the napkin right into his collar. My fingers scrape his neck which is red and hot and doughy. Just as the napkin is securely in place and I'm about to step away, I see something from the corner of my eye. His manhood has come free from his breeches and is standing stiff and pink beneath the table. I shrink back, my face flooding and burning with heat.

At that exact moment, Ma'am returns with a bottle of wine. Colonel Martin tugs the napkin from his neck, cool as a cucumber, and drops it on his lap. 'Is she new?' He jerks his head at me. My whole body trembles. What if he complains about me? What if Ma'am sees the water stain on her best linen? Mrs Martin looks at me through eyes screwed so tight they're like peppercorns.

'Ann is usually in the scullery, Colonel,' says Mrs Acton. 'But our regular serving maid is indisposed. I do hope she hasn't caused you any trouble? I do hope everything is to your satisfaction?'

'Oh, certainly,' says the Colonel.

'I'll get a decanter,' says Ma'am, and she is gone, leaving me alone with the terrible Colonel and his peculiar wife.

'Over here!' The Colonel beckons me to him. I move very gingerly, for now I know why Hatty has been taken sick. 'My napkin has fallen to the floor and my gout restricts my movement. Could you ... ?' He points at his napkin, lying crumpled beneath the table. I glance in the direction of Mrs Martin but she is staring hard at the window.

I kneel down and pick up the napkin, being most careful where I look. Then I stand up, throw the napkin on his lap and run to the kitchen.

Chapter Thirteen

Eliza

Pigeons Roasted in Vine Leaves

I wake early, my eyes snapping open. In those first blurred seconds I wonder why my blood seems so wildly alight in my veins. Then I recall the previous evening – the success of my most ambitious dinner yet. Colonel and Mrs Martin ate everything, mopping up the veal gravy with slabs of bread and requesting second helpings of batter pudding. The Colonel smacked his lips with satisfaction and declared my Madeira sauce 'the best wine sauce I have ever tasted with a sweet pudding'. I know this because Mother hovered anxiously at the dining room door, eavesdropping.

I stretch and smile to myself. I didn't tell Mother the sauce recipe was almost entirely mine: the orange zest, the extra egg yolk, the little touches that made it so distinctive, so light and frothy. Ann suggested the nutmeg, and she was right. It provided an extra depth and spiced sweetness ...

The sun pushes its warm saffron rays through the shutter slats so they fall in stripes across the counterpane. For a moment I feel inexplicably happy, a feeling of lightness – a bird-in-the-air feeling. And why shouldn't I? My recipes are working. I can cook as well as I can write. The poems I sent to the *Keepsake* are among the best I've ever written. The kitchen, that I thought to be my gaoler, has inspired me in ways I never imagined. Even the ill-composed recipes of former writers have inspired me, enabling me to sniff out a great dish of my own. Like a dog that smells a body buried in the snow and coaxes it back to life with its warm breath.

And then there's the sheer joy of writing recipes that sing! I smile again and wonder if perhaps I should write poems about cooking, or food, or eating. But no – that would be hopeless. Mr Longman would laugh in my face. I can hear him now ... *No, no, no ... Poems are the preserve of fine feelings ... And no one has fine feelings in a kitchen, Miss Acton ...*

How strange this world is – that no woman must admit to the pleasures of the table. She must prepare the table, of course. But without feeling. And she must eat of it – if only to live – but without expressing any pleasure in the process. For us of the fairer sex, food must be merely functional.

This chain of thought returns me to our boarders: what shall I treat the Colonel and his dour wife to today? Pigeons. And tiny peas fragrant as flowers. The last peas of the year. And the smallest potatoes I can find, poached, then buttered and sprinkled with coarse salt. I stretch out beneath my sheet and it comes again – the bird-in-the-air feeling, the swallow-on-the-wing feeling. Only this time I hear its song too: I am, I am, I am.

I get up, push back the shutters and let the light flood in. I have a sudden urge to fill my room with autumn branches – rosehips, scarlet-and-gold leaves, the last bright greenery of the year. But then I look around my room and my joy slips clean away. The uncluttered spinsterish emptiness of it … Reminding me that spinsters are living confessions of failure. And that little chiding voice pipes up. *Your poems, your writing … all conceit and pride and immodesty.* No doubt my poems will be returned to me today … *Imposter … Imposter …* My wings clipped. Again. My punishment for craving an audience.

When I get to the kitchen, Ann is on her knees scrubbing hard at the oil stains on the flagstones. The dewy soles of her boots hang loose and darkly damp, and on the table is a basket of rosehips. The girl must have been up since before dawn. My eye slips to the range, but it's been newly blacked and laid, and the hearth is swept clean.

'You've picked rosehips?'

'Yes, miss. I thought you might be wanting to make a syrup. Mam always made it in September when the hips were fresh.' She looks up, her eyes like two dark holes.

A sharp lump rises in my throat. I swallow it and say, 'As soon as you've served breakfast to the Colonel and his wife, I want you to go directly to William Gale's shoe shop, and get yourself some boots.'

Ann gapes at me.

'I know you haven't been paid yet, but I will buy your boots. Think of them as a gift.'

'Oh, I c-can't do that,' she stammers. 'I can't accept such a generous gift, Miss Eliza.'

'Well, I insist. Would you disobey your mistress?'

'What about Hatty?'

'She doesn't need new boots and you do.'

'I mean won't she be serving Colonel and Mrs Martin today?'

I tip the rosehips into a large bowl, tasting them on my mind's tongue ... folding in thyme ... or rosemary ... or would a hint of something more exotic work? A stick of cinnamon? The quick dip of a vanilla pod? I try to recall the rosehip syrup Mrs Durham used to make, and a rich French rosehip preserve – with apples? Elderberries? – I tasted a decade ago.

'Will Hatty be serving today, miss?'

I sigh at her intrusion. Summoning flavours from memory and combining them imaginatively on my tongue requires concentration. One interruption and the flavour – so fleetingly recalled – is lost entirely. 'I know you weren't expecting to be in the dining room but we're a small private establishment and we must all pull together. Even Mrs Acton must overcome her prejudices and help serve at table.'

'I-I don't think I'm so good at it,' Ann mumbles into the soapy flagstones.

'Well, let's wait and see if Hatty is recovered. Did you see her this morning?'

'I was up before she was, Miss Eliza. I haven't seen her.' She buries her face in the scrubbing brush.

'The Martins won't be down before nine but you can set the breakfast table – put out the porcelain cruets and don't forget the sugar bowl.'

'And dinner?'

Her question pleases me. 'I am thinking the exact same thing, Ann. Your culinary curiosity is such a delight! A brace of pigeons came last night and is hanging in the cellar. I'll need you to pluck them.' How shall I prepare them? Juniper ... Sage ... Possibly an apple sauce. Or could I use the rosehip jelly?

'It's not my place, Miss Eliza, but ...' Ann stands up, hopping from one foot to another as if she is perched on hot cinders.

'You know how to pluck game birds, I presume?' My tone is brusquer than intended, but I need to concentrate and Ann's hopping is distracting me.

'Yes, b-but what about pigeons wrapped in vine leaves? Only I saw a vine in the garden and ...' Her voice peters out as she disappears into the scullery with the pail of dirty floor water.

I stare at her departing back. But I don't see her. I see an image from my past, formless at first then filling out with colour, smell, sound ... the pruned twigs of vines alight and burning ... an iron grill, roughly hammered ... Someone pulling the innards from birds – larks, gulls, pigeons ... A basket of fresh green vine leaves ... An ache rolls up beneath my ribs.

Ann returns, the pigeons swinging from her scrawny hand, and looks at me with alarm. 'Are you all right, Miss Eliza?'

'I ate meats roasted with vine leaves in France.' I regret my words immediately for I have no desire to relive those frenzied days. Before Ann can ask any further questions, I say, 'But enough of that. Why do you suggest vine leaves?'

'My brother, Jack, has seen it. He works for a Monsieur Soyer who comes from France.'

I look at Ann for a long time, my fingers slowly circling my temples as I try to remember Mrs Rundell's instructions for preparing pigeons. 'When they're plucked, remove the heads, and cut their toes at the first joint. Then fetch me some vine leaves, the largest you can find.'

Ann disappears into the scullery, the soles of her boots flapping so generously I see the blistered skin of her feet. The girl has no stockings on! I wonder what sort of mother sends her daughter into service with broken boots and no stockings. But as I think this, a shutter closes in my mind, as if it is too cramped to dwell on thoughts like this. 'And yarn,' I call out. 'When you are measured for new boots, ask Mr Gale for stocking yarn.'

My mind veers back to roasted pigeon. And from pigeon, I travel effortlessly, unrestrainedly back to France ... the pots of rillettes fragrant with garlic, the boned forelegs of ham yellowed with breadcrumbs, the blood puddings curled up like snakes, the terrines and pâtés, the sausages from Lyons and Arles, the jowls of salmon cooked à la génoise, the hundreds of cheeses resplendent beneath their glass bells, the perfumed

melons and honeyed apricots and ... I shake my head, return-
ing my runaway thoughts to roasted pigeon ...... each must
be stuffed with a pat of butter, but should the pat be rolled in
minced parsley or cayenne?

CHAPTER FOURTEEN

Ann

FRESH BREWED COFFEE

After my *encounter* with the Colonel, I tossed and turned all night. Hatty slept sound as a board. No sign of sickness. No sweats or moans. No squatting for hours over the chamber pot. Not even the smell of sickness on her breath.

But the next morning, as I'm wrestling with vine leaves in the garden and praying I won't be called on to serve at table again, she arrives all harried, her hair flying from beneath her cap, her fingers fumbling at her apron strings.

'You haven't forgotten I'm in charge, have you?' She crouches beside me, a sizzle in her eye.

'I thought you were sick?'

'Of course I ain't sick.' She gives a most careless toss of her head.

'So does that mean you're in charge of the Colonel?'

She looks at me, triumphant. 'He showed you his pork sausage and chestnuts, didn't he?'

As relief rushes through me, all my fear and loneliness fall away. 'Is that why you went sick?'

'Yes! I know his sort. Likely that's why they arrived with no maid. And so now I must scrub out their pots and lay their fire and hang their clothes and carry their water – everything!'

I frown, confused. 'You pretended to be ill so that I would have to see his – his sausage?'

'They like it when that happens,' she says, her face flushed and shining with the drama of it all. 'It's part of their little game. And we must egg him on before he gets his comeuppance.'

I snip at the vine leaves in a fog of *not understanding*. What is she talking about?

'Without the boarders we won't get no wages, so we must wait until he pays his bill. Then we'll teach him a lesson. For now, keep your eyes above table and don't be frightened.' Her nose gives a twitch and I'm reminded of Septimus when the smell of meat is in the air.

'I've seen my pa's,' I say, not wanting to be the little innocent, the dumb village girl. 'And my brother's.'

'But not like that, surely?'

'Course not! But I've seen bulls and dogs.'

'But not at table, you fool.'

She has a point. 'No, but if Ma'am were to see, surely she would ask him to leave?'

'Oh, he's too clever for that. They only flash their sausages at frightened serving girls.'

'And what of poor Mrs Martin?' I ask, feeling a prickle of sympathy for his wife, that she must sit there while he fiddles with himself and have no idea of his dirty ways.

Hatty snorts. 'She's no *poor Mrs Martin.*'

'Why doesn't she put a stop to it then?' I ask, puzzled, and thinking of all the times Pa and I had to tie Mam up to stop her undressing in public. And now she's locked up in a lunatic asylum, while Colonel Martin is dining out and taking the waters with gentlemen and ladies from London.

'It'll suit her to turn a blind eye. Anyway, I'll be serving from now on.' She stands up and sighs, as if her earlier boldness is slipping away. So I ask her what exactly she plans to do for his *comeuppance*, as she calls it.

'I can't tell you.' She puts her fingers to her lips. 'But there's nothing to be afraid of now I have a plan.'

Then she leans in and gives me a quick hug. A small thing but it makes me forget the Colonel altogether. I'm still smiling when I return with the vine leaves.

'Ah,' says Miss Eliza. 'I see time with nature makes you joyful.'

I don't know what to say, but she's smiling brightly and I'm still grinning like a buffoon so I nod and think to myself ... *I have a friend ... I have a friend ... and no more serving at table either*!

'The Colonel and Mrs Martin want coffee today, and you shall make it,' she announces. 'Warm the coffee berries in a stew pan high over the fire and keep turning them.'

I've never seen a coffee berry but she has a stone jar of them and as they roast over the fire a wonderful smell – dark and brooding – fills the kitchen. When she crushes them in her special grinding box, I long to taste this berry that smells of the forest, of leather and honey. And something else ... which I think is hazelnuts, like those Mam once picked and cracked between two rocks.

All the time, Miss Eliza is telling me what a disgrace it is that no one can make coffee in the right way. 'There's no economy in cheaper berries ... and they should always be roasted and ground at the very last minute.' She gives a final heave of the handle on her grinding box and adds, as if it's an afterthought, 'The milk must be boiling and the cream must be fresh and cold.'

I'm still thinking of Mam cracking hazelnuts when Hatty comes for the coffee pot and winks at me in a most obvious way. She disappears in a whirl of banging doors and steam, and I feel a shiver of excitement – whatever is she up to?

As I clean out the stew pan, Miss Eliza pours some of the thick dark liquid into one of her porcelain cups that is no taller than my little finger. She stirs it slowly and then asks, 'With what do you think Monsieur Soyer would stuff his pigeons?'

I think hard and wish I'd asked more questions of Jack when he last came. 'Perhaps just a pat of butter,' I say eventually.

She smiles at me, one of those smiles that sweeps over me and makes me think I am walking on a cushion of warm rosy air. 'I shall roll a nut of butter in cayenne, I think. Or we could stuff them with small mushrooms and offer them with a mushroom sauce. And shall we serve them on crisp fresh watercress?'

I never know if she is talking to me or to herself, but I nod anyway. She's about to finish her coffee when she sees me staring at it. 'Would you like a sip?'

Mrs Thorpe's voice crowds in upon my head: *remember your place . . . remember your place.* I ignore it. 'Yes please, miss.'

She pushes the porcelain cup towards me and watches as I taste. Bitter, rich, slightly grainy on my tongue. An image of what a coffee house might be like comes into my head . . . all the gentlemen in their coloured stockings, the rustle of news-papers, the smell of pipe tobacco, the heads buried in talk and books. Jack has told me of coffee houses, and theatres, and the carriages of gentlefolk that race through the streets of London. And now my mind is racing in the same way.

'What are you thinking?' asks Miss Eliza. And I tell her I'm imagining a coffee house. She smiles and says, in her gleaming voice, 'Let's see if the good Colonel finds our coffee to his liking. He is from London so no doubt he's accustomed to the best.'

I wonder if he's waving his sausage and chestnuts in Hatty's face this very minute. Then I think of Mrs Martin, and how she must sit there while he does it, feigning ignorance. Something sickly shifts in the pit of my stomach.

When Hatty brings the coffee pot back to the kitchen and says the Colonel sends his compliments to the chef, Miss Eliza claps her hands with delight.

Later, when I'm taking the ash to the blackcurrant bushes, I pass the Colonel and Mrs Martin climbing into their cur-tained carriage. I stare at her large round rump disappearing up the steps and wonder if she feels the shame I felt when

Mam disrobed in the fields. Or the feeling of helplessness when I knew I could not stop her. How would the Reverend Thorpe advise Mrs Martin, I wonder ... But after she has settled herself among the carriage cushions, she turns to the window and sees me standing there with the ash gusting into my face. She shoots me a look of venom, then her lip curls and she turns away. Leaving me feeling small and despised.

I summon back the taste of Miss Eliza's coffee. And as it broods upon my tongue, I feel my mood restored. Jack was wrong when he said God is in a crust of bread. God, I think, blasphemously, is in a sip of coffee.

CHAPTER FIFTEEN

Eliza

A COMPOTE OF WILD BULLACES WITH THICK CREAM

When the letter comes, I slip it into my bodice, tie on my bonnet and tell Ann I'm off to collect bullaces. I cannot open it under Mother's prying, disparaging eyes or Hatty's meddlesome stare. Besides, I want to open it in a country lane, where only flocks of finches will bear witness to this momentous occasion. Because this is my moment of truth. If the *Keepsake* wants my poems, I shall persevere. And perhaps I shall become a published poet after all. If not, my life in verse is over.

When Bordyke House is no longer in view and the town – with its sprawl of mills and tanneries and brickworks – is left behind, I tear open the envelope. My eyes race across the few lines ... *A most charming poem ... We would be delighted to print it ... Many of our regular poetesses, publish either as 'A Lady' or 'Anonymous' ... But married or maiden names are, of course, acceptable ... We are unable to offer a fee of any kind ... Yours sincerely.*

I raise my face to the sky and sing 'Yes! Yes! Yes!' A startled pigeon beats its wings and flaps in an upward direction, as if carried by the current of my voice. I glance along the wooded path, see that no one is in attendance, and chant aloud 'I *am* a poet!' My words have such weight and heft I could reach out and pluck them from the air. Finches flit from the hedgerow and in their chirpings I seem to hear an echo of myself: *I am ... I am ... I am.*

There is such a spring in my step, it's as if I walk on whipped meringue. *Charming,* I think. My poem is deemed *charming.* When the exultation fades, I look at the letter again. But on a second reading I am struck by something else entirely. *Anonymous? A Lady? My married name?* E. Acton, I think. Ernest ... Edmund ... Edward ... Edgar. Should I take my brother's name, Edgar Acton? Anger and indignation flare inside me. Why must I creep around in disguise? Why must I efface myself? Eliza Acton, I say aloud. As if in affirmation the finches start up their noisy chorus ... *I am ... I am ... I am.*

When I return to the kitchen, I cannot hold my tongue. I go to the scullery where Ann is scouring the pots and pans and put my basket of bullaces beside the sink. 'Ann, do you like poetry?'

She blinks, takes a fresh handful of sand from the bucket, and starts scouring the fish kettle. 'I've not had much time for it.'

'No, no, of course not,' I say hastily. 'But would you like to learn?'

'Learn poetry, miss?' She repeats my words as if she's a bit slow-witted this morning.

'I've had some good news,' I pause, drumming up the courage to say the words aloud to another human being. Then they rush from me, without any finesse. 'I'm a poet!'

'You, miss? A poet?' Her voice is so full of veneration, I could fall to her feet. Except her feet are in a puddle of cold water, shiny with grease.

'An annual called the *Keepsake* wants to publish one of my poems.' I can barely keep the pride from my voice.

'That's very good, miss,' she says, resuming her scouring.

'Yes it is,' I agree. 'And I'd like to teach you poetry, Ann.'

She nods, then asks what I'd like done with the bullaces.

Normally, this would send my mind into a tumult of flavours and tastes. But I'm too intoxicated by my own poetic success. I bat at the air and say 'Oh, something will come to me, don't worry!'

'How about a simple compote, miss?'

I'm so taken aback at her using the word *compote* – and at how unexpectedly right it sounds on her lips – that I'm lost for words. All my poetic pride ebbs away.

'With thick cream and a dusting of cinnamon,' she adds.

'Indeed,' I say. And my voice comes out flat, as if her talk of bullaces has taken all the glow from my moment of glory.

Chapter Sixteen

Ann

A Simple Sponge Cake

A few days later I'm sent to the post office to collect two packages. One is large and heavy, with corners that have burst through the brown paper, so I know it's books. The other is thin and flimsy, but the address has been written in a very fine hand with flourishes and inky tails on all the letters. I hurry home and find Miss Eliza in the kitchen, writing in a little notebook. Whether she is writing poems or recipes I can't tell, for her face is very still and calm, but when she sees the thin package her face falls and all the light goes from her eyes.

She opens it while I'm busying myself with my cap, which

has slipped half off my head. I watch her from beneath my lashes and feel a great relief when her eyes brighten again and her beautiful lips curve into a smile.

'My collection of poems, returned at last,' she says.

I wait, hoping she will start to read aloud from them. But she doesn't. She flicks through them and, as she does so, her smile fades. From the hall comes the sound of Ma'am's heels on the flagstones and, quick as a whip, Miss Eliza slips her poems beneath the breadboard.

'I come bearing good news,' says Ma'am, patting at the jet crucifix she wears always at her neck. 'The Colonel and Mrs Martin are delighted with their rooms and with your cooking. They want to extend their stay for another week.'

My heart falls as I think of Hatty who must now endure still more of the Colonel's hands upon her *arse* (as she calls it) and his endless fumblings below-table. And how can she deliver his *comeuppance* if he extends his stay on and on? But then Ma'am says something that makes me anxious.

'Mrs Thorpe is paying us a visit this morning and I'd like you there, Eliza. Not lurking in the servants' quarters.'

Miss Eliza nods and agrees, but I'm swilling with nerves. Does Mrs Thorpe have news of Mam? Or Pa? Or worse – far worse – Has the asylum refused to keep Mam? Has she run away and not been found? All these thoughts rush through my head in a great torrent.

Ma'am points at the unopened parcel still sitting on the table. 'Not more books, surely?'

Miss Eliza picks up the package, unties the string and pulls the paper off. Even as my mind spins, I notice her fingers working at the twine – so long and white with their nails of the palest pink, like rosebuds.

'Do you not have anything to do, Ann?' says Ma'am. 'If there's no kitchen work, you can dust the drawing room and make it fit for Mrs Thorpe.'

I have plenty of work, but I get the feather duster from the scullery and as I do so I hear Miss Eliza explaining each new cookery book.

'This one is by a *professed cook* ... and this one is from a Mr Henderson ... but what I find so objectionable is the great quantities these cooks require. Listen to this ... a simple sponge cake.' She starts to read aloud. 'Take twenty-four eggs ... How many private families need a cake on this scale? These are for feast days and nothing more!' She slams the book closed.

Whereupon Ma'am asks, in a strained voice, 'Why must you purchase these books if you cannot use their recipes, my dear?'

'I learn from them,' says Miss Eliza. 'I've drawn up a list of people who might donate a favourite recipe. I have a lady who is renowned for her Jewish dinners and—'

And then Ma'am interrupts Miss Eliza, in a voice as cold as iron. 'Surely you don't intend to include Jewish food? English families will not want Jewish food – of that I am certain!'

I shuffle past them, my head bowed and my fingers wrapped tight around the feather duster. The air is so thick with tension you could run a blade through it. I dash upstairs to the Colonel's rooms where I know Hatty is airing the beds.

'Hatty,' I hiss. 'What does "Jewish" mean?'

'It's a sort of religion,' she says, not sounding very sure of herself. 'And they lend money ... even on the Sabbath.'

'Do they eat differently from us?' I ask, baffled.

She pounds her fists into a pillow, then looks at me all quizzical. 'I don't know about that. You ask the oddest questions, Ann Kirby.'

I scurry to the drawing room and swipe at the window frames with the feather duster. My head feels like a butter churner and, for a second, I wish I was back at home planting out some turnips and thinking of nothing more complicated than how to keep Mam from straying.

CHAPTER SEVENTEEN

Eliza

FILLETS OF PERCH WITH CRISP FRIED PARSLEY

Mrs Thorpe's superiority radiates from her garments, her shoes, the ivory drops at her ears, the violet silk sash at her waist, the lace that sits so confidently at her bosom. Her gestures – the flaunting of the wedding-ringed finger, the lifting of her *married* chin – all consign Mother and me to a lesser life, a diminished life. They remind us that she is a player in the drama of life, while we are merely spectators.

'What a pleasant aspect this room has.' Her eyes swivel round the room, taking in the brass fenders, the heavy velvet drapes, the mahogany cabinets with their clutch of leather-and-gilt books, the Brussels carpet. 'All rented, is

it?' Her head jerks backwards and forwards like a strut-
ting pigeon.

'We have leased Bordyke House fully furnished,' nods
Mother. 'It suits us very well, doesn't it, Eliza?'

'And is Ann Kirby to your satisfaction?' Mrs Thorpe drums
her fingers on her skirts, as if anxious to move on to more
interesting topics.

'She has barely been with us long enough to tell,'
says Mother.

'I like her,' I say, with a great effort at serenity. 'She is with-
out insolence or malice and she's keen to learn.'

'Quite, quite.' Mrs Thorpe gives another roll of her fingers.
'I hear you are a poetess, Miss Acton?'

For a second I contemplate telling her I am indeed a poet.
But then Mother fills the silence with her picked-clean voice.
'My daughter was a poetess but now she has an important
writing commission from an eminent London publisher.'

Mrs Thorpe's lips tighten into a pout, as if she cannot
decide what her response should be. 'Oh, do tell. A novel-
ette, perhaps?'

'We cannot talk of it now.' Mother presses a forefinger to
her lips, a picture of reluctant secrecy. 'But rest assured you
will be the first to know.'

I feel a flash of gratitude. Mother has tried – in her own
uncertain way – to redeem me, to redeem us both. To show
Mrs Thorpe that we are more than shrivelled husband-less
ladies running a rented boarding house. Naturally, she
couldn't own up to my writing a cookery book. But still her
words have bound us closer.

'How are Ann Kirby's parents?' I ask.

Mrs Thorpe's eyes widen and her jaw swings. 'I have no idea. I cannot be expected to discourse with every member of my husband's congregation. Naturally, Ann Kirby always attends his sermons. They are known the length and breadth of the county.'

' I wouldn't want to lose her.' I smile stiffly at Mrs Thorpe. 'Was there anything in particular you wished to discuss with me?' I can feel Mother's furious eyes upon me but the tug of the kitchen is stronger: my new books, the fresh perch gleaming in the larder, the trugs of field mushrooms and damsons and pippin apples still with the dew upon them, the curly green parsley I shall fry until crisp ...

'I am merely here to welcome you to Tonbridge, to offer the hand of friendship, Miss Acton.' Mrs Thorpe's head wobbles on her shoulders, a flush rising up her neck.

'Please forgive me, but I have matters to attend to.' I leave the room with Mother's blistering fury at my back. I half-run to the kitchen, light with relief even as I feel the guilt of betrayal. My departure is rude, a failure to reciprocate Mother's uncharacteristic gesture of support. But a few minutes of Mrs Thorpe's eyes scraping over us and our *rented* furniture is more than enough. And how can I be a writer, a cook, a poet, if I am expected to make conversation with every smug snooping woman who appears in our drawing room?

In the kitchen I find Ann preparing a bowl of damsons, halving them with a fruit knife and easing out the stones. This is the third batch of damson jam we have prepared this week and yet none has been quite good enough, either too stiff or too liquid or without the right notes of sweetness and acidity. I wonder if it is me at fault or the damsons, too watery from the August rains perhaps.

'These are beautifully ripe and very fresh, Miss Eliza,' Ann says, as if reading my thoughts. She passes me one and I squeeze it briefly between finger and thumb so that a runnel of juice drips over my hand.

'Let's cook this batch for a little longer.' I lick absently at the juice on my hand. It tastes of hedgerow and sunshine and autumn leaves.

'D-did Mrs Thorpe say anything of my family?' Ann stops her work mid-damson, her knife aloft, juice skimming down her wrists and into the rolled-up sleeves of her dress.

'Were you expecting news?'

'No, Miss Eliza. But might I be allowed a half-day this week? To visit my father?'

I pause. She's entitled to a half-day each week ... But how am I to feed the Colonel and Mrs Martin on my own?

'I appear to have become rather dependent on you, Ann,' I say at last. 'If you can help with breakfast and be back before four o'clock, I can manage.'

'Thank you, Miss Eliza.' She slices open the last damson, removes the stone and places it in the long-handled pan, batting away a drowsy wasp.

'Why do you ask for time to visit your father but make no mention of your mother?'

She wipes her hands on her apron, her tongue running quickly over her top lip. 'My father is at home alone.'

'So you have a father at home and a mother who is away, and

I have a mother at home and—' I stop abruptly. Mother and I have agreed that John Acton is not to be mentioned, that our clean start in Tonbridge could be jeopardised if his bankruptcy is known of. Boarders might be deterred from taking rooms. Butchers and bakers would deny us credit. And who knows what would happen if the landlord were to hear. Everyone – including our servants – must believe Mother is a respectable widow, living with her respectable daughter. Hatty knows, of course. But Mother has bribed her into silence.

'I'm sorry for your loss.' Ann turns quickly back to the damsons. But she's not quick enough and I see the tremble in her top lip.

For a moment I say nothing: *let her think, like everyone else in this town, that he is dead.* But there have been too many lies in my life, and my yearning for a friendship – just one – untainted by half-truths and concealments gets the better of me. 'He's alive, living in Calais. But he mustn't be spoken of.'

'I'll never mention him.' To my surprise Ann thrusts her small, knuckly hand at me. 'Pa says to always shake hands on a promise.' Her cheeks flush pink as if her gesture was too hasty and she now sees its inappropriateness.

I take her hand as if it were a butterfly and I might crush it. I feel the cool skin stretched over the small bones, the knuckles like glass beads, the roughened fingertips, the scabs and cuts and callouses. Why haven't I noticed them before? Something tips and lurches, queasily, inside me. I steer it away and disappear to the larder, returning with the perch and a scaling knife.

'Would you like to hear what I've learned from my new

books about buying fish, Ann? Every housewife should know how to choose a truly fresh fish. Look first at the eyes' – I point to the perch's head. 'The eyes should always be bright, the gills a fine clear red, the body stiff, the flesh firm yet elastic to the touch, and the smell not disagreeable.' The perch glitters, its scales like old gold.

CHAPTER EIGHTEEN

Ann

BOILED EELS WITH SAGE, GERMAN-STYLE

Today I'm called on to serve the Colonel and Mrs Martin at table again. Hatty has hurt her shoulder turning the mattresses and Ma'am doesn't trust her not to spill hot coffee on her best Irish linen.

I put on a clean apron and quickly buff up my new boots, which shine like oil and hug my feet so neatly there's no more dampness between my toes nor wind whistling round my ankles. Then I tell myself the Colonel is a dirty old man – about to get his *comeuppance* – and nothing to be frightened of.

I keep my head bowed and take the silver coffee pot and cream jug to the table. Mrs Martin sits very straight, as if all her muscles are stiff and clenched in expectation. She must get terrible indigestion, I think, and without meaning to, I look up and meet her glare hard upon me. Her eyes are like cold black marbles. Even the air around her is trying to escape, so that she sits in a little rigid space surrounded by the poison of her own thoughts. I'm concentrating on placing the pot very carefully on the woven mat, when the Colonel says, 'You can pour my coffee, one third cream.'

I hear the rustling silk of Mrs Martin's dress as she shifts upon her chair. 'I can pour, my dear.' Her voice is tight and clipped.

'We are paying good money to be here, Jane. I will not have you lift a finger.' The Colonel flaps his red gouty hand at the coffee pot. The other hand is nowhere to be seen. No doubt beneath the table fumbling at his breeches. I hold the spout above the cup and am on the brink of pouring when I see the slow crawl of his gouty hand. He's shifting it towards the sugar bowl which is perilous close to the edge of the table. It strikes me than that he must have put it there, for Hatty and I always place the sugar bowl at the centre, next to the silver cruets. Quick as a flash I see his game. I push the sugar bowl back to the middle of the table. Then I take the coffee pot, and his cup and saucer, to the side table – where there's nothing to distract me – and pour it there. When I serve his cup, all neatly poured and not a drop in the saucer, he is furious. Angry globs of spit bubble at the corners of his mouth.

Mrs Martin glowers. 'You may pour mine at the table,' she says. 'No cream.' Then she turns to the Colonel and adds, 'This is how Roman slaves poisoned their masters, is it not?'

I am so confused and afraid that I don't speak. I just stand there, as if I'm a tree putting down roots. All of a sudden words stream into my head, as if God sent them. 'Ma'am, I beg your pardon, but the lip of the pot is misshapen and this is Mrs Acton's best linen tablecloth. Besides, if I had wanted to poison the coffee I would have done so in the kitchen.'

They both stare at me, with outraged eyes. Then Mrs Martin does something most peculiar. She gets up, takes the Colonel's coffee to the window – which is open to let in the air – and pours it onto the street.

'You will serve my husband's coffee at the table.' She puts the cup, smeared with dregs, in front of him. His hand is still beneath the table, his wrist and elbow moving in a most robust way, as if he's struggling with the buttons of his breeches.

I do as I'm bid and pour the coffee. Very slowly. Keeping my eyes tight upon the spout. I try to think of Hatty's words about not being frightened but my arm is shaking terrible and coffee starts to splash from the cup into the saucer. And then from the saucer onto Ma'am's best Irish linen.

Mrs Martin is sipping at her cup, her eyes fixed on the oil painting of a girl and a dog that hangs above the fireplace. All at once she puts her cup down and jerks out her elbow so that the salt cellar is knocked to the floor, landing right at the Colonel's feet.

'Pick it up,' she commands, and the glittering beam of her black eyes bores into me. And that is when I know she doesn't deserve one ounce of my sympathy. I think of Hatty's words – about keeping my eyes from *it*, and not showing a morsel of fear for them to feed upon – and I pull my puny frame up to its full height. I want to turn on my newly booted heel but I don't: I know I must keep my job, that their words will always have more weight than mine.

I go down on my hands and knees, and crawl beneath the linen tablecloth. It smells of rotting fish and something I take to be gentleman's cologne. Eyes tight closed I grope for the salt cellar, curl my fingers quickly round it and come back up, very calm and still. I replace it beside the pepper pot and then I say something I will regret for ever.

'Would you care for some more of the *unpoisoned* coffee?'

'The what?' gasps Mrs Martin. She starts fanning at her face with her fingers as if she's about to go into a swoon.

The Colonel's face is a livid red, his eyes bulging and popping in their sockets. I look away, startled at my own brass. But an odd hoggish sound comes from the Colonel's mouth and I know I've gone too far this time. And then he brings his hand from beneath the table and strokes at the air. 'Now, now, Jane,' he splutters, breathless. 'Let's not disrupt this most enjoyable breakfast. Baked mackerel is on its way.'

'Bring my husband's mackerel, girl. In plenty of butter.' Mrs Martin has stopped her feigned swooning and her voice is curt and snappish. She flaps her hand at me, but I dare not look her in the eye.

I run to find Hatty, who is in the washroom pressing pillowcases in a swirl of hissing steam. She agrees I've gone too far. 'But you showed him,' she adds proudly. 'You showed him how fearless you are and no doubt that will stop his dirty ways.'

'Will I lose my position?'

'Likely they'll say nothing – they rarely do – but you must say nothing too. And we must get that tablecloth soaked in brine before Ma'am sees it.'

'Why does Mrs Martin have no shame of him?'

'Not to us, because we are no one. She'd be ashamed if society ladies found out. But they won't, will they?' Hatty gives my hand a little squeeze. 'I'm teaching you the ways of the world and they ain't always pretty. Now, you take over these and I'll take 'em their mackerel. And watch your lip next time, Ann Kirby, for we can rarely beat 'em at their own game.'

Later, as Miss Eliza and I struggle with an eel, I think of Hatty's words and they fill me with an unspoken savagery. The eel is as long as my arm, writhing and twisting upon the table. I grip its slippery body as Miss Eliza peers at her recipe book.

'Split the skin at the neck and remove in a single motion,' she reads. 'But first we must secure it to a board with a fork.'

The eel thrashes madly as Miss Eliza stabs at its head with a toasting fork, shuddering and grimacing as if she's been asked to stab a child. 'This is unspeakably cruel,' she gasps. 'Boiling it first would surely be more humane.'

'I will do it, Miss Eliza,' I cry. 'It's only a pond creature!' And she throws me the fork with great eagerness, no doubt thinking I've killed a writhing eel before. I haven't but Hatty's words have made my blood pump like liquid fire. I grit my teeth, think of the Colonel and plunge the fork into its body, so the eel stops his thrashing and lies quite still.

Miss Eliza steps back and looks at me in awe. 'Why, Ann ... and you so small and slight.' She laughs in relief. 'You are barely much bigger than this beast.'

I blink at her, my body shaking beneath my bibbed apron.

'You are full of surprises,' she says. 'I will leave you to skin it. Then can you open it, clean it and cut it into finger-length pieces. I think sage will pair well, don't you?'

I don't tell her it was pure fury, and nothing more, that caused me to kill the eel so effortlessly. As her footsteps recede, I curse myself – for now she thinks I have a true skill at murdering eels, so I must skin it perfectly. I place my hands upon the eel and am wondering how best to open and empty it when all of a sudden the eel twitches and its head rears up. Panicked, I jump back against the wall of the scullery. Why will this blasted eel not die! I grab a brass skillet and hit the eel. Over and over I hit it, 'til the sweat is running into my eyes. When I stop, a strange calm falls over me. My shoulders are where they should be, not up by my ears. The coil in my stomach has gone. And I feel drained, like a wrung-out cloth. But there's no time to rest. The eel lies, lifeless, on the board and now I must skin it. I pierce it with the tip of a knife and try to grip a flap of skin. The eel slips and slides from my grasp, leaving its slime upon my fingers. Tears of frustration and exhaustion prick the backs of my eyes. Suddenly I long for Mam, for how she was. What am I doing here fighting with eels and dirty old colonels with their devilish wives? I should be looking after Mam . . .

Just as I'm thinking this, Miss Eliza returns and sees the eel has slipped half across the table.

'We'll tackle this beast together,' she says, standing so close I can smell the fresh-picked sage on her fingers, the lavender from her laundered clothes, the lemony cleanness of her skin.

'You hold and I'll pull.' She takes the loosened skin from the eel's neck and eases it down. It peels off clean, like the pelt of a well-hung rabbit.

'Next time we will boil it, like a lobster, with culinary kindness,' she says. Then she turns to me, stooping her head so it's the same level as mine. 'Ann, are you happy here?'

I nod, but tears fill my eyes. No one – since Mam a decade back – has ever asked me if I'm happy. I sniff and tell her it's just my monthlies giving me pain.

She studies me with great concentration. Then says I must go and rest and she will bring me something warm to lay against my stomach. Immediately I regret my hasty lie. Although what was I to say? That my mam is a lunatic? That Colonel Martin likes to frighten servant girls with his sausages and chestnuts? That I have ruined Ma'am's best tablecloth? The truth is I've never felt happier than I am in Miss Eliza's kitchen. The near-constant bubbling of the stockpot, the endless eggs in straw-lined baskets, the trays of mulberries drying above the stove, the quinces and medlars laid out in lines. Just seeing it all and knowing – every single day – that I won't go to bed aching with hunger. But it's more than that: it's *her*. Her very presence makes my heart leap like a spring salmon. I will bear anything to stay beside her. And nothing the Colonel can do will frighten me away.

'The cramps have passed,' I lie.

'Good! Bring me a fresh knife with a keen edge and let us clean the beast together,' she says, and the lines slope away from her brow, leaving it as smooth as china again.

CHAPTER NINETEEN

Eliza

RICE PUDDING

When I take Mother her morning tea, she is sitting up in bed against a mountain of pillows and cushions, her nightcap flopping from her head like a pale wilting flower. Instantly I know something is wrong: there are violet crescents beneath her eyes, her lips are thin and tight, her shoulders braced.

She holds up her arm to prevent me speaking. 'The Colonel and Mrs Martin spoke to me last night. I have barely slept a wink.'

I think immediately of the money we've borrowed. If the Martins fail to pay us, we shall all be fleeing to Calais. 'They cannot pay?'

'Don't be silly, Eliza!'

I stare at her. 'Well, what?'

'Ann must leave. They were most insistent. She has to leave immediately.'

'Leave?' I repeat, stupefied. 'And for what?'

'Her impudence is inexcusable. We cannot have a servant who threatens our livelihood, Eliza.'

'What has she done?' I reach out to steady myself on the bedpost, for Mother's words are ridiculous.

'She said our coffee was poisoned. Mrs Martin was so upset, she was plagued with stomach pains all day. Luckily the Colonel convinced her that Ann was joking. A joke in very poor taste, I might add. But it will not do, Eliza. It will not do!'

'Surely you do not believe them?'

'Why would they lie?' She leans back against the cushions, her eyes closed, her face set hard. 'I have heard so many tales of servants like this ... they loathe their mistresses and find any way they can to sabotage them. If we allow it, we will go the way of France, where the servants chopped the head from every master and every mistress.'

'How can you say this without hearing her account of events?' I shake my head, confounded. There's not a whiff of Ann in all this talk. But Mother carries on.

'I have seen you with that girl, Eliza. I have seen how you dote on her. I do not find it ...' She pauses as if searching for the right word. 'Wholesome,' she says, at length.

I swallow, and make myself count to three before I respond. My knuckles are blanched white from gripping the bedpost and I am so angry, red sparks tumble through my head. 'She is a good servant, Mother. The best I have ever known. I cannot complete my book without her.'

'Without our boarders, there will be no book. Who do you imagine is paying for the kitchen, the ingredients, your precious time?' She opens her eyes, looks at the ceiling, sighs. 'The Martins are adamant. They are powerful people in London.'

'Hatty can serve and we can keep Ann in the kitchen.' I steady my voice but it's impossible to miss the note of pleading. 'Out of sight and out of mind.'

'If Ann Kirby has been rude to our first boarders, why will she be any different with the next? The baths at Tunbridge Wells are a small place. There will be gossip. We cannot afford to make another blunder, not after your father . . .' Her voice tails off. She drags the back of her hand over her eyes and sighs again. 'If we lose boarders like this we shall be forced to take in schoolboys. Is that what you want? To spend your days producing rice pudding for unruly boys?'

I chew my lip. And from some distant place come lines of poetry, whirling through the past to hover in the present:

> *Darkly, darkly, Misfortune's wing*
> *Is o'er thee rolling its heavy cloud;*
> *Slowly, slowly, 'tis gathering . . .*

'And if we have no schoolboy boarders, we are destitute!' Mother's voice snaps at the air.

'I shall speak to Ann. And if the fault is not hers, I suggest we ask the Martins to leave.' I straighten my shoulders and turn to go, feigning a defiance I do not feel. A bitter blend of self-loathing and self-pity rolls slowly through me. I should have defended Ann more vigorously, I think. But Mother is right: we need the goodwill of our boarders. Without them, we shall be forced to crawl on our impoverished knees to Edgar in the jungles of Mauritius, or to my married sister Mary, to live at the mercy of their charity. And yet without Ann how shall I write my book?

Ann is stoking the fire in the stove. She turns as I enter, her face flushed from the heat of the flames. 'Shall I make you some tea, Miss Eliza?'

'What has happened between you and the Martins?'

She looks away, chewing on her lower lip.

'You must tell me the truth. I cannot have a servant who lies to me.' My hands are pressed so tightly together, an ache begins to spread from my wrist up my arms. Ann's small head is bowed and I notice that the nape of her neck is a mottled pink. In the silence I hear her gulp, then the fire spits and sparks spray from the open door of the stove and die, one by one, upon the hearth.

'The Colonel has peculiar habits,' she whispers. 'He likes to sh-show himself.'

'Show himself?' I repeat. 'Whatever do you mean?'

'The parts of him that no one but Mrs Martin should see.'

'He has had you in his room?' I am so shocked my mouth hangs, open and slack.

'No, miss. He does it at breakfast or at dinner. He sh-shows himself to Hatty too but she is m-more used to it than me.'

'At table?' The idea is so ridiculous I want to laugh out loud.

But Ann's face is crimson with shame. And I know all about shame. 'So you threatened to poison his coffee?'

'No.' She stops and I see her eyes welling with tears. 'I can leave today, Miss Eliza.'

And then I do something that no mistress should do with her kitchen maid. I take her in my arms and hold her to me, stroking her hair, patting her back. 'I am so sorry, Ann. I am so very sorry,' I whisper. And in my mind's eye, I am imagining her as Susannah. My Susannah.

CHAPTER TWENTY

Ann

BREAD AND AN ONION

I walk the half-hour home through a damp white mist, my thoughts turning over and over. I am grateful for my dry feet, so snug in my new boots. Or are they my boots? This is how my mind is working, question after question. What will Hatty be told? What am I to say to Pa? How is a girl meant to deal with a man like the Colonel? I think on Ma'am's words as she ushered me from the back door: *He did no one any harm and yet your insolence has hurt us all*. And it's the truth of her words that cuts me to the quick. For my departure has hurt Hatty and Ma'am and Miss Eliza, who must now find another scullery maid. And it's hurt me and will hurt Pa and Reverend Thorpe who found me the position and Mrs Thorpe who lent me her old frock. I feel their disappointment, like buckets of water on my back.

Most of all I think of Miss Eliza. How her hair smelt of lemons, the sob that caught in her throat so she could not speak. I will never find another mistress such as her. My chest heaves and the tears rise up in me again. Why have I been such a fool? Is it such a sinful thing for a man to want to show his private parts beneath a breakfast table?

The smell of bruised apples reaches me of a sudden. And in that moment I am back in Miss Eliza's kitchen, rich with cooking odours: the nutty smell of roasting coffee berries, the syrupy scent of fruit upon the stove, the pierce of a fresh-cut lemon, the sweet warmth of a split vanilla pod, the earthy heat of a crushed clove. And her, showing me how to separate a yolk from its white, or how to hold a blade, or how to skin a tomato. A tear rolls down my nose. Then another and another.

When I reach the cottage, my heart is so heavy I nearly turn away. Perhaps Pa will be at the graveyard and I will have time to pull myself together. Septimus comes bounding to the door. I scratch his ears in the way he likes, then I kneel down and push my face into his neck.

'Who's there?' Pa's voice slurs towards me and my heart sinks as heavy as a stone.

'It's me. Why are you not at the graveyard?'

'Ann?' I hear his crutches crashing against the wall as he staggers and swings through the darkness of the cottage. I peer into the gloom. The cottage reeks, as if a rodent has died and been left to rot in a corner. I push the door back and remove the rag that hangs in front of the window. Pa coughs and curses.

'What has happened?' I whisper.

'Nothing, Ann. Nothing.' He clutches at my arm and I see his hand is streaked with mud and his nails rimed with earth. A good sign. He must have done some work in the graveyard.

'But 'tis hard on my own . . .' His breath is heavy with the stink of ale.

'Are you going to the graveyard today?'

He shakes his head and gives a long rattling cough that makes his whole body judder. 'I'm not well,' he says, easing himself clumsily onto the mattress.

'This place needs cleaning.' I look round the cottage. There's a pile of gnawed bones in a corner. The grate is empty but for a charred log and, beneath it, a thin layer of ash. The mattress has no bedding on it and hay spews from the single pillow. Mam's things have gone and the room seems bare and decaying.

I find the dead rodent – a rat – behind the grate, flies crawling over it. I wonder if I can make a meal from it but decide it's too far gone, so I carry it out by its tail and throw it as far away as I can. I turn the mattress over, sweep out the ash from the hearth, swish a leafy branch into the corners to catch the cobwebs. I fill a bucket from the stream and scrub the cottage floor and wipe the walls, changing the water several times until my arms ache from the filling and carrying and my fingers are numb with cold. My stomach growls, but there's no food in the place, not even an old potato. I pat my pocket, checking for the five shillings Miss Eliza gave me.

'I must go and buy bread,' I say. 'It'll be bread and an onion for supper, like the old days.' Pa nods and coughs, liquid gurgling on his chest. 'Before I go, tell me how Mam is?'

'And how would I know that?' he answers, his voice hoarse from the coughing.

'I-I supposed Reverend Thorpe would have kept in touch with the asylum ... to see that she was well settled ...' My words peter out, hollow and half-hearted. Why did I think such a thing? Reverend Thorpe is a busy man with an entire parish to look after. And all this time I have been thinking only of how to dress an eel, or how to spice a pork chop, or whether four or five eggs makes the lightest Madeira cake. I feel such a rush of self-hatred all the strength leaves my legs. I crumple down, next to Pa. The mattress is damp – whether from the mist or his sweat or spilt ale I cannot tell. For a second Pa looks surprised. Then he reaches for my hand and grips it.

'Why are you here, Ann?'

I look into his pink eyes and can't think how to explain. After a full minute's silence, I tell him I must buy food and visit Mam. 'Do you have an address? For the asylum?'

He shakes his head. 'Ask the Reverend.' He lets go of my hand, lies down and curls into a ball, like a baby.

'Will you come with me? You can lean on me.' And when Pa shakes his head, I know something is amiss, that he's surely lost his position. Like me.

'Did Reverend Thorpe give you any money?' I ask, softly. 'For the work you did?'

He shakes his head, then coughs so fierce his body quivers from head to toe.

'You should see a doctor. I have money from Miss Eliza.'

Pa shakes his head and croaks into the pillow, 'No, please no.'

I find a scrap of blanket and put it over him. As I kiss his bearded cheek I feel the damp heat of him, as if he has a fever. I wonder if he has the White Plague – and my heart drops into my feet. Why did Mrs Thorpe not say anything? Why has no one told me of his illness? I'll visit Mam, I think. Which means I must go to the rectory and ask Mrs Thorpe for the address. Even if it's the last thing on earth I want to do.

CHAPTER TWENTY-ONE

Eliza

ROAST WILD DUCK WITH CUCUMBERS

The butcher's boy brings eight mutton kidneys and two wild ducks to the back door.

'The mallards 'ave 'anged for six days,' he says, 'and I'm to tell you the kidneys is fresh as daisies.' The ducks hang upside down from his bloodstained hand. He gives them a jaunty swing, making the light catch, flash, on their bottle-green heads.

'I hope there are no maggots crawling around in those ducks?' I haven't the disposition for Hatty's shrieking indignations today. The girl hasn't an ounce of Ann's practical stoicism and my nerves are already in tatters.

'Tell the maid what picks 'em to use a deep bucket,

otherwise your house will be full of feathers with every gust of wind.' He wipes some drool from his nose with his cuff and turns back to his barrow.

I take the ducks to the scullery, stepping with irritation over the night's chamber pots that are lined up in front of the plate room. Why hasn't Hatty emptied them? The scullery reeks and the sink is choked with unwashed pans sitting in a puddle of oily water. Beside the sink, unscrubbed turnips and parsnips sprawl amidst clods of clag. The sugarloaf has been left unwrapped and is alive with wasps. The egg baskets are empty. The dishcloths have been discarded in a damp mound. Crumbs snap and crunch beneath my feet.

The kitchen is no better. I need a brisk fire for the ducks, but Hatty has not roused it and both the log basket and the coal scuttle are empty. My teeth grind and gnash with furied frustration. But without Hatty, the wretched Colonel and his gimlet-eyed wife will have no dinner, so I silently seethe and re-read today's recipes: Mutton Kidneys à la Française and Roast Wild Duck with Cucumbers à la Poulette. The cucumbers are the last of the season and have toughened skin and overlarge seeds but it can't be helped. The recipe I'm using appears to be for a banquet and requires twenty cucumbers. I must scale everything back: butter, parsley, veal stock, flour. I've just started paring the cucumbers, when Hatty flies in.

'Miss Eliza, I must speak with you!'

I am on the verge of scolding her for her slovenly ways when something in the wild look of her stops me. I put aside the paring knife and twist my lips into a congenial smile.

'About Ann,' she continues, her hands fidgeting at the brim of her cap.

I nod and keep my face blank. No one must know of the swill of guilt and anger that has kept me tossing and turning these last two nights.

'Ma'am is talking of placing an advertisement, but it ain't right. This,' she pauses, sweeping a scrappy arm around the kitchen, 'is Ann's position and no one else's.'

I'm about to explain that Mrs Acton – mistress of this house – has made her decision and we must abide by it. But Hatty starts hopping from one foot to the other in great agitation. 'Why did no one ask me, Miss Eliza? For it was my fault . . . all my fault.' Her hands are back at her cap, tugging at its scalloped edge as though she wishes to draw it directly over her face.

'Explain yourself,' I say gently. Beneath my ribs, something leaps. As if a galloping breeze has fallen upon a dying fire and caused a flame to catch.

'The Colonel was always at it, under the breakfast table, wanting to show us his – his . . .'

'Yes, yes,' I wave an impatient hand at her. I need more than this if I am to convince Mother that Ann should be returned to us.

'I told her some gentlemen do this and they like it when the maids are scared. I think she had a mind to be particular brave after that. Most of us girls have a mother or an older sister who explains the ways of certain gentlemen.' She pauses briefly for breath, then runs on, words spilling out of her: 'And new girls that have none of these will likely be instructed by the cook or the housekeeper. But Bordyke House don't have either. So, you see, it's not Ann's fault, miss.'

A lump appears in my throat, forcing me to cough in as delicate a manner as I can muster. But the lump is lodged fast, so I must speak through it. 'Have you had much experience of gentlemen,' I pause on this word which now seems so evidently misapplied, 'like this?'

'Oh yes, miss. And worse. Taking rougher liberties and the like. My ma warned me of their ploys and tricks, so I know when to step away and how to escape without 'em losing face, but Ann—'

'But Ann has no mother.' I reach for the paring knife and the cucumber. My hands must be busy. I must peel and cut and slice. 'This knife is blunt, Hatty. Sharpen it, please.'

She strikes the blade against the whetstone. 'I don't think Ann Kirby knows much about gentlemen, miss, and anyways it was not she that spoke of poisoning the coffee, but Mrs Martin herself.'

The lump in my throat cools, hardens, so that I can only croak 'Oh?'

Hatty gingerly puts a fingertip to the blade, then lays it on the table in front of me. 'Yes, her hand was shaking and she didn't want to spill coffee on Ma'am's newly pressed Irish linen. It's a devil to get out, only the hottest water will shift it, and hours of brine scrubbing so that your hands is painful raw.'

As I gouge the seeds from the cucumbers, Hatty explains what happened between Ann and Mrs Martin. My mind turns over, question upon question. As I salt and steep the cucumbers, and slice the fat from the kidneys, I think of how we have mistreated Ann. None of this would have happened if she'd had a mother, if she'd been in service with a *proper* cook, if she'd worked for an establishment with a *housekeeper*.

'She did not say any of this to me,' I say, batting at the metallic odour of butchery and blood drifting from the sliced kidneys. And yet I know the fault to be mine. For I did not press her. And I did not sufficiently defend her to Mother. I put the knife down, wipe my hands on my apron and go to the drawing room where Mother is reviewing the household accounts.

She sits hunched over her ledger but straightens up when I enter. There is a small smile playing over her lips which strikes me as peculiar given our present circumstances.

'I have good news,' she says. 'Exceptionally good news!'

'There can be no good news while Ann Kirby is not here!' I burst out.

She looks peevish and the smile slips from her lips. 'That's as may be, but you forget yourself, Eliza.'

I am not inclined to waste time on explanations or justifications, nor do I feel like hearing her *good news* which most likely involves some small saving she has made. 'Hatty has told me the truth about Ann and the Martins. We have treated her most unfairly and I want her returned.'

Mother frowns then closes the ledger and pushes it away.

'I wish to pay her more and to hire a scullery maid to work under her.' I pause and wipe the back of my hand over my forehead. How tiring, how humiliating it is to have conversations like this with my mother, at my age. In a final rush of fury, I add, 'If she is not returned to me, on my terms, then I shall produce my cookery book elsewhere!'

'Let us not fight, my dear. If you were married and had your own household you would be free to make your own decisions on servants, furnishings, bills of fare . . . Indeed, all aspects of domestic management would be yours and yours alone.' She looks at me in a pointed way, as if this twisting conversation is leading somewhere and I am too truculent to see it.

'I know I'm an old maid – to be pitied and loathed in equal measure – and that I must submit to your will,' I say through clenched teeth. 'But I want Ann back. I shall serve the Martins myself if necessary.' I turn on my heel, for the room has become airless and oppressive, as if our combined presences are too big for it.

'Patience, my dear! Your temper is most unbecoming. Wouldn't you like your own household? With every Ann Kirby you might want?'

'Of course.' I turn back into the room. 'But your jibes are hurtful – as you must surely know. And I wish to discuss Ann Kirby, not my lack of matrimony.'

'My dear, you may have Ann back. The Colonel and Mrs Martin are now unable to extend their stay but have generously offered to pay us the full amount.'

A lightness sweeps over me, followed at once by a feeling of panic. What if Ann has found a new position? What if she refuses to return? 'And the extra wages? The under-maid?'

Mother twists her wedding ring with a conspicuous flourish. 'You must find the money, Eliza. I have heard of cooks who turn a tidy sum selling feathers and bones to the rag-and-bone men, or selling beef dripping from the back door. Even rancid fat can be sold for soap, I'm told.'

'You expect me to do that?' I ask, startled. For this is exactly the sort of thing that would shame Mother. More shaming, I suspect, than having a common cook for a daughter.

'No, no, no!' She throws her hands into the air. 'Ann Kirby must do that. She must earn her own extra wages. At least until we are financially stable.'

'You know full well that we use everything, that I am the thriftiest housekeeper in all of Kent,' I say coldly. But Mother ignores me.

'Don't you want to hear my good news?' The smile returns to her mouth, as if she cannot suppress it. 'We have a new boarder coming. A single gentleman in possession of a fortune.'

Now I understand why she looks so pleased with herself.

'He's an old friend of your father's. John's business may have crumbled but Mr Arnott's enterprise stretches to the ends of the earth.' She pauses, as if for effect, then adds, 'And he is a widower!'

An image of Mr Arnott forms in my mind: old, stooped, balding, jowls that fall in doughy rolls around his neck, a stomach of pork fat that flops over his breeches. 'And he's come to take the waters at Tunbridge Wells? Gout? Kidney stones?'

'I did not like to pry. But be practical, Eliza. At least keep an open mind.' She gives her ring another sharp turn. And it's as though I can read the pattern of her thoughts: he is elderly and sick and rich, and the prospect of being a wealthy wife is bettered by one thing only – being a wealthy widow. The shamelessness of her machinations makes my innards shrivel.

As I leave, she calls out after me. 'You have not enquired about the nature of his enterprise!'

But I'm in no mood to ask. Besides, I have ducks to roast, cucumbers to braise, buttered kidneys to toss in parsley, thyme and cayenne.

And after that I must find the address of Ann Kirby. Before it is too late.

CHAPTER TWENTY-TWO

Ann

A PIECE OF BREAD

Mrs Thorpe doesn't comment on my hair, which is blown wild around my face, or compliment me on my new boots now covered in dust and mud, or ask why I'm not at Bordyke House. Nor does she invite me in, not even to the scullery. So we stand in the back yard while the stable boy and the butcher's boy come and go around us, and she has one eye on them and one eye on the kitchen maid who is taking delivery of a bunch of dead rabbits.

'I have no idea where your mother is,' Mrs Thorpe says, impatient. 'I'm very busy, as you can see.'

'Please, ma'am, Reverend Thorpe might know,' I say,

persistent, but with my eyes cast meek and humble to the ground. 'I was told he took her there.'

'Took her where?' She doesn't wait for an answer, but turns away and shouts, 'I hope those rabbits are fresh and young? I will not have rabbits beyond four months, Florence. Do you hear me? Four months!'

I look at Florence, a poor bitten-down creature as thin as a gnawed bone. But something in me sings, for Miss Eliza never shouted at me, never spoke to me as if I were dirt scraped from the floor. And with that little bit of knowledge I feel myself swell and grow.

'Where can I find the Reverend Thorpe, ma'am?' I look her straight in the eye, as bold as brass.

'My husband may be anywhere – he's in great demand. If you wait here, Florence will bring you a piece of bread and then you can be on your way.'

'No thanks, ma'am, I need to see my mother. Reverend Thorpe took her away and I have no address.'

Mrs Thorpe blows out a huge angry breath. 'I. Have. Told. You.' She flaps her hands at me, as if I'm a stray dog. Then she pauses, narrows her eyes and fixes them on mine. 'Why are you not at Bordyke House, Ann Kirby?'

My cheeks go hot, and all my boldness vanishes. 'I'm dismissed,' I say, my head bowed so that I'm like a cringing dog.

'Dismissed? I bent over backwards to get you that position!'

Her anger is like a tongue of cold fire.

'Just like your father, Ann Kirby! My poor dear husband had to dismiss him too. On his first day of work! We have done everything for you Kirbys and this is how you repay us.' She shakes her head and turns away as if she can't bear the sight of me. I feel smaller than a beetle. As if I've been gobbled up by my own shame.

She walks towards the rectory but I cannot move, even with the butcher's boy gawping at me. Then at the door, she turns back. 'Kent County Lunatic Asylum, that's where your mother is. Safely under lock and key. Where all you Kirbys should be!' And she's gone, the door slamming behind her.

'But where is that, ma'am? Where is that?' I cry, but I know she can't hear me behind her big closed door. Tears shove at the backs of my eyes but I won't let them out. Not in front of the butcher's boy. I squeeze every muscle in my face as he steers his cart towards the street, the iron wheels clattering over the cobbles. But then he shouts over his shoulder, 'Ain't far from here, missy. Barming Heath, near Maidstone. Fifteen mile or so.'

'Fifteen miles?' I echo. I can walk fifteen miles easy, only I have no directions.

'You can follow the river or you can ride with Jones the miller,' he adds. 'He has a lady friend who works there. Visits regular, he does.'

Hope skips inside me. 'Thank you!' I say. 'Thank you!'

Chapter Twenty-Three

Eliza

An Apple Hedgehog, Iced, with Almond Spikes

I scrub the taint of kitchen from me – onions, gravy, boiled bones – and put on my good stout boots. With my plaid shawl round my shoulders I walk to the rectory, a distinct spring in my step. The despicable Martins have paid and left. The Colonel had the audacity to enter the passageway to the kitchen after their last breakfast – for which he demanded cold beef, Cochin eggs, crumb muffins *and* baked mushrooms to *fortify them for the journey ahead*. I found him lurking, like the miscreant he is, and assumed he was checking we had dismissed Ann Kirby.

'I wish to compliment the chef,' he simpered. 'We suppose him to be French. Is that so?'

I snorted into my neckline, before remembering myself. 'You are right, sir. She is an excellent chef and I shall pass on your kind words.'

'Oh? A plain cook? In which case our conjectures were entirely wrong.' And he turned so quickly I thought he might trip over his varnished shoes.

Needless to say, his compliments to the *French chef* have added a bounce to my step. As did this morning's post which included two annuals: the *Literary Gazette* and *Friendship's Offering*. Having no boarders to cook for and not wanting to arrive too early at the rectory, I was at liberty to read. I settled myself in the drawing room and feasted on the words of Mrs Hemans, Mrs Howitt, Miss Jewsbury and, oh marvel that she is, L. E. Landon. When I read her verse I seem to observe myself in a looking glass of words. As if she sees inside me, understands me. I found myself repeating lines aloud, committing them to memory that I might quote them later, that I might educate Ann on England's finest poems.

Her poignant words return to me now . . .

> *With what still hours of calm delight*
> *Thy songs and image blend;*
> *I cannot choose but think thou wert*
> *An old familiar friend.*

For that is how I feel about my fellow lady poets. They are like intimate friends of mine, appearing when I am most in need.

By the time I arrive at the rectory my head is swimming

with verse – lines from L. E. Landon, a stanza from the formidable Mrs Howitt that refuses to leave my tongue, my own feeble attempts. A melee of words, images, illuminations that raises my spirits even as it reveals the inadequacies of my own verse. I lift the brass knocker – the maned head of a lion – and bring it down so firmly it echoes through the house. The shuffle of feet, the grate of a turning key, and the door opens on its well-oiled hinges. A bobbing housemaid with frightened eyes hurries off to announce my arrival.

When Mrs Thorpe appears, it is with ill-concealed astonishment. The muscles beneath her cheeks and round her thin mouth twitch. As if she cannot decide which facial pose to adopt. Eventually she welcomes me with a watery smile.

'I'm here for Ann Kirby's address,' I say. 'We have had a misunderstanding and now I must ask her to return.'

My words, as ever, are too blunt. Mrs Thorpe's eyes become cold and clouded, like the dulled eyes of a dead trout. 'You were so clever to find her, Mrs Thorpe,' I add with obsequious haste.

Her expression softens. 'Let us take some tea together, or perhaps you would prefer coffee?' She brings a carved silver bell from the folds of her skirt and jerks at it. The little housemaid appears, bobs, disappears. Mrs Thorpe leads the way to a drawing room – wallpaper patterned with rosebuds, an oil painting of Mr Thorpe above the fireplace, a pair of chairs upholstered in green leather.

We discuss the weather, the havoc wreaked by this year's late frosts, the London East Enders who have arrived to harvest the hops, the difficulty of finding good servants.

The latter is my cue and I pounce, like a cat upon its prey. 'A simple, foolish misunderstanding,' I explain, looking demurely into my tea where stray leaves float like drowned insects. 'Entirely my fault and now I must retrieve her, if I am not too late.' And God forbid that I'm too late, I think, with another heave of regret.

Mrs Thorpe puffs up at my words and puts her teacup on the table in such a way that a shaft of light catches, holds, sparkles on her wedding ring. After a short silence – her hand carefully preserved in its shaft of light – she says, 'Yes, it's possible she's joined a gang of hop pickers.'

My throat turns dry. Mrs Thorpe knows something. She knows I am too late. Lines of verse whirl into my head ... *Affection's chain was all too rudely wrench'd in twain ... Blighted hopes and friendship fled ... She is flung neglectedly abroad, where fostering love is not ...*

Bizarrely, I have a sudden image of my feelings in recipe form: one pound of fresh despair, three pecks of firm frustration, five ounces of pure guilt, a strewing of newly cut regret and a few grains of self-pity.

'Are you well?' Mrs Thorpe is peering curiously at me, her ringed fingers dabbling at the slender gold crucifix hanging at her neck – a gesture that informs me of both her matrimony and her piety.

'I would like to visit Ann.'

She draws her eyebrows together. 'You don't need my permission for that.'

'Yes, but I have no address.'

'Did you not record it when you hired her?' She opens her

eyes righteously wide. As if I am more of an imbecile than she imagined.

'Oh, I am such a novice at these things.' I try to remember what Ann said about her home. Did I ask her anything? When I add up all I know of her, it amounts to very little. To my chagrin.

Mrs Thorpe purses her lips and appears to think. 'Perhaps you should come back when my husband is here, and then we can discuss your poetry too. Although I must tell you that my dear husband is not in favour of scribbling ladies, particularly unmarried scribbling ladies. I am broadly of the same opinion, but you may be able to sway me, Miss Acton.'

I am so taken aback that for a second I cannot speak. I want to tell her that no less than thirteen clergymen subscribed to my first book of poetry, that the Reverends Cobbold of Ipswich, Fletcher of Woodbridge, Kirby of Suffolk and Mortimer of Kent all acknowledged receipt with appreciative notes, that one – Reverend Kirby? – wrote gushingly of my sincerity and charm. Then I remember the returned volume, with its terse and disapproving note, from Reverend Bull of Tattingstone Rectory. The hairs on my arms rise up, as if an icy blast of air has swept into the room.

I push away the memory of Reverend Bull's scowling hostile words and stand, my head held high and my back as straight and unyielding as a butcher's blade. 'If you cannot give me Ann Kirby's address, I will find it elsewhere.'

Something about my bearing or the tone of my voice makes Mrs Thorpe change her mind. She sighs and pulls the little silver bell from her skirt. A most ungodly feeling of triumph – I have won! – runs over me, mingled with relief. The housemaid is dispatched to bring paper and ink, whereupon Mrs Thorpe writes three lines of directions in her best copper plate.

'I cannot answer for what you will find,' she says, passing her folded notepaper to me with obvious reluctance.

I frown, wondering what I am to find at Ann's home. But when I leave the rectory the sky is so high, blue, scoured clean, that I immediately dismiss Mrs Thorpe's sour words. I walk past the Rose and Crown, past the wine merchant's shop and the bookseller's, past the Mechanics' Institute, past the brickworks and the paper mill. Then out beyond the water meadows and through the hop gardens, golden-green and blurred with October sun. The air is grainy, thick with chaff, and the land swarms with pickers. Barefoot children, black-haired gypsies, wizened men and stooped women with heads wrapped in handkerchiefs, all of them crouching, bending, stretching between the endless rows of hop poles.

I keep an eye out for Ann, but instead I catch sight of a hedgehog shuffling into the undergrowth – an unexpected glimpse for they are shy nocturnal creatures. Something about his gait, his spines, makes me imagine a sweet dish in his image. A hedgehog pudding ... How might I make the spikes? Slithers of blanched almonds ... impaled in a stiff white icing? Browned in a hot oven to recreate his russet colour? And beneath his armour of icing and almonds ... a Madeira sponge? A stiff blancmange? As I ponder how to make the hedgehog's body, I notice an apple tree, its boughs stripped of fruit but for a single split pippin at its apex. An apple hedgehog! A thick puree of apples drained until almost dry ... with a centre of apricot jam flavoured with lemons. I imagine Ann at my side as we construct our apple hedgehog – and suddenly I have my skirts in my hands and I am marching, almost running, in the direction of her home.

CHAPTER TWENTY-FOUR

Ann

DAMSON CHEESE

The miller doesn't talk much as we make our way to Barming Heath. I'm glad of this, for it leaves me free to spot blackberries and bullaces, codlings and crab apples, and to fancy the pretty dishes they might make. I wonder if Miss Eliza is making blackberry jelly or damson shrub. And when a pheasant runs squawking from the road, I wonder who is picking the fowl now. Hatty is too squeamish for such things. Miss Eliza must have a new girl. But I don't want to think about Miss Eliza or Hatty because it makes me feel emptied, as if I have nothing inside me.

'The asylum is a new building.' The miller speaks with great pride, as if he built it himself. 'Designed by the same gentleman as built Maidstone Gaol.' He nods in a satisfied way, and points ahead with the willow stick he's been using as a whip on his old nag.

Iron gates loom up and beyond them a road unrolls. At the end of it I can just make out a building, very big, very grey. All corners and angles and scaffolding. My heart gives a little bound. I am soon to see Mam! And the nurse that cares for her. Maybe even her doctor, her room . . .

'Still building it,' adds the miller, with the same proud note in his voice.

As we get closer I see the asylum is very grand, with a fine clock and great squatting columns and long thin chimneys that point to Heaven. Round the building runs an iron railing with spikes on top. On either side of the iron gates are a pair of matching gatehouses, oil lamps flaring from their small square windows.

'Hundreds in there,' says the miller. 'And all of 'em raving lunatics.'

He drops me at the gatehouse and tells me to be ready for collection at four sharp. When the nag clops away I'm struck by a feeling of loneliness, as if everyone has died of plague and there's just me left. An odd feeling and one I never had at Bordyke House. But then a small hatch opens in the wall and a face is peering at me, red like a steak and riven with pox scars.

'I'm here to see Mrs Jane Kirby please, sir,' I say, lifting my chin like Miss Eliza did when she was talking to Ma'am.

'We're closed.' The hatch is pulled shut. My chin tumbles. Why did no one tell me asylums close? I thought they were like churches, open all hours.

I tap on the hatch with my fingernails. 'Please, sir! I'm all the way from Tonbridge to see my mother.'

He pulls the hatch back, sharpish. 'It ain't visiting day.'

'I don't know anything about visiting days,' I say, my voice cracking.

He sighs and asks if I have anything for him, his fingers scratching at a scab on the side of his nose.

'I have my wages, sir,' I say, relieved I brought all my shillings and pennies. Which I did only to stop Pa spending them on drink.

'How much?' he asks, and has the decency to look away. 'Only I must share it with the nurses. To make it worth their while to bring her to you, seeing as it's not a regular visiting day.'

'Bring her to me?' I frown but the man looks blank. 'I wanted to see where she's living . . . her room.'

He laughs as if I have made a very funny joke. 'Her *room* . . .' he says, wiping at his rheumy eyes with a filthy handkerchief.

'I have near enough five shillings,' I say. 'But I must keep some by for the man who rode me here.'

'How about three shillings?'

I nod, wanting to be rid of the grasping, greedy man. I push the money – the best part of my earnings – through the hatch. He snatches it up and slides the hatch door closed. While he's gone I look down the long drive and examine the big grey house – the closed windows, the chiming clock tower, the rows of bony yew saplings. All at once, I see a figure at a window up on the third floor. Beating at the glass with their fists. And then gone. Just like Punch at a Punch and Judy show when the puppet master whisks him from the stage. I train my eyes on the window, for the sight has unnerved me. But the window stays blank, so I tell myself it's my mind playing tricks on me.

Eventually the lodge keeper returns, his hand scratching at the fork of his trousers. 'Mrs Jane Kirby don't have no daughter,' he says. 'She is assured of that.'

'I'm her daughter! I swear it ... she has no memory. That's why she's here.' My voice climbs higher and higher. And then I remember: I must make myself agreeable if I'm to stand any chance of seeing Mam – or getting my three shillings back. 'Please, sir, I'm her only daughter, come to wish her happy birthday.'

'She hasn't mentioned no daughter or birthday,' he says, suspicious.

A strange thought comes to me. Perhaps they don't want me to see Mam. I can't think why this might be, but a small voice speaks, soft and cunning, in my head. *They are keeping her from you. Even for three shillings, they are keeping her from you.*

'Four shillings!' I say, desperate now.

But the man shakes his head. 'It ain't up to me, missy. They'll have her ready for visiting day. I'll let 'em know Mrs Jane Kirby is to have a visitor.' He returns my three shillings, hot and greasy from his pocket, and shuffles back into the gatehouse.

Oh my Lord, I think. He turned down four shillings ... what have they done to her? My stomach is turning over like a bottle jack, and there is a cold sweat in the pits of my arms.

I rap on the hatch and when he slides it open, with an irritated expression, I ask, 'When is visiting day, please, sir?'

He tells me the next one is a fortnight Saturday, adding 'A little sweetener for the nurses never goes amiss. Shall I tell 'em to expect something?'

'Yes, and there'll be coins for your kindness too, sir.' I slip a penny through the hatch and wonder if perhaps he'd like a square of damson cheese. If I could afford just a small bag of Lisbon sugar, if I could collect enough furze for a clear brisk fire ... I have an hour before I must meet the miller. I will hunt for kindling, I think.

I turn back for a last look at the lunatic asylum. Its empty windows gape at me, like hollow eyes that cannot close. From the chimney tops, carrion crows whirl up and flap their wings. And from a small barred window beneath the clock I see a face peeping out. Is it Mam? It's too far away to make out any features but I wave my hand and smile. Then I blink – and the face is gone.

CHAPTER TWENTY-FIVE

Eliza

TEA-KETTLE BROTH

Mrs Thorpe's directions are faultless and within thirty min-
utes I arrive at the alehouse she described. I hear it before
I see it: the sound of scouring throats, hawking, coughing,
raised voices. A straggle of navvies, labourers and truant
pickers lounge in the dust, drinking from pots and pewters,
and sucking on little black pipes. They doff their caps with
feigned obeisance. One spits loudly, another shouts out with
the coarsest and most uncouth of words. I quicken my step.
But as I pass, something hits me from behind. Something
small, hard, round. A crab apple? A stone? Their rough laugh-
ter rings in my ears as I hurry round the corner, my petticoats
tangling at my legs. I feel a goad of anger at the thriftiness

that compelled me to come on foot. I should have taken a waggon and paid the price.

Ahead of me lies a copse of elm trees, and at its mouth a mud and stud hovel no bigger than the scullery at Bordyke House. Can this really be Ann's home? Although I have seen many such dwellings from a carriage window, to connect this hovel with someone I *have feelings for* is a shock. I expected a cottage, with chickens scratching in a small but well-tended vegetable garden, perhaps a munching goat, a decent window at the very least.

But that is not what I see. The thatched roof is threadbare and fissured, with thin bundles of straw hanging, drunken and dishevelled, from the eaves. The little chimney is cracked and tilts perilously to one side. Ivy rampages over the single window which is no more than a hole in the wall stuffed with rags. Paint peels and flakes from the front door, which is open and hanging from its hinges. There are no goats. No chickens. Just a dog with protruding ribs that has been tied to a post and is barking and jumping at me.

I call Ann's name. The dog strains on his rope and barks with greater ferocity.

'Mr Kirby?' I push the door and my fingers sink into the spongy wood. Inside is a single room: low-ceilinged, reeking of stale beer, mildew, the cheapest tallow. A mattress, straw bursting from its corners, lies in a shallow puddle of water that appears to have seeped up from the floor of beaten earth. There is an open fireplace, over which an iron pole hangs, and on the stone hearth sits an iron kettle, a single frying pan and two tin plates. A square of worn oil cloth acts as a rug on the puddled floor, which bears the marks of bird droppings that have fallen through the ragged thatch.

My eyes adjust to the gloom, and I notice a dented metal chest in the corner. The flour chest? I ease open the rusting lid. Inside are four blemished apples, a covered jug of water, a jar of lard, two small eggs streaked with chicken faeces, a dish of blackberries, and a bowl of flour so coarse it better resembles grit from the road. I close the lid, thinking of the larder at Bordyke House and how it spills with meat, fish, butter, cream, sugar ... I think of Colonel Martin's careless demands for plover's eggs and Finnan haddock cooked in cream and fine salt, of how Mrs Martin left half a roasted pigeon and the best part of a salmon pudding upon her dinner plate, of all the lavish food served and wasted in monied kitchens everywhere.

A queasiness comes over me and a line of poetry tumbles into my head ... *'Few save the poor, feel for the poor: The rich know not how hard it is to be of needful food ...'* Why did I allow Mother to dismiss Ann? Why did Colonel Martin leave victorious and Ann in ignominy? For a minute I am lost inside my head. Then I pull myself back to the present and scan the room for any sign of Ann's dead mother. In vain. The clothes hanging from pegs hammered into the wall are those of a man, all of them patched and fraying. There are no shoes laid out, no books, no pictures on the walls, no linen, no lamps, no good china or glassware. The mattress has a single flattened pillow and is wrapped in a balding blanket. There is no washtub – how does she wash the dishes, the clothes, her own body? A throbbing builds behind my eyes.

I pull from my pocket the note I wrote earlier and leave it under a stone in front of the door. The dog starts barking again, showing his yellow teeth in an angry, stinking snarl.

I look behind the cottage, thinking foolishly that perhaps Ann or Mr Kirby is tending a vegetable bed. A narrow roughly dug plot, no longer than a broomstick, has been squeezed between the cottage and a lurching wooden fence. Beyond the fence lies pasture, a vigorous green, grazed by fat contented bullocks who flick their tails and amble curiously towards me. I wonder who owns this land, who takes rent from Ann's family and gives so little in return.

On my way home, and in spite of the insistent throbbing in my skull, I decide to look in at the alehouse. Perhaps Ann will be there, I think. As soon as it comes into view, the labourers start their catcalls and cussing. They are still squatting in the dust but I stride past, lowering my head to enter. The room, which is quite unlike any of the inns and taverns my father once owned, has smoke-blackened beams that graze the top of my bonnet. There is a table in the centre that carries the remnants of a week's ale and ash, the ash in little heaps as if tapped from many pipes and not yet cleared. The greasy dribblings of a tallow candle run through the ash and ale, like wax tributaries.

The waft of boiling giblets, gizzards, bones, fat – from an iron cauldron suspended on a pot-hook above a meagre fire – adds to the oppressive odour of drink and smoke and unwashed clothing. My eyes begin to smart from the chimney smoke, the tobacco smoke, the thick greasy fug of the place.

A woman appears from the shadows, a pipe between her teeth, and scowls silently at me. I want to ask how she lives and eats, but her expression does not invite questions. I cast around, instinctively, for the nearest exit. There is only the front door, now blocked with a cluster of filthy, half-naked children who watch me with soup-bowl eyes. From beyond, the labourers – rick burners? Cattle thieves? Poachers? – begin to sing a bawdy, tuneless song about an old maid. They have noticed I am without a wedding ring.

'Are you wanting summat to drink?' The woman speaks through her pipe, pointing at a wooden pail of scum beneath the table.

'No, thank you,' I say, suddenly fearful for my safety. Whatever impelled me to step inside this lair? I move swiftly to the door but the children block my exit with their stick-thin bodies.

'Tea-kettle broth then? Boiled with the best mutton bones.' The woman wipes her hands up and down an apron stiff with dried blood and dirt. 'A ha'penny to you, lady. Unless you want parsnip peelings too?'

A labourer cuffs the head of a child, pushes past and weaves his way to the table where he dips his tankard into the scummy bucket, a string of oaths flying from his lips. Seeing the sudden breach I throw a shilling upon the table and make a dash for the door. I have seen enough, I think. Indeed, I have seen more of how the poor live in one hour than I have seen in three decades. As I walk away, their lewd song follows me ... *Was an old maid from Tunbridge Wells, made her bed on old seashells, invited me to join her there, I dropped my breeches without a care, she jumped up and I held her down* ... on and on it goes, until finally I can hear no more. Only then does it occur to me that perhaps Mr Kirby was among that crowd of drunken oafs. Mrs Thorpe's cryptic, vinegary words float ominously back to me ... *I cannot answer for what you will find.* I have no need of an answer, I think. I merely want Ann back. And now I have seen her threadbare, loveless home I am quite determined to get her back.

CHAPTER TWENTY-SIX

Ann

QUINCE JELLY

I am back to Bordyke House today. I rose early, before Pa
was awake, feeling as happy as a lark. Even the sun seemed
to greet me as it nudged its rays over the hop gardens, the
orchards, the pickers stumbling from their canvas tents. I
was so happy that when the boys throwing stones at the
crows turned a few pebbles on me, I just laughed and threw
them back. I sang below my breath all the way to Tonbridge:
ballads, lullabies, nursery rhymes. And when my throat was
dry from singing, I danced. Jigging and country dancing
until I arrived at the quarry on the outskirts of town. Then I
made myself grave and sober, fit to be a kitchen maid – yes,
a kitchen maid now – for Miss Eliza Acton.

She left the nicest note on our doorstep, kindly asking me to return as a kitchen maid with wages of six shillings a week. And at the bottom of her note, which I swear was perfumed with vanilla essence, she had drawn pictures of a three-tiered cake, a moulded jelly, a raised pie and a boiled pudding on a platter. I smiled for three hours straight. When Pa came home, he was not best pleased about my grinning. But when I said my position was returned to me – and as a kitchen maid – he grinned too. I didn't have the heart to tell him about the asylum. And he didn't ask.

I start work on the range, blacking and polishing 'til it gleams like coal. It's not until I stop humming and rubbing that I hear a sound from the scullery. As if someone is playing with the copper pans. I stiffen, for who could it be? I creep down the passage to the scullery and put my head, very cautious, round the door. A tiny girl with frightened eyes is polishing the coppers. Hares and rabbits and a brace of pheasants swing from the rack above her head.

'I'm Ann,' I say, relieved. For this child must be a new scullery maid. 'What's your name?'

'Mary, o' course.'

I look at her, dumbly. 'Why of course?'

She stops looking frightened and looks confused instead. 'All sculleries are Mary. But my real name is Lizzie.'

'I was the scullery maid before you,' I say softly. 'And I was always Ann. Miss Eliza likes to use our real names.'

She grins shyly. 'I like Lizzie better than Mary.'

'Are you picking those pheasants and skinning those

rabbits and hares today?' I ask, wondering what dishes Miss Eliza has in mind.

She nods and I wonder how old she is. Ten? Eleven?

'There is a gentleman boarder coming today,' she adds, as if that explains why the scullery is swinging with birds and beasts.

'Have you done much picking and skinning?'

She nods and I notice her hands, which are raw and calloused with no nails to speak of. Her presence makes me feel most peculiar, as if I'm grown in stature. As if I am older and wiser. Only I am not. But there's no time to dwell on this for in bustles Mrs Acton who greets me, very brief, and says Miss Eliza has gone for a haunch of venison and I must get a good brisk fire going and then pare and quarter four pounds of quinces from the larder.

I can tell she's in a state of some excitement because her fingers are constantly at her ring, at her cuffs, at her neckline. As if she cannot still them. She flaps around the kitchen as I lay the fire, opening and closing the window, moving things on the dresser, running a finger over the salvers and the soup tureen, squinting at the sherry glasses, looking for fingerprints and dust.

I go to the larder for the quinces and stop in amazement. For the larder is brimming over with food. Baskets of field mushrooms. Trugs of green apples and yellow pears. A metal bath containing two pink crabs. Slabs of newly churned butter as bright as a dandelion flower. Wheels of pale yellow cheese the size of my head. An earthenware bowl of cobnuts. A ham soaking in a pail of water. Who is to eat all this food?

And why has Miss Eliza gone for a haunch of venison when we have supplies to feed a king?

'How many boarders have we this week, ma'am?' I know it isn't my place to ask questions like this, but I'm too curious to hold back.

'Mr Arnott arrives this afternoon,' she says, and her fingers fly to her neckline, arranging it for the umpteenth time. 'He's from London and only eats the finest food. Do not disappoint me, Ann Kirby.' She looks over my shoulder at the quinces and I wish she would leave me be. I cannot peel these knobbled monsters with her breathing down my neck.

'Has that knife been properly scoured?' she asks. 'Mr Arnott has been in France and French gentlemen greatly object to the flavour of the knife. Indeed, Mr Arnott has been everywhere. He is exceptionally well travelled and we must not appear provincial.'

I want to ask what 'provincial' means. Instead I ask, 'How is Miss Eliza to serve the quinces, ma'am?'

But she does not answer me, for she sees something from the corner of her eye that makes her fly into a fit. She swoops her arm behind a serving dish on the dresser – the china one wreathed with oak leaves and acorns – and pulls out a book that is so prettily bound in crimson watered silk, my eyes are on stalks. Ribbons are threaded through the cover, in pink and white – it's the most elegant and fashionable book I have ever seen. Mrs Acton flings the book onto the table, then starts moving all the china on the dresser, looking behind the platters and tureens, then opening the drawers and rummaging among the linen. I try to concentrate on peeling the quinces but it's impossible with the elegant silken book in front of me, and Mrs Acton breathing like a bullock behind me.

After a few minutes she cries out, victorious: 'Ah-ha!' And pulls a huge book from the drawer in which Miss Eliza stores the boxed cutlery with the bone handles. I get a glimpse of the book and it is so beautiful I long to open it and see inside. The cover is of green leather tooled and gilded with twining flowers and fat cherubs. Even I know these aren't Miss Eliza's cookery books, which are all of dull brown calfskin. Mrs Acton sweeps up both albums beneath her arm and flounces out. I am so surprised I gape into space, until little Lizzie creeps into the kitchen, her eyes shooting in all directions.

'Do you need help?' I ask.

'No,' she says, in such a small hoarse voice I wonder if she hasn't got something wrong with her throat. 'Miss Eliza showed me everything last week.'

'You've been here a week?'

'Yes. All the talk has been of the gentleman boarder who arrives today – I just came to tell you.' She tiptoes back to the scullery, leaving me to wrestle with the quinces so as they don't carry any *flavour of the knife*. But I can't stop thinking of Mrs Acton's queer behaviour ... *confiscating* Miss Eliza's special books.

I'm so deep in thought, I don't notice Miss Eliza until she's sailed in, her cheeks glowing, her eyes shining. 'How marvellous to have you back, Ann!'

I wonder if she will take me in her arms, like she did before. Although circumstances were different then. She doesn't but

I know she's pleased because her smile is stretched very large across her beautiful face. 'Yes, Miss Eliza, it's good to be back. Thank you.' I bob my head to show how grateful I am.

'We have a busy day ahead of us,' she says. 'Mother has doubled our food budget for the duration of Mr Arnott's stay. No expense is to be spared for our gentleman boarder.'

'What is it to be tonight?' I ask.

'Hare soup, hot crab served in its own shell, then roast haunch of venison with gravy, and the sweet dish will be a meringue of pears. I have been practising all week!'

I feel my face flush scarlet, for I suddenly remember Miss Eliza has seen my home. And the image of it beside her fine food fills me with shame. All at once I feel unworthy. Of her, of Bordyke House, of the food we must prepare.

'Ma'am asked me to peel these quinces,' I say, to cover my hot shame.

'Oh, they are for a quince cheese. They must go through the jelly bag overnight.'

Then she leans in very close and says, 'My mother wishes to impress Mr Arnott, so everything must be as perfect as we can make it.' She arches her brows, then rolls her eyes in a manner that flummoxes me. Why all the effort, all the mountains of food, for a single boarder?

'When you have poached the quinces,' says Miss Eliza, 'I have some books I wish to share with you. Indeed, I shall lend them to you.' Her eyes are shining like new pennies.

A tingle runs up my arms, for there is nothing I like better than to look at Miss Eliza's new books, to picture the puddings and preserves, the sauces and gravies, the sweets and ices. To fancy myself as a good plain cook, slicing and stirring, tasting and seasoning.

But Miss Eliza is not reaching for the shelf where she keeps her recipe books. Instead, she's at the dresser, opening and closing the drawers and looking behind the serving platters and the salvers.

'How peculiar,' she murmurs.

'Ma'am took them.' I stare hard at the paring knife in my hand.

She wheels round. 'This is becoming intolerable! At moments like this I wish to God I was my own mistress.'

'They were beautiful books.' I put the quinces in a pot and scrape some sugar from the loaf. *But they were not recipe books.*

'Two can play at her game,' mutters Miss Eliza. I don't understand her words and must concentrate on the sugarloaf that is as hard as rock.

'As it happens, I have memorised one for you. Should you like to hear it?' She starts reciting, one hand at her breast:

> *My heart's in the kitchen, my heart is not here,*
> *My heart's in the kitchen, though following the dear,*
> *Thinking on the roast meat, and musing on the fry,*
> *My heart's in the kitchen whatever I spy.*

She claps her hands and laughs. 'It's a parody of a verse by Mr Burns,' she says, seeing my blank look.

I have no idea who Mr Burns is or what the word 'parody' means but I smile because I'm so happy to be back.

'I am determined to teach you the art of poetry, Ann,' she

says. 'We shall do it as we cook. But perhaps not until Mr Arnott has left and we no longer have to produce five-course banquets for a single gentleman.'

An image of Mrs Thorpe shouting at her girl, Florence, floats before me and it seems that every inch of me grows, expands, bursts with joy. And then I hear a voice in my head, struggling, swelling, muscling Mrs Thorpe aside. It's Mam. I reach for her words: *Sound on, thou dark unslumbering sea ... Thou sea-bird, on the billow's crest ...* Is she reciting to me? Reading to me? The words seem familiar but I cannot place them.

'Poetry has been the greatest solace to me.' Miss Eliza avoids my eye and I know she's thinking of my home, my *hovel*.

She pushes the slate and chalk towards me. 'I want you to record weights, measures and timings today.'

We spend the next few hours preparing dinner, which Mr Arnott has asked to be served at five o'clock. It turns out Miss Eliza has cooked all these dishes several times over – with the help of Hatty and little Lizzie – and is now adjusting the cooking times, seasonings and quantities. She writes everything down in her notebook, and for two hours I hear only the scratch of her nib. Finally, as I am emptying the cooled quinces into a jelly bag, she lifts her head and says, 'When you write down your timings and measurements, I would be grateful if you could add any other observations.'

I frown. 'Observations?'

'For instance, when I stewed quinces last week the juice was almost scarlet, but your juice is dripping through in a glorious golden hue. So your blancmange will be prettier than mine. Why might that be?'

I blush. 'Your instructions were to simmer them for an hour but they were soft at a half-hour. So I took them from the fire early. I beg your pardon, Miss Eliza.'

'Marvellous!' she says. 'That is exactly the sort of observation I wish to include in our cookery book.'

Our cookery book? *Our*? I am so flooded with feeling I cannot speak. And then I realise she means Mrs Acton, of course. What a dunce I am! It is to be the cookery book of a mother and daughter. I can see the frontispiece now: Mrs and Miss Acton in their best clothes, drawn in pen and ink, with the best Dresden china behind them and pheasants and hares dropping from the ceiling. Like the frontispieces of other recipe books Miss Eliza has.

There is a wrench in my heart. *Mam*. All of a sudden I am seven years of age again. Mam is lifting quince pips with a tin skimmer. She chops the flesh and gives me the cores that I may suck at the golden clinging fruit, which is melting soft, sweet, perfumed, and slips down my throat like cream.

'My mother always left the quinces in their liquor overnight,' I say tentatively. 'With the pips and cores. She said it set firmer and faster like that.'

Miss Eliza gives me a long, unblinking look. After a while, she tells me to add *that sort of detail* to the slate. I hope my spelling is good enough for *observations*, I think, glad of all the nights I crept to bed with a cookery book in my apron. And when her back is turned, I press my hands together and murmur, 'Please make my spelling good enough, dear Lord.'

CHAPTER TWENTY-SEVEN

Eliza

PEAR MERINGUE WITH BON CHRÉTIEN PEARS

I am changed into my velvet dress with the silk bodice and pearl fasteners when Mr Arnott arrives. I've scrubbed the onion and garlic from my fingers, rinsed my hair in lavender water, daubed my wrists and throat with rose oil. Mother has instructed me to play the hostess, saying I am to take credit for the fine food but without admitting that I cooked it and without showing too much enthusiasm which might *reveal my appetites*. She has also forbidden me from saying anything about poetry, except to admit that I read and appreciate it. And the cookery book? Not a word to be breathed, she hissed, adding that no man wishes to marry a woman who *worships at the shrine of ambition*.

'So how exactly are we to converse?' I replied, my voice edged with sarcasm.

'Express an interest in his business,' she said. 'It should not be too difficult.'

'And what is his business?'

'I have told you several times, Eliza!' she said, most exasperated with me. 'You have had your ears closed all week. He is a spice merchant, importing spices from all over the world. He is an exceptionally well-travelled gentleman.'

'A spice merchant?' I repeated. That was the exact moment I began to think of Mr Arnott as, possibly, the key to my freedom. A gentleman who is frequently abroad, who can discuss flavour and food ... I heard again, that little, tempting voice of hope: *A chance for liberty, respect, motherhood?*

Mother's words burst into my thoughts. 'Yes, an *elderly* spice merchant. But not too elderly to beget children, my dear. Exactly like you.'

I peer through the back window, for he has arrived by carriage and the yard is full of sleek prancing horses and men in tight frock-coats. Half of me watches his footman lifting travelling trunks, while the other half of me frets over what is happening in the kitchen. Ann will have to manage, I think, for I cannot be both cook *and* demure discoursing lady. I sniff at my cuff for any residual odour of roasting marrow bones or chopped onion. There is only the faintest smell of washing lye, and the rose oil Mother insisted upon. No doubt to mask any exposing taint of the kitchen.

To my surprise, Mr Arnott alights nimbly from his carriage. He has a full head of hair, silver but thick. And when he turns I see that his skin is the colour of a hazelnut, his figure is trim and his clothes are of the latest fashion – a dark tail-coat, a cravat of twilled silk, narrow, fly-fronted trousers that strap beneath his gleaming shoes. He is not what I expected. My fingers race to my hair, pushing the loose strands from my face, then quickly pinching at my cheeks.

Mother scuttles out to welcome him. My instructions are to await him in the drawing room, where he is to be offered tea, my freshly baked almond macaroons – and conversation. I half-expect him to desist, for surely he will be fatigued after his journey. But no, I hear him and Mother approaching, the door opening – and behold!

As soon as he is seated, I study him. His face is closely shaved and handsome, although he cannot be less than sixty. His tailcoat is of Irish tweed and when he moves there is a flash of gold from the heavy watch chain beneath. Every time he lifts his hands, the diamond studs at his cuffs wink encouragingly at me. Of course we must discuss his journey and the weather and the virtues of Tunbridge Wells and its waters. And then we must talk of the old days when he and my father were acquainted.

Hatty brings a tray of tea. Mr Arnott takes a macaroon and bites into it. 'Exceedingly good,' he says. 'I believe Jordan almonds have been used.'

'Indeed,' I say, regarding him with interest.

'Your cook is accomplished,' he adds. 'If I'm not mistaken, the almonds have been browned first in a slow oven, for this macaroon has a pleasantly toasted flavour.'

Mother leaps in. 'We are fortunate to have a good plain

cook, but she works entirely to the orders of my daughter. Eliza is the brains behind everything you shall eat here. She would be delighted to dine with you, should you want company. She can talk you through the menu at the same time.'

I look at her, askance. How am I to produce a five-course feast if I am sitting at Mr Arnott's table for hours?

'I should enjoy both the company and the instruction,' he says, appraising me with a keen and narrowed eye.

My smile fixes stiffly upon my face and a panicked tightness comes to my throat.

As soon as Mother takes him to his rooms I dash to the kitchen, all decorum forgotten. Ann is calmly making mayonnaise in the manner I have shown her, whisking oil into egg yolks, drop by drop. Her serenity fades once she knows she must prepare and garnish every dish and that I will not be in attendance for a single second. Her eyes fill with dread and her hands begin to shake so that the oil falls too fast into the yolks.

'We can manage,' I say. 'The crab can go to the table cold instead of warm – so we can prepare it together. The hare soup is simmering and all you must do is season it with salt and cayenne, then send it to table very hot. The venison is on the spit but you will have to carve it and prepare the gravy.' I stop for a moment and take a long calming breath. 'Let us cook the potatoes plain, in the Lancashire way. The pear meringue we shall do now.'

'I c-cannot carve,' Ann stammers, laying down the whisk.

'I shall teach you, exactly as my father taught me,' I reply, keeping my tone steady to conceal the racing of my pulse.

'Carving with propriety and self-possession is a skill every woman should possess.'

Two hours later and Ann is calmer. But I am so fretful I have to clasp my hands beneath the dining table to stop them fidgeting – even as Mr Arnott regales me with amusing anecdotes about his recent trip to Amsterdam. I feel as if only a slender fraction of myself sits at table while the larger part of me is in the kitchen.

When the soup tureen comes, I run my finger quickly round its rim. Clever Ann has remembered to warm it on the hearth. Mr Arnott, who seems not to have noticed how distracted I am, takes a spoonful of soup. I do the same, letting it run around my mouth. The temperature is perfect. And every drop of fat has been properly skimmed, so the broth is clean and meaty and leaves no greasy residue upon the tongue.

'Excellent soup,' says Mr Arnott, his lips making an appreciative smacking sound.

'Thank you,' I say, greatly relieved. 'It is my own recipe. Do you think the herbs strike the right note?' The question leaps from me, as if of its own accord. Immediately I regret it: will he think my question suggestive of *appetites*? I'm about to smooth away my hasty question with something more appropriate, when Mr Arnott nods vigorously and asks a question that surprises and delights me.

'What spices have you used?'

'Mace and cayenne, of course,' I laugh, with relief and gratitude.

'I am resolved to broaden your cook's use of spices,' he says. 'May I have a delivery sent directly to you?' He proceeds to tell me about blends of currie powders, the benefits of fresh spices, the tamarinds he is now importing in the shell. I am so absorbed I forget the kitchen – and my unfeminine blunders – entirely. He describes the smoky flavour of cumin, the black bitterness of fenugreek seeds, the sweet richness of fresh coconut flesh, the fierce blast of fresh ginger root.

Hatty clears the soup bowls while Mr Arnott tells me of his favourite curries. I try to commit his words to memory, repeating everything after him. 'Grate and simmer the flesh of two coconuts, you say?'

'They must be fresh – a rancid coconut is not a thing of beauty. You seem uncommonly interested in my trade, Miss Acton.' He eyes me over his glass of claret, and for a minute I wonder if he's assessing my *appetites*. But his eyes are so frank and bright and honest I resolve to stop any pretence of being appetite-less.

'I am,' I reply. 'Your knowledge of spices and curries and oriental food has impressed me greatly.'

When the crab arrives, I realise I've barely given any thought to Ann and her ministrations. To my surprise she has added a few finishing touches of her own. The crab sits snugly in its pink shell, beside a neat mound of delicately green mayonnaise. How has she coloured it green?

'This could be made into a currie,' pronounces Mr Arnott. 'In Madras curried sea-oysters are considered the pinnacle of fine food. Anything can be curried . . . fish, fowl, even eggs.'

'Eggs?' Again, he has intrigued me.

'Indeed eggs,' he says. 'Hard-boiled and placed in a hot curried gravy, they are quite delicious.'

I taste the mayonnaise, trying to fathom how Ann has greened it. Simultaneously I try to commit Mr Arnott's recipe for curried eggs to memory, while also checking the seasoning in the crab.

'Do you think the crab would benefit from a little more lemon juice?' I ask. 'Or perhaps chilli vinegar should have been used.'

'It is certainly fresh.' He slowly savours the crab upon his tongue. 'It tastes of the sea.' Then he turns, quite suddenly, and fixes his eyes upon me. 'I have never met a lady so fascinated by food. So curious ... so knowledgeable. It is most refreshing.'

I feel myself swell beneath his admiring eye. And when Hatty clears the plates, I hardly notice her. My moment of conceit passes as I anticipate the venison that is to come, and everything that can go wrong with a spit-roast haunch. Even when served with plain boiled potatoes and a simple gravy of beef stock and port. But Mr Arnott distracts me yet again by describing his favourite soup, a curried dish he calls Mullagatawny, cooked with marrows, cucumbers, apples and a currie-powder of his own blending. He pronounces it to be the most delicious soup ever, excluding my hare soup, of course. I half-suspect him of flirting with me, for he keeps looking piercingly into my eyes. And I wrest my gaze away with the greatest reluctance.

The venison follows, thick moist slabs of it. The potatoes swim in melted butter and the gravy has been expertly sweetened with a little redcurrant jelly. Ann has forgotten nothing, I think, until I feel the dinner platter and it is stone cold.

Our conversation turns to Hastings, where Mr Arnott first befriended my father. It is such a relief to talk of my father without having to pretend he is dead, that I am quite overcome for a moment. 'In Tonbridge we must maintain the pretence that my mother is a widow,' I explain haltingly. 'Just while we establish ourselves. It has been a testing time.'

'Yes, I can see that.' He reaches over and touches my arm, and something about this little avuncular gesture makes me feel deeply content.

The venison is taken away, replaced by the pear meringue, which we eat with long-handled spoons. The grainy sweetness of the pears bursts and melts in my mouth, adding to my deep sense of contentment.

'What variety of pears are these?' he asks.

'They are Bon Chrétien pears,' I reply. 'I make a point of always knowing the variety of fruit I'm using and cooking only with the ripest.'

He raises his eyebrows and I know instantly that I have revealed myself. A slow scarlet heat crawls up my throat and over my cheeks.

'It is delectable,' he says, after a long pause. I look at the bronzed peaks of meringue and feel his brain turning over and over, as if he is trying to comprehend me.

Hatty appears with the coffee tray, Mother close behind her. As we sip our coffee, she questions Mr Arnott on the size of his business, the location of his London house, his servants, his two children, his health and how he likes to spend his leisure time – a full interrogation which she conducts without a shred of shame. As he patiently answers her litany of questions, a white spark turns, flashes, skims across the table. His diamond studs. Yes, I think, perhaps marriage to a man like Mr Arnott might suit me. Perhaps, just perhaps, my heart is mended – and I am ready.

Chapter Twenty-Eight

Ann

Turnips in Butter

Mr Arnott is spending the weekend with relatives, so Miss Eliza gives me a day's leave. I think she'd like me to visit Jack in London because she keeps asking about Monsieur Soyer. But today is visiting day at the Kent County Lunatic Asylum and that's where I'm headed.

I'm bone-tired, for while *she* has been dining with Mr Arnott, I have been cook *and* kitchen maid. My arms ache from kneading and whisking and beating. My wrists are sore from chopping and cutting and grating. My legs throb from standing for hour upon hour. And my hands are riven and blistered with cuts and burns. In fairness, Miss Eliza has also worked to the bone. Most mornings I have come down at five upon the hour, and she is already in the kitchen, poring over her books. I have done the same whenever time permits – even by moonlight after Hatty has fallen asleep and I can barely keep my eyes open. No matter how tired I am, the recipes jump from their pages in a great swarm of smells and tastes: possets and syllabubs; stews and soups; boiled puddings and baked puddings; potted meats and pies; jellies and jams. Already I have surprised Miss Eliza with my own touches to her dishes. On these occasions she comes to me, in very good humour, and asks, 'What did you slip so expertly into that dish, Ann?' And my heart turns right over in a somersault.

Now that Mr Arnott is enticing her from the kitchen with his wily ways I'm more determined than ever to please her. Hatty says they have eyes only for each other and that it's only a matter of time before he asks for her hand. She says they barely notice the food I've slaved over. But when Miss Eliza appears, she showers praise upon me, looking at me all the while with such fondness that when I think on it later, tears stand in my eyes.

Recently Miss Eliza has not been quite herself. This morning I came down and she was not at her books but staring at the dresser, where the everyday china hangs. I waited for her to make a comment about greasy fingerprints on the soup bowls. Instead she said, 'It is a dreadful thing for woman's lip to swear the heart away . . .' She sounded so wistful I was emboldened to ask her meaning. 'I am quoting from poetry, Ann,' she replied. 'You know what a solace it is to me.'

I wondered if she needed *solace* because of what I'd

overheard the previous day. All I'd wanted was some instruction on how best to truss a corncrake, for they are small skinny birds. But when I sought her out in the drawing room, the door was closed – which is not usual. And I could hear high angry voices. Miss Eliza and Ma'am were shouting, quite out of turn. I knew it was private and I should turn away, but I listened at the door instead. Miss Eliza was demanding to know the whereabouts of her poetry books and manuscripts. And Ma'am was saying nothing, until Miss Eliza raised her voice very loud and cried, 'If you will not return them, I will not keep quiet about certain other things which you find infinitely more disgraceful than my writing of verse.' There was a very long silence, so I crept back to the kitchen and trussed the corncrake as best I could.

What did she mean? Why is Ma'am so quick to hide Miss Eliza's books and poems? There is still this itch in me to read her verse, but it's dawning on me that there is something amiss in those poems, something Ma'am wants none of us to know. And the more this notion settles in my mind, the more curious I become. It makes my head hurt, thinking over and over, and then it strikes me that perhaps Ma'am has sold the book of verse. Or buried it. Or ... A memory of Mam and Pa creeps, unwanted, into my head. He is tearing the pages from a book, twisting each one to make a paper spill, pushing it into the little fire, shouting that we will freeze and starve, while she sobs with her head in her hands, her scrawny hands that are red-and-blue with cold. A chill runs over me so I push the memory away and think what a pleasant bright day it is, how fortunate I am to have a day's leave, how pleased

Mam – in her big warm house brimming with food – will be to see me.

The asylum is ahead of me now, rearing up from the flat fields, its circle of iron railings glinting in the low autumn sun. I have a few shillings saved for the lodge keeper and the nurses, and for Mam I have Mr Arnott's leftover dinner (a slice of pink roast beef, potted mushrooms, cold buttered turnips and a scoop of brandy trifle). The lodge keeper slides back his hatch, scowling.

'Mrs Jane Kirby please, sir.' I slip him a shilling, which he grabs most zealously.

Then I must wait for a long time, while word is sent that Mam has a visitor. Eventually the lodge keeper returns and says Mam will meet me in the grounds. He points at a staked yew tree and says she will be out in a minute.

I thank him and say, by way of conversation, 'It's awful quiet for visiting day.'

'No quieter than normal,' he replies. 'The lunatics don't much like visitors. And visitors don't much care for the lunatics either.'

His words strike me as heartless and cruel, but I hold my tongue and stare at the yew saplings blowing in the wind. When three people appear from behind the building, he unlocks the gate and lets me through. I run towards them, one hand curled tightly round the coins for the nurses and the other round the little basket holding Mam's lunch. I want to run to her, but something stops me. She has a nurse on either side of her, both of them wearing bibbed aprons and with their sleeves rolled up to show their brawny arms.

They appear to be guiding her towards me, cajoling and wheedling.

'Mam?' I say. 'It's me, Ann.'

She looks blank at me. Her eyes have a strange lifeless quality, like a dead river trout.

'She is settling in very nice,' says one of the nurses. 'Very nice indeed.'

'Her memory is gone,' says the other nurse. 'She don't recognise anyone.' She raises her voice to a holler, adding 'Not even her favourite nurses, do you, Jane?' And she leans round and pinches Mam's cheek, as if Mam's a pet child who is short of hearing.

'Mam, it's me,' I say again and I reach out to stroke her cheek where the nurse has left a scarlet thumb mark. Then I remember my sweetener for the nurses and give them each a shilling. The cheek-pinching nurse bites the coin between her teeth and then slips it inside her dress. The other nurse holds her coin to the light, then rubs it on her apron and grins.

'You brought her up nice, Jane,' bellows Cheek-Pincher and gives Mam a little shake. 'Have you something to say, Jane?'

Mam looks confused, then a dull light comes into her eyes. 'I am very happy here,' she says, in a single breath. And when the whispered words are out, the light disappears from her eyes as quick as it came.

The nurses nod in a satisfied way, their arms still upon her. 'Oh yes, she is happy all right. Will you be coming every visiting day?'

'Yes,' I say, very definite. 'And if she's well, there'll always be something for your kindness.' I know these are rash words and that much of my wages will go to these women. But there is something about them and this place that unsettles me. And I must see Mam right in the only way I can.

'Good, good,' says the cheek-pinching nurse in a low, soothing voice. 'We shall take special care of your mam, won't we, Fran?'

The other nurse nods and leers. 'Our special lunatic,' she agrees.

'Can I hug her?'

The two nurses share a look I can't decipher, and then Cheek-Pincher says, 'You can hug her while we hold her. Only she might harm herself if we let go.'

'Or try and escape,' Fran cackles. 'Ain't that why she's 'ere?'

'We treats her like one of our own daughters, don't we, Fran?'

'Better than we treat our own daughters,' Fran nods, her square head wobbling on her thick shoulders.

I put my arms round Mam's waist, all skin and bone she is. The reek of the nurses' breath is everywhere. A reek I know only too well: ale. I feel Mam flinch beneath my touch, so I offer up my basket. 'I have roast beef for you, Mam,' I say. 'And turnips in butter. And brandy trifle with Kent cherries. Shall I feed you like I used to? With an egg spoon . . .'

'Oh no, no, no,' says Cheek-Pincher, her tongue clicking angrily against the top of her mouth. 'Those fancy victuals is too rich to eat now. But if we feed it to her at the regular hour, it will do very nicely.' She turns to Mam and shouts in her ear, 'You will enjoy this later, won't you, Jane?'

Fran drops Mam's arm and snatches the basket from me,

her greedy hands pulling out the roast beef wrapped in waxed paper, the pot of mushrooms, the jar of trifle, the tin box of buttered turnips. She opens each container and sniffs loudly at it. Then she unwraps the beef and smells that too. 'Oh, Jane will enjoy this fine fancy food, won't you, Jane?'

While Fran examines the food, I glance at Mam's dangling arm. The sleeve is pulled down as far as it will go, but I can just see her wrist, hanging loose. The inside is a strange yellow colour. Cheek-Pincher follows my gaze and says, very sudden, 'Your mam is in fine fettle. We treats her like a princess, you can be sure of that. Now, how did you come by this fancy grub?' And she winks at me.

'I work in a kitchen,' I say, for I know by that wink she has me as a thief.

'Of course you do,' she says, nodding and smirking. 'We believe you, don't we, Fran?'

Fran nods and hooks the basket onto her wrist. 'We'll give your basket back when you comes next. Your mam will be waiting on tenterhooks, won't you, Jane?'

Mam nods, like a docile child. Her empty eyes blink. Then she opens her mouth and whispers, 'I am very happy here.'

Fran pats her on the back and says, 'So you are, Jane. So you are.'

'We have to take her back now,' says Cheek-Pincher. 'Time for her daily visit with the doctor.' She turns to Mam and bellows, 'You like the doctor, don't you, Jane?'

'She sees the doctor every day?' I ask, relieved.

'Every day,' nods Cheek-Pincher. 'As regular as rain. And if she's late, we get a flea in our ear, don't we, Fran? And your mam don't like that. Your mam likes us happy, don't you, Jane?'

Mam looks at me, confused. Her nose twitches. Her eyes roll. For a second I think she's about to speak to me. 'Mam?' I say again.

But she shakes her head, very fast, frantic. So that her cap falls askew, tilting to one side and covering an eye.

'Quick, Fran. She don't want to miss her appointment with the doctor. I can feel her getting agitated.' And the two nurses turn and march her back to the asylum. I wonder if she will look back at me, acknowledge me with her eyes. But she doesn't. She doesn't look back once.

As I watch them go, I notice something peculiar. It's the back of her head. Where her cap has risen. Is there hair missing? A bald patch? I fix my eyes upon the spot, but the nurses are hurrying and Mam's head has become a blur.

I walk the fifteen miles home in a stupor, not knowing what to think. Her dress was clean, her hands and nails were scrubbed. She had proper shoes on, with good strong soles. She has two nurses all to herself and a doctor that visits daily. She lives in a grand house with walls as thick as my arm and real glass in the windows and its own clock tower. And yet my heart is heavy. For Mam was a ghost of herself. But she isn't running round half-naked and she's safe, says my voice of reason. She has a fine thick roof over her head and food when she's hungry and no one throttling her when she wets herself by mistake.

Too thin, too yellow on the wrists, too subdued, says my other voice. After a while I can bear the two battling voices no more and I make myself think about Bordyke House. What is Miss Eliza doing? What are Hatty and Lizzie doing? What dishes will be in the larder when I get back? As I left, Miss Eliza had just taken delivery of a basket of new-laid pullets' eggs, still warm from the nesting box. Yes, she will be making custard, I bet. Flavouring it with nutmeg, or perhaps with finely rasped chocolate or lemon-grate. Or maybe with honeyed liquor or a sweet German wine. I quicken my step, keen to get home. Home.

Chapter Twenty-Nine

Eliza

Indian Curried Fish

For three consecutive days I dine with Mr Arnott. He entertains me with his travelling tales, interspersed with accounts of how spices grow and dollops of culinary information which I suck up with an unladylike enthusiasm. He teaches me how to avoid cayenne pepper that has been thinned with brick powder or mahogany sawdust. He explains how to cook Patna rice the Indian way so that it never clots. He tells me of dishes so ferociously hot they would make an English lady swoon. And afterwards I rush to the kitchen and make notes lest I forget.

Then he goes to visit family in Hastings. On his return, three days later, he does not request my company at dinner.

This is a grave disappointment to Mother who is convinced he's heard gossip about me. But, at the very point she is most deeply in despair, he sends a request, via his footman, for my company. I confess: my heart danced. Rather to my surprise.

Mother leapt from her bed and hugged me. 'I knew it, my dear! You have charmed him with your wit and seduced him with your menus! If you can lure him to a proposal, we can bring your father home from Calais and Catherine and Anna can be released from their governess positions.'

Her words sent a shiver down my spine, for I saw then the full extent of her machinations. And I felt the weight of responsibility, like huge logs upon my shoulders: I am to rescue the Acton family from ignominy. I took the chance to pounce.

'Well, may I have my poetry books returned?'

She brushed at the air with her hands, in that irritating way of hers. As if I am a tetchy spitting cat that must be mollified. 'All in good time, my dear. But with his footman and manservant snooping around, we cannot take any risks.'

I did not press my point, for our recent squabbles have robbed me of all energy. And today I need my full wits about me, if I am to be cook, hostess and prospective wife, all rolled into one.

The mood in the kitchen is calm and unrushed. Ann is inspecting a delivery of carp using the methods I have taught her. She suggests, in her shy and tentative manner, a cucumber sauce.

'The season for cucumbers is over,' I say, but she tells

me there is a fresh firm cucumber in the larder, delivered only yesterday. I cannot help smiling. Since her return, she has blossomed into a competent plain cook, making herself wholly indispensable to me.

She begins scraping at the carp's scales, then pauses and gestures at the larder, 'There's been a delivery of spices for you, miss. From London.'

I clap my hands with delight. Mr Arnott is certainly a man of his word, and prompt to boot. 'Dare we attempt one of Mr Arnott's favourite dishes?'

'May I ask if you are to be in the kitchen or in the dining room tonight, Miss Eliza?' She looks up and I see her eyes are ringed with dark shadows, like purple bruises.

'I must dine with Mr Arnott tonight,' I reply. Her face falls. 'But don't fret – curries are best prepared in advance. I think we'll attempt a curried fish recipe he has described in glowing terms.'

The spice delivery has been unwrapped from its chest. Black enamelled tins, tiny glass jars, little hessian bags, each labelled by hand, are laid out for me to examine: cloves, turmeric, cayenne, blades of mace, whole nutmegs, powdered ginger, dried red chillies, a jar of pickled capsicum, woody scrolls of cinnamon bound with twine, black peppercorns, green peppercorns in brine, and various spice blends that Mr Arnott has composed himself. I pick out a small tin, labelled 'Arnott's Bengal Currie-Powder'.

'We shall use this,' I say, placing the tin upon the kitchen table. 'If it's successful, the recipe can sit in the *Foreign and Jewish* section of our book.' Unless Mother forbids it, I think.

But then I am reminded of a new future ... in which I am Mrs Arnott and need take no notice of Mother's imperious ways and antiquated thinking. A future in which the countless petty slights I've endured as an *old maid* have been whisked away – for ever. I hold up my left hand and imagine it with a ring upon my wedding finger. For a second I feel the old void, the emptiness in the crook of my arm, but then Ann asks, in a quavering voice, 'Will you be the first of your sisters to marry, Miss Eliza?'

The question startles me, reminding me once again of the uncommonly frank relationship we have. We are more like cook and kitchen maid than mistress and servant, I think. Which is as it should be, for am I not more cook than mistress at Bordyke House? And is she not of unusual intelligence for a servant? But then Ann blushes and apologises and lets slip that the kitchen gossip is all of me and Mr Arnott. I like this in her – so candid and guileless and yet shy and humble at the same time.

'No need to apologise.' I ease open the tin of Bengal currie-powder. A dust of heat and spice rises, pungent and dry, into the air. 'I have a younger sister who is married. She is a doctor's wife.' I offer Ann the tin. 'Mr Arnott has composed this blend himself. I think it may be rather fiery for the English palate.'

'How about I start with a salt spoon, and then taste as I go?'

I nod and give her bony hand a little squeeze. 'You are the perfect pupil,' I say, and her fingers push back, briefly, against mine.

We spend the day preparing dinner, working together

as smoothly as the wheels of a clock. Only Lizzie's hoarse
and toneless humming from the scullery perturbs me, but
I push it aside, telling myself it is Lizzie's presence that has
allowed Ann to bloom as a cook. And it is Ann's 'blooming'
that has enabled me to turn my charms to Mr Arnott. As Ann
chops, slices, fries, stirs, scrubs and keeps the fire at the right
briskness, my mind lingers on Mr Arnott and what he might
expect of a wife. I have conditions, of course. Delicate condi-
tions that must be raised very carefully. Conditions I have not
discussed with Mother. I am unsure how to raise them, but
raise them I must. My thoughts flip to and fro as I note down
Ann's cooking times and the weights and measures she uses,
as I taste from her proffered spoon, as I advise on seasoning
and flavour, as I dwell on Mr Arnott.

Later, at dinner, Mr Arnott beams at me. The waters of
Tunbridge Wells are working, he says. He has never felt in
such fine form. Then he looks straight into my eyes and says,
'Miss Acton, there is another reason I am of such a genial
disposition at the moment.'

I look demurely at my bowl of apple soup, which has
been artfully flavoured with his gift of ground ginger. 'I
am pleased for you, sir.' Oh, how I dislike all this pretence!
Why can't I look direct into his eyes and tell him I am a
published poet, with a chequered past and a commission to
write a cookery book. But no, I must maintain my silence,
as I've promised Mother. For the sake of the disgraced
Acton family.

'It is you, Eliza,' he says. 'May I call you Eliza?'

I nod, concentrating hard on all he has to offer. Money.

Freedom. Respect. A family of my own. Possibly. Am I too old to bear a healthy child? My left hand stumbles unbidden to my womb and clutches it beneath the table.

'My wife – God bless her soul – died in India, three years ago. Since then I have buried myself in my business, to the detriment of my health. Hence I am here.'

I meet his gaze, for I cannot stare at my soup any longer. Not after seeing a thin trail of oil snaking over its surface. Soup should always be thoroughly strained of fat, I think, with mild irritation.

'And now I feel my spirits lifting, my health improving.' He pauses and tugs the napkin from his collar, tossing it onto the table as if to signify his renewed vigour. 'I think I may be ready for matrimonial life again.'

The grease in my soup moves, slithers, twists into a shining tendril. A blush slides across my cheeks. Hatty comes to clear the table and I know full well she will scurry back to the kitchen with talk of Mr Arnott's dramatically discarded napkin and my burning face.

'With you, Miss Acton,' he adds, as soon as Hatty is out of earshot. 'If you will have me . . .'

The bluntness of his proposal deprives me of breath for a moment. But if we are to continue in this straight-talking vein, there is something I must tell him without further ado. 'I have no dowry,' I murmur.

'Not a penny?'

'My father lost everything,' I say. 'This house is rented.'

'I assumed there would have been something hidden away, but no matter. I have more than enough.' He coughs, as if to cover his embarrassment. I wonder if he will see me in a different light, now he knows I'm a penniless old maid.

'Let us speak honestly, Eliza,' he says, seizing up his napkin and dabbing at the corners of his mouth. 'I need a wife who can run a household, deal with servants, oversee a kitchen, entertain the wives of my business associates, stimulate me when I return from work. You know ...' He waves his hand carelessly across the table.

'And what else do you expect of your wife? I mean, what freedoms will she have?' My questions – stripped of any finesse – blurt from me and hang, like soup steam, in the air between us.

'She may do as she pleases,' he says, frowning. 'Unless, of course, it affects the good name of the Arnott Spice Company.'

Hatty returns with a platter of Indian Curried Fish and a bowl of pilaw rice. She arranges them, very slowly, on the table, then makes a lengthy show of repositioning the glasses and the cruets, and polishing the serving spoons.

I glare and she leaves. All this talk of matrimony – which appears no more than a slightly distasteful transaction – has made me long to lose myself in the food. I taste the fish and feel a jolt of pleasure. The buttery sauce is unctuous and rich, its flavours unveiling themselves in layers: garlic, white ginger, bruised coriander seeds, lemon juice, the subtlest hint of turmeric. The flakes of fish are meltingly soft but still with bite. For a few seconds I can think of nothing but the sauce upon my tongue. Mr Arnott, however, carries on talking.

'I believe I am an easy man to live with. My wife made no complaints. She was an ideal companion and you have many of her traits, so I do not see why we shouldn't live a long and contented life together, Eliza.' He tastes the curried fish, his mouth working enthusiastically. 'Excellent. As good as my own cook. You will enjoy overseeing him, although he has become used to working without any supervision.'

'Him?' I ask. And now it is my turn to be surprised, for only the grandest households have male cooks.

'Yes, his name is Louis. He likes to be called a chef, but I prefer the English word, cook.' He puts his knife and fork down and gazes upon me again, but I am too flustered to meet his eye. I have a sudden wish to be alone. So that I can concentrate on my palate, on the way in which the spices are unfolding upon my tongue. Would it be improved with more garlic, less butter, a different type of fish, chilli vinegar instead of lemon juice? But my mind is darting here and there ... a French chef who has not been supervised for three years ... the chance to have a child ... marital love ... my dishonesty ... reclaiming Father from Calais ... My mental turmoil comes to a sudden end when I hear the whine of floorboards from beyond the door. Mother is listening.

'Would you care to be the next Mrs Arnott?' he asks, at length. The hall floorboards creak again. Mother clearly cannot contain her excitement.

'Sir, I like your proposal,' I say. And suddenly it occurs to me that I like his proposal very much indeed. And I am tired of Mother and I am tired of poverty and I am tired of the relentless indignities of being old and unmarried and poor, of having to pander to the likes of Colonel and Mrs Martin, of being answerable to my mother at the age of thirty-six, of having to put up with slighting letters from Mr Longman – who has sent me yet another dictionary. As if I cannot spell! I am so weary of it all.

'Would a short engagement suit you?' He reaches over and takes my hand, covering it with both of his. I am briefly conscious of how it must feel, my scabbed *cook's* hand. But he holds it very lightly as if he understands the tenderness it carries – and does not mind.

'I shall tell you in the morning,' I say. But I leave my hand in his. And it feels good.

Chapter Thirty

Ann

Mauritian Chutney

Everything at Bordyke House is at sixes and sevens. Miss Eliza is to be Mrs Arnott and Ma'am is like a woman possessed. Hatty can talk of nothing but the wedding and even little Lizzie is excited, although I cannot think why for she will have to wash scores of pots and pans for days on end. Reverend Thorpe has been summoned for discussions and Mrs Thorpe is offering advice on everything from wedding gowns to the dressing of the church.

Only Miss Eliza seems subdued. One morning I find her in the kitchen, in the ladder-backed chair she sits in when writing her *observations*. Only she's not writing. She's staring at her hands. I wonder if she's fretting over the burns and cuts and how they will look now she is to wear a ring. Over the weeks her hands, which were so pale and beautiful, have become a bit like mine. Not red and calloused, but bearing a few scars of the knife and a burn on her thumb that is shiny and bright pink.

'Good morning, Miss Eliza!' I say. And to cheer her, I add, 'Shall we be testing that Indian breakfast recipe this morning? I kept a nice piece of cold turbot for it.'

'How thoughtful of you,' she says. 'I think Mr Arnott would like that indeed, for he leaves us this morning, as you know.' She gives such a wan smile, I think my eyes are playing up in the poor light. For isn't a newly engaged lady the happiest in the land? But then – fool that I am – I realise it's his departure that's making her sad.

I go to the larder and find the turbot, the Patna rice he likes, butter, cayenne and two freckled eggs, which I know to be his favourites. When I return to the kitchen, she's still sitting there, staring at her hands. I start raking the cinders from the stove but she doesn't move. Eventually I ask if she's unwell.

'I am quite well,' she says. 'I have been thinking of a verse I wrote. Would you like to hear it?'

I nod and she starts reciting in her soft voice, and it's like a melody, like the wind soughing in the trees:

> *Pause – 'ere thy choice hath clasp'd the chain*
> *Which may not be unloos'd again;*
> *For though of gold the links may be*
> *They will not press less painfully.*

'That's beautiful, miss,' I say, hoping she will carry on reciting, for the sound makes me feel like I do when she touches me. Less alone, I think. That I am not by myself.

But then she frowns and looks at me, worried. 'In all the excitement I have not given you your wages, have I?'

'No,' I say. 'I didn't like to ask with all the – the excitement.' I don't tell her it has been heavy on my mind, for I must give the nurses their gift when I next visit Mam and I need coins for Pa, who still owes the carpenter that made his new crutches.

'That was remiss of me,' she says, vexed. 'Most remiss and I apologise.' She gets up and goes to the dresser drawer where she keeps her money tin. But as she rises, something falls to the floor. I assume it's a cookery book and she's been planning menus. She doesn't notice and is busy sorting shillings and pennies from her tin, pressing an extra sixpence piece upon me in a most apologetic way, then locking the tin with her curly key.

'May I take my wages to my room now, miss?' I cannot risk losing even a ha'penny, I think, hurrying to the attic where my purse is safe beneath my mattress.

When I get back to the kitchen little Lizzie has arrived and is tying on her apron. But Miss Eliza has gone. My eye falls on the dark shape of her book, still lying beneath the table. How distracted she must be, I think. For Miss Eliza is a most organised and tidy lady and would never leave a cookery book on the floor. The sorting of my wages must have taken her mind off things.

I stoop and pick up the book and that's when my heart

misses a beat. It's not a recipe collection. It's a book of poems. Her poems. The poems I've longed to read since first I came here. What happens next is not worthy of me. But I cannot help myself. Instead of placing the poems where Miss Eliza will find them, I slip them under my apron and scurry to the attic. Hatty is at the washstand, splashing cold water on her face. I slide the book under my mattress and go back to the kitchen, heart beating like the wing of a bird.

By the time I finish cleaning and laying the stove my fingers are iced with cold and black with coal dust. I refill the scuttle and light the fire, prodding and blowing at it until the flames are good and fierce. I'm about to flake the cold turbot onto a plate when Miss Eliza returns and starts looking round the kitchen, most anxious.

'Ann, have you seen a small book? Bound in blue silk?' She circles the table, her hands wiping at her skirts, her eyes darting here and there.

Now is my chance to be honest and truthful. My tongue flaps, bewildered, and my brain blurs. And when the words shoot from my mouth it's as if someone else is speaking. 'No, Miss Eliza.'

'Have you been here the entire time?'

'I nipped to my room to hide my wages, miss.' My face feels scalding hot and I am thankful for the dimness of the kitchen, which is always gloomy and short of light.

'Oh yes, so you did.' She starts opening and closing the dresser drawers. 'Perhaps Mrs Acton has been in here.' She goes to the scullery and asks Lizzie if Ma'am has been in the kitchen. Or Mr Arnott's footman ... or Mr Arnott's manservant. I hear Lizzie saying she's been in the scullery and not seen a soul.

'I am going quite mad,' she says to me. 'I must have moved it myself and forgotten, in all the excitement.'

'Moved what, Miss Eliza?' Oh, how I hate myself as these words spring from my wicked lips. Every part of me cringes in self-loathing. But it's too late. I'm a thief and I cannot confess my crime now. Only last month a man was sentenced to transportation for life, just for taking a bushel of apples. Stealing a book is far worse. Men have swung from the gallows for less.

'I was reading some verse before you came down,' she says, her brow creased, her hands still clenching at her skirts. 'I must have placed it somewhere safe and forgotten where.'

I nod, unable to speak. I have such an urge to confess, to fall at her feet and beg forgiveness. But I cannot risk being sent to Botany Bay or to the gallows. And the thought of her disappointment in me is horrible. That decides me: I'll return her poems secretly. I'll run to my room, pull it from under the mattress, then place it behind a serving platter – or some such place – for her to find. Something tells me she's fretting it might fall into the wrong hands and that the *wrong hands* are Mr Arnott's. Although why this should be so, I can't think. Wouldn't any man be proud to have a writer for a wife?

'No doubt it will turn up. There is too much on my mind.' She gives a nervous laugh. How jittery she is this morning, I think. And now I've made her more so with my nosy, prying, lying ways. Dear Lord, I say in my head, please forgive me my sins.

'We must finish preparing the kedgeree. Mr Arnott wishes to breakfast with me early today.'

I reach for the slate so that I can chalk up my *observations* but she throws up her hands and says, 'Don't bother with your observations, Ann. They won't be necessary.'

Confusion sweeps over me, blotting out my guilty spirit and my heavy heart. And then it comes to me in a flash of understanding. *There is to be no cookery book.* I feel my insides turn to liquid, as if all the substance of me has been sucked clean away.

'Oh, Miss Eliza,' I gasp. 'Is there to be no cookery book now you are to be Mrs Arnott?'

She sighs, such a big sigh the room echoes with it, like a wind from the chimney that has no escape. Then a silence falls across the kitchen. I notice my fingers are shaking as they tear the turbot apart.

'I hope you will come with me, Ann. But the truth is Mr Arnott has his own French chef who will not want my interference.'

All at once I see my future dwindle to nothing. My throat goes dry and a gulping, choking noise bursts from my mouth. For if I am not cooking with Miss Eliza, what am I to do? I want only to cook . . .

'Oh, Ann,' she cries. But then her voice goes very firm. 'All will be well,' she says. 'Let us not become histrionic.'

I don't know what *hiss-tree-on-ic* means, so I blink away my tears and escape to the larder to pull myself together. When I return, Miss Eliza is her old self, beating up the eggs with a brisk hand and asking me to find the Mauritian chutney we made the other week. We finish our cooking in silence, each of us absorbed in our own melancholy thoughts. Then she passes me a clean wooden spoon and asks me to taste the kedgeree.

I put a spoonful to my lips and instantly my mind calms. The turbot is warm, almost silky, on my tongue. The grains of rice are coated in a buttery smoothness. The heat and spice plunge me into another world – of foreign shores and exotic lands, of man-eating tigers, snake charmers, camels and elephants, rajas in jewelled turbans, hot dusty plains. All the oriental things Jack has heard talk of in London float into my head as the kedgeree slips down my throat.

'More salt? More cayenne?' Miss Eliza's questions bring me directly back to earth. 'Mr Arnott has a predilection for heat, as we know.'

I pause and think. 'A touch more cayenne . . . a salt spoon's worth, I reckon.'

'Good!' She claps her hands together, her spirits fully restored. 'I must go and prepare myself for Mr Arnott. Put the chutney in the silver sauce boat and remember he likes plenty of leaves in his tea.'

I nod, my mind swooping back to the book I've stolen. I must return it to the kitchen. Before Hatty finds it stuffed beneath my mattress. Before God can punish me. Before I'm caught red-handed and must swing from the gallows.

CHAPTER THIRTY-ONE

Eliza

KEDGEREE

Mr Arnott (whom I am now to call Edwin) has received some bad news. He is not in his usual jocular spirits, but admires the kedgeree all the same. I am not myself either. I have mislaid the only copy of my verse, after going to great lengths to retrieve it from Mother's hiding place. She thinks I know nothing of her *hiding places*, or where she keeps her *secret* keys. But I know of both. My poetry books have been taken and hidden for my own benefit (she insists), but last night I had such a yearning to remember who I was, who I am, only a look at my own verse would suffice.

I found my book, re-read my paltry puny efforts, relived that terrible time when only the writing of poetry kept me from insanity. Mother says Edwin – Mr Arnott – must never know. But what sort of a marriage is that? He may not love me and I may not love him, but surely we must have trust? And honesty? I have this odd feeling that all that I am – my tenacity, my courage, my pluck – are being stolen from me, wiped away. I no longer know who or what I am. And into this blank space creeps a vast chilling shame.

Mother is entirely pragmatic, insisting I owe it to my family and reminding me that with marriage comes money and respect and dignity and protection from loneliness. When she said the word *loneliness*, her voice faltered and a tear came to her eye. 'Father will return from Calais,' I said to comfort her. But then she pounced, reminding me we're still at the mercy of his later creditors, the Ipswich brewer and the butcher who missed the proceeds of that horrid public sale where our worldly goods sat for all and sundry to pick over, like carrion crows. 'Only marriage and money bring freedom, Eliza,' she said, dabbing at her pink eye. 'Without them, you will grow old and lonely and bitter, a hated old maid who must serve others for a pittance.' When she said this I heard again those coarse vile voices that followed me from the alehouse, taunting and jeering ... *there was an old maid from Tunbridge Wells* ...

'Eliza, my love,' Edwin places his hand over mine. Such a large warm hand. A tingle skims up and down my spine and I long to lean my head against his chest, to feel the steady beat of his heart, to hold him to me. I imagine him, fleetingly, as a recipe: take one wealthy widower with two substantial houses and three thriving businesses, add one thirty-six-year-old failed poetess with a bankrupt discredited father. Add one practical deceiving mother. Scatter with three secrets. Press him to you. Stir . . .

'Yes, Edwin, dearest?'

'I would like to open an account for you with a London seamstress. You will need a new wardrobe as Mrs Arnott.'

I look down at my dress and see it through his eyes. Tired. Shabby. Unfashionable. The dress of an old maid.

'And jewellery. I notice you have none. Mrs Arnott must drip with pearls and diamonds. Whatever takes your fancy.'

How do I tell him that I *chose* to sell my jewels and keep, instead, my poetry books? How do I tell him of the joy I feel slipping on my bibbed calico apron and inspecting a brace of rabbits or a delivery of fresh perch? I must tell him. I must be honest . . .

'Would I have your permission to undertake some chari-table works, Edwin? If I'm not to help Mother with boarders I will need something to keep me occupied.'

'Which is exactly why I mention jewellery and dresses.' He pats my hand, then pronounces himself 'full to the gills', pushing half his kedgeree to the side of his plate. Something about the carelessness of this, the brief harsh scraping of the knife on his platter, makes me feel an unexpected twinge of anger. A fine turbot died and was carefully gutted, cleaned, scaled, poached and flaked that you might eat, I think pet-ulantly. I recall Ann's face as she tasted this dish an hour previous, the look almost of rapture, of beatification. Her first taste of turbot, no doubt.

I retrieve my hand from beneath Mr Arnott's – Edwin's – and

begin to eat. The kedgeree is perfectly spiced, rich, buttery, moist. My mind drifts off and I begin wondering where best to place kedgeree in my book: *Foreign Cookery* or *Fish*? Or should I include a section on Breakfasts? And then I remember – I am not to be Eliza Acton, writer of a comprehensive cookery book. I am to be Mrs Edwin Arnott.

'But after I have a full wardrobe,' I persist, 'might I do some charitable work?'

'I fear you will be infinitely busier than you anticipate, dearest Eliza. I have many servants, many business associates who must be flattered and cajoled. Your feminine charms will be put to full effect as Mrs Arnott.' He chuckles quietly, as if he knows things that I do not. 'I have been remiss since my wife died, entertaining only at my club, which has none of the intimacy of a home.' He pauses, wipes at the corners of his mouth with his napkin. 'I fear my business rivals have stolen a march upon me, for at the club I cannot host wives. I know, for a fact, that my most significant rival has a wife who is assiduous in her efforts. Luncheon parties for ladies, dinners at home that are widely talked of . . .'

In an instant, I see myself not as Mrs Arnott-at-the-seamstress-and-milliner but as Mrs Arnott, hostess. I see myself in my new garb of the latest fashion and the highest quality, presiding over a table of Edwin's most important associates and their embellished wives. I see the table . . . etched Bohemian glassware, twisted silver candlesticks that shout their price, bone china dinner plates and cutlery polished until it gleams like gold. Is this not the life I have always longed for? The life I was made and educated for?

'My houses are kept fastidiously clean,' he continues. 'But they lack ... character, a woman's touch, those little things of whimsy that make a home. I need you, dearest Eliza, to do all that for me.' His takes my fingers in his. 'You may do anything you wish to my houses. Change the drapes on the beds, order new swags at the windows, purchase some Turkey carpets or a new pianoforte.'

'That is generous indeed,' I murmur. 'And will your French chef have no objections to me supervising him?'

'Oh, he is a little indisposed at times, because he is French,' Mr Arnott says, with a stoic smile. 'But you can humour him, speak to him in his native tongue. Preparing ladies' luncheons and lavish dinners will allow him to parade his French genius.'

'And the servants?' My voice is tentative. 'May I change them if I wish?' I am thinking, naturally, of Ann. But his talk of the French 'genius' chef has left me with a sense of disquiet. I would rather hire a good plain cook ... as Ann is turning out to be. A good plain cook happy to have me – with all my quirks and demands – as her mistress.

'You may change any of the servants that do not please you.' He gives my fingers a final squeeze, then pushes away his coffee cup and tugs his napkin from his neck. 'Any except Louis.'

'Thank you,' I say, smoothing at the small frown on my forehead. I want to ask Mr Arnott a final question. I want to ask if I may write poetry. But why do I need his permission? Why should I not pen my verse when he is working and I am neither choosing clothes nor entertaining the wives of his associates nor adding whimsical decorative touches to his houses? Isn't this why I am marrying – to have freedom?

'Oh, dear Eliza,' Mr Arnott gazes upon me. 'I am so pleased to have found you, lurking here in Tonbridge. What an asset you shall be to the Arnott Spice Company!'

And the thought of spice cheers me. At least – as Mrs Arnott – I will always have the purest and freshest of spices.

CHAPTER THIRTY-TWO

Ann

LEEKS WITH WOODLICE

While Miss Eliza has her last breakfast with Mr Arnott, I dash to the attic bedroom which Hatty has left in her usual state of disorder. Her bed unmade, her nightgown on the floor, water splashed from the ewer, the rag rug rucked up, the chamber pot unemptied and reeking. No time to dwell on Hatty's messiness, I think, heaving up the mattress, and reaching beneath for Miss Eliza's book of verse.

My plan is to return it to the kitchen and tell Miss Eliza I found it on the dresser, behind the fish platter, and hope she's so bewildered she doesn't remember *not* putting it there. I know this to be devious, but I cannot think what else to do. The book gawps from my hand in an accusing sort of way. As if it sees what I'm doing and would speak out if only it could. It's tightly bound in blue silk, the colour of a cornflower. Fancy gold lettering on the cover: *Poems by Eliza Acton.*

I don't want Hatty bursting in upon me so I lean my back against the door. Very slowly, I turn the cover. The first page declares the printer to be Mr Richard Deck of Ipswich. The next page has the title and her name again, in an elegant script that is all lines and sharp corners. I know I should stop immediately, that I should ask Miss Eliza's permission, that I am behaving like a common thief. But something is tugging me on, as if I am borne upon the current of a mighty river. I run my fingers over the lettering and my heart lurches, although whether from fear or penitence or excitement I can't tell.

I come to the first poem, run my finger below each word as I read, feel my lips move. It takes a few seconds for the meaning of the words to strike me. And when they do, I close the book, startled and confused.

Then I open it and read on.

A moment later I sink to the floor. The anguish in her verse is terrible to read. Shocking and terrible! Poems that speak of wanting to die, of having to *go forth to the cold bleak world again,* of being *vile dishonour's slave,* of *remorse ... wretchedness ... shame ... scorn ... servile guilt.* And I am flummoxed. For Miss Eliza has everything one could want. Has she ever felt the grinding gnaw of hunger? Has she ever been so cold she cannot sleep for shivering? Has she had a mad, naked mother strapped to her waist for days on end? And yet it seems she has been sadder than I've ever been.

I do not know her, I think. I have never known one tiny bit of her. All the days we spend side by side in the kitchen. Me thinking of her as *my friend* ... All at once I feel very small and very far away, as if I have been lifted to Heaven and am looking down on everything, tiny and squeezed together.

I close the book, sharp. My curiosity has fled. I'm ashamed of looking, uninvited, into her soul, for her verses seem more written in blood than in cold black ink.

And fused with my shame is confusion. As if I am standing upon shifting sands. As if all I thought was certain in life, has gone.

I hold the book beneath my apron and hurry down the back stairs to the kitchen. Mrs Dolby has arrived to take the laundry and is tying everything in sheets. Hatty is carrying a tray of dirty breakfast china to the scullery for little Lizzie to wash.

'Some nice leeks for you to clean, Ann,' she says, jerking her head at the table where the muddiest leeks I have ever seen sit in clods of sticky earth, with woodlice crawling all over them. It will take an hour to have them washed proper, by which time my hands will be raw from the cold water. But today I'm glad of it. Glad of the distraction. I feel a sudden – and peculiar – friendliness towards the leeks, towards Hatty and little Lizzie and Mrs Dolby with her red meaty arms.

I slip the book of poems behind the fish platter. When Miss Eliza comes in I say, as innocent as pie, 'I think I found the book you were looking for.'

She is so relieved, her face lights up like a candle. 'Oh, Ann, wherever was it?'

'Behind the fish platter,' I say, staring hard at the leeks and making a show of brushing the woodlice into a bowl. I feel wretched and despicable and hot-in-the-face.

'How odd!' Miss Eliza says. 'But what a relief – it's my only copy.' She goes to the dresser, peers behind the fish platter and pulls out her book.

'Have we new boarders coming, now that Mr Arnott is gone?' I ask, wanting to change the subject as quick as possible.

'All going well, we won't be needing boarders for much longer.' She gives me one of her tender smiles that usually melts the corners of my heart. But today it only makes me feel wicked. 'Mrs Acton thinks we should stop taking boarders now, so that we may concentrate all our attentions on Mr Arnott. But I – I am not so sure.'

I say nothing, for she seems to be talking more to herself than to me. Instead I take the leeks to the scullery and start stripping them of their outer leaves and the lumps of mud that cling to them and the worms burrowing around in them. 'Oh, Lord, forgive me, forgive me,' I say beneath my breath. 'And make her happy. Please make her happy.'

CHAPTER THIRTY-THREE

Eliza

ORANGE-FLOWER MACAROONS

Today is *her* birthday. As we have no boarders, I was able to sit up in bed and attempt some verse. I began by writing a poem for her. But every word I wrote was thin and inept. My first stanza was so stale and clumsy, so blundering, I tore it into tiny pieces. I can't help but wonder if all that grief – once so savage, so keenly felt – has been pushed too deep inside me, squeezed into a narrow crevice between my heart and my ribs. So that I can barely feel it now. Except as a dull ache. Not enough for a poem. Or perhaps I am no longer a poet?

These questions vex me, but I feel much improved once dressed and in the kitchen. Recently I've noticed how the creation of verse mirrors the creations of the kitchen – the sense of being truly alive, the utter concentration so that one exists solely in the moment of exertion. These apply equally when I prepare a dish or when I write a recipe and must use the perfect prose. Before, I gave the gift of my poetry and now I give the gift of my food. So if I cannot write a good verse then I shall bake a cake in her name. I get straight to work, testing a recipe for soda cake.

'I need fresh butter, sifted sugar, currants that have been cleaned of grit and stalks, and three well-whisked eggs,' I say to Ann.

The girl is quieter than usual and keeps her head bowed very low over the currants as she sorts and cleans them.

'We're testing a recipe for a good soda cake,' I explain. 'I will also need grated nutmeg, fresh lemon peel and fine dry flour free of weevils.'

'Is it ... is it ... for the cookery book?' she asks, frowning into the currant jar.

'Yes,' I say staunchly. 'A soda cake resembles a pound cake but is much less expensive and far more wholesome.'

I comb through recipes from Mr Henderson, Mrs Glasse and Doctor Kitchiner, and make some notes on quantities. I am just re-calculating the weights of flour, when the front doorbell chimes, long and deliberate. A minute later Hatty appears, in her usual breathless swirl of excitement.

'Ma'am requests you in the drawing room. The Reverend Thorpe and Mrs Thorpe are come. Shall I do a tray of hot chocolate and buttered toast?'

I throw up my hands in irritation. 'I am just about to test a soda cake! Why are they here now?'

Hatty stares at me, flustered, then ventures, 'To talk about your wedding, Miss Eliza?'

I shake my head by way of an apology. 'I did not mean to snap at you, Hatty. Ann, you'll have to proceed as best you can.' I untie my apron and fling it on the table, then add, 'No hot chocolate or buttered toast, please. That will merely prolong their visit.'

In the drawing room, the scene is not as I expect. Reverend Thorpe is pacing, his hands gripped behind his back. Mrs Thorpe perches primly on the couch, prattling away. She stops when I enter, a thin sculpted smile frozen upon her face. The room is briefly silent and I have a sudden presentiment that they are not come to discuss my wedding.

'Eliza, my dear, the Reverend wishes to talk to us of Ann Kirby.'

My body stiffens, as if bracing itself. Mother gestures to me to sit down and as she does so, the iron keys at her waist rattle.

Mr Thorpe gives a flash of well-picked teeth, then strokes at his moustache. 'Ann Kirby's father has been accused of poaching. He was caught snaring rabbits by Mr Mugridge's gamekeeper.'

I smile sweetly at him. 'And what is that to do with Ann?'

Mrs Thorpe coughs into a lace handkerchief. 'My dear husband, who has done so much for the Kirby family, forgets to mention that Mr Kirby was also drunk when he was caught. We think it might be better if Ann returns home to keep him out of trouble and away from the ale. We all know the duties of an unmarried daughter.'

'I have no intention of releasing Ann. When I leave this parish as Mrs Arnott, Ann Kirby will be coming with me.' My words – with their flair and finality – ring boldly in my ears. *As Mrs Arnott* ... no longer burdened by *the duties of an unmarried daughter*.

Mother rises from her chair, flustered. 'Nothing has been decided, my dear. And if Ann Kirby has inherited bad blood we might not want to subject her to all the temptations of Mr Arnott's accumulated wealth and London's ... depravity.'

I stare at her, struck by the arrogance of their comfortable allegiances, the singular lack of kindness or compassion. When I am Mrs Arnott, I think, I will be free of people like this. Cruel, small-minded people ...

'Mother, when I'm married I shall be making my own decisions,' I say. 'Mr Arnott has already said I may choose my own servants and dismiss his, should I wish.'

'Even the French chef?' She cocks an eyebrow, and I know full well she has listened at every dinner Mr Arnott and I have shared.

Mr Thorpe flexes his fingers so that his knuckles crack. 'Forgive our intrusion, ladies. Mrs Thorpe and I are particularly proud of the sobriety of our parish and we would like to keep it that way.'

'Of course,' says Mother. 'My daughter can be most contrary, but she does not mean all that she says.'

I wince. Knot my fingers together. Bide my tongue.

Mrs Thorpe smirks and says, 'You have lost a husband and Miss Acton has lost a father. It cannot be easy.'

I make my face suitably sombre, behind my clenched jaw

and my tight eyes. All these lies … But Mother looks appro-
priately sorrowful and gestures at a framed sampler on the
wall bearing the words 'In God We Trust'. I wait for her to say
'God rest his soul' or some such thing, but to my relief even
she is not brazen enough for that.

'What is to happen to Mr Kirby?' I ask.

'He will be punished at Mr Mugridge's discretion.'
Reverend Thorpe flexes his fingers again, each cracking
knuckle like gunshot. 'Lesser crimes have meant the Hulks
and transportation for life.'

'I believe he lives in considerable poverty.' I keep my voice
soft and placatory. 'No doubt he trapped the rabbit as food.'

'He stole the rabbit, Miss Acton. Stealing is a crime.' Mrs
Thorpe rises from the couch and adjusts her peaked bonnet,
as if she's had enough of this conversation and wishes
to depart.

'But surely Mr Mugridge has hundreds of wild rabbits,'
I protest. 'And what if Ann does not wish to look after
her father?'

'You sound like a French revolutionary, my dear.' Mother
gives a nervous laugh.

I ignore her and look squarely at Mr Thorpe, who is still
pulling on his fingers. 'And the mother who taught Ann to
read and write? Was she also a felon?'

He says nothing but gives a violent tug at the knuckle of
his index finger, then bows to Mother.

As soon as the door closes Mother turns to me, shaking
with fury. 'Why must you be so argumentative and contrary,
Eliza? You know exactly the predicament we're in. You know

full well that we cannot afford to make a single enemy among the local gentry and clergy.'

'Do you think I care about our *predicament* today?' I say coldly. 'Have you forgotten what day it is?'

Her expression changes rapidly and a glimmer of kindness and understanding seems to flash across her face. But then it shifts again, hardening into something cold and immutable. 'We agreed *that* would not be mentioned. Ever.' She looks away.

'I want to speak of it to Mr Arnott,' I say. 'How can I marry him if he does not know?'

'It has been discussed and agreed, many years ago. And if Mr Arnott hears anything, rest assured he will call off the marriage. And then what of us? And your father? And your sisters who are slaving as governesses up and down the country?' She moves towards me and puts a hand in the small of my back. 'We must be sensible, my dear. And once you are married, with a ring upon your finger and perhaps with child, you may decide to mention your past. But until then . . .'

I shake her hand off my back. 'Very well, but I am baking a cake in honour of the day. In *her* honour.'

Mother's voice drops to a hiss. 'The servants must not hear anything of this.' The iron keys at her waist clank furiously as she sweeps out.

In the sudden silence, some past words of mine tick into my head:

> *Let not the cares which round me cling,*
> *Obscure one moment's bliss for thee.*

And in their wake I think of orange blossom, newly gathered, picked from the stem and snipped swiftly into fresh Lisbon sugar, then whisked with the whites of several freshly laid eggs until the whole resembles snow-bound mountains. Orange-flower macaroons, I think. A soda cake is far too dull. I should have made her orange-flower macaroons.

CHAPTER THIRTY-FOUR

Ann

A GOOD SODA CAKE

I take the soda cake from the baking oven. The kitchen fills with the smell of nutmeg and sweetness, folding soft around me like a wool blanket. Or like Mam's arms when I was little and the air was hard and tight with frost. As I ease the cake from the tin with the blade of a knife, Hatty runs in, flushed and wide-eyed.

'They are talking about you, Ann Kirby. Nothing to do with the wedding!'

'Me?' I think instantly of Pa and his drinking, then Mam and her lunacy. Then I think of Miss Eliza's poem book. And my skin goes cold. Was I seen putting it under my mattress? Did God see me and report me to Reverend Thorpe? Oh Lord, surely I will burn in Hell!

'Yes, you, Ann. Have you missed church?'

I shake my head. My mouth is dry as autumn leaves.

'You must have done summat. Why else would they come here to talk of you?' Her eyes narrow to slits. 'Did you take a bit of dripping or some candle wax?'

I cannot speak. Because I *did* take something.

'Ain't we friends?' Hatty stares at me through her slitty eyes. 'You can tell me, Ann.'

I shrug. 'I haven't taken anything.' *That I haven't given back . . .*

'Likely your name just cropped up.' Hatty grins, as if her suspicions have faded clean away. 'They found you this position, ain't that right?'

I nod.

'It don't matter where you work, they always think you've stolen something from 'em. First place they'll search is our room, so if you've put the family silver there, best move it now.' She laughs, as if she's said something funny. Then she squeezes my arm, straightens her apron and goes out to pump a pail of water.

I wait for Miss Eliza to return, unable to settle. I sieve a pail of cinders, then scrape last night's wax from the pewter candelabra, then I shave sugar from the sugarloaf so the cake can be strewn with it. I dust the day's soot from the dresser and the open shelves, shake more coal into the range and lay out the silver tea service for polishing – the teaspoons and the sugar bowl and the curly milk jug.

When Miss Eliza comes back to the kitchen she is most queer in her manner. And her face is glum, with pinkish eyes and a red mottle all over her neck. After a few minutes, in which Miss Eliza sniffs and scribbles in her notebook, she says, 'Ann, put a candle on the cake.'

'A candle?' I say, startled. 'On the cake?'

'Yes, a good beeswax one. And a full candle, not a stub.'

Her instruction distracts me. Candles are expensive and why she wants one on a cake makes no sense. Surely the cake will be spoilt by dribbling wax? I wonder if I've misheard her, but she reads my mind and says, 'It's a continental custom I came across on my travels. You'll need to make a small well in the cake's surface to keep the candle stable.' Then she goes to the dresser, unlocks her money tin and gets out five shillings, which she pushes across the kitchen table. 'Your father needs money,' she says. 'This is for him.'

A huge wave of relief washes over me. So there was no talk of his drinking or Mam's lunacy. Or – praise be – of me stealing Miss Eliza's poem book. But then my mind goes into a foggy muddle. Why is she giving me money for Pa? Why is she looking so downcast?

She reads my mind again. 'Your father is in trouble for poaching. Five shillings should buy his freedom.'

'Did you hear of it from Reverend Thorpe?' I dare not look her in the face. I know poaching is a heinous crime, that Pa must have been half-starved or else too drunk to know what he was at. I slide the shillings into my apron pocket, my cheeks burning with shame, and my skin cold with worry.

'Yes,' she says. 'The Thorpes want me to send you home, to keep your father from crime and drink.'

I gulp, then take a deep breath. How do I say I love my pa

but that I cannot go back to my old life, that I cannot leave our book of recipes? 'We would have no money but for what Jack sends home. Pa cannot work the fields like other men for he has just the one leg.'

'He started drinking after your mother ... died?'

'Yes,' I say, very low and soft. And I hate myself for the lie. And for denying Mam, for murdering her ... which is how it feels. And I hate myself for not wanting to go home, for feeling only shame of my pa.

'I thought as much.' Miss Eliza walks round the table and places her hand upon my arm. And I cannot bear it. Every little bit of me wants to shrivel up. I am desperate for comfort, but I am overflowing with disgust. At Pa. At Mrs Thorpe who made me promise never to tell of Mam's lunacy. At the whole world with its cock and bull. But mostly at myself.

'I will find that candle, Miss Eliza,' I say. And I disappear as quick as my feet will take me.

The larder is gloamy, for there is only one small window, very high and covered with mesh. A thin light trickles through, wobbling over the flagstones. Enough light for me to see my reflection in a silver tray. I hate what I see. My lying, filching, selfish face.

When I get back to the kitchen with a good wax candle, Miss Eliza is standing very straight reading a letter.

'We are to go to Mr Arnott's London house, Ann,' she says. Her beautiful face is glowing at this news, her eyes as bright as a bird's. She has such a broad smile it near stretches from one ear to the other. 'Is this not the good news we deserved today?'

'Yes, Miss Eliza,' I say, thinking 'we' means her and Ma'am and that soon I am to be discarded, returned to my poaching drunken father and his wretched hovel. Doubtless Mr Arnott has many servants already. London girls without the foolish notions of poor country girls like me. London girls with respectable fathers who can hold their ale and have no need of stealing.

'We shall meet his French chef,' she says. 'And view his house so that I can suggest changes to the decoration. He is a generous man indeed! He has invited you too, Ann. He knows how highly I think of you.'

I gape at her. Me? To London? 'Am I to come with you, miss?'

She nods and goes back to her letter, while I stand with a huge stupid grin plastered over my face. Pa stumbles into my head – who will look after him while I'm gone? – but then he vanishes and I think only of London. At last I am to see London!

'We shall leave next week,' she says after a few seconds. 'Perhaps you can visit your brother?' She puts the letter down and smiles. And then she does something I've never seen her do before. She lifts her skirts and jigs around the kitchen. I feel like jigging too but I can only stare. When she sees me staring at her, she stops, brushes down her skirts, pats at her hair and tells me to put the cake upon the cut-glass stand and take it, with the candle, to the drawing room. And so I do, keeping my hands as steady as I can, for the thought of seeing Jack in London has made my heart race, even as Pa creeps back into my head. Making my skin go clammy all over again.

Chapter Thirty-Five

Eliza

Ortolans Garnished with Cocks' Combs

Mr Arnott's house is in Albemarle Street and from the second I step down from the coach, I am enchanted. The steps are scrubbed white, the shutters are newly painted, the brass door knocker gleams. The entire façade is neat and well tended. Even the pavement has been swept clean of the chewed bones, clods of dung, mouldering rodents and rotten vegetables that litter most of London's streets.

Mr Arnott, in an embroidered waistcoat bulging with shiny buttons, comes bounding down the steps. I feel a rush of joy. This is to be my home! This is the house where I shall – at last – be mistress!

'Welcome! Welcome,' he cries, bowing low to Mother and me. While Ann and the footmen unload our luggage, we are ushered inside, where a line of uniformed servants shuffle and stare: housekeeper, butler and six maids. They bob and bow, although Mr Arnott seems not to recall their full names so that the housekeeper must jump in and make the introductions in a dialect – Scottish? – I can barely understand. Behind them ticks a longcase clock with a painted face of cherubs. A mahogany table groans beneath a gold-rimmed vase of hothouse flowers. Pictures of men on horseback, in fat gilded frames, adorn the walls. Hundreds of candles glow from sconces and two glittering chandeliers, so that the maids, the furniture, the flowers, rugs and paintings seem to ebb and flow, one minute in shadow and the next illuminated in rippling light. I look sideways at Mother. I can tell she is calculating the value of each item and every good wax candle, for her fingers move one by one against her skirts.

Our tour begins in the dining room, its floor buffed to a shine, its walls thick with mirrors and portraits. Twelve dining chairs covered in maroon leather are arranged around a long table with a mahogany buffet server on brass casters at each end, and a silver candelabra, surrounded by small pineapples, as its centrepiece. The fireplace has beside it a substantial plate-warming box painted with Chinese ladies lurking seductively behind ornate fans.

'I thought you didn't entertain,' I say, with just the smallest hint of flirtation. Mother nods approvingly.

'Everything is as it was when my wife lived here. You

may change anything you do not like.' He indicates the room with a grand flourish of his hand. 'There is little of fashion here.'

'Chintz curtains would be an improvement on the shutters, which are very plain,' says Mother.

'Do not change anything,' I say. 'I cannot abide waste in any shape or form.' Mother glares at me.

From the dining room we go to the morning room, then the drawing room, then the library, where the meagre collection of books causes me to raise my eyebrows. As we leave, Mr Arnott says, 'I cannot very well show you my bedchamber, and you will see your own chamber later, so I suppose the tour must end here. Now, how about some tea, ladies?'

I muster my courage, cough, twist my hands together. 'I would like to see the kitchen, dear Edwin. May I?'

Mother glares again, then interjects, in her most imperious voice, 'My dear Eliza, the kitchen is for servants. Fashionable London mistresses never see their own kitchens. Is that not so, Mr Arnott?'

'I believe that is the case,' smiles Mr Arnott. 'But if you would like to see it, you may. I dare say you will never want to see it again.'

We trail down the stairs, Mother breathing furiously through her nose. At the rear of the building we come to a flight of dark narrow stone steps, whereupon she says, 'I won't descend any further, thank you, Mr Arnott.'

Edwin looks uncomfortable, as if he is not sure what to do. 'Perhaps we should stay above stairs,' he says. 'Louis dislikes my presence anywhere near the kitchen. I have keys for the wine room and the silver room, but I do not poke my nose elsewhere.'

'You stay with Mother and I will take a quick glimpse,' I say, hurrying down the steps to the kitchen corridor, which is low-ceilinged and stained with damp. Beyond the storerooms I can sense the kitchen, feel its heat spilling over, smell the scum of a simmering stockpot, frying onions, mutton fat. And struggling beneath this odorous skirmish, the wooded scent of chopped rosemary.

The kitchen is painted blue, but its walls and ceiling are blackened with smoke. From its narrow rafters hang strings of onions, cured hams, long bunches of dried sage and bay leaves, dangling threads of red chillies. One wall is lined with barrels and tins and against the other is a vast dresser crammed with pots, copper jelly moulds, platters in all shapes and sizes, dish covers, dripping pans, graters, sugar nippers, spice tins, biscuit presses, strainers, hair sieves. On the table are stacks of wooden boards, knives, pastry trays, several rolling pins and a bolt of tammy cloth.

A thread of dusky light falls from a high window, through which I can see the boots and shoes of passers-by on the pavement outside. It is quite unlike the kitchen at Bordyke House, which is lofty and airy and where the smells of food sit comfortably side by side. Here, in this dark constrained space, they brawl and scrap. And although my kitchen also has a single north-facing window, I keep it open at all times to allow for a wholesome circulation of fresh air. Here, the glass-less window is grilled and barred and no bigger than a fish kettle. The walls run with steam, so the whole room is like a miniature furnace – hot, damp, airless, noxious.

'Who is in my kitchen?' I hear the clear twang of a French accent and in walks the man I suppose to be Louis the Chef, followed by a girl carrying a box of sea-coal. He is not a tall man, and the kitchen is gloomy, but in spite of this he casts a long shadow.

'I am Miss Acton,' I say, assuming he will know my name. For surely he has been briefed as thoroughly as the rest of the household staff who stood in line to welcome us on arrival?

He looks me up and down as if he cannot tell whether I have entered via the tradesman's door or the front door. And then he pushes his hand roughly through his thick black hair and says, '*Mais oui*, Miss Acton.' It is the first time I have heard French in ten years and I falter for a second, but then I notice his apron is filthy, stained with blood and grease. And I think it odd he has not deigned to change into a fresh apron.

'You need more air in your kitchen. The maids will asphyxiate in here, as will you,' I say, holding his insolent gaze. 'I will look at the larders now, if you have no objection.'

'I do,' he says, most impertinently. The girl looks up from the stove, where she has been shovelling coal, and titters.

I straighten, and lift my chin a fraction. 'Very well, Louis. But I must inform you that I plan to take a considerable interest in the kitchen when I become Mrs Arnott.'

'The master calls me Chef,' he says. 'I would ask the same of you, please.' The girl titters again, then burps and slips out.

I nod, shocked at their impudence. Are all London kitchens like this?

'The last Madame Arnott never comes 'ere.' Louis glides his hand through his hair again. His nails are rimed with dirt and his fingertips stained a greyish maroon, as if he has been handling red cabbage. I have an overwhelming urge to point out how unhygienic his *hair-fiddling* is, but I decide not to. When I am married, I think.

'I intend to run things differently.' I dab discreetly at the perspiration building on my face, trickling from my temples. Whether it's from the heat of the stove or from his impudence I know not.

'English women cannot cook,' he announces. 'You ladies learn to paint a pretty picture or play a tune or you learn to speak my language, but you do not learn to cook.'

I know I should turn and leave, but for some reason I remain rooted to the spot.

'English food is very bad,' he continues, in his heavy accented drawl. 'Why do you think London gentlemen eat at taverns and dining halls and chop houses? The only good food is from French chefs. We are artists. Artists!'

I finally find my tongue. 'I cannot agree with you. I shall take a close interest in Mr Arnott's meals once I am mistress here.' For the first time I feel no thrill, no ripple of satisfaction as I say the word mistress.

'You English have no ... taste. No palate. Always vinegar and cayenne. Always to disguise that you cannot cook, that you can only poison.' He puts his greasy hands to his throat and mimes the act of strangulation, then laughs.

'I must return to Mr Arnott,' I say, desperately in need of air and shaking with fury beneath my new dress, new hat, new mantle, new gloves.

He bows. '*Au revoir*, Mademoiselle Acton.'

I turn and walk, trembling, up the two flights of stairs to where Mr Arnott and Mother are discussing whether brocade curtains would be a welcome addition to the morning room.

'What I would like,' Mr Arnott is saying, 'is to have the ceiling painted with golden cherubs perching on the spreading branches of an English oak tree.' He motions at the ceiling rose then notices me standing at the door.

'I have met ... the chef,' I say, adjusting my cuffs to conceal my disquiet.

'Yes, insufferable is he not? I have nothing to do with him, neither did the late Mrs Arnott. But his cooking is remarkable, as you will see this evening.'

'Does he cook only French dishes?' I ask, thinking of my future husband's predilection for currie and spice.

'I insist on a weekly currie, which he prepares with great reluctance, and then he sulks for days.' Mr Arnott laughs and Mother joins him, catching my eye to indicate that I should laugh too. But I'm still inwardly trembling at the chef's insolence.

'And can I ask what you pay him?'

Mother's laughter stops abruptly. She glowers at me and then opens her mouth to speak but Mr Arnott is too quick. 'Sixty pounds per annum, my dear Eliza. But he is absolutely indispensable to me. Besides, he would get the same wage at any good London house. Indeed, I'm told Lord Melrose pays sixty-five pounds per annum for his French chef.'

His answer renders me speechless. A good female cook is paid just £10 per annum. I could make a saving of £50 if only I can persuade Mr Arnott to dismiss the loathsome *Chef.*

'Think of the lavish and enviable dinners you can host, Eliza,' says Mother in a coaxing voice that belies the cold anger in her eyes. 'Think of how you can help Mr Arnott's business.'

I want to cry out, 'But think how many more I can help with my cookery book or my poems!' Instead I close my mouth and face, hard and tight.

'That is the beauty of Louis,' agrees Mr Arnott, nodding affably. 'We need never venture to the basement!'

Later, we prepare for bed in Mr Arnott's guest chamber and Mother berates me for my *unseemly interest in the kitchen* and for my *unforgivable question regarding the chef's wages.*

'But if I am to be mistress of this house, surely I must know these things?'

'You do not even have a ring on your finger yet, Eliza. Why must you be so impatient, so contrary, so wilful?' She pushes her hair into her nightcap with angry prodding fingers. 'Fashionable London ladies do not bother themselves with the filth below stairs. They are charming, amusing and clever. That is how you will maintain Mr Arnott's place in society.'

I pull the quilt over me, turn away from her and snuff out the candle. She continues, snapping into the darkness. 'And you saw the magnificence of the chef's creations ... sippets shaped as swans, ortolans garnished with cocks' combs, a meringue pyramid shaped as a woman's head ... that dinner was in *our* honour, Eliza.'

'I know, Mother.' Louis's dinner had been magnificent and extravagant, six courses that had my tongue so tied I could barely make conversation.

'I saw you prodding obstinately at the soup,' she adds. 'And examining the sippets, like a – like a medical man! Why can you not eat like a lady?'

'There was too much food. Half of it went to waste,' I mutter into my pillow. The truth is Louis's food is still upon my tongue and I know I shall spend all night chewing over its intricacies and complexities, or else I shall find it in my dreams. The scorched sweetness of his roasted viands; the fish – brill? – which appeared to float upon a tepid cloud of rising steam; the delicate herbs – chervil? – strewn across the peas and suffused in every sauce; our names inscribed in spun sugar over a meringue as light as pollen. And yet who can afford to make or cook food like this?

'And why would a bit of waste matter? Really, Eliza! Your thrifty ways have no place here. And nor do your ... appetites.'

I sigh into my pillow and remind myself that one day this will be my home and I will be a wife, not a daughter. And the future I once envisaged – pushing a petulant mother around in a cheap shoddy bath chair – is whisked away. Gone!

Chapter Thirty-Six

Ann

Orange Crumpets Left by Gentlemen

London is all pitched roofs, rearing up, tall and black, for mile upon mile. The roads are one great jostle and shove: waggons and barrows, donkeys heaving water carts, hackney carriages, small traps they call Hansom cabs that duck and dive, ragged boys that dash beneath their wheels to grab at tossed apple cores or fallen farthings. The noise is deafening: hundreds of ironclad wheels clattering over the cobbles, the cries of the coachmen and the lashes of their whips, the ceaseless hollering of the costermongers, the wailing of the beggars. I hear it all – even in Mr Arnott's underground kitchen, even in the back scullery where I sleep upon a pallet of straw with four snoring housemaids and hundreds of scuttling cockroaches.

London, I decide, is also the dirtiest, most reeking place I've ever been. Excrement and dung and rotting fish and decaying cabbages, then waves of roasting chestnuts and bubbling pea soup and baking apples, which makes me by turn queasy and hungry. In Kent, the stench comes and goes, depending on where you're passing, or the direction of the wind. Here it is constant, so that by our second day I am already accustomed to it.

Two days after we arrive Miss Eliza says I can visit Jack. She draws me a tiny street map and says I am to speak to no one except to ask directions. I leave the next morning, while Ma'am and Miss Eliza are still in their chamber. I'm glad to leave Mr Arnott's home – for the house boys are always grabbing at my skirts and the footmen keep pressing against me in the narrow halls and the butler has put his greedy hand inside my bodice three times already.

But from the minute I appear alone on the pavement, blinking like a rabbit out of its burrow, the costermongers are at me. Would I like to buy . . . sheep's trotters, rat poison, hot eels, oysters in their shells, baked potatoes hot from the brazier, kidney puddings and penny pies, shoe polish, turnips, hair tonic made from tree bark, milk that has already curdled, scabbed apples, wooden pegs, leaflets, scrubbed beach shells. Until I'm so dizzy I must walk with my head down, looking neither to right nor left and stopping only to examine my map. And only when not a single eye is upon me.

By the time I reach Pall Mall, my mouth and nose are coated in soot and my head throbs from the din. But all of this I forget the minute I see the Reform Club. My courage is forgotten too, for it's a huge building, very grand and clean. Gentlemen with top hats and bursting with golden buttons and rattling watch chains sally in and out of the entrance, swooshing their canes as they go.

I find the tradesmen's entrance and say I have come to see my brother, Jack Kirby. And then Jack appears, startled, and so spotless white I think he must be an angel. He hugs me hard enough to crush the breath from me, then steps back so he may see me better. I tell him my business in London, that I am soon to be living here, and he grins from ear to ear – the two of us standing and grinning like a pair of clowns. 'I've missed you, little sister,' he says, and passes me a long white apron, stiff with starch. 'Put this on, and I'll slip you in.' He takes me to a door where I get a quick peek at the kitchen. It's like a great white ballroom, only full of cooks and servants, all in white. All so clean, so orderly. There is a strange smell I cannot place, but even that is clean-ish, not like rotting meat or milk that has spoiled.

'That's him, the great chef, Monsieur Soyer,' Jack points at a man all in white but for a red velvet beret that sits aslant on his head. The man is moving around on the balls of his feet, dipping a ringed finger in and out of pans. 'But he must not see you, for he will know you are an imposter.'

'I'm a visitor,' I say, indignant.

'He will know you as an imposter because you are plain and he only hires pretty girls,' says Jack, tugging at my arm. But I cannot tear myself away. I want to stand and watch the cooks for ever. They have such grace and purpose. One chops herbs on a board, then passes it to another who adds something from a spice tin and pounds it in a huge mortar. Then it is passed to another who scrapes it from the mortar and stirs it into a vast stew pan. Then Monsieur Soyer is called. He tastes and grinds in a little pepper, then he calls to another who comes with a straining spoon and skims the surface. 'It is like . . . a dance,' I whisper.

'A dance?' Jack rolls his eyes and gives my elbow another tug. 'Since when did you see a dance?'

'My notion of a dance,' I say. 'Where everyone must move together to create a story.'

'I wish you could see the dishes that go to the dining room. You wouldn't believe them, Ann. They would feed the whole of Kent for a month. Come – I'll sneak you into the meat room.'

'Why isn't it boiling hot in here?' I ask, realising all of a sudden that I haven't smelt smoke, or tasted soot upon my tongue, or wiped boluses of sweat from my brow. Like I do in Mr Arnott's kitchen.

'Gas,' Jack murmurs in my ear. 'There ain't no charcoal used here now. All the lighting is gas too. Can't you smell it?'

I sniff at the strange-smelling air and nod. 'Will you be poisoned?'

'Likely I will.' He steers me towards a room where the air is so heavy with frost and ice, I shiver and pull my shawl tight around my shoulders. The carcasses of sheep, bullocks and roe deer hang from hooks along one wall and from another hang hundreds of birds, their claws tied with twine: tiny larks, plovers, quails, woodcock, snipe, wild ducks, pheasants, pigeons, partridges, capons and geese. So that the whole wall is a mass of feathers, beaks, scaly claws. At the far end is a wide marble shelf on which lie rabbits and hares, stretched out as if in sleep.

'So much meat,' I whisper, thinking of Pa poaching a single rabbit, on his own, with his one leg and his wooden crutches. And his punishment not yet decided, even though he has the good word of Reverend Thorpe and Miss Eliza's five shillings as a sweetener.

'That's my work for today. I must skin fifty rabbits and pluck all those fowl. And then I must gut five-and-twenty carp we keep in iced drawers.' Jack's hand is on my elbow again, manoeuvring me towards the door. 'Is Pa still working the graveyard?'

'Yes,' I lie. For I cannot bring myself to tell him the truth. And lying seems to come so easy to me now.

'Oh!' Jack hits his palm against his brow. 'Wait there.' He disappears into a long white corridor and I think how beautiful it is to have everything white, just how I fancy Heaven to be. Not that I will ever see Heaven now, not with all my lies. While Jack's gone, I slip back to the huge white kitchen and look through the gap where the door hinges are. Monsieur Soyer is laughing, his red beret bouncing up and down. The cooks stand at the long table, cutting, slicing, mixing, rolling. Others are at the huge smokeless stove, stirring, shaking pans, tasting from long wooden spoons. I fancy myself one of them, all dressed up in a crisp white uniform, coming every day to this calm white place that has more food than I can dream of.

Jack returns with a hessian sack that smells of old blood.

'For Pa. Some catsup and pickles, and a few orange crumpets that the gentlemen diners left this morning.'

I try to find words to say how proud I am to have a brother working in this heavenly palace – where the master wears a red velvet beret and where fish is kept in *iced drawers* – but they don't come. Instead a gulp rises up my throat. Pride. Envy. Sorrow. Awe. All trapped in my chest so I can't speak.

'You've put a bit of flesh on your bones,' says Jack. Then he looks down and adds, 'I can't send money for a bit, Ann. My rent has doubled and there's nothing spare, but I'll send some as soon as I find cheaper lodgings.'

As he says this I have a strange feeling of being rolled very flat, like pastry. The air knocked from me. Winter is coming and fancying myself a chef isn't helping anyone. Nor is imagining myself in Mr Arnott's grand house, a million miles from where I should be. Because Pa is all down to me now.

CHAPTER THIRTY-SEVEN

Eliza

SADDLE OF MUTTON WITH GRAVY

All night I toss and turn while Mother snores soundly beside me. My discourse – if it can be called that – with Mr Arnott's *Chef* repeats and fragments in my mind, spinning me down such a multitude of avenues I become quite giddy. *English women cannot cook ... we have no palate ... all vinegar and cayenne ... taught to paint pretty pictures but not to eat ...* And his face, louring and yet familiar, swims in and out of my restive brain. Eventually I fall into a fitful slumber and dream I have returned to France and that he, the chef, is making love to me beneath a market stall groaning under a vast weight of Smyrna figs. I wake, hot and full of self-reproach. Mother is still sleeping but light rushes, rosy and golden, over the skyline, so I know it's after my habitual time of rising.

I dress quickly, splash some water on my face from the porcelain ewer on the washstand and make my way down the freshly waxed stairs. It was my intention to work in Mr Arnott's library, to compose a private verse, a poem to give him at our engagement dinner. For wouldn't such a gesture smooth the way for a frank discussion of my poetic aspirations?

But my feet acquire a life of their own and take me past the library door, down the next flight of stairs. And then on until I am descending the narrow stone steps to the kitchen corridor. Not one sound breaks the spell in which I walk. Not the whinge of the water pump nor the rattle of coal. Not the slam of a door or the clinking of glass. Instead my feet move on, past the coal cellar, the wine cellar, the silver room. Past the washroom, the side pantries, the scullery. All of them draped in a chill dark gloom.

And that's when I hear him, faintly sneering, curious.

'Mademoiselle Acton, eh?' He leans on the frame of the kitchen door, arms folded, watching me.

The spell is broken. What am I doing here? Why am I not in the library? I turn to leave, fumbling for any words that might explain my presence in the kitchen at this hour. But he finds the words before I do.

'You wish to see how I prepare the master's breakfast?'

I nod. 'And I wanted to see Ann, my servant girl.'

'Oh, Ann,' he says. 'She is already gone to find her brother.' His eyes roll over me, up and down my body in such a slow and insolent way, I know I must assert myself. As his mistress-to-be. Before it is too late.

'Very well,' I look at the floor, willing myself to turn away, ascend the stairs, find the library. But his voice is like a strange narcotic to me. All those memories of France, of love, of ungovernable passion. All of it rushing back, as he speaks with his soft loose lips. As his dark eyes rove so candidly across my breasts.

'I am sorry, Mademoiselle Acton.' His eyes lift to my face. 'I was too rude about the English.'

'You were right, in part.' I force myself to meet and hold his gaze. 'We are not taught to cook, only to amuse gentlemen with our singing and piano playing. I ran a school for many years, for private ladies of means. I sorely regret that I did not teach them to cook.'

His heavy-lidded eyes open a little wider. Then he jabs a finger at me. 'You English had the best food, the best dishes, in the world. A long time before the French. And then ...' He shrugs. 'Your bread is full of poison now. Your coffee is an abomination.'

'I was in France, fifteen years ago,' I say, speaking in a voice clipped tight to smother any wistfulness. 'The food was very good and I learnt much about your use of herbs, your appreciation of delicate flavours, how you use olive oil and lemons.'

His face is suddenly alight in the dimness, as if a candle has been placed inside his skull. 'If I had known I would not have been so rude to you. Most English ladies ...' He throws up his hands but his eyes have acquired a new lustre.

'They all want you to cook saddle of mutton with gravy?'

'*Vraiment!* Always saddle of mutton, always with gravy, always with cayenne. And so I come here,' he points at the ceiling and smiles. 'And the master says I can make any dish I want, but one day a week I must cook currie.' He gives another expansive shrug.

'You do not favour currie or food from the Orient?'

'It kills the tongue. How can you enjoy an elegant flavour – like chervil or bay – if you eat currie?'

'You may be right,' I say, thinking how peculiar it is that talking to Louis is so much more enjoyable than talking to Mother or Mrs Thorpe. Snatches of my dream come back to me ... the sweet sticky scent of splitting figs ... Louis ... I swallow quickly, as if to swallow down the self-disgust that accompanies such a perverted dream.

'There exist very old books on English cuisine,' he continues. 'Gone now, but my last master had some. Written by English ladies. Ladies who would rather cook than paint a silly picture or play badly a tune upon the pianoforte.'

'And if I am more like these ladies, will you permit me to come into your kitchen?'

He pauses, his full lips pouting as he thinks. 'London ladies do not do this,' he says at length. 'But if you will watch me, I will teach you.'

'Very well,' I say, thinking of the dinner he cooked the previous evening, the sauces of cream and wine – each suffused with a different herb: thyme, sorrel, parsley, tarragon. Each sauce had opened like a flower upon my tongue, one flavour floating into another. Until Mother kicked me beneath the table, forcing me to swallow my food expeditiously and with none of the contemplation or reverence it deserved. Of course the dinner was excessive, each dish flaunting its own convoluted brilliance. And yet, those flavours unrolling in my mouth ... the soup, like green velvet ... the sippets, golden and with perfect crunch ... the milky-white sweetness of a mousse as light as suds. Hardly surprising I could not sleep!

'And if the master does not wish it?' He raises one black eyebrow.

'Mr Arnott knows of my culinary interests,' I reply, and my voice seems to flounce coquettishly, so that I barely recognise it as my own. 'What time should I return?'

'I will show you Potage Bonne Femme.' He wipes his hands on his apron in a gesture of exuberance, as if he would like to begin my lesson this very minute. 'No one makes soup like a Frenchman. Come at midday. I will be waiting.'

Only as I climb the stairs to the library do I realise how foolish I have been. I shove the thought away. Just one lesson, I tell myself. All the better to understand the workings of my future kitchen and the temperament of my future chef. My own words convince me and when Edwin asks, over a fashionably late breakfast, if Mother and I would care to take a carriage through Hyde Park, I ask if I may have a half-hour to watch his chef prepare a French soup ... *in order to better understand the workings of his kitchen that I may manage it to my very best abilities.*

His brow furrows briefly, then he nods and says, 'If you think that would be beneficial, my dear, although it is rather hot and dirty down there.' Mother protests, her knuckles white upon her knife and fork, until Edwin says, 'My daughter and her husband are dining here this evening, Mrs Acton, so Louis is unlikely to want dear Eliza in his kitchen for more than a few minutes. Just long enough for her to feel at ease – as mistress here.' He raises his voice on the word *mistress* and Mother puffs pink with pride and stops her scowling protestations.

When midday comes, and Edwin and Mother have left for their carriage tour, I find Louis in the kitchen, inspecting a delivery of carrots and parsnips. He throws a clean apron at me and, without a single word of welcome, begins his instruction.

'The stock must never boil. Only simmer. You English are boiling everything.'

I nod curtly and say, a little snappishly, 'Yes, yes, but tell me how you made those sauces last night.'

He looks up, surprised. 'A fine dish can stop time, eh?'

A small sigh escapes from me, and he seems to understand it for he frowns and asks, 'You were not able to – to concentrate on my flavours? You were not able to groan with the bliss of the moment? To enjoy the tingle and joy on your tongue?'

I laugh. 'They were exceptionally good sauces.'

He shakes his head so vigorously drops of sweat fly from his hair. 'No, no! Not *good*. They were divine. They had rhythm, balance. Like music. Like the very greatest music.'

I think of how the flavours had unfolded, one after another, how each one had brought to mind a scene, an image, a memory, as if in that one moment I had travelled to and fro through my own past. Until the toe of Mother's slipper had prodded angrily at my calf.

'When you eat my sauces, you feel as if you are sucking the very bones of life, eh?' His eyes flare in the gloom of the kitchen. 'But you feel also the joy of being an animal, eh?'

I want to say there was too much food, that we left stuffed to suffocation. But the passion of him mesmerises me and I can only nod.

'You English have only one sauce. Butter. Always butter. But I have many. And each one will stop time so that, for one minute, you live truly in your body and soul.' He pauses and knocks his fist on his chest. 'That is my art. To give joy and life, even as Death snaps his jaws.'

He leans over and, before I have time to move away, his thumb brushes my cheek. The sensation is like lightning. As if his thumb has sent a shower of scarlet sparks through my body.

'Kitchen dirt,' he explains simply. 'Now, the soup. The secret to a Potage Bonne Femme is fresh sorrel leaves, with a little sugar to balance the sharpness. And parsley root, plenty of it, added to the stock. Egg yolks and cream, beaten in at the very end. And you must use only a silver spoon.'

I try to focus on his words, his *lesson*, but my body is still trembling from his touch, the lightning heat of it. From somewhere I hear the sharp clang of a pan lid dropping upon the flagstones. My eyes widen and blink, like those of someone jettisoned from a trance. What am I doing down here? What on earth was I thinking? Dazed, I turn and mumble an excuse. I quicken my pace, hurry up the steps, ascend two flights of stairs, find myself a chair in Mr Arnott's library. My body shakes and my mouth is as dry as sawdust. In my craven mind's eye, Louis leaps before me. Disrobed. His loins as smooth and brown as the shell of a hazelnut. I shake my head with all the force I can muster. No, No, No! It must not be. It cannot be. I look frantically round the room, seeking out something. But what? A key, I think. I want the key to lock tight this Pandora's Box.

'Eliza, whatever are you doing?' Mother is at the door, removing her bonnet and frowning at me.

'Bonne Femme,' I croak. 'Potage Bonne Femme.' I put my head in my hands and start to weep.

Chapter Thirty-Eight

Ann

Little White Lies

We returned to Bordyke House earlier than expected. Miss Eliza was feeling unwell, showing all the signs of a fever, and Ma'am was most anxious to get her home.

As I lie in our little attic room, I tell Hatty of my London adventures. She is only interested in wedding talk, but I want to tell her of Jack's master and his place of work, how white and shining clean it was. And of all the filth and vermin of the London streets and of how the footmen flirted with me and how I felt nothing for them, although the kitchen maids said any footman would be a fine catch. All this I say, but she can only ask, 'Has she a ring?' and 'Did a London seamstress visit for the making of a wedding dress?'

Finally, the talk peters out and I turn over to go to sleep. That is when she springs a most peculiar question upon me.

'Why does Miss Eliza favour you so, Ann?'

'She doesn't,' I say, surprised. 'I am her only servant, that's all.'

'No,' says Hatty. ''Tis more than that. Talking to you of poems, making you from scullery maid to kitchen maid so quick, buying you new boots with leather soles.'

'I had no boots,' I say softly. I do not say that my appearance shamed Miss Eliza, that it reflected poorly on Bordyke House.

Hatty ignores me and carries on. 'And the Reverend Thorpe coming to discuss you. And you going to Mr Arnott's London house rather than me who has been two years with Ma'am who is mistress here.'

'I suppose it's because I may be going to London too,' I say, keeping my voice gentle so as not to hurt Hatty's feelings.

'No, something else is at play,' she says, decisive. 'I seen how she looks at you. It's not normal.'

I feel a strange thing when she says this. Confusion and pleasure – rolled up like a hedgehog, soft and prickly at the same time.

'How do you mean?' I regret the question as soon as it's out. For Miss Eliza is mine and I do not want her tarnished by Hatty's jealous words.

'It just ain't normal that a lady would favour someone like you. And so soon, so quick.'

I know nothing of how ladies treat their servants so cannot reply. But part of me is overjoyed – *I am special to her! And*

Hatty has seen it too! I hug my knees to my chest beneath the thin sheet, my lips curling into a smile.

'It ain't normal,' repeats Hatty.

'Maybe,' I say, very tentative, very quiet, 'it's because she has no little ones of her own.'

Hatty snorts into the darkness.

'Or maybe she feels sorry for me,' I say. 'For having a father with one leg and no – no mother.'

'I think it's strange, that's all.' Hatty rolls over, very heavy, so that the frame of her bed grunts and groans. And then all goes quiet. And I listen to my untruth about Mam echo in my wicked ears. A lie begets a lie, I think to myself. But then that other voice – the wicked one – pops into my head telling me it's not a bad lie, just a lie of convenience.

I close my eyes and listen to the wind stirring in the trees outside. A lie of convenience ... Mam had a word for lies like that. Little white lies, she called them. Lies that never hurt anyone. I screw my eyes up tight and a picture moves across my inner eye: Mam, sleeves rolled up, arms plunging in and out of the stream as she washes Pa's clothes. I'm sitting beside her, perched on an eel trap, scraping mud off dirty clothes with a sharp-edged flint while sunlight scatters all around us. 'Little white lies, my dearest one, are always forgiven by God,' she says. And her smile catches me and holds me, like a bag of softest silk. 'If they make life more bearable for others, they are white lies and nothing more.'

My eyes snap open. Hatty is breathing from the back of her throat and shifting on her mattress. Outside a barn owl screeches. Mam and all the ghostlands of my past go as quick as they came. But her words cling on. Whose life is made more bearable when I pretend Mam is dead? The attic sours around me. I drag back Hatty's talk of how Miss Eliza favours me. But it's too late. The words that cheered me a few minutes ago have lost their shine – for I have seen and felt my own wickedness.

I push my hands together, press them hard against my chest and close my eyes. 'Dear God, forgive my untruths and have mercy on me. Make Miss Eliza better and take away her fever. Make her the happiest woman that ever lived. Make Mam better too and take Pa from the ale so that I may stay with Miss Eliza ... Make it so I have no need of lying, Lord. Amen.'

CHAPTER THIRTY-NINE

Eliza

SWAN'S EGG EN SALADE

I soon grow tired of feigning fever – my disposition is by nature a restless one – so when Mother flounces into my room announcing jubilantly that Father has written from Calais and intends to do everything possible to attend my wedding, I know the time for honesty is upon me.

I draw breath and smooth at the eiderdown, inviting her to sit beside me. 'Mother, there is something you must know.'

She sweeps past and tugs the curtains back, so that buttery light falls in neat squares upon the floorboards. 'Your dear father has it all planned. He shall slip aboard a ship he knows, where no questions will be asked. We must be very careful that none of his creditors hear.' She pauses and inspects my face in the light. 'Why, you look much better, my dear. It was the London air and the foul city water, I'm quite sure. You never were a strong child. Perhaps I shall buy him a hat with an especially broad brim. What d'you think, my dear?'

'Mother, there is to be no wedding. I have broken off my engagement with Mr Arnott.' Silence falls over the room. I stare at my hands twisting white in my lap. Exactly as they had when I broke the news to Edwin in his drawing room. The words had blurted from me then, just as now: *Edwin, I cannot marry you.* He had asked – in a voice flat with stoic disappointment – for an explanation. As he had every right to. And I had given him one. For didn't he deserve to know? He had shown me nothing but kindness and he deserved to see my wilful, contrary self, to hear its brag, to know its restive spirit.

'I cannot marry Mr Arnott.' My hands knot and unknot. Mother stares at me, astonished. Then she frowns and says, 'You still have fever, Eliza. I will send Hatty for Doctor Collins immediately.' She moves towards the door, her tongue clicking with irritation.

'I have told Mr Arnott. That is why we left his house with such urgency, the illness was a ruse that suited us both. I'm sorry.'

She stops and turns, the lids of her eyes blinking rapidly, her face pleated in confusion. 'Not because of . . . ?'

I wait for her to say Susannah's name. But she doesn't. Instead she reaches for the bedpost, a soft whimper gurgling from her throat.

I get out of bed and go to her, but she backs away, her face hardening, her mouth a pout of wilful intent. 'Explain yourself,' she says, her hand gripping harder at the bedpost so that it resembles the claw of an old hen.

I take a long breath, then climb back into bed and pull the eiderdown up to my chin. I have a sudden need to be swaddled, to feel the muffle and warmth of my bed linen. 'Yes, in part because of her. Of course I didn't tell him that. But there are other reasons. More pressing reasons.' Mother visibly relaxes, then knots her face again and waits.

'I could not be the Mrs Arnott he wanted. I have inside me ...' I pause and try to recall the words I used with Edwin. He had seemed to understand, had nodded with an aura of sympathy. As if he too were familiar with the throbbing sense of purpose that afflicts me. But Mother ... she will never understand.

'And what exactly do you have inside you?' she prompts, her eyebrows shooting into her hairline. 'What can be so important your family must suffer for it?'

'No one is suffering. Catherine and Anna have excellent positions in good families and Edgar is making his fortune in Mauritius. And Mary is contented and well married. My marrying Mr Arnott would never have saved Father from his creditors.'

'And what of me? Serving boarders with my spinster daughter lurking in the kitchen like a miscreant!'

I sigh and push away the eiderdown. Now is not the time to hide behind its quilted floral panels. Now is the time for honesty. 'I realised, in Mr Arnott's kitchen, that there are things I must do. Things I need to do. That I cannot do as Mrs Arnott, but can do as – as Eliza Acton.'

Mother snorts and pouts. I ignore her and continue, like a cook that must butcher a hog however hard, however unwieldy. 'The English are losing their ability to cook, to understand good food. Not the fancy French food of London kitchens and clubs, but the food we've eaten for centuries. Bread, properly baked. Pies, properly raised. You heard Mr Arnott's daughter ... she has never set foot in her own kitchen. Imagine a generation from now. We shall be at the mercy of overpriced Frenchmen and the foul contaminated food of the street.'

'Don't preach at me, Eliza. Where is your feminine humility?' Her hand loosens on the bedpost, as if her body wilts beneath the weight of my words.

'I feel as if my book of recipes has never been more needed than it is now.'

'And so you chose your foolish book over marriage to Mr Arnott.' She shakes her head in disbelieving fury.

'It is not a foolish book. It is an important book that I have slaved over for months, that I love almost like a husband. Why should I give it up to spend time being measured for dresses and hats? What good is that?'

'Very well, Eliza. But your sisters shall hear of this. I shall tell them how you refused to stoop to marriage. That one day, there will be a kitchen book bearing your – our – name in circulation and that this book is the reason they are governesses and not the ladies they were bred to be.' She sniffs and draws herself up. 'And I will tell Mary too.'

I stiffen. 'Let me write to Mary. I can explain it myself.'

'Oh no, no, no.' She prods the air with an angry finger. 'I

see no reason why our little agreement with Mary should be breached. I will write to Mary. And if she chooses to write to you one day, then so be it.'

I close my eyes and hear the sharp clack of the latch. Mother's footsteps disappear in the direction of her chamber. My pulse is racing so I lie very still and listen to the crows collecting on the chimney pots, the whinny of a horse, the cry of a barrow boy, the slow chime of the church bells. Mother's fury, her disappointment, is as I expected. And now it's spent, my mind calms and my pulse slows. I think of my book – *our* book, for it is no less Ann's than mine – and imagine how it will be, how it will feel in my hands. In my mind's eye I see it in kitchens, smeared with butter and flour, sticky with sugar and fruit, fingerprinted and stained and ringed with oil, blood, the cracked sheen of egg white. I see it in bookshops and bedrooms, in drawing rooms and parlours. Why not? I hear it discussed at table, over breakfast, over luncheon. I hear it talked of in butcher's shops and fishmongers, in the gilded kitchens of gentlemen's clubs and in public houses. Why not?

A sudden sense of urgency whips through me. Time is running out. We have barely touched on soufflés and ome-lettes. And what of baked puddings? Or milk puddings? And syrups, vinegars, liqueurs? And so much more to do on forcemeats, entremets, shellfish, potted meats. And swans' eggs! We haven't a single decent recipe for swans' eggs. I must write to everyone I know, request their favourite recipes, attempt them in my own kitchen. My thoughts swerve back to swans' eggs. Such splendid things – their whites are purer, more translucent than those of any other egg. Perhaps their boiled yolks might be mixed with firm fresh butter, essence of anchovies, minced herbs, even a chopped shallot. And then returned to their hard-boiled whites in softly beaten mounds. A swan's egg en salade, I think, smiling.

I had such a dish in France, all those years ago. Louis reminded me of those times too, of memories best kept locked away. Of feelings best kept locked away. I did not tell Edwin any of that, naturally. And nor do I want to think of it now. I want to think only of how I might recreate – and improve upon – a swan's egg en salade. What herbs might taste well? Tarragon? And perhaps a dash of cucumber vinegar ... And to follow? Something good and plain – and English! A pot of tender cutlets swimming in a sticky, meaty gravy, richly flavoured with life and death ... and everything that falls between ...

I throw back the covers, and leap from my bed. Outside the crows flap and shriek. Get up! Get up! Get up!

Yes, I reply. Work to do! Work to do! Work to do!

CHAPTER FORTY

Ann

A GOOD PLAIN IRISH STEW

I am in the scullery helping little Lizzie scour the pans with sand when I hear Miss Eliza in the kitchen, humming to herself. I poke my head round the door and she smiles at me.

'Ann,' she says, 'We have a busy day. Can you pump plenty of water and make a good bright fire, please.'

I do as she asks, lugging in pail after pail of water and heaping the stove with coal 'til my arms ache. She sits in her ladder-back chair, poring over her books. But books I do not recognise. 'Have you new books, Miss Eliza?'

'Yes, Ann,' she says, looking up with such a cheery expression I figure she must have had good news already. Perhaps her betrothal ring is coming today. But then she points at the books and says, 'These came from Mr Longman while we were in London. They are no longer printed and I do not know how he came by them for they are a hundred years old, but ...' She pauses with a triumphant smile ... 'They are by ladies.'

I tie on a clean apron and wonder why cookery books by ladies make her so cheery, particularly as she is soon to be mistress of a house where she won't need to go within a mile of the kitchen. As always she seems to read my small mind.

'What did you think of Mr Arnott's chef, Ann?'

'I thought he was a fine cook,' I say, not wanting to mention how oft he placed his stinking garlic hand upon my arse.

'Yes, indeed. But too fanciful for most households.' She taps at the cover of her notebook with a knuckle. 'Today I shall compile a list of all the people I know who might like to contribute a recipe to our book.'

'Oh?' I cannot hide my surprise, for how is she to complete her book in Mr Arnott's house? Is she to dismiss the loathsome Louis?

'And prepare yourself for new boarders, Ann. I shall be placing an advertisement today.'

'New boarders?' I echo, confused.

'I shall not be marrying Mr Arnott,' she says, very flat, so I cannot tell if she is sad or happy. 'Mother has taken to her bed, but my mind is made up.'

I stare at her, shocked. Why would she not want to marry a man as rich as Mr Arnott? Why would she not want servants and footmen at her beck and call?

'We have an important job to do, Ann. Our book must be completed and it will not be completed in Mr Arnott's house.'

'Can't you finish it now, and then be wed in the spring?' I ask, although I know it's not my place to ask such questions.

She shakes her head, most vigorous. 'No, no. Such a book as this will take ten years to test and write. It must be done properly. And by then I will be too old to wed.'

I am so flabbergasted I cannot reply. Ten years! She would rather spend ten years writing a book and be an old maid than be married with a fine London house and possibly a babby of her own? For a second it crosses my mind that *she* should be in the Kent County Lunatic Asylum. For surely she has gone quite mad?

And then she says something even more peculiar. 'Mr Arnott's chef has renewed my sense of purpose.' She lifts her eyes to the narrow window and adds, 'In so many ways.'

That odious, arse-groping French man? How can that be ... ? I frown so deeply she sees how bewildered and troubled I am. I wait for her to say *Close your mouth, Ann Kirby, and mind your own business.* But she doesn't. She says something most unexpected.

'As you know I spent some time in France. It was a difficult time for me. The happiest and the saddest of my life. Talking to Louis reminded me of ... of certain things that I cannot speak about ... but he helped me see how ill-prepared I am for marriage.' She pauses, her eyes stuck above my head so that I cannot tell if she is speaking to me or to the copper pans hanging from the ceiling. I think of her poems, the man who broke her heart. *God forbid that her heart still isn't mended after all these years ...*

And then she starts talking again and I can sense she is in

a chatty mood. 'Mr Arnott's chef thinks English ladies have lost all interest in the kitchen. He is right and nowhere is this more apparent than in London. They have been turned into silly little dolls. Mr Arnott's married daughter was a grave disappointment ... She could talk only of her new lace collar, the flock wallpaper she selected for her drawing room and other such fripperies. I do believe she has never set foot in her own kitchen!'

'But she did sing beautiful,' I say, for I had overheard her singing the evening she and her plump red husband came to dine.

'She was out of tune, toneless and without any expression,' says Miss Eliza, sharpish. 'But no one had the wit to tell her.'

'Oh,' I say, wondering if I should point out how pretty Mr Arnott's daughter was with her golden ringlets and her rouged cheeks. For it seems to me that Miss Eliza is being quite harsh on the poor lady.

'Mr Arnott's chef told me that London gentlemen prefer to eat out at private clubs and he intimated that his last mistresses have been entirely disinterested in his menus. Do you not see where this takes us, Ann?'

'No, not wholly ...' In truth I have no notion where this talk is going, for Miss Eliza is rarely so direct. It strikes me I should feel more disappointed than I do, for there will be no wedding. And I won't live in London, near Jack. But I feel more pleased than disappointed. I would have been sore pressed to look after Mam and Pa from London. And all those footmen and cooks handling my arse like it was a bag of turnips ... No thank you!

'The kitchen is a place where ladies used to reign, as queens,' she gestures at her new-old books in their scrappy bindings. 'We have relinquished that and now we are at the mercy of French chefs or scoundrels who ply their poisonous pies from the streets. I trust you didn't eat from the street in London, Ann?'

'Only a pickled herring, miss,' I reply, thinking of the chewy soused fish that had me gagging with its bones and vinegar.

'In London I heard of new foods being invented so that people no longer need to cook. Apparently there are factories along the banks of the Thames making powdered sauces and custards.' She pulls a face, like she's bitten into a rotten egg, but then her face lightens. 'It is our mission, Ann, to change this. Nothing is as nutritious or wholesome as proper food cooked in the kitchen.'

I nod, but in a blank, not-understanding way. Why does she always include Ma'am when she talks of her book? Even today, when Ma'am has taken to her bed, she speaks of *our*. Yet even I can see that Ma'am is not best pleased by *the book*.

'You and Ma'am will print a fine book.'

I pick up the water buckets and am just leaving the kitchen, when Miss Eliza calls out, 'My mother is nothing to do with it.'

She's talking to herself again, I think, continuing towards the scullery where Lizzie's wooden pattens are clacking up and down on the stone.

Her voice follows me, higher and louder now. 'When I say *our*, I mean you and I, Ann. Not my mother.'

I stop in my tracks, frowning. *Our* mission? *Our* book? She means *me*? The stiff iced air of the scullery is like a blast to my senses. I must move to keep warm so I start pushing and pulling at the water pump but all the while my heart is dancing.

And when I return, my shoulders hunched forward from the weight of the water buckets, I ask, 'What recipe are we to try today?' My voice bursts from me so loud and strong, Miss Eliza blinks in surprise.

'My sense of purpose must be contagious,' she laughs.

And I laugh too, for I feel as if I've swallowed a bushel of happiness and it is flooding out of me, out of every pore in my skin. 'Oh, it is, Miss Eliza, it is!'

'Well, let us perfect an Irish stew, shall we?' She motions at the dresser. 'Bring down the brown Nottingham jar from the top shelf and then you must run to market for some mutton cutlets. We shall show everyone how to make a good plain family dinner.'

As I reach for the jar, the ache in my arms and shoulders vanishes and I feel as light as a lark. I am to be with Miss Eliza for ten years, working on *our* book!

'And swans' eggs,' she adds. 'See if they have swans' eggs today.'

'Yes, miss!' And my smile is so broad my cheeks smart from it.

CHAPTER FORTY-ONE

Eliza

JEWISH ALMOND PUDDING

For two weeks the house is calm and undisturbed. Every day Ann takes our tested recipes on a tray to Mother's room. Hatty collects them, the soup bowls and platters invariably as clean as a whistle. Mother's *shattered nerves* have clearly had no effect on her appetite.

Eventually she appears, pale and tight-lipped. She comes to the kitchen, her head held very high and her eyes refusing to meet mine. 'I need a little broth for dinner, but nothing more,' she says.

'We have a new boarder arriving on Monday.' I brace myself for a histrionic display of nerves at this pertinent reminder of our future.

She pauses, then sniffs. 'Who?'

'A Jewish lady, come to take the waters.'

'I am sure you can manage without me.' She sniffs again, as if to remind me that her nervous frailty is all my fault.

'You might enjoy her company. Her name is Lady Montefiore and I believe her to be very well connected.'

Mother's head tilts and her eyes brighten for a second. Like a bird that has spotted the writhing end of a worm. 'Oh well. If I must.'

'She's written to tell us what she can and cannot eat. I shall need more money to buy oil, bitter almonds and orange-flower water.'

'There is no more money, as you well know.' She shoots me a look of such bitterness I turn swiftly back to Lady Montefiore's letter – thick watermarked paper, expensive ink from an expensive nib, perfect copperplate.

'We will be reimbursed.' I pick up the letter and read out the opening lines: *'We Jews are forbidden to mingle butter or other preparations of milk or cream with meat at any meal, so oil is much used in our cookery of fish, meat and vegetables. Although these restrictions are not rigidly observed by many Jews in this country, I follow them. I will gladly reimburse you and I shall bring my own Jewish almond pudding which will suffice as a sweet dish while I am boarding with you.'*

'She is bringing her own pudding?' Mother splutters.

'Nor can she eat pork, shellfish, hare, rabbit or swan,' I add, my eyes scanning the remainder of her letter.

Mother gives another haughty sniff then leaves, closing the door with unnecessary force so that it shakes in its frame. I glance at Ann and think how it might have been if she didn't know her place so well, how we might have shared a rebellious and irreverent chuckle at Mother's expense. As sisters might. As friends might. But Ann is too dutiful, too submissive to overstep herself like that. A shame, I think. For there are times now when my melancholy rears up and I am sorely in need of a friend. A life with Mr Arnott would have put paid to loneliness. Isn't that what marriage is for? A chance to be rid of loneliness? Have I made a terrible blunder?

As I'm pondering these thoughts, Mother returns, her chin wobbling.

'Your father educated you to be a lady, a wife to someone exactly like Mr Arnott.' A sob breaks in her throat. 'And now I must write to John and tell him it is not to be, that he must stay in those vile lodgings in Calais, that we must continue taking in boarders, that your sisters must remain as glorified servants. How could you do this, Eliza? After all he spent on your schooling ...'

I busy myself chopping sage leaves. *Thy heart, thy heart is cold as stone, and feels but for itself alone* ... Old words of mine rise up, are borne away, replaced ... *giant clouds of shame, in dark'ning masses, clust'ring came* ... Until my head reels and I must lay down the chopper before I draw my own blood.

'How could you?' she repeats. 'After all I've been through. I have only risen from my bed because today is the anniversary of Lucy's death.'

Every organ inside me shrinks and cringes with guilt. How callous I am! I have been so bound up in myself, my *mission*, I have given no thought to Mother's pain. I put my hand upon her arm but she shakes me off.

Briefly my mind flits back, more than twenty years. That terrible piercing shriek that I mistook for the keen of a squabbling gull. Mother running down the stairs shaking Lucy as if she were a ragdoll. Lucy's head lolling. The two dark recesses of her eyes. Her tiny arms hanging limply at her sides. The nursemaid running behind, whimpering with fear, her feet slipping on the painted stairs. Then me running like a hound to fetch Papa from the brewery, even as a stitch split my ribcage asunder. We were too late. When we returned Mother had Lucy so tightly pressed to her we couldn't tell if the baby breathed or not. And as Mother's tears ran over the baby's head, the nursemaid stood and stared, yellow trails of vomit on her apron, her cap, the sleeves and cuffs of her dress.

'You could have saved Lucy,' gulps Mother. 'You were with her. You could have stopped the nursemaid from feeding her enough laudanum to sink a ship.'

'No, Mother,' I say softly. 'I was twelve. It was a horrid accident, a mistake. Let's not dwell on it now.' The memory has returned so vividly it seems as though my baby sister's vomit lingers in the air.

Mother's upper lip trembles, her chin shakes. I take her hand, veined and wrinkled now, and feel a sudden sympathy for her. This was not the life my father promised. An image of our Ipswich home swims into my head: the huge library of books, the prints and gilt-framed looking glasses, the velvet curtains, the silver service and candelabra, the mahogany furniture inlaid with mother-of-pearl, the

Turkish rugs. All gracing the homes of other more fortunate people now. I had the chance to return Mother to that life. And I turned it down.

Her face sags. 'How can we live together, like this, if I cannot forgive you?'

'You must. And you must have faith in my book. It will be our salvation, I promise.'

'Oh, your wretched books!'

'He would not have married me anyway, Mother. The truth of my situation would have come out.'

'Everyone else manages it. You are stubborn and belligerent, Eliza.' She puts her handkerchief to the corner of her eye. 'Perhaps I will go and live with your brother in Mauritius.'

I know she says this to punish me, so I say nothing. I steer her to her bedchamber and give the bolster a good pounding, but she insists on sitting at her dressing table where she demands paper, pen and inkpot. I beg that *I* may write to Papa and explain my reasons for remaining unmarried. But she insists on writing in her own hand.

All my recent cheer fades as I watch her struggling to pull the cork from the inkpot. She seems so small, withered almost, the skin on her face hanging in leathery folds, her fingers gnarling at the joints. I have aged her, I think. I have pushed her to the brink of her own grave.

'You may as well have your books of verse back. No need to hide them now you are to remain a spinster.'

'Thank you. Where are they?' I know full well where they are – hidden in her wardrobe, behind her good winter coat with the fur collar. I pile the albums, annuals and books into my arms and feel as if a limb has been mysteriously returned to me.

As I descend the stairs to the kitchen, my thoughts turn to Lady Montefiore and the Jewish almond pudding she will bring. We shall need other puddings, of course. Sweet dishes made without cream or butter or milk. Perhaps made with rich amber syrups instead. And perhaps I can make an almond cream to substitute for milk in soufflés, custards, blancmanges. Blanched almonds, pounded and mixed with boiling water, then wrung through a tammy cloth. I can hear Ann in the kitchen – the comforting chop, chop, chop of a blade on a wooden board as she hews herbs. Their green fragrance reaches me like balm. My spirits lift, my step quickens. And I can think of nowhere I would rather be than in my own kitchen with its endlessly altering perfumes, its familiar sounds that are as music to my ears, its warmth and daily rhythms that mark the rising and setting of the sun and the turning of the seasons.

Take one capacious kitchen, I think to myself, add a brisk fire and ten well-lined copper pans, throw in five moulds, seven wooden spoons, a good set of steel blades, and one competent and devoted assistant. Strew over a variety of gravy strainers, dredgers, sieves, strainers, nippers, rolling pins, chopping boards and paste brushes ...

CHAPTER FORTY-TWO

Ann

DRIPPING

The house keeps on quiet, with Hatty creeping around and Ma'am in her bed and little Lizzie looking at us with her big frightened eyes. Knowing there's to be no wedding has been a grave disappointment to everyone except me and Miss Eliza. Even the Reverend Thorpe and Mrs Thorpe came visiting with their condolences, their sharp noses twitching like dogs after a scent. There was no one home to see them, but Hatty took the message and said she near burst into tears on the doorstep. Afterwards she came to the kitchen, wiping her eyes on the corner of her apron and asking why there was to be no wedding. I didn't answer, just shook my head. It's not my place to share Miss Eliza's confidences. Not even with Hatty.

One afternoon I slip out and deliver Jack's bag of preserves to Pa. I thought to find him in the alehouse but to my surprise he's at the cottage, planting out seedlings. Nor is there any stink of beer upon him. Just the smell of autumn smoke from all the brushwood being burnt along the fields. I'm even more taken aback when I push open the door and see how spick and span the cottage is. The mattress has been sewn up where the straw was leaking out and a line of moleskins is pegged across the floor, so I know he's been skinning the creatures for a few coins. Septimus bounds up from the hearth, rubbing his wet snuffling snout into my skirts.

I tell Pa there won't be money coming from Jack for a bit. He sits upon the turned earth, tamping the last seedling into the ground, and says, very solemn: 'I'm giving up the drink, Ann. I'll ask Reverend Thorpe for another chance.'

'I don't think he'll want you,' I say, glum.

'I've given up the poaching too.' He gives an indignant pout. 'Mugridge said he'll let me off this time but if he catches me again, he'll shoot me with his own hand.'

An idea comes to me, like a clap of thunder. I crouch down beside him and take his muddy hand in mine.

'I could bring you the candle stumps and the bones and the meat dripping we don't use. Miss Eliza is most frugal but there's always leftovers and I learned in London that most cooks sell these bits and bobs and pocket the money for themselves.'

'How would it work?' He looks at me, all curious.

'I bring them here, you melt down the stumps for new candles, and pick the dripping clean for potting. Then they're sold at market.'

'Have you the time?'

I shrug. 'We can try it. And I'll have a few pennies from my wages, although the rest is for Mam's nurses.'

He opens Jack's sack and brings out a jar of pickled onions, a bottle of mushroom catsup, three orange crumpets now hard and stiff as tree bark and the broken remains of a spun sugar flower. 'A feast,' he says, rubbing his muddy hands together.

'Miss Eliza likes me,' I say, feeling a flush of pride. 'Even the other housemaid has noticed that I am ... special to her.'

'Rich people don't ever care for their servants – they care only for themselves and their money.' He puts a strand of spun sugar into his whiskery mouth and sucks it. 'She may think you can chop a nice onion, but she won't be thinking you're *special*. And nor will she be *liking* you.'

'But she talks of *our* book and *us* working *together* for ten years.'

'She treats you well because you're a good hard worker, not because you're special to her. If a better worker came along wanting less money, she'd drop you like a hot cinder and take the new lass.' He leans towards me and smacks a beardy kiss upon my cheek. But I pull away, hurt.

A new thought pops into my head. 'She's not like other rich folks. She just turned down marriage to a man as rich as a king.' I'm determined not to be infected by Pa's doubt.

There's a silence and I hear the mice scratching and scurrying in the thatch.

'Likely he wasn't so kind, or so rich.'

'What I think is that she wants to live like a man.'

'Like a man?'

'She wants her own money, not a gentleman's money. She doesn't want people telling her what to do.' I pause and look up at the sky, huge and white today, with a single crow beating and cutting above us. 'She's been teaching me about poems,' I add, hugging my knees to my chest as her fine words flow through my head ... *There is no joy on earth to me, where thou art not* ... 'You see, Pa. She's not like other ladies.' *And she doesn't treat me like a servant either* I think to myself.

'Well I never.' Pa rubs at his wiry beard in a thoughtful way, as if he doesn't know what to make of Miss Eliza. 'Sometimes I wonder if all women ain't a bit daft in the head. All, excepting you, Ann.'

She is what I want to be, I think. *She is strong and true. She has courage and honesty.* I stand up, brush the earth from my skirts and offer Pa my hand. He has perfected a means of raising himself from a seated position to a standing position, without using anything to support him. He shows me this with such pride, my heart swells up.

All the way back to Bordyke House I think about how I can help Pa. Winter is coming. I can feel its edge on the wind, its snap in the broken branches beneath my feet. Will melting down candle stumps and gouging the marrow from old bones be enough? Can he turn a living from a few mole-skins? At least Mam will be warm and dry and well fed in her big fancy asylum. And for that I gratefully offer God a few words of thanks, my palms pushed hard together and my eyes skewed to Heaven.

CHAPTER FORTY-THREE

Eliza

MINCEMEAT PUDDING

As I put my notes and recipes in order I feel my book flutter into life. It is a most peculiar sensation, as if there were something at the heart of it, a pulse or a soul.

With life comes responsibility: I must lay out plans for my book as a parent plans for the arrival of a child. I put a clean sheet upon the table, dip my pen into the inkpot and write *People to Whom I Shall Send My Book*. I place a ruler beneath the title and underline it not once but twice, all the while thinking *it must go to those with influence*. I start my list with a single name: Charles Dickens. He writes regularly in the *Evening Chronicle* and I sense that he and I share a feeling of compassion for the less fortunate. He shall be the first to receive a signed copy.

Recipes now come in the post regularly, for I have spent
several days writing to both acquaintances and strangers,
requesting their most favoured dishes. I lay out the newest
donations: a potage of pearl sago, veal stock, eggs and
cream from Sweden; an apple cake and custard sauce from
Germany; an Arabic recipe for pilau rice in which the fowl
is boiled almost to rags. Oh, and an unsolicited recipe from
my little married sister, Mary, that I have quite overlooked.
Her cramped lettering is all angles and points, and she has
had the audacity to name her own dish the *Good Daughter's
Mincemeat Pudding*. Laughter of the unkind and sarcastic sort
bubbles up in me. Clearly Mother has been writing to her,
bemoaning my *bad daughter* traits. Compared to me, Mary is
a veritable angel.

Although I have not seen Mary for a decade, I can recall
clearly her pink complexion, her brown hair peeled calmly
back from her face, her serene haughty manner. Of course
she may be grey-haired and flustered now, with a face full
of broken veins. But still, she is married and living an irre-
proachable life of compliance. While I am unwed and have
published *divulging* poems under my own name, and now
keep myself buried in a kitchen with servants. And worse,
far worse, I have rejected the hand of a man who could have
plucked me (and the entire Acton family) from the ignominy
in which I live as a scribbling *cook*.

I run my eye over Mary's recipe. It is a simple, wholesome
one, thick layers of bread and mincemeat baked in a creamy
custard. I am just about to file the page with my other donated
dishes, when I notice my sister has written something on the

back. I turn it over and see her spider-leg writing amidst ink
blots and smears. To my surprise it is a note, hurriedly writ-
ten, I suppose from its inky messiness.

My dear Eliza,

*Now that a great many years have passed and I have a
fine brood of children, I think we should renew our sisterly
relations. I know my insistence on discretion lies counter
to your belief in honesty, but I think the time has come for
us to meet halfway, in a compromise of sorts. This is all
the more pertinent now that you have chosen to remain
unwed. Of course, Mother may disagree or disapprove. But
without Papa her opinion carries less significance. And so
I would like to invite you to Suffolk. Does the latter half of
November suit you?*

*I trust you will not take umbrage at my title for the
mincemeat pudding recipe . . . it is meant only to amuse. So
change the title as you will.*

Your sister,
Mary

I read her letter a second time and then a third. For I know
Mary's earnest ways, and this decision will not have been
made lightly. She is pitying my unmarried plight, I think,
knowing I will never experience maternal joy or familial
bliss, that I will be – for ever – only half a woman. Or less.
The mere ghost of a woman.

But buried in her words is an olive branch, as if she reaches to me, begs my forgiveness. An odd feeling of sadness and regret rushes over me. For all that has passed and gone and can never be returned. And then I taste something else – at the very back of my throat. Anticipation. Yearning. I write and accept her invitation, and then I force it from my mind for Lady Judith Montefiore is due tomorrow and I have dishes to plan and ingredients to buy.

In the kitchen Ann is making quince marmalade, stirring ceaselessly at the pan. Perfumed steam hangs in the kitchen, collecting on the glass panes of the window, trickling down the cold northern wall. A fly buzzes over the sugarloaf where Ann has been scraping and rolling fresh sugar crystals.

'Tonight we shall serve a roast beef heart stuffed with a veal forcemeat,' I say. 'You'll need to pound the veal until perfectly smooth. It must be quite smooth, you understand.'

I wait for Ann's assent but all I hear is the scrape of the spoon on the bottom of the pan and the soft bubbling of the quinces.

'If you can find some mild, finely grained turnips at the market, we shall serve them alongside the heart. But be sure they're not woody or tunnelled by root maggots.'

Still she does not speak. Nor nod. Nor give any indication she has heard me. 'Is something amiss, Ann?'

'In London, the cooks are given the candle stumps and the fat from the dripping pans, and the old bones and pelts too,' she blurts. 'And I would like the same.'

I am so startled at her outburst, I take a long breath. 'You know full well that we make broth from our bones and dripping from the old fat. You may take the feathers, hides and pelts, if you must.'

'And the candle stumps?' she asks in a most determined way. 'Whatever for?'

'My father will work them into new and sell them. My brother can't give money anymore, for his lodgings has increased.'

I run a few calculations in my head. I know that Ann spends no money on herself, not even for a lace collar or a few ribbons when the pedlars come to the back door. 'Where do all your wages go?' I ask gently.

She does not reply for several seconds. Then she says, all in a rush, 'My father needs new crutches.'

I unlock the metal money box and take out two florins, which leaves me a mere eleven shillings to feed Lady Montefiore. A little elegant economy will be required. Perhaps we should replace the veal forcemeat with a plain sage and onion ... or one of mushrooms. The field mushrooms are plentiful and flavoursome at the moment, mixed with a few wild ceps they could rival a veal forcemeat.

I pass her the florins.

She blushes scarlet. 'I'll pay you back, Miss Eliza.'

'From candle stumps and bone marrow? I doubt it.' My words come out more sharply than I intend and she flinches as if I have raised my hand to her. But Reverend Thorpe's words are repeating in my head ... and I cannot fathom where her wages are going. On her father's drink habit?

'We shall be tested to our culinary limits, but fortunately Lady Montefiore brings her own pudding. And it will do us no harm to cook to a budget,' I say, but Ann's face is crimson and she merely nods.

Lady Montefiore arrives in a rustling, clattering swirl of silk and jewels, and is swept to her rooms by Mother who introduces me very swiftly as 'my unmarried daughter, Eliza'. Previously, I was her 'dear daughter, Eliza'. But it seems I have been demoted. I put my apron back on, disappointed but determined not to care.

Later that evening Lady Montefiore sends word that she would like to see the cook. My heart jumps a beat. Her plates were returned quite clean, so we can't have broken any Jewish rules. But evidently she is unhappy. Did she notice the frugality of the ingredients? Is she to quiz me on the recipes? Perhaps she will demand we reimburse her.

She looks surprised when I appear in the dining room. 'Surely you are not the cook, Miss Acton?' Her thick black eyebrows rise up her forehead, as voluminously extravagant as a pair of darkly exotic caterpillars.

'I am, Lady Montefiore. Was the meal to your taste?'

'It was splendid. So light and fresh. English food is usually too heavy, all that meat soaked in gravy with liberal lashings of cayenne. But the apple and ginger soup was delicious, although it did not need a rice accompaniment in my opinion.' She gestures at the empty chair. 'Please sit and talk with me, Miss Acton.'

I take the chair with such a sense of relief I feel almost light-headed. She leans forward and looks at me closely, her head on an angle. 'Do you always cook?'

'Yes, although we do not speak of it. My mother prefers our boarders to think there is a professional chef in the kitchen.'

'Nonsense! There is no shame in cooking or eating. Indeed,

they are two of life's greatest pleasures.' She dabs neatly at her lips with the napkin, then scrutinises me again, as if I were a fascinating specimen of some rare breed. 'Can you hold a secret, Miss Acton?'

I nod, startled at this turn of the conversation.

She lowers her voice. 'My dream is to write a cookery book of Jewish dishes. I have started collating them, but it is slow and delicate work.'

'I too!' I say, enthralled at meeting someone with the same impudent ambition as me.

Her eyebrows shoot up her pale forehead again and lie there, beneath her tightly drawn hair that is blue-black like a mussel shell. 'Is that so? Well, we must share recipes. You served my pudding in a very clever manner. The puddle of blackcurrant syrup was well done. Did you taste my pudding?'

I flush and confess that a small crumb passed my lips.

'The important thing is that all the ingredients must be intimately blended, and the sugar must be thickly sifted over the entire pudding. I can write down the recipe if you would like?'

For the next twenty minutes, Lady Montefiore and I exchange recipes and cooking tips and talk keenly of the need for freshness and how best to maintain delicate flavours. Jewish food uses much fine olive oil, she tells me, and does not drown in butter or lard. The oil can be re-used, she says, promising to give me directions to her London oil merchant where I am assured of finding the greenest-goldest olive oil. We compare how best to cook fresh salmon so that its delicacy is preserved and we agree that salmon – which she tells me is often served cold in Jewish circles – is perhaps the finest of freshwater fish. We are so absorbed in conversation we do not hear Mother enter the room.

She coughs loudly and says, 'Was everything to your satisfaction, Lady Montefiore?'

'Your daughter and I are becoming the firmest of friends.' Lady Montefiore flashes such a dazzling smile Mother is quite disarmed.

When I return to the kitchen I feel as though I am gliding, like a swan, but on a vast meringue cushion of air. I grab my notebook and inkpot and jot down all Lady M has told me. She has promised to share her favourite dish – Jewish Smoked Beef. I feel a tingle of excitement in my fingertips, but then I remember how little money we have left. Enough for a thick flank of beef? I doubt it. Perhaps I shall fry rosy cubes of salmon in olive oil and serve it cooled … I cannot help thinking that a Mauritian chutney would make the perfect accompaniment to cold fried fish … And then I remember my sister's invitation, her olive branch. It has been the perfect day, I think, making no attempt to suppress the smile upon my face.

CHAPTER FORTY-FOUR

Ann

JUMBLES

Miss Eliza is in such good spirits and so pleased with Lady Montefiore, I take the chance to ask if I may have an extra hour's leave today. She lifts her head from her notebook, where she is always writing now, and says I may, but only if Lady Montefiore's meals are all prepared in advance.

'I've made a quart of almond milk,' I reply. 'And there is oxtail in the larder, ready for the gridiron. And poached quinces too.' I don't tell her of my sly addition to the poaching syrup: the hard black seeds of a cardamom pod, crushed and then strained so the eye will never know.

She blots at a gout of ink. 'I'm away for a few days at the end of the month, so Mother will need you here, even on your afternoon off.'

'Are you going visiting?' I ask, curious, for Miss Eliza never takes a day of leave.

'I'm going to my sister's.' Her eyes fall back to her notebook and her quill jabs, impatient, at the inkpot.

'Oh, to one of the governesses,' I say, for I know she has sisters who are governesses in grand houses.

'No,' she says, 'To stay with my sister, Mary.'

Mary? I've heard no mention of a *Mary*. I know of Catherine and Anna, both governesses. I've heard her speak of her brother, Edgar, who is in Mauritius. But no Mary.

'Does she live very far?' At the back of my mind I recall Miss Eliza mentioning, very curt, a married sister. A doctor's wife . . . Is she Mary?

'My sister lives in Suffolk,' she says, which is a surprise to me because Suffolk isn't far at all. 'Why don't you take the Jumble Biscuits for your father? They're too brown at the edges for Lady Montefiore.'

So I pack the Jumbles in a tin box with some windfall pears and start walking to the asylum, hoping I might get a ride along the way. The apple orchards and hop gardens are quiet now – the trees stripped bare and the hops cut to the ground. But the lanes are busy with labourers cutting the hedges with bills and slash hooks and clearing the ditches of old wains and rotten harrows and the rubbish left by the pickers and hoppers.

After much walking and two waggon rides I reach the gatehouse of the asylum. I give a shilling to the lodge keeper and tell him I have more for Mam's nurses. He looks a little mournful, as if I haven't given him enough, so I offer him a

Jumble which he takes and puts whole into his mouth. I can hear his molars crunching into it as he shuffles off.

When he returns, he has a nurse in tow. But she is neither Fran nor Cheek-Pincher. And there's no sign of Mam. He goes back into the gatehouse, leaving me with Mam's new nurse who has a coarse face and a forehead full of scars. She wears a dress of thick grey worsted with a chain of iron keys attached at the waistband, and stout thick-soled boots. I smile, polite, and tell her I'm here to see my mam, Mrs Kirby. And perhaps I can see Mam's doctor too. But the nurse doesn't return my smile. Her face is grim and pinched and she has her arms crossed tight over her chest. Quickly I offer her a Jumble.

She takes the Jumble and slips it in her apron pocket. 'Your mam ain't well,' she says.

'Not well?' I repeat, like a fool.

'She had a fall, 'tis all. But she can't get down the stairs. So 'tis best you come in January.'

As she says this, a queer shiver runs down my spine even though the day is mild and I'm wearing an old India shawl of Miss Eliza's that's good and warm.

'Can I see her?' I lift up my basket and point to the apples and pears that sit aside the tin of Jumbles.

The nurse shakes her head. 'No one is permitted to go inside. But I can take the basket to her and you can collect it in January.'

I look over her shoulder at the big grand building with its iron-framed windows. The afternoon sun falls, dappled, on its walls and windows. I think of Mam in there, all cosy, being looked after by a proper doctor. She is better there than in Pa's cottage where the winter draughts bite like teeth and the frozen rain rises up through the ground and turns the bottom of the mattress to ice.

'Is she hurt very bad?' I ask.

'Don't you fret, she'll be fine in January.' The nurse takes my basket and peers inside, as if she's appraising the contents. 'She'll like these morsels.' Her tongue creeps out of her mouth and I see it's coated with a yellow crust. But then my attention is torn away by the sound of screaming, coming on the wind from the big grand building.

'Last night's full moon has sent some of the lunatics into a near frenzy . . .' she explains, her eyes lighting up. She turns, all eager to get back, but I have more questions and I've come fifteen miles. So I thrust a shilling at her and say, 'Please take this for your troubles, Nurse.' And when she takes it, which she does with great speed, I ask how Mam came by her fall.

'She was gardening.' The nurse waves into the grounds where several elm saplings have been newly planted. 'Tripped over a shovel, poor thing.' She stops and rubs my shilling on her sleeve. The screaming has stopped, as sudden as it started, and there's only the soughing in the trees now.

'So she's broken a bone? And the doctor has set it?'

'Exactly!' She sounds as pleased as punch at my reply.

'Can she write?'

'Don't be daft! None of 'em can write.'

'My mam can write,' I say. 'Can you ask her to write me a letter?'

She slips the shilling into her apron and winks at me, as if we're sharing a joke. 'A letter! Leave it with me, dearie.'

Only as I walk home do I understand the nurse's wink. She doesn't believe Mam can write and she thinks the lunacy has been passed to me, that I have Mam's madness. I make a note in my head to send Mam a book. Why have I not thought of this before? I've been too wrapped up in my own affairs, I think. Too fond of Miss Eliza. Too eager to progress at work. Too busy stealing poetry books ... At least I have a shilling left over for Pa. I curl my fingers round the shilling and hold it so tight it cuts, sharp, into my palms.

CHAPTER FORTY-FIVE

Eliza

GREEN PEAS WITH CREAM

My friendship with Lady Montefiore blooms day by day until I am quite disheartened at the prospect of her departure.

After every meal Lady Montefiore invites me to sit with her and discuss the dishes I've cooked, their flavourings and seasonings, where I purchased the ingredients, how I prepared them. I've never met a more curious woman. She wishes to know everything: do I weigh by eye or weight? Do I prefer the flavour of an onion or an eschalot? Do I use an earthen pan or a tin pan? Do I cure my beef with bay salt or common salt? Do I prefer a brick oven or an iron oven? And when she is quite satisfied, her talk turns to Jewish food – the dishes she has taken in Palestine and Jerusalem, the Passover recipes she favours, the thin matzos biscuits she likes to send as gifts. She speaks with such animation, her fan snapping open and closed, that I am utterly absorbed.

It's invariably at this point that Mother enters, pushing her way into the conversation like some sort of battering ram. After which our discourse turns to more mundane subjects. As if Lady M is as uncomfortable as I am talking of the kitchen in Mother's presence. As if she too is aware of its implied shame. The kitchen, with its labour, heat and reek, is humiliating enough. But our interest in food carries a taint and shame of its own. *The hint of profligacy, of appetites, carefully concealed in weights and measures and instructions. But there nonetheless ...* Louis the Chef's words swim into my head: *the joy of being an animal.* Sometimes, as Mother laments the inclement weather or the price of lace, Lady M glances at me over the top of her ivory fan. Her black eyes smile and her eyebrows rise, infinitesimally. As if we are conspirators occupying a secret world.

On Lady M's last evening at Bordyke House, Mother goes out to dine with Mr and Mrs Thorpe, leaving me with Lady M all to myself. As soon as her pudding plate has been cleared, I dismiss Hatty and take the tray of coffee myself. Lady M gestures at the empty chair beside her, her jet drop-earrings swinging from her lobes, her dark eyes flickering in the candlelight. I pour her coffee and she compliments me on the stuffed baked ox cheek, telling me I *simply must* visit her London butcher.

'He's at 34 Duke Street in Aldgate,' she says. 'He's Jewish, so you'll find the beef far superior. Jewish butchers aren't permitted to sell animals with a single spot or blemish.'

'I had no idea,' I say, thinking of some of the animals I have seen at the cattle market, their hooves crusted with fungus and their hides balding and speckled with disease. I am about to quiz her on Jewish butchery, when she abruptly changes the subject with such speed butchery is immediately forgotten.

She leans towards me, her eyes as bright as a sparrow's and a gleam upon her lower lip. 'I have an idea for something you should write.' She opens her fan, then shuts it so quickly the candles in the candelabra gutter, and shadows shoot across the table, rippling over the silver coffee pot, sugar bowl, cream jug. For a second the table seems almost alive, as if quaking streams of quicksilver have replaced the linen cloth.

'Can you guess what I'm thinking?' she asks.

I shake my head.

'You mentioned a book of poems.' She pauses, lays her fan upon the table and observes me shrewdly. 'I would love to see it.'

'It's out of print,' I say, unsure whether I wish to show her or not. Those poems are no longer me, no longer mine, I think. And I want Lady M to see me only as I am *now*.

'No matter,' she waves her hand. 'It is not poetry I was thinking of.'

'Oh?' I feel something flare inside me. A peculiar sensation that begins in the lower reaches of my stomach and seems to spread through me, warm and vaguely disquieting.

'I have a friend,' she continues, nodding softly into the candlelight. 'She's a brave, bold woman called Miss Kelly.'

I say nothing for I have no knowledge of a Miss Kelly. Is she a poet? A writer of recipes?

Lady Montefiore leans more ardently towards me, so that I am inches from her luxuriant, arched eyebrows, her pinked cheeks, her perfectly preserved skin. 'Miss Kelly is an actress ... from a theatrical background. Like you, she talks freely and forcibly.'

My eyes open a little wider. Lady M's fingers twine impatiently through the pearls at her neck, as if she is waiting for me to speak.

'An actress?' I echo. I've heard talk of London theatres, of actresses. Lewd and scurrilous talk.

'She is about to open a theatre and dramatic school in the West End of London where girls can be trained in the dramatic arts. She's looking for new plays.' She stops, picks up her fan from the table, bats at her throat with it, snaps it shut. 'It is quite respectable, her patron is the Duke of Devonshire.' She pauses as if for effect, and her eyes seem to grip mine. 'Have you thought of writing a play?'

'I have years more work to do on my cookery book. And when it's done, I have a vague idea for a second book,' I say slowly. 'Very vague at present ... A cookery book for invalids, for those with delicate health.' I've told no one of this idea, not Ann nor Mother nor Mr Longman. But as I say the words, a sense of regret comes over me. And I seem to feel her disappointment, as though she has some inborn understanding of my predicament. I look down into my coffee cup, at the dark oily sediment, and wish I had the gall to show her my poems.

'Wholesome food for the sick is certainly important, but so

is the need to determine oneself, to speak out on the subjects that flame inside one. I sense you have a strong flame, like my friend, Miss Kelly.'

'I do,' I say. And as I speak I realise that Lady Montefiore is the first person who has noticed this, who has seen inside my soul, observed the flickering flame – and dared to speak approvingly of it. Dared to encourage it.

'The recipes you've copied out for me are so much *more* than recipes,' she continues. 'They are small works of art. And why should they not be so?'

'Oh no,' I say, with a self-deprecating laugh. 'Recipes cannot be compared to poems.'

'Why ever not? Yours are beautifully written, perfectly composed. I read your recipe for green peas with cream and it was as if I was reading poetry ... *Boil a quart of young peas, perfectly tender in salt and water, and drain them as dry as possible* ... See I have committed the first line to memory.'

'You are most kind,' I say. 'But a play is ...' My voice peters out, lost in the tumult of my thoughts. Why shouldn't I try my hand at play-writing? A play about the subjects that I care most about ... An image of Ann comes into my head, her scant and spartan cottage, her crippled father and dead mother. How I would enjoy revealing her impoverishment to all those Londoners who think only of their next carriage or whether to have brocade or chintz curtains ... and who believe country people dwell in quaint cottages with roses round the door.

'You have an innate sense of drama – I've seen it in the way you bring dishes to table. And you have an organised mind, a fine turn of phrase and . . .' She pauses, as if searching for the appropriate words. 'And I sense you have a yearning romantic soul beneath that tidy exterior. Am I right?'

'There *is* something striving within me, although I'm not sure precisely what it is,' I mumble, suddenly embarrassed at the personal turn our discourse has taken. But Lady Montefiore is not the tiniest bit embarrassed. She plucks a small square of writing paper from her cleavage and passes it to me.

'My friend's address,' she says. 'Mention my name and send her something.'

'I very much like the sound of Miss Kelly.' I take the paper, warm from her breast, and slip it into my neckline.

'She is the boldest of my friends.' Lady M lowers her chin and puts her hand over her mouth as if to quieten her voice. 'She has a daughter out of wedlock who lives with her, quite openly.'

I lean away, startled at this news.

'Yes, shocking indeed. One must admire her audacity though.' Lady M stops and tilts her head. In the silence we hear the squeak and scrape of the front door, the grating of a key in the lock, Mother's step in the hall.

Lady M puts her finger to her lips and whispers, 'Enough talk of boldness. I fear the waters have exhausted me as ever, Miss Acton. I must bid you good night.'

She leaves the room just as Mother sweeps in. I pick up the two coffee cups, thinking I can escape to the kitchen before Mother inflicts a lengthy account of her evening upon me. But her voice stops me in my tracks.

'Have you heard the news of your poetess, Miss L. E. Landon? Mrs Thorpe was quite full of it and could talk of nothing else. I would have informed Lady Montefiore if she had not left for her room in such haste.'

My throat tightens. 'What has happened to Miss Landon?' I whisper. Already my head is swarming with lines of her verse. But they do not swarm loudly enough to blot out Mother's voice in all its triumph.

'She was found dead on the floor of her bedchamber, somewhere in deepest Africa. An accident apparently ... She was taking Prussic Acid for an ailment and drank the entire bottle by mistake. I don't know where Mrs Thorpe gets these lurid stories.'

I put down the coffee cups. Close my eyes. Clutch at the tabletop. Hear a candle fizz and splutter and die. I want Mother to go. I feel her eye upon me. Watching me. I want her to go.

'Good night, Mother,' I say, stumbling to the hall, down the corridor, down the stairs to the kitchen. To my sanctum. I can hardly breathe, each inhale laboured and tatty. Ann is arranging platters and dishes on the dresser, but when she sees me she runs and helps me to my chair.

'Miss Landon is dead,' I say between gulps of air. 'She is gone.'

'I'm sorry to hear that, miss. Shall I get the brandy bottle?'

I lean forward and press the heels of my hands against my eyes. 'It was she who inspired me to write.' I try to find words to explain the presence of Miss Landon in my life, how she has been as guide, as mother, as companion, as teacher. But no words come. Instead I blurt out something else entirely: 'She should never have married!'

'Miss Landon is married?'

'Just this year. She went with him to Africa. I can't bear to think of her dying so far away, so alone.' I feel a sob creep up my chest. I do not want Ann to see me like this, so I ask her to go to my room and bring down all six volumes of Miss Landon's verse. While she is gone I pour a glass of brandy and toast Miss Landon, even as tears run down my face.

That night my sleep is charged with dreams. Of Miss Landon lying dead upon the marbled floor of her African palace. Of Miss Kelly and her illegitimate daughter dancing upon a London stage while labourers jeer and catcall. Of Louis making love to me in a coal cellar while Mr Arnott urges him on with wild cries. Each dream floats seamlessly into the next, until I am trapped in a tableaux so terrifying I awake sodden with perspiration. I slip from my bed, sink to my knees and pray for Miss Landon. I pray that Jesus will take her unto him, that she is somewhere more tolerant, charitable, joyful. And through my prayers, her words weave a ragged path ... *Oh, what a waste of feeling and thought have been the imprints on my roll of life ... to what use have I turned the golden gifts which are my hope and pride ...* All Miss Landon's golden gifts have gone, I think. Just as she foresaw ... Amen, Amen, Amen.

Eventually the sun struggles up and I remember it is Lady Montefiore's last breakfast at Bordyke House. I decide not to tell her of Miss Landon's death for I cannot fall into another unseemly fit of weeping. Instead I involve myself most

particularly in her breakfast preparations, making sure a
spotless lace-hemmed napkin has been laid at her table, that
the cruets have been polished to a shine, that her favourite
breakfast of devilled kidneys is garnished with the freshest
greenest parsley.

Later, when she leaves, after much talk of exchanging let-
ters, she calls out from her carriage window, 'You won't forget
to write to my friend, will you?'

Her words come to me like the call of a bird to its mate,
rousing me from my misery. I will do it, I think. I will do it
for Miss Landon!

As her carriage bowls away, dust and grit rising in its
wake, I raise my hand to wave. Above, the sky sprawls, vast
and faintly blue. And it feels to me as if I lift my hand to
Heaven, to the spirit of Miss Landon, to my own destiny.

I have no early flowers to fling ... But I shall write a play for
Miss Kelly's theatre and I shall dedicate it to the brave and
bold spirit of Miss Landon.

CHAPTER FORTY-SIX

Ann

TEA AND BREAD, BREAD AND TEA

After the departure of Lady Montefiore – and the death of *her Miss Landon* – Miss Eliza changes. Or so it seems to me. She still cooks, but with a vengeance now, as if the wind is at her heels. And she is jumpy, even a little snappy, in spite of Bordyke House having no boarders at present.

I tiptoe round her, as meek as a mouse, wondering if it's me that's made her as tart as a codlin. Have I disappointed her in some way? Every now and then, as she's writing at the kitchen table, she lifts her head and asks me the oddest of questions. Yesterday, she asked if I thought a recipe could be a work of art, like a poem or a picture. I was on my hands and knees scrubbing fat stains from the flagstones. I thought about it for a bit and then I said, 'Reading a nicely written recipe must be very satisfying for a lady.'

She peered down at me, as if she was surprised I'd answered. As if she was surprised there was someone else in the room.

'Do you really think so, Ann?' She rested her chin in her hand and studied me, as if I was a stray cat that had chanced into the kitchen. 'I dream of a time when people read recipe books for pleasure, as they read novels or verse. Can you imagine that?'

'You mean ladies sitting in their parlours reading aloud from a book of recipes?' I'll admit I laughed at that. I could not help it. Such a strange notion of hers, for everyone knows that kitchen work is despised by ladies.

'I'm serious,' she said. 'I like to imagine Mrs Thorpe and all her good church gentlewomen reading a cookery book for the sheer pleasure of it. And gentlemen too! Why should cookery books be relegated to dark greasy shelves in dark greasy kitchens? I foresee a time when they're stored in libraries or displayed in parlours!'

I snorted with laughter. But then she shot me such a peevish look, I muffled my snorting and scrubbed harder at the floor so that the damp coldness of the stone pushed further into my bones.

'Our book must be a pleasurable read, Ann. I am quite determined to make it so.' And she bowed her head low over her paper and I heard nothing but the scratching of her nib.

Our conversation has given me two thoughts. First, I should like to send Mam a cookery book. Which means I must find the pluck to ask Miss Eliza if I can borrow one.

Second, I should like to read Miss Eliza's writings, her recipes that are as beautifully penned as poems. She keeps her recipe-writing in a portfolio of marbled card with a leather spine and brown ribbons that she ties in a bow to stop the pages falling out. It wouldn't be right to open it, but what if she were to leave her papers out?

It's not until a few more days have passed that I get the opportunity to peek at her writings. I'm removing the stones from six ounces of olives with a paring knife, to make an olive sauce that Miss Eliza says is commonly served in France with ducks, stewed fowl and beefsteaks. My fingers are aching and stained a dull brown when she puts down her quill and stretches her arms wide into the air, as if she is very stiff and must get some blood moving round her.

'Would a cushion make you more comfortable?' I ask as she starts rubbing at the small of her back and twisting her neck from side to side.

She rises, her hand still circling on her tailbone, and says she will go to the parlour herself for one. I notice that she hasn't slipped her papers inside the portfolio, so I wipe my hands on my apron and glance, sly, at her pile of pages. The first thing I notice is that there are no numbers. Which is odd because her recipes usually include lots of numbers, for weights and measures and such like. I go to the table, all the time listening for her steps in the hallway. The next thing I notice is that the page isn't laid out for a recipe. Miss Eliza likes to list her ingredients at the end but this page has no list. Nor is there mention of any foods. Is it a private letter? A secret journal?

I start looking over her longhand – which is not so tidy as it should be and has many underlined words – and I know, quick as a flash, that this isn't a recipe. Nor is it a verse. I feel my brow crinkle up as my eyes strain to read what she's written. Something to do with *a lady of independent means* and *a baker who thrusts violently his closed knuckles into a huge mass of tenacious dough*. I am puzzling at the word *tenacious* when I hear, quite sudden, Miss Eliza's determined tread approaching the kitchen door. I spring back to the chopping board and take up my paring knife. In my haste, it slips and slices deep into the side of my finger. The brine from the olives goes straight into the cut, making my eyes smart and silent cusses spring from my mouth.

Miss Eliza arranges her cushion in the seat of her chair and gives a long sigh. Yesterday I would have put it down to her grief for Miss Landon, or maybe to the tragedy of her past which I saw in her poems. But now I've seen her writings I'm not so sure. It seems to me she is grappling with something new, something I know nothing of.

'Are you well, Miss Eliza?' I ask, binding my cut finger tight with my handkerchief and being careful to sound solicitous but not prying.

'It's only my back,' she says.

'They say winter is coming early this year. Likely your bones are feeling it with today's poor weather.'

'And how will your father cope if we have snow?'

'He has blankets and he can build the fire high with furze from the common,' I answer. I don't mention how long it takes him to do this, the hundreds of hobbling trips, the hours of twisting and bending to get the furze basket on and off his back. How could she possibly understand? 'And I will take him these olive stones if I may? For burning.'

'Yes, of course. And what do your people do for food in winter? For bread?'

'Bread?' I echo, thinking of the *tenacious dough* I saw written on her page. Perhaps she is writing a bread recipe and I have misunderstood.

'Yes, what will he eat when frost clings to his beard? When his limbs are numb with cold? When ice presses at his door?'

I love hearing her words when the spirit of poesy is upon her, but today her words make me cross. I want to tell her Pa is not a poem. He is a real man, crippled and poor but still a human being. But that is not my place so I play along as if I too am a poetess: 'And when his stomach growls, savage, with hunger?'

'Exactly, Ann. Describe it to me in all its coarseness. I must see and hear and feel and smell every detail.'

And so I tell her, as vivid as I can, how it feels to be always hungry so that one can think only of food; how it is to wake up with frost upon the blankets and a sharp wind whistling through the rags at the window; how it is to have fingers so iced they can barely pick up kindling from the ground; how it is to be cheated without mercy because you have nothing.

'Cheated?' she asks. 'Why cheated?'

'The very poor can buy only the lowliest of things,' I say. 'We must buy the dirtiest bread and the rankest ale and tea leaves half full of wood shavings.' I stop and hear my voice, which has changed and is as bitter as a dandelion leaf. But beneath its bitterness I hear another note. I cannot put it into words, I know only that it is not shame.

Miss Eliza makes an urgent waving motion with her hand, as if she wants me to continue, as if she hasn't noticed that my tongue has lost its usual meekness. And so I tell of how Mam made 'tea' by soaking crusts of burnt bread in boiling water, how Pa took the roof from his mouth by eating only raw onions with his bitter mouldy bread, how cheese rinds were bought for me and Jack so we might grow, how we all got sick from eating meat from diseased animals not fit for market, how Pa's leg stump made him cry out in pain every night, how Mam lost one baby after another and four in a single weekend.

When I've told her everything except the worst bits – which aren't fit for the dainty ears of a lady – I stop talking and go in search of a skillet, for the olives must be blanched in boiling water and then soaked to remove their saltiness. It's only when I turn around that I see her eyes are wet, that she is wiping discreetly at a tear. I twist quickly back to the fire for the sake of her pride. But something inside me soars like a bird. I have made my mistress cry with the force of my words. In the same way that her words, her poems, brought me to weeping, so mine have done the same to her. Strange, that my spirit is soaring even as I recall the harshness of my past. At least Mam is in her grand asylum now and Jack is in his shining white kitchen and Pa has money from his moleskins and the candle ends from Bordyke House.

A silence falls over the kitchen and in it I seem to hear my own heartbeat and it is steadfast, strong. And then Miss Eliza speaks, her voice loud with feeling and fury.

'If bread is the sole food of so many, it must be good and wholesome. These iniquitous practices must end. They must end!' She slams closed her portfolio, tucks it under her arm and goes to the larder. I hear her rummaging through the shelves, the tin boxes clanging and the earthenware jars clinking. When she returns, she says, in a most decisive tone, 'We shall start a chapter on bread when I'm back from my sister's. I want to experiment with unfermented bread . . . and potato bread . . . and German yeast.'

'Yes, Miss Eliza,' I say, happy that my words have brought her to this, to a new chapter in *our* book.

'Everyone should know how to bake a loaf of bread.'

I nod in agreement. And suddenly I feel assured enough to ask if I can borrow a cookery book. It may not be my place, but I will do it. Tomorrow, when she is calmer, I will ask.

CHAPTER FORTY-SEVEN

Eliza

BUTTERED CELERY ON TOAST

So. I have overcome my anxiety and started work on a stage play in Three Acts, about a spinster who befriends a young impoverished girl. The girl – she has neither name nor age as yet – has a secret. It is only when the spinster discovers that her young friend can read and write that she realises something has been kept from her. There will be two roles only, for Lady M informs me that her friend's theatre is most intimate, with a stage measuring a mere ten square yards.

I'm still working on the cookery book, of course, but the death of Miss Landon and Lady M's comments reminded me of the necessity for something more expressive, more imaginative in one's life. And I like the challenge of writing something new – although a play is more demanding than I expected. I must think not only of words and plot, but of motion, of stage props, of music even. I am pondering this, and experimenting with a dish of boiled buttered celery, when Ann returns from market, her basket bursting with thick stems of Brussels sprouts, Jerusalem artichokes clod in Kentish clay and a fine red cabbage so fresh it squeaks.

As she unpacks the basket, she asks if she may borrow a book.

'Of course,' I say, lifting bunches of boiled celery from the pan. 'Which one in particular?'

'I thought perhaps *The Frugal Housewife*.' She points at the small volume in its brown leather bindings, veined with gilt.

'You may read any of my cookery books, Ann. You know that.' My mind veers back to my play, which is to make several important points about how Christian ladies could better spend their time and money. I cannot make it too contentious, for it must be well reviewed. But I have to speak out on poverty and education and the fouling of food and—

'It isn't for me.'

'Oh?' I say, surprised. 'Is it for your brother?'

'Yes,' she says very quickly. Too quickly, I think.

'And he would like *The Frugal Housewife*, would he?' I am loath to lose a single volume of my cookery books for I must constantly check that my dishes are new and original.

'I shall not let him have it for long, Miss Eliza.'

'Is he tiring of Monsieur Soyer's collection of books? No doubt they are all French and lily-gilded in the French chef way,' I say.

'Yes,' she says, again too quickly and too full of relief. 'That is right, miss.'

I examine her face, bent over the red cabbage as she cuts away the outer leaves. Her cheeks and neck are flushed pink, even as her voice is oddly determined.

'I rather rely on that particular book,' I say. 'Would he like to borrow *The Cook's Oracle* instead? Its author is a constant irritation to me, with his pompous verbosity.'

'Jack would be very appreciative, only I was thinking of the size. A smaller volume would be less costly to post.'

She keeps her gaze on the cabbage and I notice her knuckles, red and rough, gripping the handle of the blade. I remind her to remove the stalk of the cabbage by splitting it first in quarters. Still she will not meet my gaze.

'It is not for your brother, is it, Ann?' My mind is darting now from the scenes of my play to the scene spilling out in front of me. Secrets and lies, I think. Here – in the kitchen of Bordyke House, my sanctum. 'Jack cannot read, can he?'

'No, miss.' She bows her head. 'How would you like the cabbage cooked?'

'Stewed very slowly in butter,' I say. 'Then we shall add vinegar and serve with broiled sausages and good gravy. To whom do you want to lend my book?'

There is a long silence, as if Ann is preparing an answer for me. Or deciding whether or not I can be trusted with the truth, whatever that may be.

'Aren't we friends, Ann?' I say gently. 'If you tell me your secret, I'll tell you mine.'

Her head jerks up and she looks straight into my eyes, quite startled. Her upper lip quivers as she puts down the knife. I cannot tell if she is shocked at my possessing a secret or terrified at the prospect of revealing her own.

'When two people work together as closely as we do, it's difficult to keep secrets,' I say. 'And not always beneficial.'

'How do you mean?'

'Secrets inevitably mean lies and it's not right that friends lie to each other, is it?' I keep my voice soft to hide how much her distrust has affronted me. Indeed, I am rather hurt by it. Haven't I been good to her?

'Oh, miss. I didn't mean to ...' Tears well in her eyes and she wipes at them with her hands that are stained a deep purple from the cabbage. 'It's my mam. She's not dead.' Ann starts to weep in copious gulps, her slight shoulders shaking. I turn away, suddenly overcome by disappointment. I have this odd sense of something curdling inside me. As if some inarticulate hope has separated and soured.

'So your mother is alive?'

Ann nods limply. 'Yes and no,' she says, but is so choked by sobs she can say no more.

'Where is she?'

'A lunatic asylum.' She presses her eyes with her cabbage-stained hands and something about them – the red-raw knuckles, the grazed, scabbed fingers, the stem-thin wrists – moves me to tenderness. In spite of her lies. In spite of the sour stream of regret and discontent winding and looping within me.

'And she would like to see a cookery book?'

Ann swallows noisily. 'I could not tell you, miss. I am sorry for my lies and deceit.'

Words from long ago spill into my head: *I woke to the dark truth ... Rous'd from dreams of bliss to know thee false ... To feel that there was agony in this ...* And suddenly I know that this is not her doing, that others have put her up to this. 'Did Reverend and Mrs Thorpe ask you to keep this concealed from me?'

'They said I would not find a situation if anyone knew. What's bred in the bone, they said ...'

'Bred in the bone indeed!' I feel my loathing and contempt for the Thorpes gather inside me, spreading from my blood to my bones to the backs of my eyes.

Ann blows her nose on her sodden ragged handkerchief, then returns to slicing the cabbage, which she does very slowly and cautiously as if she thinks the blade could slip at any moment. 'She's in an asylum and the nurses don't believe she can read and write. I wanted her to see what I'm helping with. She's not seen a new book of recipes – the one she had was fifty years old.'

'Of course you may lend her one of my cookery books. And when ours is published, she must have her own copy.' I pause, and as my disgust at the Thorpes ebbs, something in Ann's story piques me. 'How did your mother come by her education?'

'I don't rightly know. She lost her mind when I was eleven years old, a little bit at a time, until she no longer knew who we were or what was what.'

My mind swerves back to my play. Could I set a scene in a lunatic asylum or would that be too unsavoury for the ladies and gentlemen of London? Could I split the tiny stage in two, one half a country hovel and the other a richly decorated drawing room? I prod absently at the bunches of celery simmering on the fire. I can feel Ann's eyes upon me, as if she is waiting for something, but I'm absorbed in my plot, in its twists and turns, and how they are to convey my feelings and rouse the audience from its lethargy.

When Ann speaks, it is in such a quiet voice I barely hear her over the bubbling of the celery and the slicing of cabbage and the clattering of Lizzie's pattens on the scullery floor. 'You wanted to share a secret with me, Miss Eliza?'

Chapter Forty-Eight

Ann

Potatoes in the French Way

I don't know how I have the gall to ask, but the question flies from my mouth like a baby bird tumbling from its nest. And once it's out, there's no putting it back.

I'm in such a state, after showing myself to be a liar and talking openly of Mam, that my thoughts are all hither and thither. It was the way she called me her *friend* that most overpowered me, flipping the cheeky question from my gullet. For I'm quite sure that Ma'am would never call Hatty a *friend*. Nor would Mrs Thorpe call her maid a *friend*.

I concentrate hard on what I'm doing: weighing butter on the scales, melting it in a pan, sliding in the cabbage. Will she answer me? Will she tell me of the lover from her verses?

Or something of Mr Arnott that made her change her mind about marrying him? A shiver of expectation and excitement and fear runs down my spine. For I remember Pa's words – that no lady wants her servant as a *friend* – and I know it was wrong to ask.

'You are right. I promised an exchange of secrets.' She lifts the celery from the pan with a gravy spoon and lays it in a colander to drain. Then she slices off a piece and puts it in her mouth. 'Too soft,' she murmurs. 'I should have drawn it from the fire earlier. It has lost its bite entirely.'

'I'm sorry, miss,' I say, for it was I that distracted her with my weeping and my talk of Mam.

'Make some toast, Ann,' she says. 'And put a pat of good butter to melt. We shall sample this celery on a slice of crunchy smoky toast.'

I busy myself with the toasting fork – and wait for her secret. I hear her nib scratching, then the sound of her shaking over the powdered chalk to dry the ink, which means she's finished her page. My face grows hotter and redder from the flames. The smell of toasting bread, browning and crisping, wafts round my face. Finally she speaks.

'My secret,' she says, pausing to blow off the chalk, 'is that I am writing a play!'

'Oh.' My voice is flat with disappointment. So those were the writings I peeked at the other day. Not love letters or a journal of the heart, but a play for the stage.

'For a new theatre run by a lady in London. If I cannot be a poet, perhaps I can be a playwright.'

'An author of plays *and* cookery books,' I say, to remind

her of *our* book, which only yesterday she was speaking of as a *work of art*. I feel disheartened by her secret. As if a fine carriage has rolled over me, with its ironclad wheels, and I have disappeared between earth and sky. I try very hard to remember the writing I saw ... something about a baker and a lady. A peculiar play, I think. Is that what London ladies like to see upon the stage? Not much of a secret though ...

'Indeed!' She gives a dainty clap of her hands, and then, most abrupt, asks if I would like to visit Mam while she's away at her sister's. 'You may take a jar of our preserves and a loaf of the bread we shall be baking next week. Take some for your father too, dear Ann.'

My heart lifts. *Dear Ann*. She has forgiven me my lies! 'Thank you, Miss Eliza,' I say, as I pull the hot toast from the fork. 'You seem very pleased to be visiting your sister and I'm happy for you.'

'I am pleased, Ann.' Her voice rises and falls and is full of her smile.

'Will she come to stay with us one day?' I arrange the toast on a platter and my stomach gives a low groan.

'I doubt it,' says Miss Eliza. 'We are too busy. Now, let us sample celery on toast. Shall we strew it with some herbs?'

I frown, but there's no time to dwell on her words for she wants my opinion on the celery. I've not eaten celery since I was a girl, but I remember its taste – warmish and savoury with a hint of lemony bitterness that goes sweet on long cooking. I run through the herbs in the garden that are still fresh and green. 'A shame the lovage is long gone,' I say. Sage, thyme, rosemary ... too strong, I think. They will overpower the celery. 'A thin grating of nutmeg?'

'Minced parsley, if we had it fresh,' says Miss Eliza. 'Let's sample a plain and then a nutmeg-strewn toast, shall we?'

As I cut the toast into four squares, I think about this mysterious sister, Mary, who is so rarely mentioned, unlike Miss Eliza's governess sisters, Catherine and Anna, who are often spoken of. My curiosity gets the better of me and as I pass the celery toast, I boldly ask if Mary has children.

'Yes, she has several.'

I wait for her to tell me more of her nieces and nephews, their names and ages, how bonny and lively they are. But she says nothing, just chaws on her toast and stares at the nutmeg grater, as if she is deep in thought about the celery. I'm right, for a minute later, she says, 'I prefer it plain. It has no need of nutmeg.'

Then she gestures at the window, where the dusk is pressing at the glass. 'How sudden the dark comes now,' she says. I clear away the plates and trim and light the oil lamp.

'Soon you will be with your sister ,' I say, to cheer her.

She nods. 'Mary's house is most comfortable. Her husband is highly respected and they have the finest carpets and the brightest silver.'

It strikes me that she's regretting not marrying Mr Arnott. But then she leaps up, as if her verve is quite restored. 'Supper! Only you, Hatty and I tonight. Shall we have salted haddock? Gently heated through upon the gridiron ... and served with ...' She pauses, her pale hands clasped upon her chest. 'Let us fry potatoes in the French way. They must be crisp and light brown, piled into a dish and sprinkled with fine salt. Such a handsome dish!'

And it's as if the thought of food, and supper, and cooking, has rescued her from melancholy, and it cheers me to know that cooking can truly lift her spirits.

Chapter Forty-Nine

Eliza

Baked Apples with Cloves and Cinnamon

The Colchester-to-Grundisburgh coach jolts along, stopping only once. Here I take a short walk while my fellow passengers – a rough, uncouth couple with faces like pickled eggs – eat in the tavern.

On my walk I look into a beer shop and observe several hovels, taking note of the filth and disease, the animals that appear to live alongside the occupants, the scrawniness and hopelessness of it all. For years I have chosen not to see such things. For years I have turned away and preoccupied myself with poetry, with love, with myself.

I ask for directions to the nearest bakehouse, but receive

only bald, feeble-minded stares. Bread – the staff of life – is much on my mind. And yet not one hovel contains an oven. How can bread be baked without an oven? Indignation simmers in me, and only when it calms do I wonder if my mind is purposefully, furiously, keeping busy. So that other subjects can be pushed, deftly, aside.

The coach rolls on and as the light drains from the sky we reach the outskirts of Grundisburgh. The air is chill here, with a piercing south-westerly wind that carries a faint tang of the sea and makes me pull my cloak tight around my shoulders. My heart beats faster, harder. My hands grow hot and clammy in their gloves. I suddenly wish I'd taken Mother's advice and refused Mary's invitation. But no, I could never have done that. Whatever olive branch Mary wishes to offer me, I am ready to receive it. I think of my portrait – a small pen-and-ink silhouette – rolled up within my shawl of saffron silk and smuggled at the last minute into my travelling trunk. Was I rash to bring it? Certainly I was extravagant to have it made at such short notice. But something about Ann, her confession, awakened in me an obscure need for something I can barely understand, let alone put words to. God knows I have tried. Perhaps Mary will have my portrait framed and hung. Or perhaps she will scathingly return it to me. Or worse. Perhaps she will hide it, burn it even.

Suddenly we are stopped and the coach driver shouts, 'This is where Doctor Gwynne lives.' Their house is jealously guarded by iron railings and tall black gates. The windows flare with light and are generously wreathed with swathes and swags of chintz and velvet. An oil lamp smokes in a porch of newly whitewashed brick, and upon the front door gleams the hulking brass head of a lion with a brass striker hanging from its brass jaws.

They must have heard the slurring wheels of the carriage or the thwack of my trunk being cast upon the ground, for within seconds a bevy of eager children, their faces as sharp and bright as pinheads, are at the window. They tap on the glass, and wave, and squash their noses against the panes so that the glass blooms with their breath. So many of them! I search immediately for Susannah, hoping to recognise a familiar feature. But in the breathy commotion I cannot tell one child from another.

And then Mary and Anthony, sleek-haired and well nourished, are at the door, kissing me on the lips and urging me inside. Instantly I smell cloves and cinnamon and baking apples. I want to follow the scent to the kitchen. I want to still my hands by slicing and chopping. I want my mind to shed its nervous clutter and think only of temperatures and cooking times and the pairings of flavours and textures. For a second I wonder if there isn't some way I can spend time in the kitchen. The two of us cooking together, conferring, tasting, while the kitchen hums gently in the background. And it seems to me that the kitchen, with its natural intimacy, is more conducive to friendship and love than any other room in the house. The steady indeterminate pattern of days spent there, the heady unforgettable smells, the warmth and succour of its confined space.

'But don't you look well,' gushes Mary, whose cushioned cheeks glow like coals. 'Do you not agree, Anthony my dear?'

Anthony takes my cloak from my shoulders and nods. 'Indeed you do, Eliza.'

And then the children – hundreds of them, or so it seems – tumble into the hall, all laughing and talking and pushing to be near me. Again I seek blindly for Susannah, but the children are all dressed alike, white-smocked, blue-stockinged. The bustle, the noise, the shrill clamour of it all overwhelms me, even as Mary calls on them to be quiet and remember their manners. How does she live with this cacophony, I wonder.

I am introduced to the children one by one: Anthony Junior, Tatham, Minna, Anna, Emily, Helen, Hammond. And finally Susannah. She stretches up and kisses me with her pink pursed lips. I smell soap on her newly scrubbed skin and wait for some sort of emotion to sweep over me. I feel only the dimmest sense of affection. I wait a moment, stroking abstractedly at her hair. But there is no sudden spurt of maternal love, no visceral desire to grip her to me, no rush of raw longing. What I feel, above all, is curiosity. As she steps away I scrutinise her, searching for myself in her features. She has my dark hair, my pale skin, my long slender neck. But her eyes are not mine ... Her eyes are deep-set, brown with tiny flecks of gold, long thick lashes that curl as if they have been scraped through a butter curler. They are *his* eyes, unshuttered, unsparing. And I am reminded, instantly, of *him*.

The younger children pull on my hands and skirts and the older ones look me over from the corners of their eyes. Anthony puts his hand on the small of my back, guiding me into the parlour where a fire flickers, red and violet, and where endless shelves display endless lines of books bound in calfskin.

Anthony sees me eyeing the books with a prying, envious expression. 'Excessively dull medical books,' he explains, batting at the air.

'They remind me of our old home, before we sold our library,' I say. 'I'm glad you have such a collection. It is right that children grow up with books around them.' I wonder if my volume of verse is in amongst the medical tomes, if Susannah has seen it or read it. But no, Mary was always shamed by my *unfettered sentiment*, as she once put it. If there is a copy of my poems here, it will be under lock and key.

The smaller children tumble upon the Turkish rug, where they push and shove, and make hideous faces, sticking out their pink tongues and waggling their fingers in their ears. They seem unable to sit still, even for a second. They poke at each other's ribcages, and fall upon one another and call each other vile names. The older children egg them on with much mirth, as if my presence is of no consequence. Surprised, I look to Anthony for discipline but he is busy settling himself into an armchair and Mary has gone to give orders to the servants.

I snatch constant looks at Susannah, observing how she tilts her head when listening, how she beats her thick lashes in irritation, how she slaps at her brothers with a peculiar flapping motion of her hands, how she wrinkles her nose and scratches at her head. And then she sees me looking at her and flashes me a smile, so blithe, so lopsided, I am reminded again of *him* and of his smile that seemed to curve in two.

'Susannah, won't you sit beside me?' I pat encouragingly at the sofa. She catches Anthony's eye and he nods his assent. The little girl, my very own daughter, creeps to the sofa and springs upon it like a cat. She snuggles beside me and I feel the warm damp weight of her leaning into me. My arm lifts, as if of its own accord, and reaches round her shoulders.

And that is how we are when Mary returns.

CHAPTER FIFTY

Ann

BAVARIAN BROWN BREAD

I get two rides to Barming Heath. The second is with a tanner who huffs stale breath all over me and blows pipe smoke in my ear. After a mile of this, he puts his brawny hand upon my knee and asks how I shall repay his kindness. I answer, very stoutly, that being a good Christian girl I want no more of his ungodly talk. My words, so full of assurance, take me quite by surprise. They come from my mouth of their own accord. Only after I have jumped from his cart, do I hear Miss Eliza in my words. The neat force of her, the determined politeness. I have learned all that from her, I think, and a warm feeling comes over me.

This warm light feeling stays with me all the way to the lunatic asylum, in spite of the weight of my basket which grows heavier with each step. In it are two jars of preserves, a pat of fresh butter and a pot of thick cream, as well as a loaf that Miss Eliza calls our Bavarian Brown Bread – from a Professor Liebig whose books and pamphlets have been arriving by mail coach all week. Underneath all this lies a cookery book, for I am determined to show the nurses that Mam can read. It will be a small miracle, of course, for she has read nothing for years. But Miss Eliza assured me that *no one forgets how to read. Ever.*

There's a sharpness on the back edge of the wind today. And when it gets into my mouth and nose I sense an ice-and-pepper tang. It blows up as I reach the asylum, whipping my hair from its cap, nipping at my chapped lips, gusting up my skirts. When the lodge keeper draws back his hatch, the wind blows straight through, making the papers on his table fly into the air so that he growls, irritated.

'I am here to see Mrs Jane Kirby, my mam,' I say, pushing him a sixpenny bit.

He looks at the coin and frowns, as if he's not sure whether to take it. I push it a little further, wondering why he doesn't snatch it up in his usual swift way.

He screws up his hog-ish eyes then looks at the paper on his desk, holding it down with a bony fist for the wind is still blowing through the open hatch. I pull my shawl tight around my shivering shoulders and hope they will bring Mam to me somewhere warm. Perhaps I can see her bedchamber today, feel the softness of her feather mattress and the thickness of her quilt. She is all bones, so a skinny mattress and skinny blankets will be no good at all.

The lodge keeper coughs, his eyes circling over the sheet of paper. Round and round.

'I can read,' I say, tentative, for I do not want to hurt his pride.

'Likely you can, missy,' he says, with another cough. 'A gentleman came for Mrs Kirby yesterday.'

'Oh,' I answer, surprised. No one has called Pa a gentleman for as long as I can remember. I wonder why he didn't mention anything when I delivered the candle stubs and rabbit ears last week. 'That must be my father. He has only one leg,' I say, wondering if he rode with the miller, and hoping he wasn't turned away like I was on my first visit.

The lodge keeper's mouth drags up and down as he peers at the paper. Then he looks up but does not catch my eye. 'The gentleman what came yesterday had two legs.'

I stare at him, confused. 'A gentleman with two legs for Mrs Kirby? For my mam?'

The lodge keeper nods slowly, licking at his dry lips. 'He took her away.'

'No, you are muddling my mam with someone else,' I say, impatient now. 'Show me that paper.' I push the sixpenny bit so it's touching his knuckles and make a grab for the paper. Perhaps there is another Mrs Kirby, or a Mrs Kirkby, or a Mrs Kribby, someone else who has been cured by the doctor and collected by her husband.

He pulls the paper back, his face colouring. 'I know what my eyes have seen and my ears have heard, missy. I have no need of reading.'

'Well then, tell me where she has gone,' I say. 'Or who has collected her.'

He grabs at the sixpenny bit and puts it in his pocket, as if he no longer feels compelled to leave it. And in that moment I know he's telling me the truth, that he's about to reveal something he shouldn't.

'T'was a clergyman. He saw the superintendent for a private meeting.'

The wind falls away and for a minute everything goes very still. Even the old, dry leaves stop scurrying along the ground. Is it possible the Reverend Thorpe – for who else could it be? – has taken her home? That she has been cured and made ready for the parish again? But as soon as these thoughts strike, I see the folly of them.

My voice falls to a whisper. 'Where did he take her?'

The lodge keeper closes his lips tight and stares hard at his sheet of paper. Only this time his eyes aren't going round and round. I take a shilling from my purse and shove it towards him.

He looks at the coin and I see his mouth working, as if he's fighting with his own soul. 'Please have the money,' I say. 'For your troubles.'

'She was in the Dead House. Likely for some time,' he says after a long pause. 'It's full to bursting right now.'

I frown, not understanding his words, not understanding what a Dead House is. 'Is she still there?'

'He took her to St Margaret's Church in East Barming.' He pushes the coin back to me. 'It's where the lucky ones go, those that aren't sold.'

'Sold?' I echo, baffled.

'That's right – their skull caps is cut off and their lunatic brains are cut open. You're lucky she had a Christian burial with a proper man o' the cloth.'

Black spots start rushing and swarming before my eyes. All at once I see nothing but the endless black spots. Behind them, the lodge keeper is blurred, his nodding head disappearing in a spin of blackness. I hear his voice, muffled: 'Are you all right, missy?'

As my mind gropes through the storm of black spots, words from somewhere rush at me. I catch them, hold them fast, say them, silent, over and over: *Life's silver cord torn apart, the golden bowl broken. Life's silver cord torn apart, the golden bowl broken ...*

'You can walk to East Barming, 'tis just over a mile as the crow flies. Look for the spire. Hers'll be the only fresh grave, all the rest is sold to the surgeons.'

Through the swirling speckled spots, I see the lodge keeper gesturing through the hatch, back to the road, down to the left.

'But she had somewhere to go,' I say, numb. *Life's silver cord torn apart, the golden bowl broken. Life's silver cord torn apart, the golden bowl broken.* 'I was her silver cord and she was my golden bowl.' Through the fading black spots I see the lodge keeper give me an odd look, his hand reaching for the hatch, reaching to shut me out.

Somehow I find my stumbling way to St Margaret's Church, tears blurring my eyes as I beg directions. All the time I am haunted by the thought that Mam's death is my fault – for if I had stayed home with her she would surely be alive. And if I had been stronger, more like Miss Eliza and less like my feeble wavering self, I would have demanded to see Mam after she tripped over a shovel, which I now know was a lie to keep me away. My tears stop when I reach the graveyard. At the back is a small mound of newly turned earth. Not a single bloom lies upon it. Not a single piece of fresh foliage. Dead curling leaves blow over it and gust away. I scour the ground for footprints and find only one. The imprint of a hobnailed boot. No sign of anyone else. Only the fresh-turned earth, black and crumbling. Only the crows screeching from the leafless trees.

I take the preserves from my basket, along with Miss Eliza's copy of *The Cook's Oracle*. I cannot leave without commemorating Mam. Without remembering that it was she who taught me to read. It was she who taught me to write. I place the book so it sits squarely in the midst of the broken earth. A tombstone of sorts. Its leather cover, stained where buttery fingers have gripped it, shines faintly from the black soil. I kneel in the cold mud and put the jar of damson jam on top of the quince marmalade and place them on the book. I have made her a sepulchre, I think. A gravestone as respectable as any. I arrange the loaf of Bavarian brown bread and the pat of butter and the jar of cream to make a crucifix. Then I kiss each one – the book, the jars, the bread, the cold black earth.

When I'm done and have wiped the crumbs of dank soil from my lips, I notice the wind has dropped to a sullen breeze. I take up my basket, pull down my cap, hug my shawl to my ribs and begin the long walk back to Tonbridge.

CHAPTER FIFTY-ONE

Eliza

CURRANT CAKE

Mary presides efficiently over the children's tea, chastising the nurse, dispatching the sulky maid to and from the kitchen, issuing a steady stream of commands. Do not talk with your mouth full. Do not eat with your fingers. Do not open your mouth when you chew. Do not pick at your nose. Do not take God's name in vain. Do not put your napkin on your head. Do not tease your sister. Do not poke the baby. Do not drop crusts on the floor.

Within a few minutes I am stupefied with boredom, while my head throbs from the relentless cacophony. I try to watch Susannah from the tail of my eye, but she is interested only in gobbling scones or elbowing her brother. I feel a curious detachment, not only from her, but from the entire rabble of nephews and nieces. It occurs to me, most uncharitably, that I would not mind if I were never to see them again. The thought shocks me with its bluntness, with its lack of feeling. Perhaps love comes with time, I think. Perhaps if I had seen more of them I would feel a modicum of affection. Perhaps if Susannah had grown up with me I would feel a mother's love.

Minna shrieks so shrilly I put my hands to my ears in an involuntary movement that Mary, with her omniscient eye, spots. 'Ah, Eliza, my dear. They are in high spirits because of you. They are not always so unruly.'

I lower my hands into my lap, where they twist at a napkin. I want to excuse myself and slip to the kitchen or to my bed-chamber, but I know Mary wishes me to observe the children at tea, although I have no idea why. No sane woman would make an old maid sit through such bedlam. I wonder what I would do if this was a play. How might I end it? How might I hold the audience's attention? Could I pull the cloth from the table so the crockery and cutlery crash to the floor? Could Mary grab the bread knife and plunge it desperately into her heart? I need something to bring an instant ghoulish hush to the stage ... For a few minutes I am completely lost in my thoughts, in my stage directions and props and when to bring the curtain down. Until Mary's voice cuts, reproachfully, into my head.

'Eliza? Eliza? Susannah is talking to you ...'

I look up and see Susannah's eyes upon me. And *he* flashes before me. A memory so vivid, so acute, my nails dig into my palms.

'I'm sorry,' I shake my head. 'I was thinking of something else altogether.'

'Mama says I may read to you tonight.'

I give a thin awkward smile. Mary, who is cutting a vast currant cake, halts and beams at Susannah. 'Why not show your aunt how you can read in French?' She ploughs the knife into the cake then turns to me. 'A French master comes to the house every week, more for the benefit of Hammond and Tatham, but Anthony thought Susannah should join the lessons. She has such an ear for French, my dear.'

'My French is much better than Hammond's and Tatham's,' adds Susannah, picking out the currants from her cake and pushing them to the edge of her plate. The currants have not had their stalks removed, I note testily.

'Do not brag, Susannah.' Mary turns to me again. 'Her French is very good, my dear. Uncannily so.'

I flinch, wishing she would cease her innuendo. Her constant references to the long-gone past – which I have worked so hard to delete – give it a weight and substance that drags on me, fatigues me. The baby starts to cry and I see Susannah flick a currant at Hammond. Suddenly I long for the composure of Bordyke House, the quiet presence of Ann, my books of recipes and poetry, my quill pen and its brass inkpot, food that has been carefully prepared, properly prepared. Food that is eaten slowly, voluptuously, morsel by morsel and mouthful by mouthful. Not like this table where it is all gobbling and devouring, or mangling to a pulp, or little sticky fingers slipping crusts and currants to the floor.

'If I am to hear you read, I must ready myself.' I make my

voice amiable, jolly. The voice of a fond maiden aunt. 'So I shall rest for an hour, if you will excuse me.'

'You must be rested for dinner.' Mary saws at the bread, which is not properly risen. Then she looks up and fixes her eye on me. 'We have important things to discuss.'

I feel a moment of confusion. As if some mystery has drifted into view, but hovers just out of reach. And then it races towards me and suddenly I understand her letter. She does not want to renew sisterly relations with me. She wants something – *from* me.

Dinner is a dull affair, each course less appetising than the one that precedes it. I gnaw my way through leathery overcooked mutton, boiled potatoes that have not been peeled with sufficient attention and are still hard at the core, shredded cabbage that has been overcooked and not correctly drained and, finally, a rice pudding that has been cooked with neither raisins, almonds, lemon peel nor flavouring of any sort. The awfulness of the food distracts me from the conversation to come, the *important things to discuss*. I have now worked out what these important things are: Mary and Anthony Gwynne are in need of money.

All through dinner I am braced and ready with my answer. Namely, that I have received no advance from Mr Longman and there will be no money for several years to come. I am also braced for questions about my refusal of Mr Arnott, for recriminations and accusations of failing Mother and Father and my sisters, *slaving as governesses*. But none come. Instead, Anthony proves to be a font of knowledge on Professor Liebig and his nutritional theories. For an hour we discuss the importance of nutrition, even as we chew on food that has been cooked dry of all goodness. The irony of it goes unnoticed by Mary who is constantly distracted by the children's scampering feet overhead or by something she has forgotten – a hem that remains undone, a sock heel not yet darned, a misplaced boot that must be collected from a neighbour.

Finally, the port arrives with a tiny crystal glass for Anthony. And with it, the *important things*.

Anthony pours himself a glass and then clears his throat. Mary clears her throat too, so I do not know who is to make the request for money. I see them catch each other's eye and so, to spare them embarrassment, I hold my hand up and say, 'Please don't worry. I know you need money for Susannah, and you shall have it. But I have no advance from Mr Longman, so it will take some time. I have given myself ten years to prepare my cookery book.'

Mary's face flames but before she can speak Anthony has both palms in the air, stroking at it, as if to stop me speaking.

'You have quite misunderstood our invitation,' he says. 'We have asked you here to offer Susannah back to you.'

The blood drains out of my face, then rushes back in a sweep of mortification and confusion and shock.

'Given your refusal of Mr Arnott, it seems unlikely you will have your own family now,' says Mary. 'We love Susannah as if she were our own, but it is not right we should keep her. Mother says you have a young girl helping with your book and we thought, now that Susannah is twelve, perhaps you could use Susannah instead. Mother has agreed.'

My own daughter, I think. I can take Susannah home with me. I shall be a mother. A mother!

'You can explain it very easily,' says Anthony, pouring himself another glass of port. 'You can say she is a niece from Suffolk come to help you. Her costs will be covered by the wages of your kitchen maid.'

I close my eyes and instantly scenes swim before me: Susannah and I at market together; me teaching French and literature to Susannah; the pair of us cooking, tasting, conversing, discussing books and baking, poetry and puddings. I shall introduce her to the verse of Mrs Hemans and Miss Landon. And when I visit the bold Miss Kelly to discuss my play, Susannah shall accompany me and I will tell the truth of her.

'Well, what do you say?' There is a crack in Mary's voice and when I open my eyes I see that hers are glazed with tears.

'Let Eliza sleep on it,' says Anthony gently.

I nod, determined not to make a hasty decision. But I am tingling all over with the promise and possibility of *my daughter*. 'I will hear her read now, as I promised,' I say, pushing away my chair and almost running from the room.

Susannah is propped up on a mound of knitted cushions in a plump painted bed. I touch the bedstead and its metallic chill gives me an instant sense of relief: bedbugs do not take so well to metal. It strikes me this may be my first truly maternal thought, and I feel slightly startled at how it came upon me, as if by instinct. Is this motherhood? Will other motherly feelings follow in the wake of a single fear of bedbugs in my daughter's bed?

'I will recite you a poem,' says Susannah, her scrubbed pink cheeks shining in the candlelight. She starts reciting, fast and in a single breath so that the words spill into one another: '"Will you walk into my parlour?" said the Spider to the Fly, "'Tis the prettiest little parlour that ever you did spy; The way into my parlour is up a winding stair, and I've a many a curious thing to show you when you're there."'

I sit beside her and put a clumsy arm around her shoulders, waiting for – for what? For a deluge of motherly feelings, I think. She is still rattling away, so I try and concentrate on the words . . . '"I'm sure you must be weary dear, with soaring up so high; Will you rest upon my little bed?" said the Spider to the Fly. "There are pretty curtains drawn around; the sheets are fine and thin, And if you'd like to rest awhile I'll snugly tuck you in!" "Oh no, no," said the little Fly, "for I've often heard it said, They never, never wake again, who sleep upon your bed!"'

'You've remembered the words splendidly,' I say, although something about them unsettles me. Images of spiders and unsuspecting flies shuffle through my mind. Which of us is Spider and which of us is Fly? If I were to pluck her from this rowdy boisterous home – where she has a respected doctor as a father – would she one day thank me or would she one day hate me? And what if I cannot cultivate feelings of fondness for her? What if it starts and ends only with the fret of bedbugs?

'Do you know the rest, Susannah?' She doesn't answer and I see she has fallen asleep. I stoop to kiss her cheek, hot and faintly sticky with the residue of cake soap. A thrill runs over me ... my own daughter! How will it be to have her at my side, in my home, the two of us cooking, reading, reciting poetry together? I kiss her cheek again, letting my lips linger, wondering if this is how Mary feels when she kisses her children good night. It is such a contented feeling, I cannot help but kiss Susannah a third time before blowing out the candle. I am just tiptoeing from her room, when a ball hits me on the side of my face. I turn, my cheek fizzing with pain, and glimpse Hammond and Tatham scampering down the hall.

My earlier contentment turns instantly to irritation. Why is Mary not here to scold them, I think, stroking my throbbing cheek. And where is the nursemaid? I try to remain calm because Anthony's words are repeating in my head ... that I must sleep on my decision, that I must not rush into anything. It is only as I creep past Mary's bedchamber that I realise why she is not chiding Hammond and Tatham. She is in her room. Weeping.

Chapter Fifty-Two

Ann

Plain Pound Cake

I don't stop at Bordyke House. Miss Eliza's not due home for another day and I have questions. For Pa. For Reverend Thorpe. For Mrs Thorpe. My feet are sore and stinging. Blisters burst and ooze at my heels and on the tops of my toes. An east wind full of spite and frost has risen from nowhere, whipping my face raw. My fingers are threads of ice. But the pain is nothing next to the din in my head. So many questions, all tripping over each other, a heaving, squirming sprawl of questions. How did Mam die? Why did no one tell me? Why did the Reverend Thorpe bury her in an unmarked grave miles from her home? And beneath these, other questions maunder. Less keen, less sharp. Like a grumbling ache that will not pass. Questions I should have asked long ago: did something make her a lunatic? Did something happen I know nothing of? Did *I* drive her to lunacy? Is her lunacy to be my fate too?

I know I should go home first and ask Pa. But I don't trust him to tell me the truth. And the rectory is on my way. I shall stop at the rectory, I think. I shall put on my *Miss Eliza voice* and insist on a proper burial for Mam in her own church.

I go to the back door, squeezing past a dog cart and a pony at its hay bag. When I ask for the Reverend a housemaid looks me up and down, says he is out, and tries to close the door.

'Mrs Thorpe then?' I ask. The wind blusters past me, lifts the housemaid's apron, tugs at her cap.

She nods and shuts the door. And when it next opens there is Mrs Thorpe, dressed in stout black silk, her face dragging in different directions. As if she doesn't know which expression to muster. Finally she settles on a look of resignation.

'Come in, Ann Kirby,' she says. 'My husband is not here but you can wait.'

'Maybe you can help me, Mrs Thorpe.' My hands shake beneath my shawl as I follow her to the parlour. I would rather be elsewhere. I don't feel comfortable among her china knick-knacks and velvet cushions. I wish I had gone home to Pa but it's too late. Mrs Thorpe points at a plain wooden chair as she lowers her thick rustling skirts into a velveteen armchair. She looks at me with her eyebrows raised, as if she wants to know the nature of my business.

'I've come about my mam.' My voice is very quiet and a gold clock in a glass case chimes as I speak. 'I believe Reverend

Thorpe has buried her, all the way over by Maidstone.' Tears prickle in my eyes.

Mrs Thorpe nods, brisk. 'That is correct. He has been very good to your family, Ann Kirby. I am sure you will want to thank him when he arrives.'

I blink, baffled at her words. 'But how did she die and why was I not told?'

Mrs Thorpe picks up some embroidery from a basket on the floor and, very casual, begins to stitch. 'She fell down the stairs and broke her neck in the asylum. Mr Thorpe was informed and took it upon himself to make the necessary arrangements. He is with your father at this very moment although I expect him back imminently.'

'Yes, that is very kind of him.' My lips wobble as images crowd into my head. Mam tumbling down hundreds of stairs in that huge, grey building. Why wasn't she tied to a nurse? She would never have fallen if I had been caring for her. Guilt presses down on me.

'Indeed it is. He is a busy man. And an exceptionally generous man – he paid seven shillings for her coffin. The Reverend is a saintly man, Ann Kirby.'

'But why is she buried so far away?' I grind my nails into my palms to stop the tears from bursting forth.

'We cannot have the dregs of lunacy in our graveyard, Ann Kirby. Our bedchamber overlooks the graveyard and we hope to have our own children, God willing.' She stabs at her embroidery, not looking at me once. 'Besides, I like to open the window for fresh air.'

I stare at her pale, tight face. Is she saying that Mam's

madness might rise from a coffin, from the earth, and infect her through an open window?

'Yes, the Reverend and I cannot take any risks.' Then she looks up, straight into my eyes. 'The truth, Ann Kirby, is that she has not been your mother for a very long time. My husband saved you – and her – from a life bereft of dignity and propriety. The time for mourning was when she first lost her mind. After that she was no longer a mother, merely a lunatic.'

I look away, at the china ornaments on the mantelpiece, at the framed embroideries and watercolour pictures that crowd the wall, at the yellow roses that twist and writhe upon the rug. I try to summon pictures of Mam before her madness, but they do not come. Not until I turn my foggy head and catch sight of a bible on a table by the window. And in that moment, she comes to me. And I am ten and crouched beside her, turning pages of a book. The air is thick and steamy and smells of apples and honey. A wasp buzzes and its drone mingles with her words. She's speaking in her low, calm voice, her fingertips stroking my cheek. She's telling me books must be treasured, that books will always be my friend.

I grip the picture to me, but it fades away. Later, Pa threw all the books upon the fire, ripping them page by page and shouting that we must have warmth or we would die. Mother was mad by then, but still she wailed and sobbed. Father bound her to the mattress so she could not hurl herself upon the flames.

'She is still my mother and I want her buried in Tonbridge,' I say, surprised at the boldness of my voice.

Mrs Thorpe bends and pulls a padded footstool from

beneath her plump chair. She rests her feet upon it, as if she has had a hard day labouring, and resumes her needlepoint. 'How did it begin, Ann Kirby?' she asks, very slow with her eyes narrowing. 'What were the first indications of her mental decay?'

I pause, unsure what to say, whereupon she rings the brass bell at her belt and tells the parlour maid to bring tea and two slices of plain pound cake no thicker than her little finger – which she jabs at the air so there can be no mistaking how thin to cut the cake.

'Think back, Ann,' she says, her features quite soft now, almost smiling. 'What did you notice first?'

I don't want to talk about Mam to Mrs Thorpe, but I'm suddenly very hungry and thirsty, and it strikes me that if I'm polite perhaps Mam can be buried proper, in Tonbridge. Where Pa and I can place wild flowers upon her grave every week.

I answer her question, uncertainly, for it was many years ago and I was but a child.

'She could not remember what seeds she had planted,' I say. I don't say that nasturtiums burst from every inch of soil, that we had no potatoes or leeks that year, that we ate nasturtium seeds until our mouths burned. Did she stop being my mother then, I wonder? Was that the moment I became *her* mother? Mrs Thorpe's words have left a sour taste in my throat, but I know there is truth in her words. At some point, my mother ceased to be the mother I had known. And yet, to me, she was still Mam ... my mam.

'She became forgetful?' Mrs Thorpe is smiling at me, a

peculiar smile that looks as if it has been stuck upon her face with clay. 'What next?'

'Her words were mixed up and she could not find them,' I reply. I don't tell her how one day, when Mam couldn't seem to find any words at all, she took the iron kettle from the fire and threw it at Pa. Or how, after that, she spent hours and hours lying on the mattress. Just lying there. Doing nothing. Saying nothing.

'When did she start ... wandering and ... removing her clothing?' Mrs Thorpe coughs and inspects her embroidery.

'That was more recent.' All at once I don't want to say any more. I don't want to think of how Mam behaved in the last year. Toppling over as if she were drunk, crying, shouting, lying-like-dead for hours and hours, pissing on the cottage floor, running half-naked up and down the stream bed. I don't want to remember her like that. 'She could not reason,' I say, simply.

Mrs Thorpe's face sets hard again. 'And how about you and your brother? Are you becoming forgetful?'

'I must get back to Bordyke House.' I stand abruptly, no longer caring about my manners or the promised pound cake or seeing the Reverend Thorpe. Suddenly I loathe Mrs Thorpe and her nasty nosy questions, and I want to be in Miss Eliza's kitchen with her poems of despair in front of me. A line of her verse floats towards me. I pluck it from the air and hang on to it, tight ... *Come to my grave when I am gone, and bend a moment there alone* ... I will find a way of getting Mam buried in Tonbridge, I think, even if I have to dig her up with my own bare hands.

CHAPTER FIFTY-THREE

Eliza

POTATO BREAD

Of course I cannot *sleep* on Mary and Anthony's offer to return my daughter. After an hour of inner turmoil I rise and dress myself. I creep down to the drawing room but the fire is almost out and the air is stiffening with cold. I make my way, uncertainly, to the kitchen quarters. Past the scullery, where a housemaid sleeps upon the floor. Past the wash house, where someone snores loudly from behind the door. In the kitchen, the stove still radiates a little stale heat, the copper pans glimmer in the moonlight, and a beetle-trap clicks and clacks as insects fall between its jaws. I close the door behind me and let the serenity, the quietude of the room soothe me. I have an inexplicable urge to do something with my hands – to write or slice or knead. Anything but this endless clenching and unclenching of my fists. I light a candle and look for a quill pen, an inkstand, paper, but see none. Unless I can still my hands, I cannot think, I cannot put my mind in order.

I had not expected Susannah to be returned to me. I had never dared hope for such a thing, although I have often dreamt of how a life with my daughter might be. But now the moment has been sprung upon me and I am plagued with doubts. For me and for her. It pains me to confess it, but I do not have Mary's sanguine motherly nature. And in the anxious hours of night I am beginning to wonder if there is perhaps something wrong with me . . . for even when I kissed Susannah I felt only contentment. Not the true, deep love I suspect Mary feels. Of course, my hand reached involuntarily to check whether Susannah's bedframe might harbour bedbugs. But what if that was only out of concern for my own welfare? Above all, my mind keeps returning to our introduction in the drawing room, when I felt merely curiosity. None of the warmth and affection I imagined would pour into me at our first meeting. Am I unnatural in some way?

I look about the kitchen and my eye falls upon a flour tin and a basket of potatoes. I find a paring knife hanging from the dresser shelf and begin scraping the potatoes, dropping long spirals of mud-crusted peel into a bowl. I give each twisting length of peel a thought as I dispose of it: would my daughter be more contented alone with me, or with a full family replete with siblings and father? Do I have the attributes of a good mother? Does Susannah belong to me because I bore her, or to Mary who raised her? What makes a mother?

As I drop the final peeling into the bowl, I have an overwhelming sense of *wanting*. Of wanting Susannah for myself. Of wanting to possess what is rightfully mine. A memory of her birth comes to me: she is in my arms, her head streaked with blood, her face crumpled like a blanched walnut. Madame le Duc, in her long white apron, bends over me, giving me brandy from a china feeding cup. Susannah gnaws on my nipple. I feel again the pain, the relief, the sheer exhaustion of it all. Pierre never visited, never saw her.

One day, as I was waiting to return to England, I received a letter from him. I didn't keep it but its words are impressed upon my mind. And the scene of its arrival is set, as if in aspic. I can remember all those vivid little details: the air pulsing with the warm scent of lilac; the Normandy light falling, like gold, across the floor; the creaking of the rocking chair with its cane upholstery; Father reading and pulling at his moustache; Madame le Duc humming to Susannah. I was looking out of the long narrow window, wishing I was well enough to walk along the beach again. The beach where Pierre and I had spent such joyful times, walking and talking, our hands fluttering, grazing, unable to keep apart.

Of course the beach had also been my downfall. The softly sloping dunes where I had taken him in my arms, where we had kissed as we had never kissed before. He had asked me to marry him. He said the French way was to make love before marriage, that there was no shame, that as his wife I would be half-French. I don't regret it. For many years I have feasted from that one night of passionate love, recalling his sumptuous skin, the touch of him, the sand sinking softly beneath me.

When I realised I was with child, it was too late. By then I'd heard the talk of his philandering. With servant girls and seamstresses, with ladies and with lace-makers. It seemed that no one was immune to his desires and yet all this had passed me by. I saw then my future ... a wife, far from home and cast aside, unable to trust a single maid, a single friend. Not for all the silver in Spain would I be that forlorn little wife.

At first the jealousy was unbearable. I could think of nothing but how he touched them, how he kissed them, the words he slipped into their ears. The jealousy bore into me, green and sour, until I could think of nothing else. Until I was no longer myself. Then one night I decided to express my feelings on paper. I wonder now if it wasn't God's obscure guidance – for the writing of verse was my saviour. A week later, I returned Pierre's ring. He fell upon his knees, begged me to think again, said all the talk of other women was lies and slander. I wavered. He was so very handsome, so dashing, so charming. So famed for his courage and bravery upon the battlefield. I felt my body melt and cry out for him, but my mind was stronger. And I was fortified by poetry.

That evening I returned to my lodgings and wrote poem after poem. A month later I knew for sure I was with child. I was bursting from my corset, my monthly bleeding had ceased, I could take no food before midday. Still my mind was resolute: I would not be Pierre's submissive prowling wife. I wrote to Mary, who had married Anthony and become stepmother to his three children and was also with child herself. I wrote only for advice: my sleep was broken every night by fierce cramps in both legs and the morning nausea was unbearable. But she informed Mother, who refused to correspond with me. Father, however, hurried to Normandy. He tried to persuade me to take back Pierre, to make a marriage of form. But I would not. I could not. I had found a voice in my writing, a voice that kept me steady. A voice that seemed to offer me a means of escape. Already I was imagining a little booklet of verse, an audience. I knew there was truth in my words and that, if they had helped me they could help others. Even as I grew big with Pierre's child, I was nurturing this other secret child – my verse. By the time of my confinement Pierre had found himself a new fiancée and Father had halted all attempts to *return me* to him. But my secret love child – my poetry – was well and truly bonded to me, warm and alive with a beating heart all of its own.

There was only one matter on which Father was intractable: I was not to raise the child myself. Already Mother and Mary had agreed the Acton family must not have its good name stained by a bastard child. Such a stain would have made marriage for my sisters unattainable, business for my father and brother difficult, a social life for Mother impossible. And as for me, the education in which Father had invested would have been worthless.

'How will you find a husband?' he asked. 'How can you be a governess or a schoolmistress or a lady's companion if you have a child?'

Pierre's letter arrived that afternoon, as the shadows lengthened, as the running swell of the sea grew louder in that long-windowed room. He wrote with a proposition:

that he and his wife-to-be adopt Susannah and raise her, in France, as their own. It was a generous offer and Father urged me to consider it. I knew then that I could lose my child for ever. I wrote to Mary and Anthony and begged them to take Susannah. Mary's letter came swiftly – she would take Susannah, but on one condition. Only if she could raise Susannah entirely as her own. Only if I forfeited all maternal rights. For ever.

Susannah was mine for a mere month. Did I love her for that month? Can that month compare with her many years as Mary's daughter? I remember the wrench of handing Susannah to my sister. For a week I suffered. For a week the emptiness at my elbow and my breast was an aching throbbing pain. My leaking milk was like a wound until Madame le Duc bound my chest in cold cabbage leaves and strips of linen. I wrote poetry day and night. But then, one bright morning, I walked out through woods of pine and birch. Foxgloves and wild clematis and briar roses were bursting from the earth. Birdsong shook the air. Swifts snipped at the sky. I knew then that I must publish a collection of my poems. Not only the tragic ones but new verse, about the glory of life, the joys of solitude, the majesty of nature. I hurried back to England and set to work, finding printers and subscribers, writing new poems, editing the old ones. Pierre was quite forgotten. Even Susannah had faded to a dim memory. After a while I struggled to recall her features, to hear the pitch of her cry, to remember the milky softness of her skin.

All this floods back to me as I chop potatoes, as I pump water into a pan, as I place the pan upon the stove and pray for sufficient heat to bring it to the boil. While the potatoes simmer I weigh out flour by rushlight and hunt for yeast in the pantry, being very careful not to wake the supine creature – a parlour maid? – sleeping upon the floor. My thoughts turn to Susannah. What is right for her? To rip her from her family? Her home?

As I tip the flour into a bowl, I hear the beetle-trap click-clicking. Not once, but several times, as if a train of insects has been gobbled up. I measure out the yeast and prod at the potatoes. I can tell they are properly mealy from how quickly they crumble. Perfect for potato rolls, I think. Only then do I remember Ann. It was she who told me of a bread her mother made using potatoes rubbed, quite hot, through a coarse sieve.

If Susannah comes to me, what will happen to Ann? If Susannah comes to me, how will I make the money I need to be truly independent? To secure *her* independence? If Susannah comes to me, how will I complete my cookery book, my play?

As I drain the water from the potatoes, my conundrum clears into a simple question: what do I most want for my daughter? And through the smoking, spitting rushlight, an answer comes. Clear and concise.

CHAPTER FIFTY-FOUR

Ann

SMOKED HAUNCH OF BADGER

I leave the rectory and return to Bordyke House. Hatty takes one look at my long face and hugs me to her, very hard.

'Go to your pa first thing in the morning. I can do your work and I'll tell Ma'am. Miss Eliza ain't due back just yet,' she says. Later that night, after she blows out the candle I tell her everything.

'You're lucky the Reverend Thorpe has dealt with it,' she says, matter-of-fact. 'At least your mam's in consecrated ground. I've heard tell of pauper lunatics being thrown into lime pits. No grave, not even a coffin. They just put 'em in a shroud and throw 'em in a hole.'

Her words startle me out of my grief. Mrs Thorpe's comment

about the cost of Mam's grave flies into my head. Seven shillings for a coffin. Why would Reverend Thorpe do that? I fling back the cover and sit bolt upright. All the hairs on my arms are on end. My mouth feels as dry as sawdust. So dry that when I speak my voice is hoarse and croaky. 'Are you sure, Hatty?'

'Oh yes. Paupers from the workhouse are treated likewise, only their hearts are chopped open. With idiots, it's the skull. Cracked open like a nut, they say. They can't very well bury them after that, can they? So they tip 'em in a lime pit.'

I don't answer her, for the darkness is seething all around me, muffling her gabble so that everything blurs. All I can think of is Reverend Thorpe, hurrying to the asylum, getting Mam's body to the nearest church, paying for the coffin, not breathing a word.

'And you ain't had to pay a penny. So Reverend Thorpe has done you a service. Anyway, it's not so far, is it? I'll come with you and we can plant it up with spring violets, make it the prettiest burial plot in the place. And you can save for a headstone.'

'But why would he do this for us? He hates us.'

'Because he's a man of the cloth and God told him, I suppose.'

I put my head beneath the cold sheet and close my eyes. Something seems odd to me, very odd. I think of the times I visited the asylum, how eerily silent it was. No other visitors, no parish officers, no hearses or carriages. I glimpsed tradesmen of course, but they had always disappeared round the back, like the miller. And yet the Reverend Thorpe had been there. A day before me.

The following morning I rise early, leaving Hatty to black the stove and pump the water and fill the coal scuttles and lay the fires. I find Pa at the cottage, pegging out fresh moleskins for the puny December sun to dry. He leans for his crutches but I put up my hand and tell him not to move. Then I squat beside him and start crying, huge scraping sobs that judder through me.

'She's in Heaven,' he says. ''Tis better for her. And Reverend Thorpe got there in time to have her properly buried. She's in God's own hands now.'

'Why can't she be buried here?' I sob. 'Near enough for us to visit . . .'

He shakes his head. 'Mrs Thorpe didn't want her too close. And then there was the extra expense of getting her body here. I couldn't ask that of him. What matters is that she's had a Christian burial, Ann.'

I nod, my sobs dying in my throat.

'Her funeral would have been a sparse and dismal affair. Best left to the Reverend.' Pa takes my hand in his and jerks his head at the neat line of moleskins beside him. 'Will you come home, Ann? I'm making a few coins from the moles and the Reverend has offered us the bones and eel skins from his kitchen. Seems he's partial to eel but he don't use the skins, which dry very nice and make a lovely garter for gentlemen with aching knees. We could scratch a living, the two of us.'

I stare at the grey moleskins with their long pale claws, pegged firmly into the ground with small wooden stakes. I should come home and look after Pa, I know that. But as I think this, something tugs at my insides sucking out all the air in my lungs. I wipe my eyes and think of Mam, of all the hours she spent helping me with my letters. Did she teach me to read and write so that I can *scratch a living*? I think of Jack in his shiny white kitchen, of Miss Eliza bowed over her quill pen. I imagine myself at market, selling Pa's greasy candles and scrawny moleskins from a barrow. I cannot believe that is what Mam intended for me.

He nods towards the kitchen. 'Can you smell that?'

I sniff at the air, catching something meaty, woody, smoky at the back of my nose. 'Are you cooking in there?'

'I've a haunch of badger smoking in the chimney. The Reverend has agreed I can lay traps in his garden. You won't go hungry here, Ann.'

All this talk of the Reverend is confounding me, unsettling me. I have a feeling that Pa is not telling me everything.

'Why did the Reverend have Mam buried? Why didn't he leave it to us? Or to the asylum?'

Pa sucks at his cheeks and says nothing for a long time. I feel the cold and wet of the soil seeping through my skirt and petticoat, spreading through my skin and into my bones. 'Does he do that for all his parishioners?' I feel confused, for everyone keeps telling me how good the Reverend is and yet I cannot forget all his little acts of meanness.

Eventually, Pa speaks. 'No,' he says. 'No, he does not.'

'So why for us?'

He strokes absently at a pegged moleskin, still sucking in his cheeks. 'You must not breathe a word, Ann. Do you promise?'

I nod, more flummoxed than ever. I feel very hot inside my

cold damp clothes, a flushing heat that comes from nowhere, and makes my skin scald, my face burn, so that I must throw off my shawl and loosen my bodice.

'The Reverend Thorpe and your mother were cousins. We were sworn to say nothing, to no one.'

My eyes grow big and disbelieving.

'And so he feels an obligation. Not much, but a little. His wife believes madness to be in the blood. She makes it hard for him, but she has the money. Not him.'

'So he is a relative of mine?'

'If we do not shame them – with drinking, or madness, or crime – they will help us. But we must say nothing of the family connection. They were shamed by your mam marrying so far beneath her but now they are shamed by other things, by my crippled leg, by us being paupers. But mostly they do not want the taint of madness upon them. Do you understand, Ann?'

I nod and stand up. The smell of smoking meat gusts from the cottage making me feel hollow and hungry. And in that second, my future is suddenly, blindingly, as clear as glass. I think of Miss Eliza, the way she always speaks with purpose. I try and copy her voice, strong and clear.

'I cannot scratch out a living here, Pa. Mam would not have wanted it. And I don't want it. I want more – I want to be a cook. I want to help Miss Eliza finish her book of recipes.' And only God knows how long is left to me, I think. Only God can spare me from the lunacy.

I help Pa up, adjust his crutches for him, motion to the cottage. 'I shall insist that Mr Thorpe takes you back. It is the least he can do for us.' As I walk beside Pa, it seems to me that I am a fraction taller, a little straighter. As if something inside of me has grown.

'You'll take a slice of my badger ham, won't you, Ann?'

'I will,' I say. 'But then I'm going straight to Mr Thorpe.' And I have never heard my tongue so determined, so decisive.

CHAPTER FIFTY-FIVE

Eliza

CHOCOLATE ALMONDS, GINGER CANDY AND PALACE BONBONS ON OSIER TWIGS

I am pulling an iron tray of potato rolls from the oven, straining to see if the crusts are sufficiently browned and crisp, when the kitchen maid appears, her hands scrabbling at the ribbons of her apron. She cries out in surprise, for the mantel clock shows it is barely six and the rushlight throws only the slenderest beam upon my person.

'It's only me – Miss Acton,' I tell her. 'I have made a fire, so that is one less task for you.'

She peers, bemused and still half-asleep, at the rolls.

'Potato rolls,' I explain. 'They stay moist longer than any other bread and the flavour is excellent. Do you have a rack?'

The girl gawps at me as if I am speaking in a foreign tongue. After a few seconds she comes to her senses and pulls a rack from a cupboard on the wall. 'I'm sorry, ma'am,' she says, blinking. 'Only Mistress Mary rarely comes to the kitchen. I thought you was an intruder.'

'Indeed not,' I say briskly. I leave instructions for the rolls to be served warm with very fresh salted butter and return to my room to find the portrait of myself I brought for Susannah. As I'd rubbed the boiled potatoes through a cullender, stirred in the flour, kneaded the dough and cut it into squares, my mind had cleared and sharpened. And now I have a plan and must put it into action.

I take the portrait from my trunk and a letter wallet from my bag. From the wallet I take a poem I wrote to Susannah after Mary took her from me ... I read it again, and think how poignantly it reads, but also how distant it sounds, as if it has been penned by someone else, someone I barely know. All that repetition of the word 'forget-me-not'. How lacking in originality it seems. How obvious.

I roll the poem into a tight cylinder and slip it inside the rolled portrait, pausing briefly to unroll it and inspect my silhouetted pen-and-ink self. She too seems another person. Even though she is so newly inked. She is no longer me, I think. In the same way that Susannah is not mine. Too much has passed. How can we be mother and daughter without that bond of time and nurture to sustain us?

I think of the expression on Mary's face when Anthony offered Susannah back to me. The way her lips trembled, the light draining almost imperceptibly from her eyes. I recall the weeping I heard from her room. I remember how she watched over the tea table – correcting the children's manners and grammar, straightening their collars and cuffs – and how she can talk of little else. Could I be like that? Do I want to be like that? I look again at the portrait, searching the eyes for signs of who I was. Could I have been like Mary? Could I have been as happy a mother as she is? I try to picture myself with a boisterous brood of children, but the picture in my mind's eye is a watercolour and will not hold, the colours bleeding and fading. Perhaps if I picture it in oils, I think. Still it tears and frays and will not hold. I look at the rolled-up portrait with its inner rolled-up poem – reassuringly firm and tidy – and speak to my old self: *Perhaps you were never intended for motherhood, perhaps you were made differently, made for something else.*

While I wait for Mary to wake up, I take ink and quill, and note down my observations on potato rolls ... More salt is needed than with regular wheaten bread. And less liquid. And the fire must be gentle, if they are to succeed. My nib scratches over the paper as I add my final observation: the potatoes must be of the best quality, the very best. Only when my notes are complete do I take a clean sheet of paper and start writing instructions for my will. Susannah may not have her blood mother but I am determined she has her independence, that she has choices. For without choices, we are nothing.

Later, when I've completed the notes for my testament, I go in search of Mary. I find her in the nursery, instructing the nursemaid on which outfits the children are to wear.

Already the room is pandemonium: the boys are fighting, the girls are bickering over hair ribbons, the baby is wailing, three musical boxes are clamouring, and Mary's sartorial instructions are being delivered most emphatically. I retreat and wait impatiently in the corridor. Now my mind is made up I want to return to Bordyke House as swiftly as possible. Ann will be there, I think. And the kitchen will be quiet, industrious, purposeful. I shall be able to proceed, unfettered, with my work.

As Ann comes to mind, I have a sudden longing to take her a gift. Something dainty and delicious. Chocolate almonds, ginger candy, barley sugar ... in a pretty bag tied with satin ribbon ... I make a mental note to ask Mary if there is a confectionery shop nearby, but already the mental note is lost, for my mind is crackling with ideas of confectionery. Our book must have a confectionery chapter, I think. Nougat, as I ate it in France, crammed with pistachios, almonds, filberts. Palace Bonbons of candied citron on osier twigs. Orange-flower candy made with the freshest blossom. How odd – no sooner does Ann come to mind than I am running over with ideas and inspiration. It strikes me then that Ann is more daughter to me than Susannah.

Mary appears, breathless and bustling, from the nursery. 'They are always full of spirit in the morning!' She laughs and fans at her face with her fingers, as if the exuberance of the nursery has warmed her. Then her face falls. 'We shall miss Susannah terribly. She is so loved by us all.' She turns away and fumbles for a handkerchief. When she speaks again, her voice is low and muffled, as if she has the handkerchief pressed against her mouth. 'But Anthony is right and we cannot keep her for ever. Not now that you have chosen to be husband-less, not now that she can live with you under the guise of a niece or a kitchen maid.'

'Mary,' I put my hand upon her arm. 'I have decided it is better for Susannah to stay with you. As soon as I am able, I shall send an allowance.' I pause and a strangled gasp splutters from my sister's throat. I continue, rapidly, efficiently and to the point. 'I shall leave her everything in my will, so there will be no financial burden on Anthony. And no difficulty for you finding her a husband. There is just one thing …'

Tears are streaming, in gullies, down Mary's pink disbelieving cheeks. 'B-but she is yours …' Her stammer is a mingled relief and shock and bewilderment. As if she cannot understand my decision, even as it fills her with joy.

'There is just one thing,' I repeat. 'I have a small portrait of myself that I would like to give to Susannah. I shall leave it at your discretion how best to explain it.'

'She must not be tainted by scandal,' sniffs Mary into her handkerchief.

'No,' I agree. '*I may have sinned … but be the curse upon my head – oh, let it not descend to her.*'

Mary looks up, her eyes pink and wet. 'That is so beautifully spoken, Eliza.'

'I quote the verse of Miss Landon,' I explain, my voice wavering. 'I was once told that husbands wouldn't allow their wives to invite Miss Landon into their homes. I do not want a similar fate for Susannah.'

'Nor for you,' says Mary, suddenly sounding cheerful and resolved. 'Scandal and shame are to the detriment of all of us.'

I nod absent-mindedly. It strikes me that, as Susannah's 'aunt', I can do more for her than I ever could as her hapless, ill-starred mother.

'I shall go and inform Anthony – he will be delighted.' Mary gives a little satisfied clap of her hands. 'And then I must deal with Cook, who is very upset and about to give warning. She is under the delusion that I have forgotten my place and used her kitchen before she was up.' She laughs as if such an idea is preposterous, then hurries to the stairs, her voice issuing commands to the air: 'Hammond, are you dressed yet? Anthony, where are you? Bessy – tell Cook I am coming . . . And can someone put the dog outside?'

It pleases me to see Mary so full of cheer, to know that Susannah is so deeply loved. But thoughts of *scandal* and *shame* pluck at me. There is a finality in those words, I think. An unambiguous instruction that makes my dream of dedicating my cookery book to Susannah a misguided folly. It will need a new dedication, I think, as I return to my chamber to pack up my belongings. Words and phrases flay about in my head: a line from Mrs Hemans? A dedication to the memory of Miss Landon? No doubt Mother will wish it dedicated to her . . . Should I dedicate it to Mary in gratitude? Or to Father who had me educated and is still in exile?

I shake my head, trying to rid myself of all these swilling thoughts, for I would much prefer to think of candied fruits and caramel. But as the coach rolls back to Colchester, and then another jolting coach to Tonbridge, Susannah will not leave my mind. I am determined she inherits something sizeable from me, be it money, or ... or ... Only when my journey is finished do I realise that I have come home empty-handed, my intended gift of chocolate almonds or ginger candy for Ann quite forgotten.

Chapter Fifty-Six

Eliza

Her Majesty's Pudding

I cannot shake the idea of dedicating my cookery book to Susannah. Back at Bordyke House I pull down my volume of *Domestic Cookery*, which states most clearly in its introduction that it was written for *the authoress's own daughters*. I read those words again and feel a prick of envy. But then my eye is caught by the frontispiece and its accompanying line: *By a Lady*. And another possibility comes to me. If I published anonymously – another unknown, nameless *Lady* – perhaps I could safely dedicate my book to Susannah. It would be my gift to her, along with the future proceeds of the book.

As I ponder this I notice a line at the bottom of the page, a line I have never previously noticed:

SIXTIETH EDITION

Suddenly I no longer want to be anonymous. Not even for Susannah. In my mind's eye I see my book – sixty editions of it – with my name emblazoned across the opening page and stalking down the spine. There is something about this image that makes me tremble, even as it makes me feel taller, less flimsy. I have lived at the whim of chance, but if my book ran to sixty editions Susannah would inherit a substantial estate. She could live freely, like a gentleman or a wealthy widow. I balance *A New System of Domestic Cookery* in my palm and imagine my own book being passed from hand to hand, from mother to daughter, from sister to neighbour, from family to friend. Of one thing I am sure: recipes speak. They carry within them their own language. And to remain anonymous is an act of cowardice. For when we strip away our name, we remove the certainty so necessary for a new housekeeper. I look at my shelf of recipe books: *Carême's Patissier Royal; Raffald's Cookery; Glass's Cookery; Clermont's Cookery*. Each name in proud, gleaming gilt. And it seems to me that these recipe-writers have been my companions, not only guiding me with their instruction, but offering friendship – even as they infuriated me with their ill-measured ingredients and inelegant prose. They have softened the edges of my seclusion, filling my kitchen with accomplices. I turn over Mrs Rundell's book and inspect the nameless spine. I shake my head, for company is never nameless. What sort of woman ekes out her friendship in anonymity?

The door rattles open and Ann appears, her gait so unusually brisk and bright that I forget all thoughts of *sixty editions*.

She asks about my journey and my sister's family, then says, 'Are we to be very busy today, Miss Eliza?' There is a glitter to her voice, as if she has swallowed a saucer of golden ingots. And for a second I am envious of how uncomplicated her life is. She has felt hunger and cold, of course. But she has never battled her own ambition, or felt the sting of spinsterhood with all its untold duties, or experienced the lashing tongue of disapprobation. She simply *lives*.

Ann looks at me, as if she can see my envy in the green glare of my eyes, then says, 'Or are you working on your play today?'

'I'm thinking of visiting Lady Montefiore,' I say, quite unexpectedly, my words bolting from my mouth as if of their own accord. 'She wishes to read my play and I wish to meet her theatrical friend, Miss Kelly.' I feel a sudden urgency to complete my play, to see it performed in London, to hear lines – that I have written – bounce from the walls of a theatre. At the same time I hear the call of my cookery book. And my head hums with hundreds of recipes impatient to be cooked in kitchens everywhere. 'So little time,' I murmur, too quietly for Ann to hear.

'I worked on a new dish while you were away. A pudding.' She ties her apron tight around her waist. 'Milk, cream, vanilla, eggs and sugar.'

'Oh,' I say, slightly unsettled at the jauntiness of her tone, at its *certainty*. 'A custard. Did it curdle?'

She ignores my question and tells me that she garnished her pudding with branches of preserved barberries. She asks if I would like to see it. But before I can answer she scuttles to the pantry, returning with a clean pudding cloth over one arm, and my best platter – on which wobbles a custard as large and pale as a harvest moon. Atop are woven branches of barberries that wink like garnets. For a second I am speechless. Her creation – for it is nothing less – is picture-perfect.

She offers me a salt spoon and jabs at the platter. 'Go on, Miss Eliza. I saved it for you to taste first.'

I dip the spoon into the custard's wrinkled rind and lift it swiftly, curiously, to my lips. As I do so, I'm aware of a sense of serenity washing through me. My anguish over dedications, the lurking accusatory voice that lives inside my head, all of it slips away. And there is only cream and vanilla. It occurs to me that although this glorious pudding is her creation, Ann is partly my creation, and I am partly her creation. Cooking and tasting have provided their own stage and we are performing on it at this very moment.

'Have you a name?' I nod at the quivering pudding, marvelling again at Ann's use of barberry branches for decoration. 'What about Barberry Custard?'

Ann smiles, more to herself than to me. 'I've called it *Her Majesty's Pudding*.'

'For Queen Victoria,' I nod, approvingly.

'Oh no,' she says. 'For my mam who died and was buried without my knowledge.'

The salt spoon clatters from my hand. Why has Ann not mentioned her mother passing away? I feel confounded and hurt but Ann merely wipes at her eye with the pudding cloth, then turns back to the custard and pokes at the barberry branches. 'I don't want to talk about my mam,' she says. 'Besides, the custard is named for you too, Miss Eliza. You are now my queen.'

Something clots briefly in my throat. But then Ann is speaking again, and her words leave me dumbstruck. 'I have a new rich relative, but I can't say anything because he is a secret!'

I stare at Ann, and wonder if the girl is touched with fever, if the death of her mother has sparked a fire in her brain. But another glance at her barberry custard tells me this cannot be the case. I feel panic at the edges of me, moving through my veins, blotting out my surprise and confusion and hurt. Blotting out the joy of hearing her call me her *queen*.

'A rich relative?' I repeat foolishly. But my mind is frothing. Is she about to leave Bordyke House to live with her *rich relative*? To look after her widowed father? Or to join her brother in Monsieur Soyer's famous kitchen? No wonder her tone is jaunty! No wonder there is a fresh spring in her step!

'Yes,' she says, her gaze swivelling to the window. 'I can't say any more, but it has made me feel ... bolder. And so did getting Pa's job back, and making and naming my own pudding.' Her eyes turn back to me and they have lost their customary shyness. 'I have you to thank, Miss Eliza. You have ...' She pauses and I see her lips working, searching for the right phrase.

'Emboldened you?'

'More than that ... Nourished me.' She tips her chin, as if pleased at her choice of word. Then she falls silent, and I wait for her to say that she wishes to give notice. Instead she turns on her heel, hurrying *Her Majesty's Pudding* back to the pantry. Leaving me to mull her newfound audacity: will it take her from me? Is my kitchen sufficiently spacious to accommodate two bold cooks?

My head feels too small for so much confusion and doubt. So I return to Mrs Rundell's recipe book, my thoughts scrambling back to my own cookery book and the problem of its dedication. I wipe at a buttery fingerprint on the spine, then dust off a smudge of flour. And as I do so a name flashes before me. Ann! I would like to dedicate my book – *our* book – to Ann ... But no, that would never do. No writer ever dedicated a book to a servant, and Mother would be incandescent with rage. I must find a dedication that encompasses Ann *and* Susannah, that speaks to anyone in need of a kitchen companion, that includes all those exiled from their kitchens ... rich and poor, married and unmarried, Jewish and gentile ... Words begin to cut and fold in my head. I need words that are clear, simple, to the point. Like my recipes. Like me ...

I close my eyes. I can hear the fire hissing with a thousand breaths, Ann humming in the pantry, the clink and clank as she arranges bottles and jars. And from this music, a line drifts into my head. A line that is clear, simple, complete. The perfect dedication:

To the Young Housekeepers of England.

I write it down and slip it inside the pages of my play. And then I repeat it under my breath. *To the Young Housekeepers of England ... To the Young Housekeepers of England.*

And I like it. Yes, I like it very much.

EPILOGUE

1861
GREENWICH, LONDON

Ann

I find her cookery book at the bottom of a chest where I keep spare blankets for Mr Whitmarsh's motherless girls: *Modern Cookery*. How sturdy and handsome it looks, in its wine-red leather bindings, embossed on the spine, stitched at the edges – and her name in gold so bright it sparkles. I open the book and turn to the title page. I can't help but smile: *Modern Cookery, In All Its Branches: Reduced To A System Of Easy Practice, For the Use Of Private Families ... In A Series of Receipts Which Have Been Strictly Tested, And Are Given With The Most Minute Exactness ...* Oh, Lord, how we tested! I turn to the contents page, laying the book side by side with my so-called gift from Mr Whitmarsh: *Mrs Beeton's Book of Household Management.* And then I go through both, recipe by recipe. By five o'clock I have barely covered a quarter. But already I can see which way the wind blows. Mrs Beeton has filched at least a third of our recipes. The very same dishes, but made flat and dull, and with new titles of her own making. Granted, her placing of ingredients at the beginning rather than the end is clever. But there's nothing more than that.

Reading our recipes all over again has made my tongue hum. Like it used to. Before I came to Mr Whitmarsh's house and he told me he would dine only at his club for *professional reasons*. Before his daughters refused to eat anything but burnt-to-a-crisp mutton cutlets with plain boiled potatoes and plain rice pudding. I lost heart when I came here. Mr Whitmarsh wanted me laundering his shirts and his daughters' frocks, and scrubbing the floors, and boiling up the rags he needs as chief dispenser at the Royal Greenwich Hospital. He gave me enough money for cutlets, potatoes, rice and milk. And not a penny more. Meanwhile his belly grew plump and soft on Green Turtle Soup and suet pudding. Gobbled at his club for *professional reasons* . . .

I put the books to one side, take a sheet of paper and write myself a shopping list. Tomorrow I will cook real food. Miss Eliza's food. Why else has the man given me a cookery book? As I write out the ingredients from my favourite dishes, the flavours and tastes return to me, reaching beneath my tongue, collecting sweetly in a pool at the base of my throat: a brace of young well-kept partridges, fresh button mushrooms, port wine, fine salt, a firm flavoursome cucumber, fresh green spinach. And pudding? Why, of course! It must be the pudding we tested over and over: *The Elegant Economist's Pudding*. How she liked that name! And how apt it was – for she was both elegant and thrifty. To my list I add: a pint of stoned raisins, fresh milk and newly laid eggs, lemon-grate, bitter almonds, a few drops of ratafia.

I say not a word to anyone, but two days later I tell Mr Whitmarsh he is to eat at home tonight. He looks at me, perplexed. I slip a hand inside my neckline, flirty, and say, 'For *professional reasons*, sir.' And then I wink, as bold as brass.

When he gets home, his girls are already fed their overcooked mutton cutlets and tired rice pudding, and I have dressed the table like an altar. Best damask tablecloth. Best Wedgwood china. Best crystal. The three-pronged silverplated forks. A fresh bunch of sage at the ceiling to keep the flies away. He sniffs at the air, confused and wary. As if he thinks I'm about to poison him. Then he looks at the table, laid for two, and frowns. 'Am I not dining alone?'

'I shall join you, if I may, sir.' I blush, for it's not a servant's place to suggest such things, even when she shares her master's bed. 'It's all cooked and keeping warm. But I can eat below if you prefer?' Oh, the bare-faced cheek! I never heard myself so brash and saucy. Mr Whitmarsh raises one sprouty eyebrow, then shrugs. And so I eat beside him, in a high-backed chair with a napkin shook out upon my knee. Like a married woman dining with her husband.

Over supper – spit-roast partridges stuffed with field mushrooms and served with a mushroom and port-wine sauce, and stewed cucumbers, and spinach turned from a mould and richly buttered – I tell him of my life before I came to him. Of how Miss Eliza Acton and I worked ten years on a cookery book. Of how she wanted it to bear my name too, but I refused. I felt it weren't my place. We fell out over that, for she could not understand it and was mortally offended. And then I found out she had a child, a girl she'd kept hidden from me all those years. It was my turn to be mortally offended. For by then I thought we were firm friends.

Mr Whitmarsh eats, drinks, nods. No doubt thinking of the medicines he must dispense tomorrow. So I continue rambling on about my past ... For reasons that were stupid and regrettable, I left Bordyke House. Miss Eliza asked me to stay and help with her next book, which was to be on nothing but bread. But we had been too long together – cooking side by side fifteen hours a day for ten years – and she had become quite the preacher. Always angry about poverty and the injustices of life although she'd never had a hungry day! Later, when she was living in Hampstead and working on her book of bread recipes, she sent me a signed copy of *our* book. In her letter she said her 'niece' was helping out. Even then she refused to say it was her *daughter*. She wrote that her play had been a great success but that she was too tired to write plays or poetry now and that her mind was going. She could not remember simple things, she said. She forgot to put her full address, writing only Miss Eliza Acton, Hampstead, London. So how was I to write back to her?

Mr Whitmarsh is barely listening to me, for when I put this question he nods and chaws and says my food is the finest he has ever eaten and why didn't I tell him I was a mistress of the kitchen?

'And now she's dead,' I say, ignoring his question as he has ignored mine. 'And I think it was the madness that came upon her because that was how my mam started her slow descent ... forgetting little things. And knowing this frightened me so that I didn't want to think about Miss Eliza, or look at our book, or cook. But now . . .' My voice trails off as I wonder how best to explain that Mrs Beeton's plundering of our recipes has reminded me that life is short, that it comes only once, that it must be grabbed and gulped at. And not left out to spoil and rot.

He cocks an eyebrow, then lifts a partridge bone to his mouth and sucks noisily upon it. 'Better than my club, far better, and all the time you've been scrubbing floors, my Ann . . .'

'I am tired of scrubbing floors and charring mutton cutlets for your girls, sir.' I put my knife and fork down. 'I want to be your cook. You can entertain your gentlemen friends here. Mrs Beeton says home dining is very fashionable in polite society.' I almost spit when I say *Mrs Beeton* – the cheek of her!

'Only in households where there is a wife who acts as hostess.' Mr Whitmarsh says, curt. No mention of *my Ann* . . . 'I cannot invite the doctors' wives if I do not have one myself.'

I take a deep breath. 'I am tired of being your servant. I wish to be Mrs Whitmarsh and to cook your supper every night and converse with your gentlemen friends and their wives. And to sleep always in your bed.' My face blushes hot but I look right at him, straight in his eye. If he says no, I'm decided: I'll go elsewhere and find a position as cook. Monsieur Soyer is dead these past two years, as is my brother Jack, but there are other places I can go. I have heard talk that Lady Montefiore has opened a Jewish soup kitchen in the East End of London. Likely she would take me . . .

He looks down at his plate and slurps at his mushroom and port-wine sauce, very slow as if he's thinking. Then he looks up and grins. 'Why else do you think I bought you a book of household management, my Ann?'

My addled brain dances. 'So you will accept my hand in marriage, my Benjamin?'

He laughs. 'Only if your pudding is as good as your partridge.'

'Oh, it's better,' I say. 'The Elegant Economist's Pudding is the best sweet dish ever baked.'

HISTORICAL NOTE

Eliza Acton's 576-page cookery book took a decade to complete. Published in 1845 as *Modern Cookery, in All Its Branches: Reduced to A System of Easy Practice, For The Use Of Private Families*, it was an immediate success and became a bestseller within weeks of publication, staying in print for over seventy years. It's now widely regarded as the first cookery book written for general use and its author as the first 'modern' cookery writer. The book – which sold over 125,000 copies within thirty years – returned to print in 1966 and has been reprinted several times since.

Eliza's biggest innovation was listing the ingredients for each *receipt*, as recipes were called at the time. *Modern Cookery* was the first book to include accurate measured lists of ingredients, a concept extended by Mrs Beeton and now followed by cookery writers everywhere. Not only did *Modern Cookery* include ingredient lists with each recipe but it also gave precise notes on timings and other factors likely to affect the outcome, often under the heading of *Obs* (a thoroughly contemporary abbreviation of *Observations*). It was also the first cookbook, according to food historian, William Sitwell, to include a recipe for Brussel sprouts.

Eliza Acton remained in great respect (perhaps more than any other historical cookery writer) by later generations of chefs and writers. She has been described by Delia Smith as 'the best cookery writer in the English language', and by food writer Bee Wilson as 'great', while *Modern Cookery* was described by Elizabeth David as 'unquestionably the greatest cookery book in our language'; by Soyer's biographer, Ruth Cowen, as the cookbook that 'took the genre to new heights'; and by Penelope Farmer as 'the parent of the modern cookery book'.

Eliza was the first known poet/playwright to become a cookery writer, a trend of combining fiction and food writing that continued with May Byron, Mary Virginia Terhune, Harriet Beecher Stowe, Crescent Dragonwagon, Hanna Winsnes, Helena Patursson, Janet Laurence, Alison Uttley, Sophie Dahl, Marian Keyes, James Salter and many others.

At some point during the writing of *Modern Cookery*, Eliza's bankrupt father returned from exile to England and Eliza's mother left Bordyke House to live with him in Hastings. This left Eliza and Ann at Bordyke House, where they meticulously cooked and tested recipes. After the publication of *Modern Cookery*, Ann Kirby appears to have parted company with Eliza. According to Eliza's biographer, Ann is not heard of until the 1851 census when she is recorded as living in London as personal servant to the widowed dispenser at the Royal Greenwich Hospital.

While my portrait of Ann is entirely fictitious, my portrait of Eliza is based on several facts. Her poems were published in 1826 and she sold 530 copies, with 352 going to early subscribers. When she took her second volume to Longmans publishers, a decade later, she was indeed told to go home and return with a cookery book. We know she continued writing poetry because a poem of hers was published by Richard & John E. Taylor in 1842, suggesting she wrote poetry for at least twenty years.

Eliza never married, but her first biographers (Mary Aylett and Olive Ordish, *First Catch Your Hare*) were lucky enough to be in communication with her great-niece. It was here that I encountered the story of Eliza's illegitimate daughter who was raised (allegedly) by her sister. This short biography also referred to Eliza's play, produced at Miss Kelly's Soho Theatre. No record of the play remains (most of Miss Kelly's plays were produced anonymously) and no one has been able to track down Eliza's illegitimate daughter, although this is hardly surprising given there was no requirement to register births during this period and illegitimate children (who were very common) were frequently hidden away or absorbed into respectable families. According to Aylett and Ordish, Eliza's daughter was known to have inherited an allowance, and to own a portrait of her biological mother, which she kissed every night, a story that travelled through generations of the Acton family.

Several mysteries hover over the story of Eliza Acton, many of which have been explored in her more recent biography, *The Real Mrs Beeton: The Story of Eliza Acton* by Sheila Hardy. Hardy never found any record of Eliza Acton's will.

Eliza would have died a wealthy woman and yet neither a will nor her letters have been discovered, leading to speculation that these were destroyed on her death, perhaps to preserve her reputation and the family name by preventing disclosure of an illegitimate daughter. Several of her poems (which struck me with their frankness and intensity) also include missing lines and dedications using asterisks only (a technique employed by Victorian newspapers to avoid libel).

After the success of *Modern Cookery*, Eliza produced a second cookery book: *The English Bread Book*. It never sold as well as *Modern Cookery*. However, during this time, Eliza became a champion of home-cooking and nutritious food, persuading the public to eat healthier food and fighting to have harmful additives removed from bread. While Mrs Beeton later plagiarised around a third of her recipes, others did so during Eliza's life, prompting her to denounce them, in an 1855 preface to *Modern Cookery*, as 'strangers coolly taking the credits and profits of my toil'.

Eliza died on 13 February 1859 at the age of fifty-nine. Oddly, her death certificate describes her – in the Occupation column – neither as poet nor writer but as 'Daughter of John Acton, Ipswich. Brewer. Deceased.' The cause of death is given as 'Premature Old Age', now thought to be a euphemism for dementia. Meanwhile her grave was inscribed only with the words 'Eliza Acton, formerly of Ipswich who died in Hampstead'.

It was in Eliza's poetry and cookery writing that I sought (and partially found) clues as to what happened to Eliza in her youth. It's known she spent time in France (probably on two extended occasions) and that she had a debilitating love affair. At this time illegitimate children were rife in France, with historians estimating that between 30 and 40 per cent of all babies born in Paris were illegitimate. Her poems speak plainly of betrayal, envy and emotional pain. I have plundered them accordingly, adding flesh to a rumour that has doggedly pursued her – that of an illegitimate daughter.

Within two years of Eliza's death, Mrs Isabella Beeton produced her first cookery book. For several decades, Eliza languished, lost in the long shadow of Mrs Beeton. It's now known that Mrs Beeton plagiarised Eliza shamelessly, cutting and pasting hundreds of her recipes and claiming them as her own, going 'out of her way to alter the formulations so that no one – and especially not the hawk-eyed Miss Acton had she lived – could point an accusing finger' (Kathryn Hughes, *The Short Life and Long Times of Mrs Beeton*). Mrs Beeton, however, cleverly moved the ingredients list from the bottom of a recipe to the top – where it has remained to this day.

Eliza's story took place at a time of unprecedented social upheaval. The early Victorian period saw Britain change irrevocably: the Industrial Revolution; a rising middle class; vast wealth but also unimaginable poverty, particularly among the rural poor; rapid change prompted by new technologies – from gas to electricity to railways. But this was also the era when the first 'fast' and convenience foods appeared, from powdered custard to imported frozen meat. The processed food we consume today had its beginnings when Eliza was writing, and her dislike of it (in particular its lack of nutritional content) informs both her cookery books.

To provide a richer and more intense flavour of the period and for the sake of narrative flow, I have collapsed events that took place over the ten years Eliza spent writing her cookery book into a shortened timescale.

A NOTE ON CHARACTERS
AND LOCATIONS

For added authenticity I have based most of the characters in *The Language of Food* on real people. However, the Thorpes and Ann's family are entirely fictitious. Mr Arnott is also fictitious, but was inspired by a man of the same name, mentioned twice in Eliza's cookery book. The *Curries and Potted Meats* chapter includes recipes for Mr Arnott's Currie-Powder and Mr Arnott's Currie, the latter taken directly from Mr Arnott's written instructions, with the ultimate paragraph as follows: 'Next put in a fowl that has been roasted and nicely cut up; or a rabbit; or some lean chops of pork or mutton; or a lobster, or the remains of yesterday's calf's head; or anything else you may fancy.' How could I resist making him a character? Incidentally, in her *Observations* Eliza makes it clear that although Mr Arnott's currie-powder is worth making, his currie is not!

MARIA RUNDELL

Mrs Maria Rundell's book is frequently referred to by Eliza. Rundell was the anonymous author of *A New System of*

ANNABEL ABBS

Domestic Cookery, published by Longman's arch-rival, John Murray, in 1806. It became a publishing sensation, running to sixty-seven editions, and is thought to be the reason Longman asked Eliza for a cookery book.

JUDITH MONTEFIORE

Judith Montefiore was the author of the first Jewish cookbook in English, *The Jewish Manual: Or Practical Information in Jewish and Modern Cookery*, published anonymously (by A Lady) a year after Eliza's book, in 1846. Some of the dishes she describes are very similar to those in Eliza's book (Eliza refers several times to a 'certain Jewish lady' to whom she's indebted for her Jewish recipes) and we know that Eliza ate Jewish Smoked Beef, which she considered 'excellent', in the home of a 'Jewish lady'. It has been speculated that the 'Jewish lady' was, in fact, Judith Montefiore of London and of Ramsgate in Kent.

Judith was an extraordinary woman: she spoke six languages, played an active role in the development of Palestine and was a dedicated philanthropist, involved in numerous charities including the establishment of soup kitchens in the East End of London.

FANNY KELLY

Fanny Kelly was a well-known actress believed to have been part of Eliza's circle of acquaintances. In 1840 she opened a

Theatre and Dramatic School in London's Soho so that young women could be trained in drama. She lived with her 'niece' who was widely believed to be her illegitimate daughter.

Mrs Hemans and L.E.L.

Mrs Felicia Hemans and L.E.L. (Miss Letitia Elizabeth Landon) were prominent and hugely popular female poets, writing at the same time as Eliza. Like many female poets of this time, they remain largely unknown. Hemans published more than fourteen volumes of verse between 1818 and 1835, becoming one of the best-loved poets of her time. L.E.L. published her first poem when she was sixteen and her many, many novels and poems sold so well she was able to maintain her mother and help fund her brother's Oxford education. However, her reputation as an independent, unmarried writer meant most men forbade their wives from inviting Miss Landon to their homes. She eventually married (after giving birth to three illegitimate children) the Governor of Cape Coast Castle on the African Coast, dying four months later in a possible suicide.

Alexis Soyer

Alexis Soyer was a French chef who became Victorian England's most celebrated cook, presiding over the kitchens of London's Reform Club for thirteen years (1837–50). A born innovator, he was one of the first to cook with gas and famously invented a portable stove. He set up soup kitchens in Dublin during the Irish Famine and helped organise the feeding of militia during the Crimean War. He also wrote several cookery books.

KENT COUNTY LUNATIC ASYLUM

The locations of this novel are also as historically accurate as I could make them, in particular the Kent County Lunatic Asylum, accounts of which make horrific reading. One of the earliest purpose-built asylums, it opened in January 1833. The site was modelled on a prison (the same architect designed Maidstone Gaol) and was described by an inspector visiting in 1840 thus: 'massive stone walls, small iron-framed windows, absence of ornament ... narrow stone stairs, low vaulted ceilings, rows of dark dungeon-like cells ... tables screwed to the floor, heavy wooden chairs in which patients were strapped, primitive wooden beds with straw for bedding ... lunatics in coarse scanty clothing, some in strait waistcoats, some in manacles or other form of restraint.' The inspector went on to describe finding two men who had been chained to their beds for four and a half years, and another twenty to thirty men and women in manacles or 'fastened in a coercive chair by a large cuirass of thick leather'.* In these early asylums it was common for dead patients to be

* Geraldine Procter, *A History of Oakwood Hospital from 1828–1982*, Kent County Library, 1982

dissected by surgeons who had a particular interest in the brains of the 'insane'.

The Kent County Lunatic Asylum later became Barming Heath Asylum, then Barming Mental Hospital and, finally, Oakwood Hospital. It closed in 1994, but its legacy endures in the term, *barmy*.

Bordyke House

Bordyke House in Tonbridge, Kent, where Eliza and Ann tested thousands of recipes as they wrote *Modern Cookery*, is still a private home, although Tonbridge is – of course – a very different town!

Poems

The painful beatings of a breaking heart are hush'd to stillness –
    'The Grave Poem', Eliza Acton

My first affections, and my last, were thine – thine only – fare
    thee well! – 'L'Abandonnée', Eliza Acton

Darkly, darkly, Misfortune's wing/Is o'er thee rolling its heavy
    cloud;/Slowly, slowly, 'tis gathering – 'Cards of Fortune',
    Eliza Acton

With what still hours of calm delight/Thy songs and image blend;/
    I cannot choose but think thou wert/ An old familiar friend' –
    'Stanzas on the Death of Mrs Hemans', L.E.L.

Affection's chain was all too rudely wrench'd in twain … blighted
    hopes and friendship fled … she is flung neglectedly, where
    fostering love is not … –'L'Abandonnée', Eliza Acton

Few save the poor, feel for the poor: The rich know not how hard it
    is to be of needful food – 'The Poor Poem', L.E.L.

My heart's in the kitchen, my heart is not here, My heart's in
    the kitchen, though following the dear, Thinking on the

roast meat, and musing on the fry, My heart's in the kitchen whatever I spy. – Maria Jane Jewsbury

Sound on, thou dark unslumbering sea ... Thou sea-bird on the billow's crest – 'The Last Song of Sappho', Felicia Hemans

Pause – 'ere thy choice hath clasp'd the chain/Which may not be unloos'd again;/For though of gold the links may be/They will not press less painfully – 'Cards of Fortune', Eliza Acton

Let not the cares which round me cling, Obscure one moment's bliss for thee – 'Le Triste Adieu', Eliza Acton

Thy heart, thy heart is cold as stone, and feels but for itself alone – 'Cards of Fortune', Eliza Acton

Oh, what a waste of feeling and thought have been the imprints on my roll of life ... to what use have I turned the golden gifts which are my hope and pride – 'Erinna', L.E.L.

I have no early flowers to fling – 'The Forgotten One', L.E.L.

I may have sinned ... but be the curse upon my head – Oh, let it not descend to her! – 'The Dying Child', L.E.L.

RECOMMENDED READING

As ever I am indebted to the work of others, in particular:

First Catch Your Hare: A History of Recipe Makers, Mary Aylett and Olive Ordish

The Real Mrs Beeton: The Story of Eliza Acton, Sheila Hardy

Cooking People, Sophia Waugh

The Short Life and Long Times of Mrs Beeton, Kathryn Hughes

A Woman's Work is Never Done: A History of Housework in the British Isles, Caroline Davidson

The Victorian Kitchen, Jennifer Davies

The Kitchen in History, Molly Harrison

Taste, Kate Colquhoun

The Last Food of England, Marwood Yeatman

The Victorian House, Judith Flanders

Alexis Soyer Cook Extraordinary, Elizabeth Ray

Relish: The Extraordinary Life of Alexis Soyer, Ruth Cowen

Feast, Roy Strong

A History of English Food, Clarissa Dickson Wright

Food: A Cultural Culinary History, Ken Albala

The Art of Eating in France: Manners and Menus in the Nineteenth Century, Jean-Paul Aron

Scoff: A History of Food and Class in Britain, Pen Vogler

Victorian Women Poets, ed. Angela Leighton and Margaret Reynolds

L.E.L. The Lost Life and Mysterious Death of the 'Female Byron', Lucasta Miller

Rural Life in Victorian England, G. E. Mingay

Early Victorian Tonbridge, C. W. Chalklin

The Victorian Asylum, Sara Rutherford

Life in the Victorian Asylum, Mark Stevens

A History of Oakwood Hospital, Geraldine Procter

Victorious Century, David Cannadine

And most importantly of all, Eliza's own works:

Poems, 1826

Modern Cookery for Private Families, 1845

The English Bread Book, 1857

Author's Note

In 1996 I was lucky enough to acquire the cookery book collection of my mother-in-law, June. After leaving school June studied Domestic Science. She started her career as a teacher of Domestic Science, then joined the *Good Housekeeping* institute, before returning to education as a cookery teacher. During this time – and long before it was fashionable – June began collecting old cookery books, eventually amassing a library of more than two hundred. It was here that I came across Eliza Acton, as well as Maria Rundell, Alexis Soyer, William Kitchiner, Hannah Glasse, Hannah Woolley, Agnes Marshall, Mrs Beeton and many, many other cooks and cookery writers. It was only on closer examination that I realised Eliza Acton's recipe-writing was head-and-shoulders above that of her peers, rooted in her personal history as a thwarted poet. Although Eliza was writing nearly two hundred years ago, the message to her readership of 'young housekeepers' is more relevant today than ever before. Thrift and the avoidance of waste, nutritious food for good health, the need to master plain cookery, cooking with care and fresh ingredients, learning from 'other nations', and the importance of making good food available to everyone … These resonate as much now (if not more) as they did in 1845. And so I leave the last word to Eliza: *It is not, in fact, cookery books that we need half so much as cooks really trained to a knowledge of their duties.*

Indeed, Eliza, indeed.

ACKNOWLEDGEMENTS

I'd like to thank the following for their continued support and inspiration: my mother, Barbara, who introduced me to the twin delights of cooking and reading recipe books when I was a mere toddler; my mother-in-law, June, for her superlative collection of English cookery books and for teaching my husband to cook when *he* was a mere toddler; my first readers – my mother, my husband Matthew, Sharon Galant and Thomasin Chinnery at Zeitgeist Literary Agency, and my friend, Rachel Aris, all of whom provided invaluable feedback; Gladstone's Library where I spoke on the subject of Eliza to an audience that listened (and kindly ate my Eliza cakes and biscuits) with such enthusiasm I was inspired to stop researching and start writing; the antiquarian cookery collections at the British Library, the London Library, the Guildhall Library and the Wellcome Library; the Tonbridge Historical Society, Beverley Matthews, archivist at Tonbridge School; and, of course, my family – Matthew, Imogen, Bryony, Saskia and Hugo – who have dutifully eaten my Eliza-inspired cooking for longer than they can remember. Thank you!

A final and special acknowledgment to the many teams

across the world who have played a part in publishing *The Language of Food* (*Miss Eliza's English Kitchen* outside the UK): my agent, Sharon Galant, has worked diligently and tirelessly; Sara-Jade Virtue and her fabulous team (Alice Rodgers, Rich Vlietstra, Jess Barratt, Joe Roche, Rich Hawton, Nicola Mitchell, Rhys Thomas, Naomi Burt, Andrew Wright, Francesca Sironi and Gail Hallett, and Micaela Alcaino, for her glorious cover design) brought their considerable enthusiasm and talent to the process of publication; in the US, my agent, Claire Anderson-Wheeler, and Lucia Macro and her equally fabulous team at William Morrow; elsewhere, the many publishers and translators grappling with translating Eliza Acton's more obscure culinary terms: I wish you luck.

Special recognition must go to Eliza Acton herself, and to all the women of history who were brave and audacious enough to write under their own names, whether it was poetry, recipes or something else entirely. I hope this novel goes some way to acknowledging how difficult, complicated and courageous this decision was.

Miss Eliza's Recipes

All recipes taken verbatim from
Eliza Acton's *Modern Cookery for Private Families*, 1845

Eliza Acton's Pickled Peaches

Take, at their full growth, just before they begin to ripen, six large or eight moderate-sized peaches; wipe the down from them, and put them into brine that will float an egg. In three days let them be taken out, and drained on a sieve reversed for several hours. Boil in a quart of vinegar for ten minutes two ounces of whole white pepper, two of ginger slightly bruised, a teaspoon of salt, two blades of mace, half a pound of mustard-seed, and a half-teaspoonful of cayenne tied in a bit of muslin. Lay the peaches into a jar, and pour the boiling pickle on them; in two months they will be fit for use.

Peaches 6 or 8: in brine three days. Vinegar, 1 quart; whole white pepper, 2 oz.; bruised ginger, 2 oz.; salt, 1 teaspoonful; mace, 2 blades; mustard-seed, ½ lb.: 10 minutes.

Eliza Acton's Broiled Eels with Sage

Kill, skin, open and cleanse one fine eel. Cut it into finger lengths and rub it with a mixed seasoning of salt and white pepper, and leave it for half an hour. Wipe it dry, wrap each length in sage leaves, fasten them round it with coarse thread, roll the eel in good salad oil or clarified butter, lay it on the gridiron, squeeze lemon juice over, and broil it gently until it is browned in every part. Send it to table with a sauce made of two or three ounces of butter, a tablespoonful of chilli, tarragon, or common vinegar, and one of water with a little salt.

Eliza Acton's Chocolate Custards

Dissolve gently by the side of the fire an ounce and a half of the best chocolate in rather more than a wineglassful of water, and then boil it until it is perfectly smooth; mix with it a pint of milk well flavoured with lemon peel or vanilla, add two ounces of fine sugar, and when the whole boils, stir it five well-beaten eggs which have been strained. Put the custard into a jar or jug, set it into a pan of boiling water, and stir it without ceasing until it is thick. Do not put it into glasses or a dish until it is nearly or quite cold. These, as well as all other custards, are infinitely finer when made with the yolks only of the eggs, of which the number must then be increased.

Rasped chocolate, 1 ½ ounces; water, 1 large wineglassful; 5 to 8 minutes. New milk, 1 pint; eggs, 5; sugar, 2 oz.

Or: chocolate, 2 oz.; water, ¼ pint; new milk, 1 pint; sugar, 2 ½ to 3 oz; cream, ½ pint; yolks of eggs, 8.

ELIZA ACTON'S BOILED SWAN'S EGG

Swan's eggs are much more delicate than from their size, and from the tendency of the birds to feed on fish might be supposed; and when boiled hard and shelled, their appearance is beautiful, the white being of remarkable purity and transparency. Take as much water as will cover the egg well in every part, let it boil quickly, then take it from the fire, and as soon as the water ceases to move put in the egg, and leave it by the side of the fire – without allowing it to boil – for twenty minutes, and turn it gently once or twice in the time; then put on the cover of the stewpan and boil it gently for a quarter of an hour; take it quite from the fire, and in five minutes put it into a basin and throw a cloth, once or twice folded, over it, and let it cool slowly. It will retain the heat for a very long time, and as it should be quite cold before it is cut, it should be boiled early if wanted to serve the same day.

NB Eliza serves these in a green salad, first removing the yolks and mashing them with herbs, spices, butter, minced onion and lemon juice, then returning the mixture to the whites and arranging the whole lot on a bed of dressed lettuce.

Eliza Acton's Tonbridge Brawn (Pig's Head)

Split open the head of a pig of middling size, remove the brain and all the bones, strew the inside thickly with fine salt, and let it drain until the following day. Cleanse the ears and feet in the same manner; wipe them all from the brine, lay them into a large pan, and rub them well with an ounce and a half of saltpetre mixed with six ounces of sugar; in twelve hours, add six ounces of salt; the next day pour a quarter of a pint of good vinegar over them, and keep them turned in the pickle every twenty-four hours for a week; then wash it off the ears and feet, and boil them for about an hour and a half; bone the feet while they are warm, and trim the gristle from the large ends of the ears. When these are ready, mix a large grated nutmeg with a teaspoonful and a half of mace, half a teaspoonful of cayenne, and as much of cloves. Wash, but do not soak the head; wipe and flatten it on a board; cut some of the flesh from the thickest parts, and lay it on the thinnest; intermix it with that of the ears and feet, roll it up very tight, and bind it firmly with broad tape; fold a thin pudding-cloth quite closely round it and tie it securely at both ends. Place the head in a braising pan, with the bones and trimmings of the feet and ears, a large bunch of savoury herbs, two onions, a small head of celery, three or four carrots, a teaspoonful of peppercorns, and sufficient cold water to cover it well; boil it very gently for four hours, and leave it until two parts cold in the liquor in which it was boiled. Take off the cloth and put the brawn between two trenchers, with a heavy weight on the upper one. The next day take off the fillets of tape, and serve the head whole.

Eliza Acton's Soup in Haste

Chop tolerably fine a pound of lean beef, mutton, or veal, and when it is partly done, add to it a small carrot and one small turnip cut in slices, half an ounce of celery, the white part of a moderate-sized leek, or a quarter of an ounce of onion. Mince all these together, and put the whole into a deep saucepan with three pints of cold water. When the soup boils take off the scum, and add a little salt and pepper. In half an hour it will be ready to serve, with or without straining; it may be flavoured at will, with cayenne, catsup, or aught else that is preferred, or it may be converted into French spring broth, by passing it through a sieve, and boiling it again for five or six minutes, with a handful of young and well-washed sorrel.

Meat, 1 lb.; carrot, 2 oz.; turnip, 1½ oz.; celery, ½ oz.; onion, ¼ oz.; water, 3 pints; half an hour. Little pepper and salt.

Obs. – Three pounds of beef or mutton, with two or three slices of ham, and vegetables in proportion to the above receipt, all chopped fine, and boiled in three quarts of water for an hour and a half, will make an excellent family soup on an emergency: additional boiling will of course improve it, and a little spice should be added after it has been skimmed and salted.